Acclaim for J'nell

"Smart, savvy, and seductive, J'nell Ciesielski's *The Socialite* takes the reader on a high-stakes thrill ride through the darkness of WWII–occupied Paris. Painting a portrait of excess from inside the top tiers of the Nazi war machine, the hopeless glitz and glamour of the elite creates sparks of tension through Ciesielski's vivid imagery and the raw experiences of those resisting their oppressors at the same time they must survive in their world. Creating balance between a brave heroine and hero—the first naive but steely Kat, reluctantly partnered with the more-than-capable Scot Resistance fighter, Barrett—their pulse-pounding journey leaves the reader breathless to the very last page. *The Socialite* shines bright as the City of Lights, and then some!"

—KRISTY CAMBRON, AWARD-WINNING AUTHOR OF THE LOST CASTLE SERIES AND THE BESTSELLING DEBUT THE BUTTERFLY AND THE VIOLIN

"In the tradition of Ariel Lawhon and Kate Quinn, *The Socialite* immerses readers in the glamor and destruction of Nazi-occupied Paris. Featuring two sisters whose travails and triumphs recall the cinematic real-life story of the Mitford family, the book is a portal into a world at times opulent and deadly as two people bound by conscience navigate the grey waters of the City of Light in its bleakest hour of darkness. A picture-perfect portrait of early 1940s Paris, this impeccably researched love story stands out in a sea of WWII–era fiction with its distinctive crystalline voice and unforgettable hero and heroine."

—RACHEL MCMILLAN, AUTHOR OF THE LONDON RESTORATION AND MURDER IN THE CITY OF LIBERTY

"With dramatic intrigue and inspiring romance, *The Socialite* will delight readers looking for World War II novels. The unique characters, riveting plot, and sparkling prose bring 1940s Paris to life. Well done and highly recommended."

—CARRIE TURANSKY, AWARD-WINNING AUTHOR OF NO OCEAN TOO WIDE AND ACROSS THE BLUE

"Readers will devour each moment leading up to the satisfying ending."

—*PUBLISHERS WEEKLY*, STARRED REVIEW, ON
THE SONGBIRD AND THE SPY

"With lovely prose and her impeccable attention to history, author J'nell Ciesielski once again delivers a riveting, romantic adventure in *The Songbird and the Spy*. In this gripping tale of espionage and romance, the perils of WWII come to life, as forbidden attraction between a German captain and mysterious French waitress threatens to expose their secrets, jeopardizing themselves and countless others trapped inside Nazi-occupied France. Intrigue, danger, and romance abound in Ciesielski's sophomore novel and will guarantee to keep you on the edge of your seat. *The Songbird and the Spy* is a must-read for those who love WWII historical Christian fiction!"

—KATE BRESLIN, BESTSELLING AUTHOR OF *HIGH AS
THE HEAVENS*, ON *THE SONGBIRD AND THE SPY*

"Unlike most romances set in this time period, this one never sugarcoats the ugliness of war. There are moral dilemmas, friends die, and survival is hard. Love grows through stolen moments, not dramatic declarations. This carefully researched novel is rich with historical details . . . Readers will relish this powerful story of battlefield love."

—*PUBLISHERS WEEKLY*, STARRED REVIEW, ON *AMONG THE POPPIES*

"Ciesielski opens the doors to a setting of WWII not yet fully explored by other authors of this genre, allowing readers to discover the intricacies of occupied France in a new and fresh way. With enough secrets to last a lifetime, readers will be on the edge of their seats, cheering on the heroes. Action-filled and captivating, readers who enjoy books with espionage, war, and romance should definitely read this one. Get lost in time in this moving story of faith, freedom, and love."

—*HOPE BY THE BOOK* ON *AMONG THE POPPIES*

"From page one, the characters pull you in and keep you reading! J'nell Ciesielski pens her story with beauty and skill."

—ROSEANNA WHITE, BESTSELLING AUTHOR OF THE LADIES OF THE
MANOR AND SHADOWS OVER ENGLAND SERIES, ON *AMONG THE POPPIES*

Other Books by J'nell Ciesielski

The Songbird and the Spy

Among the Poppies

The Socialite

THE
Socialite

A NOVEL

J'NELL CIESIELSKI

THOMAS NELSON
Since 1798

Published in Nashville, Tennessee, by Thomas Nelson. Thomas Nelson is a registered trademark of HarperCollins Christian Publishing, Inc.

Thomas Nelson titles may be purchased in bulk for educational, business, fundraising, or sales promotional use. For information, please email SpecialMarkets@ ThomasNelson.com.

Publisher's Note: This novel is a work of fiction. Names, characters, places, and incidents are either products of the author's imagination or used fictitiously. All characters are fictional, and any similarity to people living or dead is purely coincidental.

ISBN 978-0-7852-3355-8 (audio download)

Library of Congress Cataloging-in-Publication Data

Names: Ciesielski, J'nell, author.
Title: The socialite : a novel / J'nell Ciesielski.
Description: Nashville : Thomas Nelson, [2020] | Summary: "Glamour, treachery, and espionage collide when an English socialite rushes to save her sister from the Nazis"-- Provided by publisher.
Identifiers: LCCN 2019044381 | ISBN 9780785233527 (trade paperback) | ISBN 9780785233541 (epub) | ISBN 9780785233558
Subjects: LCSH: World War, 1939-1945--France--Fiction. | France--History--German occupation, 1940-1945--Fiction. | GSAFD: Historical fiction.
Classification: LCC PS3603.I33 S68 2020 | DDC 813/.6--dc23
LC record available at https://lccn.loc.gov/2019044381

Printed in the United States of America
20 21 22 23 24 LSC 10 9 8 7 6 5 4 3 2 1

For my mom. We made it.

Chapter 1

Bloody lipstick." Kathleen Whitford yanked a handkerchief from her handbag and rubbed off the uneven line of Sequin Red curving over her lip. Angling her gold compact mirror to the streetlight, she swiped the red tube over her mouth again. "Can't meet the Nazis with smeared lips."

Slipping the mirror back into its place, she raised a shaking hand to pull the silk scarf from her head and tuck it safely in her beaded handbag. She looked up at the pristine white-brick building posed as the grand dame of Rue de l'Université. Light, laughter, and music spilled out of the open windows on the top floor, chilling her to the bone despite the late-July air.

"Relax. It's only a party. You've been to a million of them before."

Her wooden voice bounced off the gleaming oak front doors and smacked her in the face with irony. Yes, a million parties filled with dukes, lords, ladies, and even the king for her presentation at court. Curtseying before His Majesty had been a cakewalk compared to this. Buckingham Palace hadn't been filled with German officers. Or their mistresses.

Her heart panged. Ellie.

Throwing her shoulders back, Kat covered her pain with a bright smile and a gentle sweep of her lashes, just the way Mother had taught her, and marched in. Her black velvet pumps *ticking* across the gray marble foyer drowned out the hammering of her heart as she climbed the sweeping staircase all the way to the top.

Following the music to the door on the right, she took a deep breath and raised her hand to knock. Before she could, the door burst open. Out tumbled a uniformed German soldier with a woman in a gold dress in his arms.

"*Entschuldigen uns.*" The man laughed, grabbing the woman around the waist before she slid to the floor.

Red lipstick smeared the woman's lips as she twisted her head to grin up at Kat. She thrust a half-full bottle of champagne under her nose. "*Vouloir quelque?*"

Kat pushed the bottle away and shook her head. "*Non, merci.*"

"*Ce est bien.*" The woman wagged the bottle, sloshing the golden bubbly down her dress.

Kat leaned back out of range of flying drops. "*Non.* I'm saving my appetite for the water."

"Water?" The woman scrunched her nose for a second before delight lit up her hazy eyes. "Oh! You joke!" She swiveled back to the man, grazing her red lips against his neck. "Did you hear that, *cherie*? She wants water."

"Yes, I heard," he said in rough French. "A jest, surely, as no one drinks water in France. Come on, *schatz*. Our night continues elsewhere."

With her welcoming party skidding their way down the stairs, Kat pushed into the flat. The temptation to turn and run hit her like a wall of ice. A crush of German soldiers in gray uniforms and women in their finest evening attire stood cream wall to cream wall. Overhead, a chandelier dripping with crystals reflected off the mirrors and gilded frames lining the walls while deep-blue brocade drapes swathed the floor-to-ceiling windows overlooking the street and Ming vases filled with white lilies stood in each corner of the spacious room.

"Madame?" A waiter appeared at her elbow, offering her a tray of champagne, wine, and cognac.

Kat shook her head and edged around him. The last thing her roiling stomach needed was spirits. Her feet sank into the thick carpet as she dodged between couples dancing to the warbling tunes of Edith Piaf blaring from a gramophone. Enduring elbows, the crushing of her toes underfoot, and champagne splashed on her red satin dress, she made it to the other side of the room. She braced her back against the archway dividing the front room and the dining room loaded with food and scanned the crowd through the haze of cigarette smoke.

Her fingernails dug into the glossy white trim of the doorway. If Ellie weren't her baby sister, there would have been no power on Earth strong enough to drag her willingly into a room full of Nazis. Then again, if Ellie had learned to temper her impulses, she wouldn't be in this horrible predicament to begin with while leaving Kat to sweep up the chaos.

As always.

Another waiter popped up in front of her with a tray of canapés. His eyes dropped to her clinging hands. "Madame? May I escort you to a chair?"

Breeding surged to the rescue. Letting go of the wall, she clasped her hands in front of her and smiled. "*Non*, I was just looking for the hostess. Have you seen her?"

"Madame Eleanor?" His brow scrunched as he glanced across the smoke-laden room. "She had gone to get new records."

A clatter of trays echoed from the double doors at the back of the dining room. The doors flew open, and out breezed a petite blond on a cloud of cigarette smoke. "Just sweep it up and get me new ones," she called over her shoulder in scratchy French. "Charles Trenet or Rina Ketty. Someone upbeat. The last thing I need is this party to drag from dull music."

The pebbles that had plunked into Kat's stomach since the second she stepped on occupied soil dropped like a boulder. Gone was the innocent girl she had known, replaced by an unrecognizable woman. A woman who radiated happiness, not misery like she'd expected to find. Air wheezed in her throat. "Ellie."

Her sister stopped dead in her tracks, her long silver cigarette holder dangling precariously from her fingers. Her cherry-red mouth formed a perfect *O*. Seconds dragged by as Kat waited for German hands to grab her and toss her out. This was a mistake. She should have waited until morning to drag her wayward sister back across the Channel without the whole of the Third Reich watching. She should have—

Ellie's feet moved, delight springing to her blue-green eyes. She launched herself at her sister. "Kitty Kat!"

Kat barely caught her little sister before she bowled them over into a stack of crackers, foie gras, and bullhead cheese on the gleaming mahogany dining table.

"Oh, Kat, you're here! Really here. I can't believe it."

Wrapping her arms around her sister, Kat squeezed her tight as a flood of relief washed away months of worry. Ellie was all right.

"Can't breathe." Ellie coughed, tapping her on the back.

Warmth rushed to Kat's cheeks as she stepped back. "Sorry."

"Take one foot off the island, and suddenly your stiff upper lip is no more." Ellie laughed and brushed a wrinkle from Kat's shoulder. Her bright smile faltered. "What *are* you doing here? Nothing bad has happened?"

Other than you running off to occupied France to become social secretary to the Nazis?

"Do I need a bad reason to miss my sister?" Kat smiled in an attempt to capture the runaway with honey rather than the vinegar eating her up inside. One false move and the girl would spring like a deer from the crosshairs. She raised a hand to Ellie's rouged cheek. "It's been nearly a year since I've seen you. How fine you look."

Ellie beamed and reached up to touch the diamond comb sweeping the blond curls up on one side of her head. Independence radiated from her every move. "Yes, I quite think the French air agrees with me."

Kat's smile twisted. It wasn't French anymore. The Germans patrolled the Louvre and Champs Élysées as if they marched in the Rhineland. If the fighting went their way, they would soon goose-step through Piccadilly Square. She took a deep breath to calm the acid burning its way up the back of her throat. The Germans weren't her priority. She'd traveled here to bring back her sister. Hopefully the process didn't involve binding, gagging, and throwing her into the back of a waiting car.

"I thought I'd have trouble finding you once I got here, since you never sent an address."

"You cannot fathom how busy I've been, and the post takes so much longer to circulate these days." Ellie took a long drag from her cigarette. Smoke curled out from the corner of her mouth. "How *did* you find me?"

The wary note in Ellie's voice hung in the air like a curtain of iron. The wrong answer—or any answer involving their father—would bring it crashing down. Sir Alfred Whitford's arm was long reaching, but his money and connections knew no boundaries, including using his university friends at Scotland Yard to track down his youngest daughter.

"I asked the concierge to point me to the hottest ticket in town. Who would have thought that meant a Brit?" Kat's throat ached on a forced laugh. Turning, she cast an appraising eye over the room. "And in such a swanky place right in the heart of the 7th arrondissement. *Trés chic.*"

A woman with platinum-blond hair swished by as she attempted a tango with a bottle of sauvignon. A frightened waiter chased after her with a cork.

"Eric would have nothing less than the best," Ellie said, uncaring for the safety of her white rugs. "The district was once for *le Faubourg,* so it's only fitting that we claim it for our own. The new nobility for the new world."

Eric. The name spoken with such intimacy screamed like a siren in Kat's head. Her baby sister, living with a man. The situation was sickening at best. As always, instead of heeding the warnings all around her, the girl had run straight into the fantasy she had conjured for herself. Only instead of boys, dance halls, and bathtub gin, she had thrown herself into the arms of a vile ideology and a man she knew nothing about. Except that he offered an escape from the crushing grip of their parents.

Hooking her arm through Kat's, Ellie guided her back into the crush of guests. The crowd parted for her like Moses and the Red Sea. "As the new queen of Paris, I shall introduce you to all my friends. You'll love them."

I bet. "I don't know if I could hear introductions over this din." Kat pointed to the gramophone now blaring "*C'est si bon.*"

"What? Oh, no. These aren't my friends. They're mainly Eric's." Ellie took another long pull from her cigarette before tapping off an inch's worth of ash into the nearest Ming vase. "I talk to them, too, of course, but my dearest friends couldn't make it tonight."

Too busy attending a book burning? Dread curled in Kat's stomach before she dared the question out loud. "Who is this mysterious Eric?"

Light sparkled in Ellie's eyes as her lips curved into a dreamy smile. "The most wonderful man, with the most beautiful blue eyes you've ever seen. Everywhere we go, men clamor to shake his hand and women purr for his attention, but he belongs to me." Her eyes clouded for a moment. "Or at least he will soon."

Kat pulled them to a stop behind the powder-blue settee. On the other side, a game of stacking empty wineglasses on the Queen Anne end table was well under way. "What do you mean?"

"Nothing at all. Darling, where are you staying?"

Kat bit her tongue. Prodding further into this Eric character would lead to nothing good. She had a big enough headache already. "The San Regis."

"Not anymore. You're staying right here with me, and we'll stay up all night chatting just like we used to do." Wetness glistened in Ellie's eye. She bit the corner of her lip. "I've missed you, Kat."

A lump bobbed in Kat's throat. "I've missed you too. We all have."

"We?" The wetness blinked from Ellie's eye. Yanking a fresh cigarette from the bodice of her gown, she jammed it into the holder and lit it. "That's why you're really here, isn't it? The Firm sent you to drag me back. Well, I'm not going. I'm staying here, so you've wasted a trip."

"I came because I haven't seen or heard from you in over a year."

"As you can see, there's nothing to worry about, because I'm doing quite well here. Free to do whatever I like for the first time in my life."

"I didn't know that back in jolly old England." *Where you left me.* Kat took a deep breath, pushing down the stab of betrayal. Different as night and day, they were still sisters. They'd shared secrets, giggled until all hours of the night, gone ice-skating together, and shopping. Their memories were wrapped together in shared childhood, but it hadn't always been easy. Kat adhered to the rules while Ellie lived to break them. Kat followed the well-ordered path the family laid before her while Ellie traipsed into the grass without a backward glance, abandoning her.

Sisters weren't supposed to abandon each other.

Whatever sense of betrayal that radiated in Kat's heart did not show on her sister's polished face. For all her grown-up airs, the past year hadn't taught Ellie to consider her actions' effect on others. Now wasn't the time to raise those hurts, nor was it something a well-bred lady would bring up. If Kat represented anything, it was a lifetime's lessons of good breeding. "How about a glass of that famous French champagne for your dear parched sister?"

Ellie raised a slender eyebrow. "Parched for champagne? And here I thought tea was the only thing running in your veins."

"When in Rome—or in this case Paris."

"Kathleen Whitford, the living prodigy to duty, dips her standards to partake with the sinners. Will wonders never cease?"

"You above all others know I'm no saint."

"Sure, and I've got a halo hanging in my closet." Never one to hold a grudge for too long, Ellie snorted and waved a waiter over. Grabbing two glasses from his tray, she handed one to Kat. "To Paris."

Raising her glass, Kat clinked it to Ellie's. "To sisters and their halos. Or lack of."

A large man with a white apron and beads of sweat dotting his forehead poked his head around the dining room wall. Scanning the room, his eyes stopped on Ellie. "Miz Eleanor."

"Are those macaroons done yet, Pierre?" Ellie drained her champagne glass.

"*Oui*, but it is not the macaroons you need to worry about." With the corner of his apron he wiped away the sweat dropping down to his ear. "Jean-Claude has delivered the oysters, and well, Miz, they are less than expected."

"What do you mean?"

More sweat popped out on his head. "They are *less*." He held his thumb and forefinger an inch apart.

"Oh, for pity's sake. I told him only yesterday to—Never mind, it's done now." She set her glass on a shelf next to Victor Hugo's *Les Misérables* and Chanel's latest fashion of 1936. "Kat, you can entertain yourself, can't you? Have another drink and mingle. Most of them don't know English, but their French is passable. *Oui, oui*, Pierre. *Je viens.*"

Mingle. Dread crawled down Kat's spine as gray uniforms danced before her eyes like a kaleidoscope of drab horror. Throwing herself into a pit of vipers would be more bearable. Grabbing another glass of bubbling champagne, she skirted around the dancers and pushed through the double doors out onto the balcony.

The smell of sweet freesia mingled with the night's gentle breeze. Kat gripped the wrought-iron handrail, the cool metal a relief against her warm palms. She dropped her chin to her chest. If appearances didn't need maintaining, she'd drop her cheek down to the smooth rail for a brief respite from the abomination of merrymaking behind her while the people of the country cowered in terrified submission to their oppressors. And her sister in the middle of it all.

An ache groaned up inside of her. How wrong she'd been to imagine a tear-streaked Ellie falling into her arms with a desperate plea to whisk her back home. Back by Tuesday—wasn't that what she'd said to her parents as they waved her off at the train station last Saturday morning? Her naivete had crashed down around her ears with the starry-eyed look from Ellie. Her sister was in pure bliss, like a fawn unaware of the prowling wolves.

A knot twisted in Kat's stomach. Father would be furious if she gave up and allowed the family name to be smeared through the German mud. He'd never trust her to accomplish his purposes again.

Taking a deep breath, she lifted her head. She'd dreamed of visiting this city of lights with its tree-lined avenues, museums, and smoke-filled cafes, but tonight the magic was doused beneath blackout curtains. Except Ellie's, of course. An eclipse couldn't shadow her sister's sparkle. It was a trait Kat had failed to grasp when weighted with the responsibility of family duty, but one that whispered wistfully to her. Perhaps when the war was finally over and Ellie safely at home, she could come back and enjoy the city in her own time. No rules and no one else deciding which parks she should stroll through or how many crêpes she shouldn't eat. Pure bliss.

Metal twanged.

Kat peered over the rail to the empty street below. The cobbled gray thoroughfare was deserted, with every window shuttered and door locked tight. Even the mice had succumbed to Nazi rule after dark.

Scuffling. More metal slapped, like something heavy hitting a wall.

Kat leaned farther over the rail, inching sideways down the balcony as the scuffling drew closer. Her pulse pricked. What if one of those legendary sewer rats had escaped in search of midnight delicacies? Like the cave-ripened brie perched on the edge of Ellie's buffet table.

She wiggled her toes. Velvet Ferragamo pumps were the wrong footwear to take on a rodent.

"You might want to stand back."

Kat jumped. "Who's there?"

A large shadow swung over the balcony and dropped next to her. She screamed.

"Shh! You'll wake the neighbors."

A second scream caught in Kat's throat as she stumbled back into the rail. The shadow leaped forward, catching her around the waist. Her hand flew up and struck hard.

"Ow!" Pain shot through her fingers.

"Careful of the buttons, lass. They'll leave you smarting."

Pulse careening, she shoved against the dark mass in front of her. "Unhand me at once, you . . . you prowler."

"'Prowler'?" The *r* rolled off his tongue in a muted burr that kicked her pulse in a completely unexpected way. The securing arms fell away on a loud snort of laughter. "Hardly."

"Who are you? What are you doing here?" She inched away, stretching her fingers out in hopes of finding a loose rail or forgotten champagne glass to clobber him over the head with. "If it's money you want, you should know I have nothing more than a hankie and tube of lipstick in my handbag, and the guests inside have undoubtedly lost all spare coins in their drunken haze."

He shifted, blocking her view of the people inside. And their view of her. "I'm afraid you have me mistaken for someone else."

"Who else but a man with sinister deeds in mind prowls rooftops in the middle of the night and scares women alone outside?" Her fingers brushed a potted geranium.

"I've been called many things, but *sinister* is a new accusation. Besides, if I'd gone out burgling, I would have worn something more accommodating." He stepped into the shallow glow of the sconce by the doors. Tall, with dark hair combed to the side and a clean, angular jaw, he was dressed in a black dinner jacket that accented his thick shoulders. He pointed to the bow tie at his throat. "See?"

Her heart tripped. Fine jackets and starched white shirts were nothing more than a required uniform in her social circle, but this man wore them with a jagged edge of danger. As if they didn't quite fit.

Her fingers curled over the lip of the pot. "A new breed of thief. Easy to slip among the guests while you rifle their pockets."

"Lass, I think you've been out here in the dark too long. Your imagination has run amok."

As he reached for the door, she grabbed the pot and hurled it. He ducked as it sailed an inch over his head and crashed against the wall.

He swung back to her, dark eyebrows slashed together and eyes wide. "What in blazes do you think you're doing? I didn't scale the side of a building to be taken down by a bucket of dirt."

"You can scale right back down or I'll scream for the police. There are close to forty German officers in there who would love nothing more than to"—she peered around him to the party still swinging inside, all hope of rescue dying—"ignore my cries for help as they spiral into a drunken waltz."

"Aye, I can see that." He brushed dirt off his shoulder and nodded as two uniformed men swung a laughing woman back and forth to the lively tempo inside. "Personally, I don't think you need their help. Your aim is quite lethal on its own. Too bad you're out of ammo."

Ignoring the knowing smile in his voice, she bent her knee and raised her foot back to grab a velvet pump. "Don't count on it."

"Before I get a shoe or hairpin or that chair over there thrown at me, allow me to introduce myself. I'm Barrett Anderson, owner of the Blue Stag." He gave a short bow. "So you see, as a businessman I have little use for picking German pockets when they can come to my club and hand over the money willingly."

"How enterprising of you." The panic surging within her ebbed. She lowered her foot. "A little far from home, aren't you, Mr. Anderson?"

"A little farther than Berkshire, for certain." A dark eyebrow raised in acknowledgment. "Same as our hostess."

"What a coincidence."

"Sisters aren't coincidental." At her look of panic, he gave a short laugh. "You look alike, same upper accent."

No point in denying it. Half of Paris's Gestapo was inside. "So you've met Eleanor?"

"Briefly. I doubt she remembers. It was a New Year's party."

"Was there champagne?"

"Of course."

"Then no, she doesn't remember." Kat pressed her fingertips to her throbbing temple. The night had turned from horrendous to excruciating, and now this man had thrown in an unnecessary tangle. "However did you get up here?"

"Drainpipe. I would've come in the door, but there was a woman greeting her guts in the potted flowers just outside the building doors. Thought it best not to interrupt."

She glanced over the rail to judge the impressive feat. What else did this mystery man have up his sleeve? "Very considerate. Might I ask what you're doing here? Most Brits have packed up and left the city by now."

He leaned forward, catching the lantern light in his dark-blue eyes. "I could ask the same of you."

Warmth fluttered up her neck as the deep blueness probed for the secrets she kept locked away. Not to mention her heart and the bruises it carried. "Perhaps it's best to each mind our own business."

"Up to you." He shrugged, a lopsided grin tilting his full lips. "As for me, I'm heading inside before all the good drinks are gone and nothing is left except for the swill one of the waiters scrounged up on the black market. Care to join me?"

She clasped her hands together to keep from taking his offered arm and shook her head. She needed a few more minutes to refasten her armor before jumping back into the lion's den, and preferably without him watching her every move. "I'll rejoin the gaiety soon."

Music poured out on a roll of laughter as he opened the door. "Enjoy your evening, Miss Whitford."

The woman was out of her league. The Germans would sniff her out in a matter of days, if that, and kill her as a suspected spy. Or worse, put her on one of those trains with the Jews and other undesirables and ship her off. Likely to the camps or factories whose true intent they were so keen on hiding from the public behind false headlines of German victory. Maybe even straight to Berlin. Sir Alfred Whitford's daughter should fetch a hefty price.

Barrett shifted as the corner wall dug into his back. He'd been a fool to agree to Whitford's request behind the Secret Intelligence Service's back. A desperate fool who craved the hefty paycheck that came with accepting the side deal. With that amount of money he could finally start his life over on his own terms.

"Champagne?"

He shook his head at the white-gloved waiter and his tray. If he was going to drink, it was going to be a wee dram of pure scotch at the end of a long and satisfying day. Today had been long, but satisfying it was not. Not with another English debutante throwing herself at the mercy of the Nazis. What was the haughty rich girl thinking coming over by herself? Did she really expect that flippity sister of hers to drop the glittering social circle, that Nazi officer she pined for, and skip back home without a second thought? She was in for a rude awakening if she believed that.

Shifting position to see over the tops of the reveling scum, he watched Kathleen Whitford trying to blend herself into the wall. If she clung any tighter, she'd be a picture. A pretty picture, at least. Softly curled blond hair and smooth skin that had never seen a day of outdoor work. She should've kept to her ballrooms and fainting couches if she couldn't handle a simple party. What was she going to do when it was time to meet that pout-worm Eric and his SS chums? Faint at their feet, most likely.

He rolled his shoulders, stretching the tight jacket across his back. He should be at the pub, training the new recruits, but instead here he was chasing a girl across Paris because Sir Alfred was too much of a coward to come after the runaway himself. What kind of man allowed his daughters to step within a hundred miles of occupied soil and then paid someone else to fetch them back?

Kathleen inched closer to a potted plant. No doubt to hurl it at the next dancer who waltzed over her fancy shoes. But as frightened as she clearly was, she was here. No matter how much he disagreed with it, he had to give her a spot of admiration for crossing the Channel just like those brave lads.

But unlike the boys, she wasn't trained for combat. That's where he came in. But not tonight. Tonight he'd let her try her own way of getting Eleanor to listen to reason, and when that didn't work, he'd step in. Sir Alfred had paid him well.

Chapter 2

"Why is it so bright out here?"

Kat turned the page of her newspaper. "Because it's midday. One o'clock in the afternoon, to be exact."

Ellie threw up a hand to shield her eyes from the sun and shuffled onto the balcony in her fuzzy pink slippers. She plopped onto the spindle chair across the bistro table and groaned. "I feel like I just went to bed."

"You did—four hours ago."

"Then why did Sylvie wake me up?"

"I told her to." Oh, to be Ellie. Never a care in the world, never the burden of responsibility beyond picking out new shoes to weigh on her young shoulders. What must that sort of freedom taste like?

Kat turned a page. She bit her tongue to keep from gagging at the oversized picture of Helmut Knochen, the German senior commander of the security police in Paris. He'd rounded up more than one hundred Jews last week in a single swoop, according to the British paper she'd read before coming to Paris. The headlines back home were filled with the dreads of war, yet to read the French news one might believe it was a pure garden party under occupation.

Her fingers crushed the paper over the ugly man's face. "I found your day planner and noticed you have an appointment at three with a minister of music."

Ellie's white satin sleep mask slid higher as her brow wrinkled in concentration. "Oh, yes. We're supposed to go over the music list for Goebbels's new film premiere." She swiveled in her chair. "Pierre! Coffee, *tout de suit!*"

Kat frowned. "Are you not rationing?"

Turning back around, Ellie waved a manicured hand in dismissal. "Eric is head of Culture and Social Movement. He's given allowances, like most of the other top officials."

And Eric's allowances transferred to Ellie. Sourness knotted in Kat's stomach. Her baby sister, mistress to a Nazi. When had their lives veered off course and come to this?

Creasing her paper in half, she laid it on the table and took a small bite of her buttered toast. A true luxury. Back home they were allowed a single pat per day, enough to thinly scrape across mealy slices of bread. Were Parisians given the same allotment, or did they find themselves feasting as their occupiers did? "When do I get to meet this mysterious Eric?"

Ellie's face clouded. "Probably tomorrow. His . . . obligations keep him rather busy."

A lifetime of sharing sisterly secrets, braiding each other's hair after lights out, and hiding together from their governess whirled through Kat's emotions. She longed to reach out and hold her sister's hand just like she used to when the latest boy broke her heart. Instead, Kat curled her fingers, digging her nails into her palm. Those boys had never been Nazis.

"Does he have many obligations?"

"Too many to count now that Paris is fully under the Third Reich. He's been tasked personally by the Führer to oversee all the museums, gardens, theaters, and galleries and bring in German influences."

Kat swiped the crumbs from her fingers to the floor and ground them under her toe. "By Herr Hitler personally. My, my."

"His family has been friends with Eric's for years. They're invited to the Berghof each summer, and Eric is supposed to take me later next month."

The Berghof. Hitler's private escape in the Bavarian Alps. One had to be a member of the Nazi Party to gain access to the surrounding towns. If Kat had her way, they'd be safely back home long before Ellie could step foot near that atrocious place. A contact waited in Calais to smuggle them on board a Red Cross ship scheduled to leave for England next week. Screaming or compliant, Kat would have her sister on that ship.

Kat took a sip from her tea, washing down the now soured taste of toast. "Quite important, this man you've snagged. However did you meet?"

"At the Garnier for a performance of *Salome*. He sat in the box next to mine, but he kept watching me instead of the stage the whole night. He introduced himself at the intermission, and we've been inseparable since. Well, nearly inseparable. Pierre! Where's my coffee?"

Pierre hurried to the table and slid a silver tray with a steaming cup of coffee and a plate of croissants in front of Ellie. Black circles ringed his eyes as he blinked slowly like an owl up past its bedtime. The man had probably never seen his pillow last night. "*Excusez moi.* I could not find the coffeepot this morning. One of the guests had stuffed it on the top bookshelf."

Leaning back in her chair, Ellie lit a cigarette and puffed between coffee sips. She closed her eyes and tilted her face to the warm sun. Without all the heavy makeup from last night she looked like the sister from years ago.

How many days as children had they spent lying in the far fields of the estate, gazing up at the blue sky to see who could count the most fluffy white clouds? Kat always let Ellie win. Hard to believe they had once been so young and innocent.

The longing crumbled to sadness. Kat had grown to accept her duties, but Ellie still chased clouds. Only this time they bore the mark of a swastika.

A fuzzy slipper dangled from Ellie's foot as she jangled her leg crossed over the other. "It's too nice a day to stay shut up inside poring over lists of music with a man who sweats through his jacket." Her eyes popped open as a grin split her lips. "Let's go to the Luxembourg Garden. It's beautiful this time of year, and there's a wonderful café to sip wine in and listen to music."

Kat fingered the crust of her unfinished toast. She had no desire to tour gardens, drink wine, or enjoy music. Not here, and certainly not now when they fiddled to the tune of "Lili Marlene" straight from Germany. She only wanted to go safely home with Ellie—obliging or not—in tow. She crushed the corner of the toast under her thumb. But how? One wrong word or move and Ellie would toss her out onto the pavement.

"I promised Mother and Father to send them word once I got here. You know how they worry." She dusted the crumbs from her fingers, heart racing. "I'm sure they'd appreciate a note from you."

Ellie's leg jangled faster. She took a long drag and blew out the smoke on a snort. "Highly doubt that."

Kat resisted the urge to snatch the cigarette from Ellie's pouting mouth and shove it down her ungrateful throat. Did she not see the pain she'd inflicted on their entire family through her selfish whims? For once, could she not take credit for the situation she'd put them all in instead of leaving it to Kat to smooth things over? As always. "You left without a word to them, and they've been out of their minds with worry. Me too. We deserve more of your consideration."

"When did they ever show us consideration? We were nothing more than Father's little soldiers, arranged to obey his every command while Mother paraded us around like prize brood mares in search of the next great lineage to marry us off to. You wonder why I left."

"Like it or not, they are still our parents."

"You don't always have to do as they command, you know. Stop allowing yourself to be forced into situations where you're nothing more than a slave to the Whitford wheel of cold power. Live a little, Kat. Say no."

Ellie's words struck a sore spot that Kat had tried to bury under familial obligation and duty. As eldest daughter, she carried certain expectations, though of late they had grown more demanding. Perhaps, if social conventions didn't exist, she might allow herself the luxury of shedding the burdensome weight. To live as Ellie did, forging her own chosen life.

A knock sounded on the front door. Pierre's muffled voice drifted outside in answer.

Shaking off her envious thoughts, Kat leaned forward, desperate to keep her sister's attention before the butler came back with another interference. "I promised them a line or two from you. It would mean so much to them."

"So much to whom?" A heavy German voice severed the string of hope she'd flung out. A tall, slender man with slicked-back blond hair and a perfectly pressed gray uniform stood in the doorway. His unblinking blue eyes bored into Kat.

"Eric, darling!" Ellie grabbed his hand and pulled him to her side. "What a surprise to see you here. I thought you couldn't come today."

"I had a few minutes to spare between appointments and wanted to see how the party went last night." Releasing her hand, he leaned down and pulled Ellie's silk robe over her bare knee. "I didn't realize you had a guest."

"My sister, Kathleen, but you can call her Kat. She surprised me last night. Can you believe it?" Ellie gazed up at him before swinging her moonbeam grin in Kat's direction. "Isn't he dreamy? I just adore a man in uniform."

Eric's shiny black boots clicked together as he gave a short bow at the waist. "Major Eric von Schlegel, at your service."

Kat's lukewarm tea threatened to come back up and spill over his despicable jackboots. "Kathleen Whitford, Ellie's older sister."

"Of course sisters. You have the same beautiful expression and—what do you call it? English-rose complexion." He smiled, but the cool reserve didn't leave his eyes.

Kat matched his emotionless smile. "The natural gloominess of England provides the perfect shade, unlike here on the continent."

"I'm sure Eleanor is delighted to see you after so long apart, but how unexpected to see you turn up without notice. Especially in Paris."

His tone clipped the stifling air like scissors. Kat didn't flinch. If he thought to intimidate her with the mighty arm of German security in their occupied countries, then he was sorely mistaken. Her mother had instructed her every footstep through the viper-laced courts of London. A pretentious military officer was barely a challenge. However, a German officer with a Luger strapped to his side was another matter altogether.

"I missed my dear Ellie and would have sailed to Timbuktu for a chance to see her." She beamed across the table at her. "Luckily, I only had to go so far as Paris."

"And how did you get here?"

"I'm sure she's told you a little about our father." He blinked. Of course she had. Ellie never knew when to keep things to herself. "He has far-reaching connections, none of which I care to know too much about as long as they can get me to where I wish to go. And this time it was Paris."

Kat leaned back in her chair and crossed her legs. *Take that, old chum.*

Eric's fingers twitched on the brim of the hat he had clasped under his arm. Despite the sun glaring from the high windows on the opposite side of the street, the light-blue eyes didn't squint. "Do you plan to stay long?"

Shrugging, she took a sip of her watery tea. "Haven't thought about it. We have a whole year to catch up on. Right, Ellie?"

"A year and two months." Ellie reached her hand over the side of the table, ready to tap off the ashes of her cigarette. "Where's that potted plant? The one with the red flower?"

Kat glanced around until spotting the shattered remains of the pot on the other side of the door. Last night it'd been meant for a man's head. A Scotsman who had swung off the drainpipe in evening attire. For one so desperate to get into a party, he'd barely spoken to anyone and spent the rest of the night watching her from across the room.

Ellie followed her gaze. "What happened there? Oh, dear. Eric, darling, you'll have to get me a new flower, as someone's broken the one you gave me. Perhaps a lily this time."

Kat smirked. Any regret she had for smashing that poor plant vanished knowing it was a gift from Herr Soldier Boy.

"Anything you wish, *schatz*." Eric dropped his hand to Ellie's shoulder, roving his fingertips over the back of her neck and skin just below her collar. His cold eyes raised to Kat in challenge.

Gathering every shard of revulsion, Kat shoved them all the way down, grinding her toes into the floor until she thought the balcony ready to bust beneath her. "Ellie tells me you're in charge of museums. Quite the cushy job." There. If there was an award for Best Actress Pretending Not to Hate Her Sister's Nazi Suitor, the prize was hers for the taking. If only she could cram it down his throat afterward.

"Cushy? *Nein*, no. It is very hard work gathering all the right paintings, music, exhibits, and lectures to showcase the wonder and might of Germany." His chest swelled, pushing out the silver buttons running down his tunic. "The Führer takes great pride in what the world will see of us, and so do I. You should come and see for yourself. I think you will be much impressed."

"Not today, darling." Ellie took a long drag, allowing the smoke to curl up from her lip. "We're going to Luxembourg Gardens to see the fountains and get some fresh air. That party left me positively confined."

The insipid smirk flattened into a long line on Eric's lips. "You have a meeting today at three with Herr Graeber."

Ellie waved her hand, scattering ash across the table. "He can pick music by himself. Or better yet, use the list we decided on from last week."

"Your job is to oversee every little detail with absolute perfection: selecting music, securing venues, organizing guest lists and invitations. I gave Dr. Goebbels my personal recommendation that you could perform all tasks to the highest of degrees. You are not taking your duties seriously."

"Of course I am, except when it's unnecessary. Besides, shouldn't my sisterly duties come first?"

"Nothing should come before serving the work of the Führer."

"That's because he doesn't like his sisters." Ellie winked across the table, pulling a smile from Kat just like she always did.

Red flooded Eric's cheeks. Taking Ellie by the elbow, he hauled her to her feet. "May I speak to you privately, *schatz*?"

Kat surged to her feet and gripped the rail to keep from going after them. Ellie was a big girl. She'd gotten herself tied up with that thickhead and she could untangle herself. Only he didn't seem the kind of man to easily unsnarl.

Far below, taxis trundled by, mixing their exhaust with the scent of warm bread from the *boulangerie* on the corner. A queue of locals stretched around the block, shifting with impatience, eyes downcast. The exiting customers looked neither left or right as they kept their heads down and hurried away with scant packages tucked tightly under their arms. A day's worth of food for an entire family. Meanwhile, the buffet presented at Ellie's party last night would have been enough to feed the block for the rest of the week. Uneaten oysters, canapés, and cakes were waiting in the rubbish bin to be taken out without a thought for the leftover waste.

"Well, I'm sorry, but she's my sister and she's staying here."

Kat's ears prickled as the conversation inside wound its way out.

"And when am I supposed to see you?" Eric's tone ended on a whine.

"You're seeing me now. Oh, don't give me that face. We'll still have time for us, and perhaps, if you behave, I'll pull out that lace slip you bought me last week."

Heat burned up Kat's neck. She tugged at the collar of her blouse.

"Yes, yes. I'll make it up to Herr Graeber. Of course I want to make you happy, and I'm doing my best, Eric, truly I am."

"Then perhaps don't sit outside where every man can stare at you in your nightgown."

Kat's fingernails curled into her palm as their voices dipped again. The front door clicked shut. Her bottled breath hissed out between her clenched teeth.

Ellie whirled back onto the balcony, her satin robe closed tight over her chest and neck. "Shall we go?"

Chapter 3

Barrett tossed the watery packet of ice onto the desk in his upstairs office at the Blue Stag and carefully rotated his arm around. Better, but he'd smart from that blow to the shoulder for a few days. Good thing Anton weighed a mere seven stone when wet, or he'd have a broken collarbone instead of a bruise.

Shuffling the worn postcards of Coney Island, New York, and Washington, DC, he carefully returned them to the small carved box on the corner of his desk. Soon it wouldn't be merely a dream. He could leave the unwashed existence of his life behind and start over with a name that didn't carry the burden of ill-fated ghosts.

Trumpet notes drifted up through the floorboards, announcing a new set. He checked his wristwatch. Nine o'clock on the dot. Greenwich could set its clocks by Sam. Unfortunately, it also meant his time of hiding was over for the night.

Wincing as he slipped on his jacket, he cast a longing look at the bottle of Ballantine's on the side shelf. "Soon, my old friend, you and I will have a wee dram, but now it's time to play for the jackals."

Locking his office door behind him, he hurried down the stairs into the back room that served as a washing station, stock area, and waiters' loitering area before the doors opened. At the moment it bustled like a hive of jittery bees.

"Get this water mopped up before someone slips." He pointed to an overflow of drips from the sink. "Did that case of bourbon arrive? What about that order for the glasses?"

Corbin, his second in command, cocked his head in exasperation.

"*Oui, Patron.* Everything is taken care of just like it always is, so I don't understand why you always ask."

"Because I need something to do while you get all the real work done." Barrett clapped him on the back, ruffling the thin man's starched black jacket. "No one I trust more to keep my ship sailing smoothly."

"Talking to me about ships. What do I look like to you, a fish?" Corbin muttered, smoothing the back of his jacket.

"If I'm to mingle with pigs, why not a fish?"

"Then there is a whole barrel of them out there waiting for you. Happy hunting, *Patron.*"

If only. Rolling back his shoulders, Barrett pushed through the swinging door. A wide room lined with dark walnut paneling and scuffed maple floors spread before him. A long bar backed by a mirror and shelves of glass bottles lined the entirety of one wall. Cozy booths lined the other wall with bistro tables and chairs dotted between. If it wasn't all a sham, he might actually take pride in this place. Not every day an orphaned brawler from the alleys of Glasgow ran a joint like this.

In the back corner on a low stage flocked by heavy, dark-green curtains, Sam led the six-piece band in his newest arrangement of "There'll Always Be an England." Thankfully, the Germans were too tone deaf to recognize the popular song. Berlin had decreed only German music to be played in occupied lands. Anyone caught playing or listening to anything else would immediately be arrested and sent to one of the work factories along the Polish border manufacturing shells and tanks for the German war machine. But the people of Paris had found a way to artistically revolt through cleverly arranged music that fooled their captors. And Sam was the master artist. There was nothing that talented man couldn't bend a trumpet note around, but no one in Paris had wanted to hire him after the Nazis invaded. No one could risk hiring a Jew. Barrett had given him a full ten-second audition before hiring him on the spot. In the passing months Sam had proven himself an expert chess player, a lover of Shakespeare quotes, and a great proponent of optimism. He was also the closest Barrett had come to having a friend.

A nervous young boy popped up in front of him. "Sir, I would like to apologize again for falling on top of you. I know the objective was to tackle, but I can do better. I *will* do better next time."

Barrett took half a step back before his newest waiter and recruit bumped his nose. "Of course you will. That's why we practice over and over, so it becomes as natural as breathing."

"*Oui*, sir."

"You did good today. Be proud." The boy beamed and turned to go before Barrett signaled him back. "And Anton, from now on let's keep the days' duties out of earshot of our patrons."

Red splashed across Anton's pointed face. "*Oui*, sir."

His patrons. Barrett gritted his teeth. They spread across his bar like a disease of gray filth with gleaming buttons, starched collars, and scrawling swastikas. Here they dared to sit, laughing, drinking, and tapping their polished jackboots to unauthorized non-German swing music. If he didn't have an operation to run in the basement, he'd lock the doors and set a match. Or fifty.

He turned to the bar. "How's it going tonight, Henri?"

The bartender sidestepped around his staff to the end of the bar and handed Barrett the clean glass of water he had at the ready. "Fair enough. Sam's keeping them in high spirits, so the beer is flowing. I told him to try a slower one soon so they'll order the wine."

Barrett fingered the rim of the sweating glass. "That horrible batch that fell off the back of a lorry last week?"

Henri nodded. "But the Germans will be so drunk by then that they'll never notice."

"No wonder you're the best barkeep in town."

Running a cloth over his impeccably kept bar, Henri leaned his elbow on the wood and smiled wickedly. "I could be the best in all of France if you'd let me add a few drops of poison to their mugs."

"The Gestapo would be on us faster than a tick on a deerhound, and I don't fancy myself locked in an interrogation room with a boy who only put on brass because his da paid for the commission. Always got a chip on their shoulder with something to prove."

"Not much for military rank, are you, *Patron?*"

Taking a long swallow of water, Barrett shook his head. "That's why they've got me here with you lot."

"And I thought it was because you loved the Parisian nightlife and its people so much that you left your beloved highland hills of Scotland to come here and open a bar."

Barrett winced at his cover story. It wasn't the worst he'd ever heard, and it had kept the Germans from sniffing around too much. For now.

Shifting to put the bandstand in view, he caught Sam's eye and gave him the wind-down signal. They needed to move that bad wine off the block before his new stock arrived in the morning. The back-door dealers got itchy when there wasn't room enough for their provisions and hiked the prices on the next turn around.

Sam nodded and eased the boys into a slow tune. The crowd's voices hummed lower between the gentle clanking of glasses and the swanky trumpet notes. Cigarette smoke blossomed over the tables like mushrooms. The acridity smothered the rich smell of wood paneling, the earthy soil in the newly potted plants by the front door, and the warmth of the brass sconces flickering along the walls. First thing in the morning, he'd throw open the front windows to air out the suffocating toxins.

Barrett took another sip of water and rolled the glass between his hands. Funny how real the place had become to him. Four years ago he'd been stuck in the same brewery his da had, and then a back-alley brawl with a politician's drippy-nosed son had changed his life.

Either spend a few years behind bars or go to work for the government, he'd been told. He didn't need a second breath to decide that one. Now, here he was in Paris training Resistance operatives for the SIS in the basement of a nightclub that entertained Nazis. As soon as he served his sentence, he'd be on the first boat across the Atlantic with Alfred Whitford's paycheck to set up a new life far from all of this with no obligations but to himself.

Disgust roiled his stomach as his eyes roamed over the brilliantine-slicked heads of the officers and soft curls of their dates. What self-respecting woman ran around with Nazis? Women did all kinds of things for love, or what they foolishly thought was love. Never was there a more wasteful sentiment.

The disgust soured as his two awaited blondes breezed in the front door with a tall man marching behind them. His new charges. Get them out safely and back to England, payment upon delivery, Sir Alfred's message had said. A cut-and-dried task. How difficult could two socialites be?

"Get that champagne ready." He handed Henri his empty water glass. "The good kind."

Henri winked. "The expensive kind."

"What else?"

As instructed, Corbin led the trio down the center of the tables to the best seat in the house. In front of the band, but just to the side so conversation could carry on without getting an earload of trumpet and bass.

Wisps of cigarette smoke curled around Eleanor's head as she laughed and waved at people two tables over. Beautiful as a butterfly and just as flighty. What a mess she'd caused them all. The man next to her, the reported Eric von Schlegel, sat as if a pipe had been rammed up the back of his jacket. And then there was Kathleen. Elegant and cool in a summery blue getup, her only giveaway was the nervous bouncing of her foot under the table and the slight looks over her slim shoulder.

Drink orders taken, Corbin glided past the bar on his way to the back. "They're all yours, *Patron*."

Taking a deep breath to calm his bumped-up heart rate, Barrett summoned his most congenial air and made his way to the star table. "You made it after all."

Eleanor spun back in her chair, her red lips parting in a wide smile. "Of course we did. After your insistence last night, we simply had to come and see what all the fuss was about."

"As you proved such a gracious hostess, I only hope I can return the favor tonight." His gaze slid to the back of Kathleen's head. "Though my views are hopeless compared to the one I found from your balcony."

Shoulders stiff, Kathleen's head turned up. Blue-green eyes slammed into his. They were more vivid than he'd given them credit for last night.

"Mr. Anderson. How nice to see you on level ground."

"The occasion called for solid footing this evening."

Eleanor rocked to the front of her seat, a silver cigarette holder dangling from her manicured hand. "Do you two know each other?"

Kathleen shook her head, slipping golden curls over her shoulder. "We met briefly last night. Though I had no idea we would be enjoying the delights of his establishment so soon."

Tapping her ashes into the ashtray, Eleanor rolled her eyes up at Barrett. "You'll have to forgive my sister. She's forgotten how to have a good time. I'm hoping the French night air opens her up a bit."

Barrett gritted his back teeth. The girl was more delusional than he'd realized. A vise had choked the French air ever since Hitler's men goose-stepped down the Champs Élysées last year. "If that fails, I have a bottle of champagne on its way that should do the trick."

Von Schlegel shifted in his chair, announcing the lack of attention directed his way.

A tick wound its way up Barrett's jaw. He forced it into a welcoming smile. "Apologies, sir. I'm Barrett Anderson, owner of the Blue Stag."

The sleek blond head tilted in acknowledgment. "Major Eric von Schlegel. Minister of Culture and Social Movement in France."

"Quite a title."

"Quite a responsibility."

"I'm sure. Promoting movies and music is difficult when trying to appease the masses."

The German's nostrils flared in disdain. "My mission is not to appease but to inform. The only difficulty is cleansing out the rot that came before me."

"Aye, I did notice a few of the floorboards going bad the last time I was at Bobino's. Miss Baker was known to drop a few banana peels during her performances, which probably contributed to the problem."

Confusion flickered in cold blue eyes. Then slow recognition that snapped to revulsion. "Miss Baker, if you can call her a 'miss,' has no place on a stage. She and others of her undesirable kind will be expunged from their hovels to make way for the pure artists of the Fatherland."

Just what the world stage needs. Bony-kneed men in lederhosen leaping to the rousing tune of an accordion. They'd have the Garnier smelling of sauerkraut in no time.

Sam's muted coronet billowed across the room like a warm breeze, assuaging the anger building in Barrett's chest. Sam was the most talented musician he'd ever met and a loyal friend. God-fearing as well, with barely two farthings to rub together, he'd give you the shirt off his back. And in the eyes of the Third Reich, he was considered an undesirable because of the blood that ran in his veins and those of his forefathers.

Before he could put his fist into the buffoon's face, Corbin rescued him with a bottle of champagne. Shooing his man away, Barrett tucked the bottle under his arm and popped the cork. Golden froth spilled from the mouth, splattering on the floor. Two drops plopped on von Schlegel's shiny toe. Kathleen's lip curled as she noticed the damage. If he wasn't inwardly grinning from his own satisfaction, Barrett would pull her aside for a short lesson in controlling her expressions better.

Pouring three glasses, he set the bottle in a bucket of ice. Kathleen reached forward, brushing his hand as she took her bubbling goblet. Her fingers tingled icy cold despite the almost-ninety-degreee temperature outside. Poor lass. The telltale nerves would give her away before long.

Snatching the cork from the floor, Barrett pushed it into his pocket. "Enjoy, and don't hesitate to call out for more."

"Oh, no! You must join us." To the chagrin of her tablemates, Eleanor patted the space next to her. "I insist, from one spectacular host to another."

Grabbing an empty chair from the next table, he settled between the sisters. He couldn't have situated himself in the viper's nest more perfectly if he'd planned it himself. "Who am I to refuse such a request? Hope you don't mind sharing the company of these beautiful ladies, von Schlegel."

"Of course not, as long as you know one is spoken for." His long fingers closed over Eleanor's hand. "And it's *Major*. We officers have earned the right for our rank to be used in address."

"Eric, you're so stuffy sometimes." Eleanor laughed on a puff of smoke. "Can you believe the sourpusses I surround myself with? Oh, dear, you don't have a glass."

Barrett waved off the glass she tried pushing in front of him. "No, thank you. I prefer to keep a clear head during work hours. Never know when you have to jump in the middle of a crisis."

Kathleen twirled the stem of her glass between her fingers, swirling the bubbling liquid into a tiny whirlpool. "Such as running out of clean glasses?"

A laugh scratched his throat. So there was a sense of humor brewing under that stiff upper lip after all. "More like breaking up drunken fights in the back alley and poring over the ledgers until the wee hours of the morning. It's a dull life I lead, but I'd have it no other way."

Her fair eyebrows lifted. "And how does one get into the dull trade of bartending? Lifelong aspiration, or profound knowledge of brews that you had to share with the rest of the world?"

"My da was a brewmaster, so it was likely I'd follow in his footsteps in some way, but being under another man's thumb was no life for me. If I have a lifetime of work ahead of me, then I'm going to be my own boss."

A dark cloud passed over her face. She blinked it away before he had time to decipher it. "Why come so far from home?"

"Not much to recommend me back in Glasgow. Came here to start over where no one knows me."

Von Schlegel snorted.

"Is that funny, Major?"

"Not particularly, only I find it amusing that you think no one knows you here. That you have slipped into this city as a stranger. I know all about you." Von Schlegel sipped the champagne, the delicate glass a perfect fit to his slim, pale hand.

The imperious tone raised Barrett's hackles. If not for the threat of jail hanging over him, he'd seek personal satisfaction in wiping the ridiculousness from the German's face. Crossing his arms over his chest, he tipped his chair back. "Tell me."

"Your mother is French. Your father British."

"Scottish, actually."

A blond eyebrow hiked. "Is it not the same thing?"

"Not to a Scot."

Kathleen shifted in her chair, bumping her agitated foot against

Barrett's leg. "It's more than an insult to confuse a Scot with an Englishman. A mistake you shouldn't make twice, Major."

The German brushed her warning off with a flick of his hand. "All from the same island and not worth deciphering the nuanced differences."

Thoroughly dismissed from his own conversation, Barrett leaned back in his chair as Kathleen's jittering foot belied the calmness of her face. "Quite a bit of difference, especially when the English marched in to rule where they weren't wanted."

"They brought law and order to a land of wild men running around half naked. It was for the best."

"That's what bullies always say."

"Bullies." Von Schlegel scoffed. "Men of vision."

"Two names for the act of taking something that doesn't belong to them. That will never belong to them." Kathleen's eyes flickered to her sister and back to von Schlegel. A perfectly polite smile slipped into place. "A lesson we should learn from history. But alas, some things never change."

Barrett dug his fingers into his knee. If not for the paycheck awaiting him, he'd wring that beautiful neck of hers. This little side job he'd taken on was already proving too much of a headache. He stretched his fingers out, rubbing them back and forth to loosen the tension.

"Ease off, Kat. I'm not a little girl anymore." Eleanor shot her sister a curdling look that was more reminiscent of a six-year-old than the elegantly coiffed woman she posed as. She leaned into her German lover. Her hand fluttered possessively over his arm. "Besides, I've got Eric now to defend my honor. Right, darling?"

Von Schlegel's eyes eased down to the creamy skin exposed by Eleanor's low V-cut gown. Grasping her fingers, he raised them to his lips. "Nothing gives me greater pleasure." As he released her hand, the passion banked in his eyes. "Straighten up, *schatz*. Your dress will wrinkle."

A vein ticked in Kathleen's neck. "How kind of you to look out for Ellie when I wasn't here, Major."

"It was my pleasure from the moment we first met, and will continue to be so long after you've sailed away." He draped an arm around the back of Eleanor's chair and trailed his fingers across her shoulders. "No one can take my Eleanor from me now. Not ever."

Like a cork ready to explode from a wine bottle, Kathleen snapped from her chair. Her long fingers curled white around her beaded handbag. "Will you excuse me a minute, please? I need to powder my nose."

Barrett jumped to his feet, but von Schlegel remained seated with smug victory curling his lip. "Behind those curtains. Second door on the left."

As she hurried off, Barrett grabbed the empty champagne bottle and tucked it under his arm to keep from smashing it over the Nazi's head. "That reminds me. I've got a few things to check on in the back, but I'll be back shortly and with a new bottle of this."

"Work is never done, *ja*?"

"No. It never is."

Swiping the lipstick across her mouth, Kathleen fumbled for the cap and nicked off the creamy tip of the stick. "Drat."

She scooped the precious red curl into her fingernail and gingerly patted it back onto the stick. Not perfect, but with rationing on she wasn't about to let it go to waste. Blotting with her lace-trimmed hankie, she slipped it and the mended tube back into her handbag and dared to glance into the vanity mirror. Normal color had returned to her cheeks. Curse that man for making her lose her cool. Tears prickled the back of her eyes. She blinked rapidly. No, no hint of tears until she and Ellie stepped safely back into England for good. And then they would be tears of joy for having escaped the Nazis' clutches.

Spinning, she checked the seam of her stockings. Thankfully, she still had a drawer full of silk ones and hadn't been relegated to the itchy cotton pairs. Yet. Or worse, to staining her legs with tea like many of the other girls. She smoothed her hand over a wrinkle near her hip, then dropped it. She'd once despised wrinkles, but tonight was quickly changing her opinion on them.

Venom rippled in her veins. It clawed the sense struggling to rule her mind. *Get ahold of yourself. Cowering in here like some ninny from a schoolyard bully. You are the daughter of Sir Alfred Whitford. Now pluck the backbone God gave you.*

Tipping her chin, she pushed the frosted glass door open and stepped into the lovely sound of a piano and violin crooning down the hall. As soon as she got back to the table she'd turn her back to that horrible man and listen to the jazzy notes—

"What do you think you're doing?" Someone grabbed her arm and yanked her behind a large potted palm. Barrett Anderson towered over her like a seething volcano. "Do you have any idea the game you're playing at? You are in way over your head."

She slapped his hand away. "Stop accosting me in dark places."

"Then stop painting a target on your forehead."

"Whatever are you talking about?"

Impatience burned in his dark-blue eyes. "That Nazi. If you have any hope of getting your sister back, then you'd better learn to smile a little more convincingly."

She took a wobbly step back. Palm leaves brushed the backs of her knees. "I don't know what you mean."

"Don't play dumb. It's not attractive on ladies of your breeding."

He knows. Blood pounded in her head. Her father's contacts at MI6 had warned of spies around every corner. With agents trained to charm the socks right off you or put a bullet in your head, she was to trust no one. *Simple is better. Just say what they told you to say.* "I'm here merely to visit Ellie."

"With the intent of dragging her back to England, by the roots of her hair if you have to." He took a deep breath, swelling the broad expanse of his chest. The irritation slowly faded from his eyes. "As comical as that would be to witness, we can find quieter ways of doing it. Ways that won't have the Gestapo chasing our trail."

"'*We*'? No, no, I'm afraid there's been a mistake." She took another step back, bumping into the pot. Why, oh, why hadn't she demanded better instruction on handling interrogations?

"You want her back, and so does Parliament before she spills everything she knows to that clod-headed boyfriend."

Kat shook her head, whirling the blood pooling there. "Ellie knows nothing beyond how to throw a smashing party, and even if she did, she certainly wouldn't betray her country."

"She's already betrayed it by coming here."

"You're wrong." Even as the words slipped from her tongue, she tasted their false bitterness.

"We'll Meet Again" crooned from the muted pipes of the trumpet as a bass strummed the harmony. She'd last heard this song the night before Ellie disappeared. They'd spent the whole evening at Lord Melford's party trying to find partners who didn't step on their feet. As Ellie hugged her good night, Kat never thought it meant goodbye. Her dear little sister had a penchant for finding trouble, but a traitor . . . She pressed a hand to the throbbing above her eyes.

"Miss Whitford, I know you have the best of intentions coming here." Barrett shifted, drawing her attention. Weariness etched his tan face. "But your best intentions won't save your sister from the shark-infested waters she's flung herself into. You need someone who's treaded the waters before."

"She never was a good swimmer."

A white scar shone above his top lip as his mouth tilted in a half smile. "At least you remembered your sense of humor. It'll come in handy for what we're about to do."

"'We' again?" Kat straightened her shoulders. He was dealing with the wrong sister if he thought to bully her. "No, I'm sorry, Mr. Anderson, but I'll ask you to refrain from barging in on our private affairs."

"The second she stepped foot on occupied soil, your affair was no longer a private matter. That's why I'm here. I'm getting you and your Rhine-loving sister back to good ol' Blighty before she has the chance to waltz Hitler straight to the gates of Buckingham Palace."

Chapter 4

The bar's blue velvet curtains had been tied back to throw open the large front windows in hopes of catching a warm breeze. Morning sunlight spilled over the gleaming tables and dark panels as dust motes danced around Kat's head. How different it was from last night when it had been filled with music and drunken Nazis.

The room stood empty except for a boy behind the long bar polishing mugs. A lively tune whistled from his lips as he focused on the glasses in front of him, but his eyes flicked up to watch her every few seconds. A lookout should she try to escape, no doubt.

Barrett strolled in through the back door. Dark-brown trousers, scuffed shoes, and a light-blue shirt with the sleeves rolled back had replaced last night's formal appearance. His eyes were deep blue rather than dark, and his hair more chestnut than what she had first glimpsed that night on the balcony. In the clear light of day, without the distraction of cigarette haze, he was quite handsome. In a rumpled devil-may-care sort of way.

"You came."

"You threatened."

A rakish grin pulled at his mouth as he swiped at the sweat dotting his forehead. "Oh, aye. I did, didn't I?"

"Most colorfully." Following his ambush by the potted plant, he'd given her no choice but to meet him the next morning. Meet him or be kept hostage among his bottles of illicit drink until she agreed.

Must you always do as they say? Ellie's words of liberation taunted her as she realized she'd been forced into another position with few given options. Not once had she been asked for consent nor even an opinion on this interloper to her already-made plans. Someone else had decided it was best.

"Now, may we attend to this business you insist upon so I may return to more important matters?"

"Don't take this the wrong way, but I admire a woman who can get down to brass tacks." He gestured to the door he'd just come from. "Shall we?"

Kat shook her head as the alarm she'd desperately kept at bay all morning came rushing back in a tidal wave. "I prefer to hear whatever you have to say out here in the open."

"What I have to say can't be said out here in the open." He dropped his hand and shoved it into his trouser pocket. Lean muscle rippled in his forearm. "You don't trust me. Another admirable trait under most circumstances, but in this you're wrong."

When she didn't budge, he moved toward her. The cordiality slipped from his tone. "I had a late night and two fights to break up, so don't make this more difficult than it needs to be. I'll toss you over my shoulder if I have to."

"Charming."

"I'm not here to charm you, merely keep you out of trouble."

She hesitated for the briefest of seconds as she read the flat line of his mouth. She should have told Ellie where she was really going in case she was walking into a trap. Too late to change her mind now. She walked through the door he indicated.

"If you're to have me swinging from balconies, then you should know my footwear is hardly adequate."

He grabbed a bulging burlap sack and slung it over his shoulder. "Lucky for you, no swinging or physical exertion of any kind is required today. If there is a next time, I'll give you warning to wear loafers, or whatever women wear for comfort, because I'm sure what you have on your feet now isn't."

Kat glanced down at her red peep toes with tiny bows at the buckles. "I can hardly wait."

Skirting around dishwashers stacking clean glasses to dry and towers of wine bottles, they wedged themselves between two barrels of beer and to a small door tucked in the corner.

Barrett opened the door and stepped down. A light glowed over his head. "This way."

This way to her death, by the look of those stairs.

Musty air filled her lungs as she took a deep breath and stepped behind him. And missed the stair. She pitched forward, and with lightning speed Barrett whirled. His arms scooped around her as if dipping her in a dance.

"Careful now, lass. Throwing yourself at a man in the dark, he might think you're after something else."

Her fingers curled like grappling hooks into his chest as the warmth of his solid body pressed against hers, folding around her like a cloak. Heated blood spun around her heart and rushed to her head. Slowly, she spread out her fingers and gently pushed out of his protective hold. "I assure you, your virtue is safely intact."

"More's the pity."

Righting herself, she gripped the wall for support and forced her heart to slow its racing as the warmth of him ebbed from her skin. She held her arms out for support as they descended the narrow stairs into a cavern of pitch black.

"Stop right there. Don't want you missing the last step and busting your head all over my stock." Barrett fumbled in front of her. *Click.* Light flooded the room. He grasped her hand. "Careful now."

Kat blinked as if the sun had popped up. She waited as dizzying spots slowly formed into tall racks of dusty bottles of reds, whites, rosés, and champagne. Holding Barrett's hand to keep herself steady, she stretched her leg down to reach the awkward distance to the floor. His warmth seeped through her glove. She immediately dropped his hand.

"There must be a century's worth of wine down here." Kat fingered a merlot from 1869. What her mother wouldn't give to flaunt such a prestigious collection. "Bet it tastes better than that swill you serve upstairs."

"The swill is for the swine. These wee beauties will go to celebrate our Allied victory." Walking to the far back, he shouldered a tall rack and pushed. Corded muscles in his forearms strained until the rack swung away to expose a low door. "Bet you can't guess what's through here."

"Torture chamber?"

White teeth flashed in his tan face. "Some might call it that. Care to find out?"

The alarm from earlier wound through her stomach like a knotted rope. "I've come this far."

"Thata lass."

After an intricate pattern of raps on the door from Barrett, it creaked open to reveal a bulbous nose and an attached face that looked as though it had been pulverized by a meat grinder.

"*Se assurer.*"

"*Stand sure.*" An appropriate password for whatever Barrett was hiding down here. Kat clasped her hands and tried not to imagine a masked man with shackles waiting for her on the other side. Her fingers brushed the bottom of her handbag, reassured by the bulky weight of the knotted life preserver resting inside. It might not save her life, but bloody well if she wasn't fighting to the end.

Shifting the bag on his shoulder, Barrett stepped through and held the door for her. "Careful now. These doors were built for wee ones."

"Not strapping men such as yourself?" Kat ducked, but the doorway still knocked her red felt hat sideways. She spat out the navy ribbons that swung into her mouth.

"Told you to watch your head." He stepped aside and gestured to the large room behind him. "Welcome to the French Resistance."

The space was a long rectangle with padded walls. Overhead lamps dangled from the vaulted ceiling, and worn rugs lay scattered over the dirt-packed floor. Tables and chairs sat neatly stacked in a corner surrounded by maps of France and Germany. A makeshift firing range had been erected along the back wall, where crudely painted targets and a variety of firearms hung. Standing in groups of twos and threes there were at least twenty men and three women with fists raised in combat stance.

She could hear a pin drop as they all stopped and stared at her.

"*Ce que vous cherchez à?*" Barrett's bark filled the cavern. His Scottish burr scuffed his French. "Come and get your fill." He tossed the burlap sack onto a wobbly table. Potatoes, oysters, half loaves of bread, and other items wrapped in wax paper spilled out. The base ingredients of the opulent offerings set before the German customers last night. The gathered men and women fell on the feast like starving wolves.

"Leftovers from the bar," Barrett offered as way of explanation. "The Blue Stag is given extra rations to keep our jackbooted clientele well fed and drunk. I've managed to stretch supplies a little further by picking up certain items from the lesser-known markets."

"The black market, you mean."

"Don't turn your nose up. It's the only way to get the good stuff if you're not a Nazi, and my fighters depend on it. The rations they're given as citizens are pathetic. They can barely keep their families fed on it. This is sometimes the only meal they get a day. Brave devils."

The breakfast of toast, eggs, and cream Kat had consumed mere hours ago threatened to sour in her full stomach as the veil of disillusion tore from her privileged gaze. Her own dilemmas paled in contrast to these visceral sufferings.

"Who told you to stop practicing?" Barrett barked as the fighters swept up the last of the crumbs with their fingers and shoveled them into eager mouths. "Do you want the Germans better trained than you? Get back to it. *Tout de suite.*"

A feather could have knocked Kat over. Running to keep ahead of the Nazis, she'd fallen into the lap of the very operation struggling to fight back. "Never did I imagine."

Barrett crossed his arms over his chest, grinning with pride. "Thought I was leading you to your deserved doom. Surprised?"

"To say the least." Kat's hand fluttered to right the skewed hat on her head. Her mind raced to connect the dots. "You're not really a bar owner?"

"I am, but it's a cover for this. The SIS needed someone who could run a successful pub while instructing how to bloody a few German noses."

Her eyes traveled to the bullet-ridden back wall. A new appreciation sparked for the mysterious man at her side. "Seems you do a little more than that."

"My recruits are trained for every possible necessity. Bloody nose, broken skull, or blown bridge. They learn it all here."

He stood straight and tall with a confident tilt of his chin. A slight dip in his nose indicated a one-time break. Or more. The scar sitting atop his lip shone white as he eased into a smile, while his large, blunt fingers tapped with impatience as if the boxing match before them called him to join in.

"Who are you?"

He shrugged, not taking his eyes from the rib jabbing. "Just a simple man trying to end this war before any more of our lads get laid low."

"Mr. Anderson, I believe you to be many things, but simple is not one of them."

"I know my way around a bottle or two and how to keep my feet in a scuffle. One day I met the right people—or rather they met me. They threw me into a few months of official skill sharpening and tasked me with training willing French citizens to fight back using guerilla attacks."

A frown puckered between her eyebrows. "Would not a Frenchman have been a better choice? As a Scotsman, surely you stand out."

"As an underground instructor, I suppose they're willing to loosen the rules a bit for proper training. Didn't hurt that I'm part French, though that hasn't made much difference." His dark-blue eyes flickered to her. "More recent, I've been tasked with babysitting."

"The British government cares about two girls? Is the war not enough to concern them?"

His eyes dropped to the ground. "Suffice it to say you're important enough to need supervision."

"I don't require a caretaker."

"And I don't need to trail after two girls who don't have the sense to stay where they belong when my efforts are needed here. Where I'm trying to keep good people alive for their country instead of dying for it."

For months she'd endured the hardships of war by conserving her lipstick, wearing fashions from two years past, and canning jams at the local Women's Institute. How grand they had felt to pitch in to do their bit before laying their heads to rest on a pillow at night. Not once was she forced to entertain the thought of picking up a weapon or laying down her life. Soldiers did that. Faceless others who courageously ran into the line of fire to protect the innocent and save the world from tyranny. *Here* were the others. Here were the faces she could not unsee, that so blithely put her best efforts of bravery to shame. Family restrictions, a wayward sibling—they held no weight in comparison to the horrors happening right here. She was a right high hat for thinking otherwise.

Barrett scuffed a toe against the corner of a frayed rug. Two men tumbled in front of them. The smaller one slipped around and pinned his larger opponent. Barrett nodded in approval. "For laughs, do you have any plan on how to get the two of you out of here? Getting in must've been simple enough. Someday you'll have to tell me how Father dear pulled the strings. But getting both of you out will prove trickier. Especially with that propaganda minister she's consorting with. He's not all he seems."

"I was told no one is in this town."

"Too right about that."

"Including yourself?"

He slid her a wink. "Especially myself."

Kat blinked and quickly looked away as heat spiraled over her cheeks. Men never flirted with her, at least not without the incentive of bending her father's ear in the political arena. Men like Marcus. His nice smile and manners had convinced her that love would come in time. Joke was on her. He'd needed the Whitford influence, and her father had wanted the blue-blooded name. When she'd discovered her father pulling together the strings of the engagement, the stab of betrayal had left her reeling. He didn't even trust her to pick the right man.

She moved away to examine the marked maps on the wall. The coolness of the air soaked into her skin, pushing out the ridiculous heat Barrett had flared. His flirtation was no more meaningful than the others, but like those who had gone before him, he wanted something in return. Cooperation.

"Now that I've laid bare my secret, it's time for you to tell me your plan of escape."

Ignoring his nearness behind her, she continued to stare at the black swastikas crawling over the French map. "I thought you said I couldn't do it without you. Having doubts?"

"Not a one, but I need to know what I'm working with. And how far I have to go to break you down to the reality of the situation."

"Not very trusting of others' abilities, are you?"

"I've found that most people lack the common sense it takes for capabilities." He came around next to her and perched a hip on the desk. One leg swung back and forth like a pendulum. "Something tells me you don't fall into the same category as most people."

A wry smile twisted her mouth then fell flat. "In truth, I don't know which category I fall into. I simply want to get Ellie and me back on proper English soil. I don't care what it takes."

"Choose your words carefully. It may just come to that."

Finally, she turned to him. No use in holding back anymore. "The International Red Cross has set up a small camp near Calais. We are to meet with a contact there who will guide us to—"

"No."

"But you didn't let me finish.".

"Reports have it that some of the Red Cross stations are controlled by the Nazis. Step one foot in there, and they'll pack you off to a work camp or hold you as spies."

Each word thrust like a thorn to her bubble of hope. Her father had told her each return possibility had a one in twenty chance of going off without a hitch. Most of them called for cloak and dagger, or crossing the Maginot Line into Vichy France to sail around Spain and the fortified coast of France. After days of plotting and arguing, her father and his intelligence mates had decided this was the best course to take. How was she to know any different?

Her head dropped as she imagined Father's disappointment. Another failure to prove her capabilities—or lack thereof. "Not what I wanted to hear."

"Facts are facts. Those pencil-pusher boys have a tendency to think they know what's best even though they've never seen a battle line besides the black marks on the map hanging over their posh desk."

"I was given specific instructions by these so-called pencil pushers who spend their entire days poring over intelligence reports from the top agencies. Reports too secret for ordinary eyes such as mine and yours."

An irritated noise furrowed in his throat. "Those reports are often out of date by the time they reach their sweaty little hands."

"Sweaty hands or not, I have rules to follow."

"And you always follow the rules, don't you? No matter who gives them or for what reason. My guess is you don't ask the reason. You simply obey." He shoved his hands into his pockets and peered at her as if he could read the inner workings of her mind. "What if these people you're trying so hard to please are wrong?"

Kat curled her toes as irritation flared. "It's the best solution with the information at hand. Until that changes, this is my course of action."

"So until then, I'll simply lie and say what a brilliant plan it is."

"Don't ever lie to me."

"Not a habit I dip much into. It has its uses in this line of work." He gestured to the secret vault filled with his trained fighters. "But do it too much and people don't trust you. And trust is what gets you what you want."

Trust. There it was again. But whom? The intelligence agents who spent their lives analyzing every possibility and outcome or some stranger who specialized in fisticuffs and whisky shots?

The air closed in around her. Heat furled up her neck and into the thick hair curled behind her ears. She reached up to loosen the strands, but Sylvie had used enough pins to keep them steady against the Second Coming.

"Miss Whitford, are you all right?"

Kat eyed the floor and its instant coolness. "Yes, of course."

"You're a terrible liar." Barrett slipped a hand under her elbow.

"A gentleman never calls out a lady about such things."

"I've been called many things, but 'gentleman' usually isn't one of them." He tugged on her arm. "Come on, now."

Back upstairs, he sat her at a table and brought over a glass and a pitcher of ice water. Sipping the coolness, she considered chucking her ladylike principles and pouring the entire pitcher down the back of her hot neck.

Barrett grabbed the chair opposite her, twirled it around, and straddled it. Surprise, caution, and concern rippled in the dark-blue depths of his eyes. "Better now?"

She nodded. "I didn't eat much of a breakfast, and all those stairs, you understand." One dark eyebrow lifted in dubiety. Flushing, she reached for the pitcher and poured a fresh glass. "Not going to call me out on that one?"

The ripples stilled in his eyes. "Maybe later."

A soft breeze drifted in the open window to cool the back of her neck. The scent of fresh bread and cab exhaust mingled in a strange concoction on the air that was uniquely "large city." Kat peeled off her white-netted gloves and placed them on the table next to her glass. "What do you suggest?"

"Not sure."

"Mine wasn't good enough. Surely you have a plan in mind." She dropped her voice and leaned forward. "One the Germans aren't dipping their hands into."

Draping his arms over the back of the chair, he tapped a rhythm on the table. "I found out about you only last week. I'll need a few more days to see your mettle before I decide which route is best."

Straightening, Kat flattened her hand on top of her gloves. "I don't understand what my mettle has to do with leaving France."

"Because if I tell you to crawl on your belly through mud and barbed wire for ten miles to get past a nest of snipers, then I need to know you'll do it without question."

"Even if it's littered with broken glass both ways. As long as I can get Ellie out of here."

"What makes you think she's going to go along with you? She's sitting pretty right where she is and from what I can tell has no intention of leaving anytime soon."

"You leave her to me."

"Your determination is admirable, but we'll see how it holds up when the fires get lit. Believe it or not, there's more at stake here than your sister's safety. A war, in case you hadn't heard." Long and blunt tipped, his fingers *tap, tap, tap*ped and fell still. "Until then I suggest you enjoy the sights of Paris."

Sit tight, go shopping, smile and sip wine, and let the men chart the path. Her whole life had followed her father's urging hand. Steady and sure, she had dutifully followed it in hopes of earning a mere smile of approval from him. When his political powers didn't reach far enough to France, he had phoned up his old regiment chaps at SIS with instructions for her. And now Barrett. A man to pour her a glass of champagne with one hand and strangle the neck of the enemy with the other.

She glanced down at her hands poised atop the table. One would never know the restlessness quaking within them.

"There's nothing I'd like to do more on my lovely holiday than stroll by the Eiffel Tower and see it littered with all those little red-and-black flags and guarded by armed men, but Major von Schlegel has organized an afternoon of viewing the latest exhibition he's set up in honor of the Fatherland."

"Play nice with him. Those officers are trained to spot dissonance and squash it immediately with the heel of their jackboot. In fact, mentioning an interest in the Anglo-German Fellowship will help ease him and the others off your back. But only if you can make it believable." His brow scrunched in doubt. "On second thought, stick to what you know."

"Like how Mr. Burgess and Mr. Philby joined the Anglo-German Fellowship in hopes of disguising their communist affiliations, or how John Macnamara has ties to the Hitler Youth?" She pressed her fingers to her mouth in mock shock. "Oh, dear. Was I not supposed to know that?" Why did men assume all women knew nothing of what was going on around them?

His full mouth twitched. "I see you'll do just fine."

Laughter announced the arrival of five men carrying large suitcases. "Morning, boss." Their eyes stopped on her. "And lady friend."

"Morning, boys. This is Miss Whitford, a special friend of mine. And this"—Barrett swept his arm out to indicate the quintet—"is the swingingist band this side of the Channel."

Kat smiled. "You boys are smashing."

The shorter one with a wide mouth that accentuated his small nose strolled over and placed his case on the ground, propping one foot on top of it. *"Bonjour, jolie dame."*

"You're the trumpet player."

His mouth widened in a smile that stretched across his entire face. "Guilty. Sam at your listening pleasure. I remember you from last night. Your face lit up every time we played Benny Goodman."

"He's one of my favorites."

"But not one of your other tablemates', I think." Sam's close-set eyes flicked to Barrett and back to her. "The gentleman might prefer a Goebbels special."

"I don't think much of anything could make him smile." *Unless it has Hitler's face plastered on it.* "I hope you continue to play those exceptional arrangements. Your take on them is a breath of fresh air to this city."

"We aim to please, eh, boss?"

Barrett nodded and slapped Sam on the knee. "Haven't found an audience yet that Sam couldn't charm with his magical fingers and big mouth."

"Mama always said it'd come in handy for something besides catching flies." If possible, Sam grinned wider, flashing crooked white teeth. "Can we hope to see you again tonight, Mademoiselle Whitford? Never too many pretty ladies in the crowd, especially ones who compliment my trumpeting."

"I'm not sure about tonight, but I will come back if you promise to play 'Moonlight Serenade.'"

"For you, I'll risk the censorship." His spicy aftershave tickled her nose as he leaned close. "And afterward you can tip a glass of champagne with me instead of the boss man. I provide more civility than he does."

"Go on with you, now." Barrett kicked the case out from under Sam's foot. "Trumpet can't play itself."

Laughing, Sam snatched up his case. "We on for a game later, boss?"

"Let's try for cards. I'm tired of losing to you at chess."

"Why do you think I like to play it? You still owe me after that last one."

"Yeah, yeah."

Still laughing, Sam ambled over to join his bandmates at the stage. The lanky drummer squeezed himself behind his kit and tapped out a beat while the others warmed their strings and mouthpieces.

"Quite an interesting establishment you run here."

Barrett's white teeth gleamed against his tan skin. "Only one of its kind."

"Aren't you afraid of discovery?"

"I'd be a fool not to be, but it comes with the job. The best we can all do is get on with it."

"Well, in the name of getting on with it . . ." She stood, gathering her handbag and gloves. "I have an exhibit to explore on the glories of the Fatherland, personally guided by a man you've charged me to make nice with even though I detest his very being."

"It's for the best."

She snapped her gloves on. "So everyone keeps telling me."

Chapter 5

Kat's ears screamed from Eric's verbal abuse. Listening to him spout on and on about the great painters and sculptors of whom he knew little was cruel and unusual torture in the hallowed halls of the Rodin Museum to which he had brought them on a cultural excursion. The first hour she had tried correcting him, but by the second hour she was too numb to care. That and she guessed his head would explode if she interrupted him one more time. So she stared blindly at the painting in front of them. Fifteen minutes was more than enough to explain the artist's self-portrait of wine drinking.

"Do you agree?"

Silence roared in her ears. Odd. Shouldn't it act more of a balm to all the screeching? She dragged her eyes from their fixed point on the frame, and they slammed into Eric's expectant face.

What on earth had he said? "Oh, absolutely I do."

His fair eyebrows slanted down. "You believe it's acceptable for the artist to display himself as a drunkard?"

Frantically, she pawed through her mental file cabinet of art classes and yanked out the closest comment regarding drink. "Nowhere does this painting indicate drunkenness. He could be toasting a birth, or marriage, or payment for commission. Cups are often used as symbols of joy and celebration in art, as the Duke of Wellington and I discussed at a dinner party a few months ago. The AGF was honoring his commitment to serving far-right-wing causes."

She held Eric's stare with as much calmness as she could muster. Four long years of training and studying with some of the world's most astounding artists and historians weren't getting squashed under his disdainful sneer.

Finally, he relented. "Your explanation is well thought out. I shall need time to consider it. But in the meantime, another of Aachen's paintings will give you a different perspective."

"Please not another one." Sitting on a bench in the center of the space, Ellie dragged an emery board across her red nails. The scratching echoed in the otherwise empty area. "I'd like to see the sculptures out in the garden, and you're boring Kat to tears. Look at her face. There's probably not one word she hasn't already heard from her professors during her university days."

A muscle jerked in Eric's neck. Kat hurried to smooth his temper before it erupted. "We studied very little mannerism, and it's always interesting to hear what others think of a piece. Millions of opinions exist for each."

Ellie's board hit a jagged nail corner. "Well, my opinion is we move on. It's too beautiful to stay cooped up in here all day."

Outside, Eric took Ellie's arm and pulled her to *The Thinker*. Kat veered right. Gravel crunched beneath her feet as she let them wander where they would. A warm breeze drifted through the immaculately cut topiaries and ruffled the bottom of her floral cotton dress. Hot grass and blooming roses mingled in a pleasant aroma of freshness as fat bees buzzed from flower to flower. The air teemed with crisp life compared to the stuffy stillness inside. Of course, Eric had a tendency to syphon the very life from everything he came in contact with. He and his fellow German officers who strolled with their French mistresses through these very gardens as if they owned them.

She veered right again to the eastern wall. The massive bronze doors of *The Gates of Hell* loomed before her. Figures poised with complete abandon to agony. Forbidden love, punishment, suffering, and even maternal love, all carved from every human emotion possible.

The chaos of the scene leaped from the structure and pressed on her chest—the figures' mouths twisted with cries of help, their faces searching for understanding—but still the gates remained closed in silence. Kat's heart pounded against the weight. They stood alone in their misery.

"Impressive."

Kat jumped to find Barrett behind her. She swallowed to force her heart out of her throat and back down where it belonged. "What are you doing here?"

"I enjoy artwork as much as the next man."

"You have animal heads hanging in your pub."

"One man's eight-point buck is another man's Renoir."

"You have me there." She looked more closely. His dark-gray trousers, white shirt with the sleeves rolled up to his elbows, blue waistcoat, and tan fedora tilted to the side indicated he'd dressed with purpose and not just for running out to get milk. "Ellie invited you, didn't she?"

He grinned, crinkling the skin around his eyes. The day's brightness did little to lighten their blue darkness. "She did indeed. Disappointed?"

"No." Kat's belly did a small flip as the confession slipped out before she could stop it. He'd come to invade her thoughts much too easily over the past few days. A quick glance over her shoulder ensured no one listened nearby. "Truth be told, I can use the backup."

"Hard time remembering to smile?"

"And I insulted his great German artist." His wince barbed her. Like everything else that day. "I know, I know. You don't have to remind me how dangerous it is to start my own private war amidst the larger one at hand. It came out of my mouth before I could stop it. If he didn't want my opinion, he shouldn't have asked."

"Probably wanted to hear his own opinion repeated back to him."

Kat groaned. "That man makes my skin crawl."

"Here I thought it was this grotesque thing you're staring at."

"It was inspired by Dante's *Inferno*, but Rodin later changed it to express the universal emotions of humans in all their misery and desire." Somewhere in the back of her mind, her art professors cheered as the commentary rolled out of her mouth on cue.

"Not something you want to sit in front of for comfort." Taking her hand, he tucked it in the crook of his arm and turned them to the path leading around to the back of the museum. "Come on. I know a better way to forget your thoughts."

"I don't want a drink."

A grin split his face. "Close, but not what I had in mind."

The hairs shot up on the back of her neck. She yanked her hand away and stepped back. "I'm not interested in that either."

"You really have to stop thinking seduction is around every corner. Plenty of that to be found elsewhere. Paris is the city of love, after all."

The weight from earlier dropped into her stomach. Love. A grandiose phrase for obligation and unrealistic expectations. She'd had enough of that to last another lifetime and didn't need that four-letter word heaping on more.

"Don't worry. Wasn't talking about that noose either." Reaching for her hand once more, Barrett looped it back through his. "Your honor is completely safe with me."

"What a relief."

Crossing the terrace, they descended the steps onto the expansive lawn and strolled along the eastern path beneath the towering linden trees. Thick green leaves wove together over their heads, creating a shady reprieve from the sun's glare.

Barrett fiddled with the buttons on his waistcoat. The small movement rippled down his arm to flex the muscles beneath where her hand rested. "I don't know if I should be offended or not by that."

Kat curled her hand in hopes of ignoring the tingling sensation of his warm skin beneath hers. Goose bumps sprang up on his arm where her fingertips brushed. "Not. As our time together is brief, I prefer to keep all personal issues out of it."

"I'd call your sister in the middle of all this a wee bit personal."

"She can't help it. Or rather, she doesn't not want to help it." Kat forced her focus onto the path in front of them and not on the hardened muscles rippling under her palm. "My point is we're here and we need to get out and safely back to England."

"Sounds rather simple when you put it like that, but your case is far from it."

"Two English women should hardly make a blip in the grand scheme of things."

"You really don't know, do you?" Pulling the fedora from his head, he fanned it in front of his face. "You are the daughters of a retired colonel who now reclines in the high circles of British government. Your father sits behind closed doors, discussing secrets to make or break this war. Do you know what the Germans would do to gain access to that kind of information? They'd take a young girl and seduce her in hopes she'd open the doorway for them."

Kat's fingers crimped the edge of his sleeve. "Ellie would never do that."

"How do you know she hasn't already? Whether she meant to or not? The two of you together could provide the blackmail of a king."

"Rubbish. My father has never breathed one word about any of that. All he talks about are his glory days back in the war."

His hat twirled on his hand, distracting the fat bees from their yellow daisies and purple rhododendron. "Germans don't know that, and they'll use any measure at their disposal to break you. Or hold you for ransom."

"If abating worries is a part of your job, you're terrible at it."

"You told me never to lie to you."

"A statement I'm starting to regret."

Dropping her arm, he stopped and turned to face her. The tiny scar above his lip shone white against his tan skin. "All right. From now on, I'll tell you life is as good as those red roses on your dress."

"They're poppies."

He looked down at the printed flowers. A frown creased his brow. "They look the same."

"That's because you're a man."

"Aye, we're not an observant bunch." His frown eased into a smile that had surely stopped more than one woman's heart. "In Scotland, the only things to stare at are wooly sheep."

She smiled. "Quite a change for you, coming here."

"I go where the job is."

He'd crashed in on her like a bomb, blasting her well-laid plans to shards and scattering them to the four winds. As she rushed to piece the fragments back together, he strutted around with all the confidence of the world weighing on his shoulders. Yet that night at the pub she'd seen the seriousness burning in his eyes and the deft manner in which he'd played around his enemy patrons. How little she knew of this man.

"Do you see much of your mother's family here? You must worry terribly for them."

He placed his hat back on his head, shading his eyes. "She left no family behind."

Kat ground her toe in the dirt to keep from stretching it back and kicking herself. "I'm sorry."

"Why? Not your fault."

"It was careless to bring up something you don't have."

"Never had them, so I don't know what I'm missing. Kinda prefer it that way."

"I suppose having no strings has its perks in your line of work."

"Aye, it does. I go where and when I please, and if things take a turn for the bad, then there's no one to pull down with me."

But no one to turn to when times were good or when there was a burden too heavy to carry alone. Who was she kidding? Standing in a room filled to the brim with Whitfords and their extended blood, she never felt more alone. Of course, she had Ellie. Or had had before the girl started taking her opportunities of freedom into her own mischievous hands. Unlike Kat, she'd ignored their father's rule that children should be seen and not heard and had drawn the attention of anyone within earshot. Then she was gone, abandoning Kat with nothing of comfort but the broken pieces of her heart.

"For good or bad, family has its way of leaving a mark on you no matter how far you roam," Kat said.

The breath eased in her lungs, stilling her like a statue at his direct stare. Dark eyebrows flattened over his fathomless eyes as he searched for something in her face. A crack? An answer? She waited for the judgment to settle, but it never came. The studious lines smoothed into something she hadn't seen in a long time: understanding.

A current moved in his dark-blue gaze. "Or connections, in your family's case."

So much for understanding. Disappointment scorched her as she ruffled a finger over the fluffy peony petals at their side. The ants gathering the sticky sweetness from its center scattered and raced back down the stem. "Is that why you've agreed to help us? In hopes my father's connections will extend to you in some way?"

"I'm not one to polish a man's shoes in hopes he'll notice me." He glanced away. "I've a job to do, plain and simple."

"For a man who seems to make his own rules, I have to think your jobs are rarely simple. You must have a good reason for risking your neck every day."

A dark eyebrow lifted. "Are you calling my patriotism into question?"

"We all strive to defend our country, but it goes much deeper than pride in one's nation. For many it's to preserve a way of life and protect family."

"And beneath all that is money. Money makes the world go round, and as long as the British government employs my special skills, my world will keep on spinning." He looked back at her, cool reserve in his blue eyes. "Not the noble answer you hoped for, is it?"

Kat shook her head, swishing hair fanning the hot air across the back of her neck. "It's not the typical answer, no."

"Maybe not for your set, but it's the world I live in. One that's all the muddied shades between black and white where nobility no longer exists."

"So says the man helping two nobodies escape from under the nose of the Nazis."

"You'd do best to stop holding people to such standards, especially me."

Why had she expected a certain depth from him? One minute charming and sweeping out of the blue to spend the afternoon strolling a garden with her, and the next slashing all her ideals of knights on their white horses. It was just as well. She was allergic to horses.

She continued down the shady path bursting with scents of delicate alyssum, sweet peas, and tangy grass. A few yards away at the end of the garden rested a round ornamental pool with a patinaed statue in the center.

Barrett's footsteps crunched slowly behind her. Never in a hundred years would she have dreamed of life plopping her here in a beautiful city thrown under a merciless shadow with a trained saboteur as her bodyguard. What was he going to do if she got into a jam? Pistols at dawn? Blow something up? How did one overcome the fear of blowing themselves up in the process of setting a trap for the enemy? It'd certainly take quite a bit of gumption.

She peeked over her shoulder. The steady gait, the confident set of his shoulders, the cocky tilt of his hat. Barrett Anderson had enough gumption for an entire army.

He looked up, a half smirk on his lips signaling he'd caught her staring. "Something on your mind?"

"How did you fall into this line of work?" A man shrouded in mystery was overrated. The more she wondered about him meant the more she thought about him. Not a habit she wanted to pick up, but she was already failing miserably at that.

"That is a long and unfortunately boring story."

"I've got time."

"No. We don't." A smooth smile eased over his face as one eye flashed in a wink. "Maybe later, darlin'."

"Caught you hiding in the shadows." Ellie's voice rustled through the leaves like a bird's *cheep*. "Hope you weren't doing anything I wouldn't."

Kat strolled out to the open lawn and joined Ellie and Eric by the pool. Barrett followed steps behind her. "What does that leave out?"

Ellie laughed and flapped a paper fan in front of her pink cheeks. "Not much."

Even with the bright sun glaring down, Eric wasn't bothered to blink. "How nice of you to join us, Mr. Anderson."

Barrett's arm brushed Kat's sleeve, his presence as solid as the statues surrounding them. "I was surprised to get the invitation, but I'm glad I did."

"So you've enjoyed the art and sculptures?"

Barrett shoved his hands into his pockets. The lean muscles in his forearms twisted. "Frankly, I respect the talent to create them, but don't get into the deep meaning behind each brushstroke or why a statue is standing a certain way."

Eric's blond eyebrow twitched. "A pity for you to waste your afternoon, then."

"Wouldn't say that. I'll never turn down the opportunity to get outside. One of the downsides of running a business is that you don't get out much."

"*Ja*, that is a problem when all the people come to you." When Barrett didn't take the bait, Eric turned to Kat. "And you, Miss Whitford. Did you enjoy the art?"

"The lines are very modern, to the point of rawness. My old-fashioned senses crave something a little . . . softer."

Eric snorted. "That sounds like those frivolous Romantic notions."

"Frivolous or not, they proved fascinating to study at university. Friedrich. And Leighton, though he wasn't strictly Romantic." Kat tilted her head, blocking the late afternoon sun with the brim of her straw hat. "My professors were so rigid about what we studied. I thoroughly enjoyed having my horizons broadened today. Thank you, Major."

Delighted surprise lit his face, and his chest swelled. "It was my pleasure, Miss Whitford."

"Oh, for goodness' sake. Can it not be 'Kat' and 'Eric'?" Ellie hooked her arms through each of theirs and turned to the gate. "If we're to be a jolly party—and I intend for nothing less—then no more of this stuffiness. Gives me a headache, and I won't abide it when I'm with my two favorite people in all of the world. I'm sorry for not including you in that, Barrett, but I'm sure you'll earn the right soon enough."

"That is my greatest hope."

At Barrett's sideways wink, Kat dropped Ellie's arm and stepped back in pace with him. "Your cheekiness is going to get us caught."

"If it's not worth going all out for, then it's not worth the attempt." Ducking through the short doorway that connected the garden to the street, he blocked her exit as Ellie and Eric stepped out to the corner to hail a taxi. "Whether you like it or not, we're stuck together for a while, so why not make it a little fun?"

"There's nothing fun about Russian roulette."

"Right about that. Unless you're the one holding the bullet, and it just so happens I am."

Panic flaring, Kat scanned his sides and hips for a bulge. Ridiculous. He wouldn't hide a gun in such a predictable place. "What bullet are you talking about?"

He dropped his lips to brush against her ear. "Me. The Germans have never met a player like me. My game, my rules, my ending."

"Your arrogance knows no bounds, does it?"

"None that I'm aware of." He hovered close to her neck. "You smell nice. Like flowers."

Kat flushed. "We're in a garden."

"No. It's you." Pushing back the door, he stepped aside and let her pass.

The fragrant quietness of the garden fled at the onslaught of the bustling street outside. Exhaust choked the air as autos rolled by. Rifled soldiers shouted at schoolboys kicking a can against the side of a building while working men and grocery-carrying women hurried along never daring to raise their eyes from the ground.

Clustered together on the curb sat three children with worn baskets at their feet. Faded clothes clung to their stooped shoulders, and dust covered their dull shoes. The two girls had tied off their long braids with string, and the little boy covered his shaggy head with a patched cap.

"Oh, look. They're selling flowers." Ellie hurried over to them. She squatted down and combed through their offerings with the same enthusiasm she showed at Marks & Spencer.

Kat bit her lip. Here was the Ellie she knew. The compassionate heart hidden beneath complicated layers of indulgence, spoiling, and lipstick. She couldn't pass by a child without stopping to coo and cuddle.

"I don't understand why she wants those ratty things when she has vases of roses filling her flat," Eric sniffed.

Smug satisfaction crept over Kat. "Perhaps she's tired of roses."

"What woman tires of roses?" Crossing his arms, he shifted like a sullen child. "If she wanted something different, she should have told me. I would have brought her anything she wanted."

The pointed lines of his face softened as he watched Ellie. The coldness melted from his eyes, transforming him into a man ten years younger. Affection had chipped its way into that frigid, manipulating, and haughty cavern of his chest where a heart should pump. Love? Surely not.

A half smile curved his lips as Ellie held a purple iris up to her nose. Unease wriggled in the back of Kat's mind. He couldn't understand love, but possession was even more dangerous.

"Look how beautifully it goes with your hair. Brings out the lovely golden tones." Ellie lifted a yellow chamomile to the older girl's hair and tucked it behind her ear. Pink bloomed across the girl's cheeks. "My goodness, I can't decide which one I like best. I suppose I should take the whole basket."

Dumping her coin purse's entire contents in the remaining basket, Ellie skipped back with her bouquet treasure tucked under her arm. "Look how beautiful. Perfect for the bedside table."

Eric picked a tiny purple aster from the basket as if it were a snake. "Did you have to purchase the entire basket? It encourages the other urchins to fill the streets, and our resources are needed cleaning out the ghettos and searching for those underground movements."

Barrett shifted next to Kat. Tilting her hat brim, she refused to look at him. He'd hidden his secret far below the German bustle on the streets, but how long before they dug him out? Those people who trusted him with their training and lives would be cornered like rats. And, like rats, they'd be taken out for extermination.

Blood swooshed in her head, spinning dots before her eyes. Plucking off her gloves, she turned her wrists to the fresh air. Her pulse relaxed with excruciating slowness. "It's about time someone took to hand the sewer-rat problem. I hate the thought of them scurrying beneath our feet."

Eric's brow rumpled. "Not the rodent problem. Vigilantes who dare to take matters into their own pathetic hands, as if they could outmatch the strength of the German army."

"Vigilantes." Like a madman refusing to accept the insanity around him, Barrett laughed. "Straight out of a comic book."

"Hardly." Eric straightened, pinning his hands behind his back. The tunic stretched across his flat chest and pulled the softened lines from his face, aging him anew. "These Resistance fighters have much in common with rats, and the only way to deal with such vermin is go after them in their holes and burn them out."

"Stop. You know I hate it when you talk that way." Ellie shuddered and raised her hand for one of the passing taxis. Three zipped by without making eye contact. "It only sours the mood, and I want us to continue this lovely afternoon into a splendid evening."

Kat dared a peek at Barrett, who looked completely unconcerned with the conversation. With the hunt for fighters escalating, he needed to keep himself far from the spotlight. If that was even possible. The man had a knack for stepping outside the lines to announce his presence.

A black-and-red taxi with rolled-up windows took pity on Ellie's frantic waving and swerved over to the curb. "Climb in the front, Eric, dear, so Barrett can sit in the back with us. I have a few requests for the band tonight I need to discuss with him."

"We can't go tonight, *schatz*."

Ellie's pheasant feather knocked his hat sideways as she swiveled to Eric. "What do you mean we can't go?"

"It's Tuesday."

His pointed look deflated Ellie. "Oh."

Despite her sister's disappointment, elation filled Kat's chest like thousands of champagne bubbles. A night away from the dreadful boor. "I'm sure we'll be quite safe with Barrett."

If he was surprised by her sudden declaration, Barrett didn't show it. "My service is at your feet, ladies. For now, I need to stop off and get a few things to take care of the rats down in my cellar. Don't want them busting up the wine bottles and causing problems upstairs."

Without another word, Eric climbed into the back of the waiting car and pulled Ellie in behind him.

Kat rolled her eyes to Barrett. "Guess we'll see you tonight. Maybe Sam can play something to celebrate our brief but very much needed liberation for the evening."

"Consider it done."

Kat climbed into the back of the waiting car and squished in next to Ellie and Eric. Barrett reached down and tucked a hanging corner of Kat's dress up on the seat before shutting the door. She rolled down the smudged window. "Good luck with your rats."

He grinned. "Always."

Barrett crushed the coded message in his fist as he watched the taxi drive off. He should've told her, but he'd barely had time to sort it himself after a carrier agent pressed it into his hand on the way to meet her at the museum.

> We know about the deal with A. W. and now the rules have changed.

Yanking the wadded paper from his pocket, he smoothed it against his knee and rolled it into a cigarette. With a flick of his lighter, he held it to his lips and pretended to take a long drag as the fire ate its way down the incriminating note. So the SIS had known all along about the deal with Sir Alfred. Good on them for sniffing it out and holding back until Kat was in Paris to turn the situation to their advantage. Whitford wasn't going to like it, but he could take it up with his mates calling the shots now. Resistance-fight trainer, pub owner, babysitter. Why not throw in spy to round him out properly?

The ashes crumbled from his fingers to the sidewalk. He ground them beneath his shoe. Now all he had to do was tell Kat they weren't leaving Paris as quickly as they'd hoped, all while keeping her father's involvement a secret. Another secret, another placement of his little pawn. Didn't she deserve to make her own choices for once?

Guilt wriggled deep inside. He had his own purposes in keeping her close for this little charade the SIS had cooked up. Without her clout he had no way of gaining access to otherwise denied circles, and without those circles of information he might as well kiss his dream of America goodbye.

He scrubbed a hand over his face in hopes of wiping clean the memory of the note. But the ashes still piled near his foot. Best to get on and be done with the whole sorry mess, because those Germans wouldn't forfeit secrets on their own.

Chapter 6

S ure you know where you're going?"

Kat hooked an arm around a sagging Ellie and stepped back up onto the footpath. The eerie silence broke with each clack of their heels. "Of course. I'm not the one who drank my sorrows into the bottom of a champagne glass tonight."

A belch rumbled out of Ellie's mouth. "The pain relief was worth it."

"Not for the one who has to drag you around in the middle of the night."

"If you'd joined me like I told you to, you wouldn't complain so much."

"If I'd joined you, we'd both be passed out under a table."

"At least we'd be together."

Propping her sister against the front of a building, Kat hurried to the corner and stretched up on tiptoe to squint at the street sign. What she wouldn't give for a torch to see what she was staring at, but the mandatory blackout was an hour into full swing. *Hate to give those Allied bombers a target.*

Like the inhabitants of the surrounding buildings who had boarded themselves up for curfew, the stars and moon refused to come out and break the inky night. She twisted her head left and right. Slick with fog, the deserted streets left no remnants of the day's props of flower sellers, café menus, and newspaper stands to give any indication of the way home. A chill sprang over her exposed arms. Why hadn't she paid more attention on the taxi ride over?

"Are we lost?" Ellie's hiccups bounced off the thousand water droplets hanging in the air and shattered the stillness like a cymbal crash.

When they'd arrived the sun was hanging over her left shoulder, which meant the flat was back . . . that way. Kat spun. She didn't recognize those buildings either. *Stupid, stupid, stupid. By far the most idiotic thing you've ever done, Kathleen Whitford. It'll only be by a miracle you don't deserve that you make it through the night alive.*

Gathering Ellie from the wall, she turned them around the corner. The stale waters of the Seine hit her nose. Good. If they could get to the river, then she could decide the better direction.

Click, click. Falling brass nails sounded quieter than their heels.

"Have I ever told you how impressed I am that you can keep it together when you don't know what you're doing?" *Hiccup.*

"One of us has to. Reliance can be rather difficult to obtain."

"That sounds a smidge resent—" *Hiccup.* "—ful to me, but that wouldn't be like you, would it? Always the perfect response at the perfect time. Perfect, dutiful Kat. Not like me. The downfall of the glorious Wh—" *Hiccup.* "—itford name. That's why I'm glad you're always there to take care of me."

The truth stumbled across the resentment Kat held locked down, pricking it open to freshened bitterness. It was never a sentiment she dwelled on. How could she when it came to helping her only sister, who hadn't a clue how to take care of herself? Yet she could not deny the growing evidence. "I may not always be here to take care of you."

"Won't you? But then I'll have Eric." Ellie's arms curled around Kat's waist as her head fell to her shoulder, oblivious to the danger creeping around them. "Eric would know where we're going. Eric knows everything."

"So I've gathered."

"Tuesday—" *Hiccup.* "—shouldn't make a difference." Ellie's bitter tone was the last remnant of the night's long tirade against him and all men who dangled women like a worm on a hook. "He's here in Paris with me. Not—" *Hiccup.* "—back there in the land of sauerkraut and sausage."

"Why does here or there make a difference on Tuesdays?"

"He's got obligations on Tuesday."

"Like what?"

Ellie's head popped up as she staggered over a crack in the footpath. "You wouldn't understand if I told you. You'd act all superior and come down on me like a mighty hand of justice. Like Father."

"Promise I won't."

"Promises. I've heard a lot of those lately." Ellie's steps slowed to a halt. Wistfulness blinked slowly in her hazy blue eyes. "He loves me."

Kat's heart squeezed. She wanted to rip the word from Ellie's mouth and gouge it from her own ears for hearing it. Hate and love couldn't exist in the same space. One would destroy the other, and for a Nazi hate was sure to win. And yet she'd seen the soft, unguarded looks he'd bestowed on Ellie. She hated the truth crawling over her lips. "I'm sure he does. In his own way."

"Loves me every day of the week except Tuesdays." Sorrow hinged Ellie's words. Dropping her arms from Kat's waist, she reeled into the street and spun with her arms out wide. "Why not every day? I'd be so easy to love. Remember that song, Kitty Kat? Come dance with me."

"Keep your voice down!" Kat grabbed her arms and forced her to a stop. "If we're caught out here after curfew, we're going to jail."

"Wer ist da draußen?"

Kat clapped her hand over Ellie's mouth. Blood pounded, spiking adrenaline through her veins like thousands of needles. *Get out of the street. Get out of the street.* Clutching the back of Ellie's dress, she pushed them to the footpath. Ellie's heel caught a sewer grate, pitching her forward.

"Halt!" Two German soldiers appeared around the corner. Rifles held ready at their sides.

"Get up, Ellie. Get up!" Kat hauled Ellie to her feet.

The soldiers sprinted across the street, shouting, with rifles pointed straight at them. Standing in front of and behind them, they dipped their rifle muzzles in surprise at their catch.

Kat shook her head as they garbled out questions. Her German was barely passible, but their heavily accented Low Saxon was impossible to follow. Passing frustrated looks to each other, they slung the rifles over their shoulders. The soldier who was more boy than man spoke again. "*Französisch?*"

Mouth as dry as cotton balls, Kat nodded. Yes, she knew French.

"Papers." With only the one French word spoken, it was clear he hadn't aced his foreign language classes. He held out his hand, fingertips beckoning with impatience.

Reaching into her handbag and Ellie's, Kat pulled out their fake papers and handed them to him. Terror screamed in her chest, clawing higher and higher until it shrieked in her ears. With a little monetary persuasion from Father, the best forgery man in Parliament's employ had created the French identifications in less than a day, but if Ellie decided to open her mouth the game was over. The Germans wouldn't take kindly to two English women out after dark with false papers. She dug her fingers into Ellie's arm to keep her quiet.

With excruciating slowness, he scanned the papers again and again before folding the thin cardboard back into its three sections. "What are you doing out this late?"

"My sister became sick while we dined out. She was too ill to move and we tried to make it home before curfew, but she can't move very fast and there are no taxis to take." Kat took a deep breath. It wasn't a complete lie. On cue, Ellie doubled over on a low moan. "I'm so sorry. Please let us go home so I may take care of her."

The man tapped the papers against his palm as he translated for his comrade. Though she didn't dare turn around, she heard the skepticism in the other man's voice.

"She smells like beer," the first man said.

A German and yet he couldn't tell the difference between beer and champagne. Kat pushed a damp lock from Ellie's forehead. A mistake. The hair was hiding her scared eyes. "The doctor thought it would help empty her stomach to get the sickness out."

"I don't doubt she's sick." The papers *tap tap tap*ped in his palm. Blowing a lungful of air out his long nose, he stuffed them in his pocket. "But you're lying about something, and that I can't let you get away with."

The soldier behind Kat grabbed her shoulders and jerked her against his chest as his friend hauled Ellie to her feet and to the alley between the buildings.

"Stop! Help!" Kat twisted, but her captor held her tight as he dragged her into the alley with his friend. The windows and doors remained shut tight as her screams clawed at the air, begging someone to open them. No one was coming. "Help!"

Her captor's hot breath hissed in her ear, his words unintelligible but their meaning perfectly clear as his fingers fumbled for the buttons on her bolero. The other soldier pinned Ellie to the wall, pushing her cheek against the brick while his hand lifted the hem of her skirt.

Kat's mind streaked clear of the man pawing her as tears burned down Ellie's pale cheeks. Her mouth contorted in pain, but no sound came out. Kat sank her nails into her captor's hands. "Get off of her! Help us!"

Her captor dug his fingers into her hair and yanked, exploding fire along her scalp. As spots of dizziness whirled before her eyes, she fumbled open the clasp of her handbag and clawed over the comb, lipstick, and hankie until at last something long, smooth, and wooden brushed her hand. Snatching the leather club, she dropped her handbag and threw her arm back with all her might. The knotted end collided with his ear.

Howling with curses, he clutched his head. Kat threw herself at the back of Ellie's attacker, but the curses of his friend warned him. He swung around and clipped Kat's shoulder with his fist. Pain exploded down her arm as she collided with the wall and slumped to the ground with Ellie clinging to her. The man sneered with hatred as he leaned over and grabbed her arm with one hand, fisting his other.

This is it. Your prayer for a miracle was a waste of breath.

Metallic thunder rang down the alley.

Numbly, Kat looked up to see Barrett, garbage lid in hand, standing over the unconscious second soldier. His eyes slanted to Kat. Her captor dropped her arm and grabbed the rifle slung over his back as Barrett stalked toward them. With a black cap shading his face and dark trousers and shirt, he moved like a terrible shadow that gathered the surrounding blackness as his strength.

The still upright German pulled on the bolt of his rifle. It didn't budge. Frantically he tried again and again, but the jammed metal refused to give. Swinging it high into the air, he brought it down with a feral yell. Barret threw up his lid shield, and the weapon glanced off before it could split his head wide open. Without wasting momentum, Barrett swung it back around to knock the gun from the German's hands.

Kat's breath filled her lungs like hot iron as the men collided in a blur of fists. Barrett's punched straight and true, springing blood from the soldier's nose. The German ducked and slipped like a snake, striking his own blows to Barrett's ribs. Tripping over the rifle, they tumbled to the ground. Barrett grabbed the front of the boy's tunic, hauling his head off the ground, and socked him on his bloody nose.

He's going to kill him. And get us dangling from the end of a noose when the Gestapo finds out.

Declawing Ellie's fingers from her arm, Kat crawled over the ground. Broken gravel dug into her knees as she splayed her hands out. *Where are you, you bloody club?*

The soldier's hand snaked around Barrett's ankle and flipped him backward. Pulling a knife from his belt, he jumped on top of Barrett and stabbed downward. Barrett's arms blocked the fatal blow.

Without thought, Kat scrambled to her knees, grabbed the rifle, and rammed the butt into the back of the Nazi's head. He fell limply onto Barrett's chest.

The gun fell from her numb fingers. Its clattering on the slick pavement jolted her back. Rolling the unconscious man off of Barrett, she fished the identification papers from his pocket and stuffed them down the front of her blouse. Turning back to a tear-streaked Ellie, she yanked her to her feet as the prostrate soldiers moaned. "We've got to get out of here."

Pushing to his feet, Barrett pressed a finger to his lips and motioned for them to follow. Ellie's feet tangled together, pitching her forward. Kat caught her before she hit the ground. Impatience flashed across Barrett's face as he hurried back, caught Ellie up in his arms, and rushed out of the alley. Kat ran behind them.

Doors and buildings blurred as they raced the length of the block. *Tick! Tick! Tick!* Kat's heels fell like hammers on the footpath as her legs pumped as hard as they could to keep her going. Rounding the corner, she threw a glance back to see if the dogs would continue their chase, but only eerie silence hounded them. More locked doors and windows passed until Barrett skidded to a halt in front of a solid black door. Slipping a key in the lock, he pushed in with Kat right behind him.

Inside, a staircase ran up in front of the door. Next to it, a long hall disappeared into the back. Turning into the lantern-lit room on the left, Barrett gently lowered Ellie onto a flower-printed settee. A cold fireplace took up the far wall, while outdated pictures hung on the faded wallpapered walls. One oversized chair with peeling leather stood in a corner next to a lamp with a stack of newspapers on the floor.

Barrett turned on her. Feet braced apart and hands fisted at his sides, his dark eyes seethed. "What were you doing out there?"

His low growl reverberated in Kat's chest, terrifying her pulse into overdrive. She ran a shaky hand through her hair. A tortoiseshell comb dangled from the end of a curl. "We—I, that is, Ellie was sick. By the time she was well enough to move, I didn't bother looking at the clock. I wanted to get her home before anything happened."

"Oh, aye? How'd that work out for you?"

"I didn't know what else to do."

"You could've asked me."

"To what? 'May we sleep on top of your bar for the night because my sister needs to sober up?' No, thank you. I can figure out a solution to our problems."

"And look where your solution got you tonight." He rubbed a hand over his mouth as if to hold back a curse. Turning on his heel, he stalked to the fireplace and braced both hands on the mantel. Muscles strained in his forearms. "Do you realize the gravity of what would've happened if I hadn't heard your screams on my way home from the pub?"

"Words can never express how grateful—"

"I don't want your thanks. I want you to swear you'll never do something so stupid ever again."

"I won't."

He spun back to her. A muscle ticked in his jaw. "Swear it, Kathleen."

"I swear." Her tongue revolted on the word. If her mother ever found out she'd betrayed her upbringing to the ill-breeding manners of swearing . . . "And we are grateful, no matter if you want to hear it or not."

The tick in his jaw slowed as his gaze swept up and down. "Are you all right?"

"Yes, yes, of course." At her insistent nod, the comb slipped from her hair and bounced across the floor. Pain burned deep in her knees as she knelt to pick it up. The rocky pavement had torn her stockings and gashed the skin. Hot tears flooded her vision as she groped around. Too many times that night she'd fumbled to keep things upright.

Blast that comb.

She heard rather than saw Barrett kneel in front of her. Brushing the hair from her face, he slipped the comb back in her ruined curls.

"You did a braw job tonight, darlin'. Those German lads sure as daylight didn't expect the whipping you gave them."

Kat buried her face in her hands as the tears broke free. "I ripped my stockings."

Arms enveloped her, pulling her into a circle of warmth and strength. His stubbled cheek brushed her forehead as he tucked her head against his shoulder, gently circling his hands across her back. "It's all right now. You're safe."

She squeezed her eyes shut, staunching the tears of weakness. What a time for emotions to take hold and throw her into the arms of a strange man. A man who smelled of wood, worn cotton, and night musk.

His palm smoothed up her back, curling around the back of her neck and tangling the hair behind her ears. Her breath held as his head dipped and his lips brushed her forehead. He slid closer to her mouth. Soft and warm, his caress dispelled the terror quaking in her bones. And ushered in a whole different kind of fear.

"Ugh." Ellie moaned and swayed to sit up as her pale cheeks puffed out. She lurched off the coach and bent over a dead potted fern to empty her stomach.

Chapter 7

Barrett rolled the worn leather stick between his palms, the knotted ball on the end spinning in a blur. His head pounded like a beast and his jaw ached, but it wasn't anything a cold beefsteak couldn't put to rights. Too bad beefsteaks remained a dream of the past.

Then there were the things from the past that refused to go away. He'd kissed many women before without a second thought. Like taking a sip of water when he was thirsty. But Kathleen Whitford was like brandy. Fiery and smooth, burning down to toast his insides. And that had been her forehead. What would her actual lips do to him?

Frustration itched through his bones. Flipping the stick, he drummed the head against the worn kitchen table. Women.

"You found it."

The stick tumbled from his fingers at Kat's voice. He caught it before it hit the ground. "Aye. Next to the one with blood coming out of his ear. He'll have a hard time hearing for a while if he's not deaf already."

Kat hovered in the kitchen doorway, hands knotted together in front of her stomach. Changed from her torn clothes of the night before, she wore a blue cotton dress with flowers that glided easily over her narrow waist and round hips. Her golden hair was gathered loosely at the back of her neck to fall in waves just past her shoulders. Much different from the elegant getups he'd seen her in before.

Hard to believe she'd taken on a patrol of Nazis a few hours before.

"Your housekeeper was kind enough to loan us a few items." She ran a hand over the worn material. "It may take a few soakings to get the stains out of our clothes."

"Mrs. Bonheur could coax a rock from a mountain, so your dress is in capable hands." A clock above the ancient stove ticked several seconds. "Coffee?"

Not quite meeting his eye, Kat shook her head. "Tea?"

"Afraid not. All I have to offer is this sludge they call coffee. Toasted barley and chicory to fuel a man's belly." Lifting his mug, he gulped back the contents before he could taste it. The acrid smell, however, would linger in his nose for hours. "My man will make his rounds next week with better options."

One of her slender eyebrows lifted at him. "'Better options' as in smuggled goods?"

"Le système se débrouiller."

Wryness twisted her mouth. "'Getting by.' Yes, I suppose that's what we're doing until this whole mess stops." She shifted her weight and drew her fingers through the loose ends of her hair.

Tick. Tick. Tick. If the clock ticked any slower . . .

Searching for something to fill the awkwardness, Barrett held up the stick. "What is this?"

"A life preserver." She moved into the room, circling around the table to stand next to the counter and far away from him. "My grandfather used to carry it. My father thought it more appropriate than me stuffing a loaded gun in my handbag."

"Logical man, your father."

The corner of her mouth twitched. "Sentiment was never an accusation that could be attributed to him. He'd say that belongs to women. He never thought I could pull a trigger, and he's probably right, hence the club."

"Did he teach you to use it?"

Her back straightened. "Of course. My father would never hand a soldier a weapon without preparing him first, much less his own daughter."

Commander through and through, Sir Alfred couldn't separate

his soldiers from his own flesh and blood. And just like every other man of highborn stock, he'd sent someone else to do the dirty work while he sat back on his cushion. At least he'd pay Barrett for the job done. But Kat? What would she get for her troubles? Worse yet, what would she be called upon to do to complete her task?

The small bludgeoner weighed like a brick in his palm. "Handy. Might have to get my own." He pushed the hand-sized club across the table.

She didn't move to take it back. "Your fists seem to do the job well enough."

"Haven't let me down yet." He rubbed the backs of his hands. Sore this morning, but not too bad. If he was to start taking on broken bones in the name of Sir Alfred's daughters, the man was going to have to dig a little deeper into his pockets. And Barrett would take whatever he was offered. No coin was too much to escape the ghosts haunting him on this side of the ocean. "'Course, my knuckles are a little more calloused than they were a few years ago."

Kat said nothing.

He should never have tried to kiss her. It had been pure reaction to her distress, a way to bring comfort with no thought behind it. But that had quickly changed when his lips charted their own intention. A foolish lack of control. Such things never ended well. Most of the women he'd kissed had smiled or pouted their lips, hoping for commitment beyond what he was willing to give past the one night of diversion. Now, the one woman he needed to keep far away from was the one woman he was stuck with. Every second with her stood as a reminder of the stirring she'd released in him. Last night he'd realized it: he couldn't *not* kiss her.

Tick. Tick. Tick.

Restless, he shifted in his chair. "Listen, about last night—"

But she was speaking as well. "Last night I forgot—" They both paused. "Apologies. You go first."

Barrett shook his head. "No, you go ahead."

"In all the tiredness of last night I forgot to thank you properly." Her shoulders inched back as she finally met his eye. "I don't know how you found us, but I'm ever so grateful you did. If you hadn't come along when you did . . . Thank you, Barrett."

He'd been on his way home when he heard the gut-churning scream. Pure, black fury had barreled into his blood when he discovered it was her. If not for her interference, he would have killed those soldiers ten times over.

"Anytime." He cleared his throat. "Listen, about that k—"

The warm gratitude in her eyes froze to ice. The unsure girl of moments before vanished as her cool exterior slipped back in place. "I'd rather not discuss it further."

Crossing his arms over his chest, he leaned back in his chair. He didn't like making women angry—too unpredictable—but he'd rather have that than fumble around with their timidity. "Afraid I can't allow that. I have a few questions that need answers."

Suspicion warred in her eyes. Today, with the help of the dress, they showed more blue than green. "I'll give you five."

Only five. Better make them good ones. "Why were you on the streets that late?"

"I told you. Ellie wasn't feeling well enough to leave until it was too late to call a taxi."

"I saw you get up and leave just after nine. Plenty of time to get back to the flat before ten."

"I'll count that as a question." Her eyes dropped to the scratched tabletop. "We didn't exactly leave the premises."

The pink crawling across her face confirmed his guess. They'd spent the remainder of the evening in the ladies' room trying to sober Ellie up while he'd been too busy upstairs reading new orders from his commander to notice if they'd gotten in a taxi or not.

Berating her for coming to the Stag in the first place would do no good, especially when he was charged with keeping her—no, *them*—safe. Burying his fists into his ribs, he fought to keep control of his words. His tightening knuckles reminded him of the bruising they'd taken. That sister needed a good horsewhipping for what she'd put Kat—and him—through.

"Why didn't you come and get me?"

A delicate eyebrow hiked with incredulity. "What for? Surely you don't have special privileges to defy curfew or any other law."

"I know my way around them enough to not get caught. I've had enough practice."

She picked the small club up off the table. As sure as a soldier handling his sword, she wrapped her fingers around the leather handle and thumped it against her other palm in a monotone beat. "Will they come after us?"

"Nazi guards pummeled by two women is hardly something they want to advertise."

Worry clouded her eyes. "They won't leave you out of their report."

"No, but they won't gain much traction with a suspect who kept his face covered." He'd spent a week in Glasgow's slummiest jail cell to learn that lesson long ago. She wouldn't last ten minutes in such conditions.

Her bludgeoner beat an erratic pace against her palm. Reaching across the table, he laid his hand on hers. "I've told you, you're safe with me."

She jerked her arm back as if he'd burned her. Every moment with this woman he seemed to take a wrong turn.

Giving up on his questions, he pushed to his feet. Best to divert her attention and channel his irritation to something useful. "Come on. I'll give you a few pointers so that the next time you can take them all on your own."

"What happened to sticking to my side from here on out?"

"I need to know you can handle yourself should my fists have too many attackers to take on."

The SIS message he'd received yesterday prodded the back of his brain like a needle. He needed to tell her about the change of plans, but not now. She was ready to leap as it was, and that would send her straight off the ledge. Best to ease her into the absurdity as painlessly as possible.

She hesitated as he started out the back door. "I can't leave. Ellie will wake up soon."

If by soon she meant late afternoon, then they had plenty of time. Laying the little drunk out on the bed upstairs last night had been like putting the dead to rest. Her wall-rattling snores had kept him awake until the wee hours of the morn from his position on the downstairs settee.

"We won't go far, and Mrs. Bonheur is here if she needs anything." He stepped out onto the back stoop and breathed in deep. Dawn's mugginess had dissipated into a late-morning haze that filled the small courtyard. "The world won't fall apart if she gets her own self out of bed today."

"You make me sound as if I have nothing better to do with my time than wait on her hand and foot."

"And do you?"

The kitchen floor creaked as she crossed the room to the open door. Leaning her shoulder against the doorframe, she considered him with half-hooded eyes. "Think you've got me figured out pretty well, don't you? Always trying to please the wrong people—isn't that what you said that day you first took me to your training room? You don't know the first thing about me and my sister."

Tugging a worn mattress from behind a stack of chipped clay flowerpots, he dragged it to the middle of the bricked courtyard and threw it down. "Prove it to me."

Her eyes jumped from the mattress to him. The club twisted in her hand. "Mr. Anderson, I've made my opinion on such things very clear."

"There you go again, thinking the worst of me. Kissing you like I tried to last night wasn't the most accurate representation." Her face blanched white. "Oh, I know your genteel upbringing forbids talking about such base things, but there it is."

Pulling the knife from his back pocket, he gestured to the mattress. "Let's move on."

The color returning to her face didn't remove the scowl. Her eyes turned upward to the surrounding buildings and windows. "Your neighbors won't find this odd?"

"Nope. Nothing new to them."

She sighed. "Of course not."

"The SIS bought up the entire block the Stag sits on to cover up the comings and goings." He pointed to the plain brick backside of the Stag that stood on the opposite side of the courtyard. "Most of the rooms are empty, but any occupants found inside are loyal to the death for the Resistance."

"Nice to know they won't run to the Gestapo when they hear guns going off in the basement."

Flipping open the blade, he brushed his thumb against the freshly sharpened edge. "Target practice happens to coincide with band practice."

"Clever." The closest thing he'd seen to a smile all morning flitted across her face as she slipped off her fancy shoes, placing them carefully on the ground with the toes precisely lined up, and joined him on the lumpy mattress. "I assume you're going to teach me to use that and not stab me."

"Too valuable to do away with you now. Hold out your hand." He placed the switchblade diagonally across her palm and closed her fingers around the brown-pitted handle. The deadly weapon looked out of sorts cradled by a hand with perfectly manicured fingernails. "Always hold it like this for better control. Hold it like an ice pick, and you can only thrust down. A novice move that's easily blocked."

"Can't have that."

A door squeaked open from a third-story flat. Two of his late-night waiters stumbled out onto the tiny balcony with cigarettes dangling from their lips. Leon raised a mug in greeting before taking a sip that curled his entire face with disgust.

Barrett waved a hand and turned back to Kat. "You'll want to cut in and out, fast, like a snake striking. Aim for the throat, abdomen, or kidneys if you come up from behind."

A frown dipped her brow as she examined each of the vital spots he pointed to. "Why not simply the heart?"

"Because you've the ribs and breastbone to get past." He tapped the hard bone in the center of his chest. "Only the most skilled should go for it, and even then it's tricky finding just the right angle. Hit the bone and you're likely to lose your knife, not to mention the numbing pain shooting up your arm. Now, when you—What's wrong?"

She was shaking her head, trying to hand him back the knife. "I can't."

Leon and Luc sat on boxes, peering over the rail to the lesson below. Across the way on the fourth story, an older woman whose daughter excelled in map reading and explosives opened her window to hang a load of laundry. Moth-eaten and still grimy from being washed in the fouled water trickling through the building's only remaining pipe, their sour smell clogged the courtyard.

"*Bonjour*, Monsieur Anderson," she called.

"*Bonjour*, Madame Gilbert."

Kat offered a polite smile to the woman, but it wasn't enough to hide the quick wrinkle of her nose. Only in that moment did he realize how ill placed she was here. The simple, worn dress did nothing to hide her born elegance and gentility. A far cry from the grime he'd grown up in.

"Bit different than what you're used to, is it?" Barrett tugged at the collar of his less than pristine shirt. It had never bothered him much, but standing in her presence was like having a torch blaze across the squalor the besieged inhabitants of Paris had succumbed to. "Such is life under occupation."

"Has all of Paris been relegated to, ah, less than satisfactory living conditions?"

If the situation weren't so revolting, he might have laughed at her attempt to be polite about their neglected state. "Only for those not in the Germans' pocket. Food, clothing, electricity, petrol, or anything else of worth goes to the Germans first, then scraps to their local informants, and whatever is left for the rest of us to fight over amongst ourselves."

"Here one cannot properly wash their clothing, while I've been changing my outfits three times a day. How shameful is ignorance."

"Aye, but you're ignorant no longer. It only matters what you do from now on. Like with this." He tapped the knife in her hand. She shook her head, relaxing her grip on the blade. "What's wrong?"

"When you talk about stabbing throats and puncturing stomachs . . . I can't do that."

"Firstly, you don't stab a throat, you slash it. And second of all, I'm not teaching you this to become an assassin. This is merely self-defense should you absolutely need it."

"If I come at someone with this, they'll simply laugh. Who's going to be afraid of me?"

"Precisely. Use it to your advantage." Taking her hand, he curled the knife back until it lay flat along the inside of her wrist. "They won't see it hidden like this, and when they get close enough to reach out, flip it and slash their wrists or biceps. Hurts like the dickens and gives you time to beat it around the corner."

Her pulse beat wildly against his fingertips still curled around her wrist. For a girl who'd bloodied an armed soldier the night before, her confidence came and went like the wind. Did she not realize the guts it had taken to do what she did in that alley? Or, for that matter, coming all the way to Paris when most expatriates had the common sense to get out while they could. Didn't say much for him and for his own common sense, but then again, he had a debt to pay.

Had she become so accustomed to having her duties drilled into her head that she'd forgotten what it was like to do something for herself? Especially when the best thing was right at her fingertips.

Releasing her, he stepped back on the sagging mattress. "Now, come at me." Uncertainty flitted across her face as if he'd asked her to conjure a snowman in the middle of July. "The only way to learn is to do it. You need to feel the movements."

Screwing her face up with determination, she lunged forward. He stepped aside and knocked the knife from her hand. "I said strike like a snake, not a wet noodle."

Snatching the knife from the mattress, she tried again. Barrett swung his forearm up to block her, stepped into her side while hooking his foot behind her heel, and levered her backward.

"If you were a real attacker I'd trip you completely and let you fall, but I'll go easy since it's your first time." She wriggled in his arms. Soft curves pressed against him, triggering a pulse he hadn't expected. And didn't need. He righted her and let go. "And I'd hate to get your pretty dress dirty."

Her pink cheeks puffed out. "Don't worry about my dress."

Laughing, he swung his arms wide and called out for the watchers to hear. "Don't worry, she says. Is that supposed to intimidate me?"

Their audience guffawed and threw down their own colorful suggestions of what she could do with the dress. Barrett's ear wasn't the most skilled with languages, but according to the red creeping up Kat's neck she understood every word.

Ever the polished blue blood, she waved away their calls with a flick of her hand before grasping a pleat of her skirt. "Not exactly dressed to kill."

The woman was blind if she couldn't see the way that flimsy material skimmed every curve like water over silk. He slowly circled her, appreciating the new view each step brought. "On the contrary. A woman in a dress is more dangerous than one in trousers. Better form of seduction, you see, and that is the greatest weapon of them all because the target will never know what hit them."

"If I was going to hit you, I'd go ahead and do it and not hide behind fluttering lashes and silk."

He should've seen it coming. He should've kept his eye on his footwork and not underestimated his opponent, like he instructed all of his recruits. But he didn't and her stretched back foot caught his. He hit the mattress facedown.

"What were you saying about using my attributes to my advantage?" Delight danced in her eyes as she loomed over him with the gentle scent of lilacs. She flipped the blade over in her hand and grinned. "Dinna even need this wee one."

Her spot-on mock brogue took the sting out of his red face, but jabbed harder into his pride. "Forgot to tell you something else. Just when you think you've got your opponent right where you want him, never underestimate his determination to win."

Grabbing her ankle, he yanked her foot out from under her. She plopped next to him with a shriek.

"I dinna need the wee one either." He snatched the knife from her hand before she could cut the lumpy mattress to pieces and moved to close it. It hesitated before folding in. Turning it upward, he ran a thumbnail to catch debris jamming the release mechanism. "While you're catching your breath, I've got my fourth question for you."

"If it has something to do with how gullible I am for that trick, then I'll thank you to keep it to yourself."

The questions rolled in his head like marbles, bouncing off one another to vie for attention. But there was one dreaded marble he needed to play sooner rather than later. His thumb rubbed over the smooth blade release. Good thing he'd taken it away from her first.

"I've been tending drinks a long time, and drunks even longer. The most common reason to drown your sorrows is in the name of love." He pressed the button, springing open the blade. "What happened between her and the major?"

Her slim shoulders heaved up and down. "There was a disagreement about his supposed duties on Tuesdays. Surprisingly, three bottles wasn't enough to loosen her tongue on the specifics beyond her being far more interesting than bratwurst." Reaching a hand behind her, she pulled forward the tail of her tied-back hair and wound the ends around her fingers. "Then there was the usual tirade against men and their lying tendencies."

Barrett frowned. "Is this a common complaint when women get together?"

"Oh, I know by now that you don't like fitting yourself into the same category as everyone else, but you can't say you've never worked an angle to get what you want."

A sliver of guilt shot through him. His whole life he'd manipulated others to get the result he wanted, whether it was a pretty girl's affections or dragging his drunk father home from the pubs. Trying too hard to keep his head above water, he'd never had time for regrets. Only chumps wallowed in remorse, or so he'd always thought—until he found himself staring into the selfless blue-green eyes of Kat Whitford.

He shook it off. Selfless though she might be, she had no clue how to pull off this ridiculous mission of hers. But he did. "They still seeing each other?"

Her face scrunched in displeasure. "Yes." She turned at his grunt of approval. "Don't tell me that's what you wanted to hear."

"Actually, it is."

She stared as if he'd suggested having Hitler, Mussolini, and Stalin over for tea. Which was nearer to the ballpark than she could imagine. Rolling to his feet, he tucked the knife back in his pocket and held his hand out to Kat.

Suspicion drew her eyebrows together. "Why is it important to you whom my sister socializes with?"

Barrett glanced up to the balconies. The lack of action had driven their audiences indoors once more. "Because we may be spending a lot more time with them in the very near future."

"We?"

"There's been a change in plans."

Her brow furrowed. At Barrett's slow nod, objection flared over her face like a thunderstorm. She shot to her feet. "Absolutely not. I refuse."

"We're not allowed to leave until we get the required information." He didn't bother mentioning that the British government refused assistance to escape should they try to leave before the job was deemed over. "I don't care for this couples arrangement any more than you do, but I can't infiltrate the higher enemy circles without a little more genteel touch. You can. So to end this war quicker, you'll deal with it the same way I will." He leaned back and crossed his arms. "You wouldn't refuse your country's request for assistance, would you?"

"Request? More like an order."

"Before you get too ruffled, no one bothered asking me if I agreed to this either."

"We'll tell them no. We refuse."

"I'm not exactly in a position to refuse them. They have no qualms about tossing me right back into that jail cell, which would leave you high and dry in Nazi-occupied territory."

She pushed the hair from her forehead with an agitated flick. "Once again I have no option in the matter."

"In that, we are together. A motto for our mission, if you will."

She paced away, likely running through every mental objection he'd raged over ever since he received those new instructions. After a lengthy minute, she came to stand in front of him. The drawn lines of her face readied for argument. "It would be treason. The ramifications of my name, the Whitfords, circulating with the Nazis is a death sentence."

"Your dear ol' dad has enough clout to keep your names from ever reaching English soil to cause any kind of political or social harm."

"You can't be certain of that. Dark secrets have a way of making themselves known."

Not if he had anything to say about it. "Then you'll be lauded as a double agent. Look, if you're going to worry over the particulars, then we won't have much success with this charade. Focus on what matters right now, and we all might make it home alive."

Her lips pressed tightly together as a war of arguments flashed across her face. Finally, her mouth eased in semiacceptance. "If we're to partner in this endeavor, you'll keep your hands to yourself."

"If we're to make this believable, then a few liberties are a must." He flung up a hand as her lips formed a flat refusal. "I swear by my finest bottle of Ballantine's that I shall behave as the utmost gentleman. Though in my own defense, I've never had complaints before."

"Then you must've been lied to before last night."

Last night hadn't been his finest hour in romance, but she hadn't exactly turned away with revulsion. He'd promised to behave, but somehow his heart refused as his gaze dropped to her mouth. "Care for me to show you?"

"Try it again and I'll crack your precious bottle of Ballantine's over your head. Unless there's a Nazi present, keep your liberties to yourself. Deal?" With a haughty tip of her head, she stuck her hand out.

Barrett's lips curled. This assignment could be a little more fun than he'd given it credit for. He took her hand and shook it. "Deal."

Chapter 8

Ellie turned right and left in front of the full-length mirror, plucking at the low neckline of her soft-pink watered-silk gown. A disapproving frown marred her powdered face. "If only I had the curves to pull off this dress."

"You look beautiful." Angling a diamond comb over her ear, Kat pushed it into the cluster of curls piled on her head as Ellie twirled behind her.

"You wouldn't know about it. You look like Lana Turner, and I look like her stick of gum." Ellie swished across the room and draped her arms over Kat's bare shoulders. Her red lips scrunched as she stared at her sister in the vanity mirror. "I think my lipstick is too dark."

"It's not. They always put terrible lighting in ladies' rooms." Kat tucked her pressed-powder case back into the beaded bag that perfectly matched her periwinkle chiffon gown. "I'm surprised you have any left after I found you out in the garden with Eric. This is his big night. You need to behave yourself."

"He needed a boost of confidence before his welcome speech. Besides . . ." She tugged on Kat's ear as a wicked grin burned her lips. "Wouldn't hurt you to misbehave a little more with Barrett. Don't deny it. I saw his arm slip around you more than once. He hasn't ventured more than two steps away from you the whole time we've been here."

Barrett played the perfect date. Never leaving her side except to refill her glass, introducing her to the brass he knew as customers, teasing her, and always with an arm or hand brushing hers. But as much as she wanted to believe Barrett's smiles, it was an act. Just like

Marcus and their orchestrated engagement over two years ago. She meant nothing more to him than one of the dozens of bottles lining the bar shelves, and when this was all over, he'd forget about her just like the others.

But could she forget about him? Nerves fluttered in Kat's stomach like a hundred demented butterflies desperate to get out.

"He is rather charming, isn't he?" Kat couldn't quite look her sister in the eye.

Ellie squealed and threw her arms around Kat's neck. "Oh, Kitty Kat! It's about time you found someone. I knew this romantic Parisian air would get to you eventually."

"I think it finally has. Without all the strict rules of home hanging over my head and seeing you so happy with Eric has made me want that for myself." Kat smiled through the disgust roiling in her throat at the hypocritical words and squeezed Ellie's hands. "I can see why you're so happy here."

"Can you really? I'm so glad." Dropping her arms, Ellie sank down on the tufted bench next to Kat. The glow on her cheeks dimmed. "Since the minute you showed up on my doorstep I've been edgy thinking you came to drag me back on Father's orders. That the old dog's so worried about protecting his own neck he couldn't come himself so he sent you."

"I came because I love you and worry about you." Kat brushed her hand over Ellie's cheek. "And despite Father's English sensibilities that prevent him from expressing it, he worries about you too."

Ellie's eyes dropped to the bunched fabric in her lap. Beneath the rouged and powdered cheeks and expensive gowns, she was still the insecure little girl crying out for attention and affection. No wonder she'd fallen into Eric's most attentive arms.

"You never did tell me why you ran away."

"Didn't I?" Ellie looked back up with the remnant of past hurts in her eyes as the carefree mask slipped back in place. "Not so much running away, but finding a place that appreciates the wealthy and their superior place in the world. The Great War upended the social ranks, but the Führer is striving to put them back in their proper places. With my connections back home and the new ones I'm making here as the social secretary of Paris, I have everything to gain from the situation."

Kat dug her fingernails into the front of the bench to keep from smacking Ellie across the face. Did she not hear how utterly ridiculous she sounded? Her sweet little sister had become the most fashionable mouthpiece of propaganda for her Nazi lover. "When did this interest in politics pick up? The last comments I heard you make about government were that they needed better-looking ambassadors."

Ellie laughed and jumped to her feet. "You're right. Politics really aren't my cup. But it'll infuriate Father, won't it?"

"You don't actually believe all that nonsense, do you?"

"I haven't thought much about it one way or the other. Not like Eric and his friends, who talk of almost nothing else but their dumb little war games. It's as if they don't realize there are more interesting topics to discuss."

Kat fought to keep her tone even, light, lest she muck up the whole opportunity of turning her sister before given a chance to start. "In case you haven't realized, there is a war on. Events are happening that we can't turn a blind eye to. Find something you truly believe in instead of latching on to the fashionable sentiments surrounding you."

Ellie dismissed her words with a wave of her hand. "Things aren't so doom and gloom. Yes, it's sad to lose a battle, but the Germans have been peaceful occupiers. They're setting up to restore glory and honor to those under their leadership. Why, in yesterday's paper—"

"Not according to the headlines in England. They report the opposite."

"Oh, Kat. Lighten up. This is a party, after all. You sound too much like Father sometimes. I'd hate to have to run away from you too."

Kat bit her tongue. Cold as he was, their father didn't deserve such childish cruelty. He'd been set to come for her himself until Kat had convinced him that Ellie was less likely to run from her. It had taken months to switch the carefully constructed plans to feature her instead of him. Reprimanding Ellie further would only put her in a bad mood, and tonight she needed every ounce of sisterly support if she and Barrett held any hope to pull off this charade.

Barrett. He was probably prowling outside the door wondering why powdering her nose was taking so long.

"Well, now that we have our beaus, how about we go enjoy this exhibit yours has put together?" Kat plastered a dazzling smile on her face and stood as she grabbed her bag.

Bubbling like a loosened bottle, Ellie looped her arm through Kat's. "What a foursome we'll make out on the town."

Pushing out of the perfumed dimness of the ladies' room, they stepped back out to the brightly lit gallery filled with boozing German officers and their cigarette-puffing mistresses. In order to put food on the table and keep a decent shelter over their heads, many of the women of France had shed their dreams of innocence and draped themselves over the arms of the enemy. Looking past their painted faces and shrill laughter, Kat wondered if a few extra rations were worth such a price of degradation.

She glanced down at Ellie's arm hooked through hers, and a sliver of shame struck her heart. In order to keep their heads above water, many of the women here most likely held the same mask she herself wore. She had no right to judge when it came to the sacrifices one made for the people one loved.

Shaking off her dour thoughts, Kat scanned the gray uniforms and fox furs and spotted her date standing next to the fully stocked bar. He was talking to three well-oiled officers and a woman who kept adjusting the diamond choker around her neck.

Barrett cut quite the striking figure in his immaculately tailored black jacket and trousers that hinted at the power of lean muscles beneath. A crisp white shirt showed his tanned skin glowing with outdoor health. He'd combed his chestnut hair to the side, but left the ends unfashionably natural to wave behind his ears. Tall and confident, he attracted more than one woman's admiring gaze. Including her own.

Barrett's head turned to the direction of the ladies' room, a slight furrow on his brow. He scanned the sea of faces, the crease growing deeper with each pass until he spotted her. The line smoothed as one corner of his mouth tipped up. She remembered the feel of that mouth close to hers, strong yet exquisitely tender. How it had begged for her to linger even after she pushed him away. Her butterflies looped in a frenzy. No. He wasn't a man for kissing. He was a confidant, an anchorage should things get rocky. Glancing around at the Iron Cross medals for courage under fire and bravery before the enemy, it wasn't a question of *if* things turned rocky, but *when.*

"There you are, poppy." His smile widened as she weaved through the crowd to join him. "Thought I might have to send out a search party."

The butterflies swooped with delight at her suggested pet name. Blast those wings. "Powdering one's nose takes an artistic hand that cannot be rushed."

"Hear, hear!" The other lady in the group raised her glass and drained the contents in one gulp. The diamonds at her throat glistened as she swallowed. "Men simply don't understand what pains we suffer to look so good."

Barrett's arm slipped around Kat's waist, pulling her close. "Kat doesn't need all that paint to enhance her already beautiful face."

Heat rushed to Kat's face. Whether it was from the warmth of standing so close to him or his intimate words brushing her ears, she didn't care to discern. *This is an act. Don't let his aftershave muddle what you're here to do.*

She playfully pushed him away. "You do know how to embarrass a girl."

"How can it be an embarrassment if it's the truth?"

The desire twinkling in his eye almost had her convinced.

"Because a lady will never admit to needing cosmetics, and now you've outed me in front of these gentleman. Whatever am I to do with you?"

"I'm sure he can think of something." One of the men with three silver diamonds on his collar leered at her as his dark eyes lingered on her body. His companions snickered as the woman looked away, the skin around her red mouth pinching white.

Clapping called for the room's attention. Eric, with a beaming Ellie next to him, stood by the curtained entrance to his newest exhibit. Rocking back and forth, he looked ready to pat himself on the back from sheer pride. "*Meine Damen und Herren, Mesdames et Messieurs! Die ausstellung ist für ihr sehvergnügen offen.*"

"Looks like the show's beginning," Barrett whispered.

Kat focused to keep her eyes from rolling. "Oh, goody."

Like cattle, the crowd slowly shuffled through the now opened doors into a large space dotted with photographs, paintings, and sculptures depicting a sun-filled Germany. The room narrowed at the end, bottlenecking the crowd into a dimmed, tight space. The art grew darker, more sinister, as pointy faces creeped in the shadows, their clawed hands raking across the sun and land while the perfectly blond inhabitants ran in terror.

Juden. Jew.

"Pathetic, isn't it?" Barrett's snort hummed in her ears. "Look at them. They're eating it up."

Kat didn't want to look around. She didn't want to see the nods of approval or the self-flamed righteous anger burning in the German eyes around them. If the people at home could see her now. No amount of Father's power could prevent her being labeled a traitor.

"How can they possibly believe this?" Sickness twisted in Kat's stomach as she neared a poster with a demon lurking around a group of blue-eyed children. She couldn't fathom such hatred toward another human being.

"Ol' Adolf's a mighty powerful speaker, and right now the Germans are looking for someone to blame for their loss of power."

"The Jews, Poles, and Gypsies have done nothing to deserve such degradation and hate. Is the Resistance not helping them?"

"Why else do you think I'm training fighters? They learn what they can and go out to fight."

"Do you not wish to join them out there?"

"I love nothing more than a good brawl, but their operations are beyond my sphere, which is right here. With you." Barrett turned, blocking her from view of the crowd. "We're trying to make friends with these people. Especially your sister's beau. We have to make him trust us if we're to get into the inner circle."

Frustration and anger chased each other around and around inside her until they clashed, with no decisive victor. Her fingernails curled into her bag, loosening the jet beads from their delicate thread. "I'm trying, really I am, but they make it nearly impossible."

"We have to do the dirty work and the fighting for those who can't do it themselves."

"I came here with one purpose: to retrieve my sister. Thinking the war at large was for someone else to fight. But then I see this and it makes me utterly sick. We cannot allow this hatred to spread."

"We're not."

"No, *you're* not. I go to parties and sip cocktails while you're instructing people to fight back. Do you not see how useless that makes me in comparison?"

"We all have our roles, and not one of them is useless." Slipping an arm around her shoulders, he turned them to face a small painting in the corner. He dropped his mouth to her ear so only she could hear. "I know you've no training and this was the last thing you expected to do, but you're doing a fine job. Most women would've crumbled by now, but not you. And as long as I'm next to you, I'll not let you."

His warm breath stirred the hairs curled behind her ear. Calm and reassuring as a summer night's air. It was enough to pick up her heart's pace.

"Canoodling in the corner, I see." Ellie's cheerful voice grated along Kat's raw nerves.

Barrett swiveled as Ellie and Eric stopped next to them. Eric's chest heaved up and down as if he could barely contain the joy bursting beneath his medal-bedecked tunic. "What does your artful eye make of the exhibit?"

Kat scrambled for words. "It's bold."

He leaned forward, eyebrows raised in expectation, but when no profuse congratulations came, he straightened. "*Ja*, it is. Just what the people need. An unsheltered view of what the unwanted are doing to our country, families, and land. Wait until you view the last room. A glance at what Germany and eventually the world will look like when it is cleansed of impurities."

Ellie rolled her eyes. "Now, Eric. I've told you that not all of them are like that. Father knows quite a few in the Treasury who are whizzes with money and have advised him on more than one occasion about stocks."

"I told you never to speak of that in public." Steel glinted in Eric's pale eyes, but his hiss did little to ruffle Ellie. "Just because they are competent with money doesn't mean we should trust them with it. They only use it to their advantage."

Barrett nodded. "He's right. Sometimes, lying and evilness are in people's blood, and you can't change blood." He took Kat's hand, lacing his fingers between hers. "When there's a sickness, it's often best to bleed it out until the blood is pure again."

Disgust tumbled up Kat's throat, hot and burning to lash out at anyone within striking distance. Her fingers dug into Barrett's palm as heat swarmed her body. Barrett's hand curled tight around her fingers, cutting off the blood flow as a silent warning until she swallowed her cry of outrage and managed a small nod. In return, his hand relaxed and offered hers a gentle squeeze. He trusted her to back him up, and she couldn't falter now.

Kat prayed her words came out with the appropriate tone and not the insults she wished to hurl at him. "Congratulations on your opening, Eric. You've really outdone yourself."

Eric blinked with shock. "Why, thank you, Miss Whitford. Kathleen. That is indeed high praise coming from you, and I shall cherish it all the more as you are Eleanor's sister."

"All right. Enough of this before your head explodes. I need it in working order if I'm to introduce you to the colonel of media coverage in Belgium." Looping her bangled arm through Eric's, Ellie winked at Kat. "You two have fun. There's a nice garden just off the east exit if you care to see it. Nice and dark. Bye, now."

Kat shook her head as the pair disappeared into the crowd. "Subtle as a brick."

"She seems delighted by our burgeoning romance."

"It'll work to our advantage, you mean."

"Aye, it will, but she also genuinely wants to see you happy. A rare thing in this cynical world we find ourselves in." Barrett's eyes glinted with approval.

"Ellie's always been like that. Wanting to have everyone happy and smiling. It's why she tries so hard." She wouldn't be smiling when she found out their true motives. Kat pressed a hand to her chest as a crack fractured her heart. Ellie might never forgive her for the deception, not even if it was to save her life.

"She'll come round." Barrett's words cut through her fog as if he knew exactly where her thoughts lingered. "If all goes according to plan, she'll thank you for using trickery to yank her out of this nightmare."

"There's that far-fetched confidence again."

"In this line of work, confidence and wits are sometimes the only link to living over dying. A lesson you're making quick work of tonight."

The warmth of his fingers still twined with hers spun Kat back to reality. This wasn't a date. She slipped her hand from his. "Shall we continue our work by joining the crowd for the grand finale in the next room?"

"As much as I'd love to see Eric's glorious vision of the Fatherland to come, we have something else to do."

Kat followed him back to the first room, where Barrett circled around a painting standing on an easel at the center of the room. With Nazi flag held high, Hitler led an army of flag-waving soldiers as the dawn of a new day broke behind them. An eagle of iron soared above him like the dove from heaven at Christ's baptism. Kat's eyes dropped to the inscription. *Our beloved leader. In him we are well pleased.*

Nausea swept up Kat's throat. "How can one man be so evil?"

"Devil needs someone to do his dirty work. But not for long." Digging into his trouser pocket, he pulled out a silver lighter and flicked it open. The orange flame danced with eagerness. "Care to do the honors?"

Kat balked. "You're not serious. We can't start a fire in here. With all these people, someone could get hurt."

A deep *V* creased his forehead. "Tell that to the lads out in the fields. The ones dying while the slop-suckers in here toast to their deaths."

When she backed away, he flicked the lighter closed. The crease reluctantly eased from his forehead. "My objective is to break their pride, create chaos in their midst, and drive them out. The French spirit is alive, but buried. The enemies' triumph tonight could very well snuff it out altogether." The lighter flashed in his palm. "While I draw breath, I won't allow that to happen."

The tempered passion blazing in his eyes leaped into Kat. This wasn't some far-off abomination. The tragedy lay at their front step, right before their eyes, and if good people remained too scared to fight, then the atrocities would swallow them whole. "You do it. I sense you'll gain greater pleasure in burning artwork than I will, even if it does have Hitler's face on it."

"It's not art." He flicked the lighter open again and touched the orange spark to the bottom corner. Flames gobbled up the edges. "It's hateful propaganda."

As the corners curled to black, satisfaction split across his face. "Ready to run?"

Kat dragged her gaze away from Hitler's melting face. "Run where?"

"For your life." Grabbing her hand, he yanked her to the side exit. "*Fire!*"

Chapter 9

Barrett was right. Instead of boasting about the city's newest exhibit to German pride, the morning's *Le Temps* was plastered with images of the burned painting. Charred black around the entire right side, the only thing left of Hitler was his hand holding the flag. A guest claimed to have seen the attacker as he made a run for it. Short, long nosed, with a terrible laugh that cackled over the roaring flames. Most likely *Juden*.

"'What more can be said of the night except that it is a terrible dent to the Fatherland's honor? A night meant for rejoicing was forever soured by the heinous acts of a saboteur.'" Eric crumpled the quoted newspaper and threw it on the ground. "They didn't even mention all the other preserved works in the exhibit. And what about that exclusive interview I gave before it opened? I suppose it'll stay buried under this rubbish."

"Calm down, darling." Ellie leaned out of her chair and snatched up the wadded paper. "I've already called the editor, and he's sending someone round this afternoon to give another interview. Simply use last night as an exciting spin about the forces out there trying to stop your good works. People love a good underdog."

"I am not an underdog." Darkness flashed across Eric's pale face. "Or are you saying the saboteur is the underdog?"

"You, of course." She smoothed the papers out on the shiny dining table. "It's not a terrible article. They took quite a dashing picture of you. And you can barely see the destroyed picture in the background."

Kat ducked her face into her teacup to keep from smiling. Last night's antics had kept her heart beating double time well into the early hours of the morning before she finally fell asleep. From outside in the garden, Barrett had made them wait until panic was in full swing before slipping back inside amongst the frantic guests. The curator rushed around with buckets of sand and water while Eric stood still as a statue in the center of the room. White as paper, with shadowed flames dancing on his tunic, he had demanded that the culprit come forward. Barrett had grabbed his arm and forced him to help usher the ladies out.

She had been beyond terrified, yet a secret pride thrilled through her at having helped destroy a Nazi foothold in something that gloated over the death of an entire culture. Perhaps she could make better use of her presence than simple cocktails after all.

She took a sip of her cooled tea. "At least no one was hurt."

"That's right," Ellie agreed, folding the paper and stuffing it under her plate. "Pierre, did you get the croissants?"

Pierre appeared in the doorway with a fresh pot of coffee. The black smudges under his eyes popped out in his flushed face. "*Non.* The baker is out of flour. I am sorry."

"That's all right. We'll try again next week when the new rations come out."

Pierre set the pot on the silver trivet in front of Ellie and backed toward the door. "New week may be the same, or worse."

Ellie refilled Eric's cup before topping off her own. "What do you mean?"

Pierre's eyes flickered to Eric before dropping to the patterned rug beneath his feet. "There is not enough flour to go around. Many of the bakers are trying rice or mashed potatoes as substitutes."

"Well, that sounds . . . interesting. Surely that doesn't include German officers. I don't know how we're expected to get by on potatoes."

"Many do," Kat said quietly, shamed by taking a place at the Nazi buffet of plenty over the past few weeks while the rest of France was reduced to scrounging for food where they could. The tide of battle must be worse than reported if Eric's table was to be rationed.

Blissfully unaware of the unspoken, Ellie sipped her creamed coffee and smiled. "At least the coffee is still good."

Pierre's face wobbled in relief before he spun around and disappeared back into the kitchen.

Kat leaned forward and dropped her voice. "Is he always so nervous?"

Ellie sighed and leaned back in her chair. She tugged her chiffon robe back over her exposed shoulder. "Yes, but more so lately. I think he's worried about losing his job, but I've assured him I'll sell the silver and furs before I see him go. Him and Sylvie. Hard times and we have to stick together."

"You'll do no such thing." Eric gulped back his steaming, sugarless brew and grimaced. "I bought you those things. Workers come and go."

"You keep saying things like that, and people will wonder if there's a heart beating beneath that starched uniform of yours." Ellie reached out and tapped a finger against his chest.

Eric captured her hand and raised it to his lips. The harsh lines softened around his mouth. "I'm sorry, *schatz*. Last night has me on edge."

"That's because you didn't sleep."

"No, I didn't." He turned her hand over and pressed a kiss to her palm. "Perhaps I could use a rest."

His husky tone indicated he wanted anything but rest. Kat shot to her feet before she had to listen to any more. "I think I'll go for a walk. Maybe to the Champs de Mar."

Her announcement fell on deaf ears. Hurrying from the room, she decided a walk was just the ticket to calm her mind and nerves. From the giggles following her down the hall, a nice *long* walk was in order. She turned the corner to her room.

"—but the rabbi has already said to hide the Torah and prayer books after the Germans raided the 14th arrondissement. We need to flee before they catch us too."

"Hiding in plain sight is our best chance. How many other Jews do you know who have kept their jobs? Almost none. Our families will starve if we leave now. Things cannot be so bad or the papers would have reported it."

"Von Schlegel will catch us."

"Not if we are careful."

Kat's slipper-clad feet stumbled to a halt as Pierre and Sylvie froze in the center of her room, a limp blanket dangling between them. "I'm so sorry. Didn't know anyone was in here."

"Excuse me, m'selle." White as cotton, Pierre slipped from the room, leaving Sylvie shaking and alone.

Kat gave her a bright smile. "I'm going to take a walk, but I believe Eleanor and the major are remaining."

"Very good." The blood had drained from Sylvie's thin face. Bobbing a curtsy, she headed for the door.

Kat caught her hand before she bolted and gave it a gentle squeeze. "You're safe with me. Both of you."

Sylvie bobbed again and flew out of the room, the blanket unfolded on the bed.

Barrett twisted Anton onto his back and wrapped his hands around his neck. "You have about thirty seconds before you lose consciousness. What do you do?"

Panic flared in Anton's eyes as he smacked against Barrett's hands. Sweat rolled off his forehead and plopped onto the thin training mat beneath him.

"Think, Anton. I know it's hard, but you must concentrate."

The boy's panicked whimpers echoed off the low cellar ceiling as he shoved at Barrett's chest.

With most men, Barrett would have added pressure to their necks so they understood the sensation of choking to death, but one small squeeze on Anton's would have him passed out. "Your hands are useless because you won't have enough force to use them properly. Besides your hands and legs, what weapon do you have to use?"

"A knife." Anton drew his leg up and fumbled in his sock until his knife slipped free. Red mottled his face as he brandished it triumphantly before Barrett.

"Unless you plan on stuffing that in my mouth, show me what you do with it. Hang on. Make sure it's closed first. I'd rather not bleed out today."

Double-checking for safety, Anton pushed the blunt end of the knife against Barrett's lower back.

"Oh, I'm terribly sorry, sir. Have I inconvenienced you by sitting on your chest like this?" Barrett leaned down with most of his weight. "If you're trying to kill me, you better do a proper job of it the first time because I won't be very forgiving if you keep jabbing me like that."

A few grunts and feeble attempts that completely missed his kidneys, and Barrett was ready to call it quits. The kid wasn't a killer. He didn't have what it took to . . . to what? Survive? Defend himself? Defend his loved ones? No, Barrett didn't believe that. Every man had it in him with the right motivation.

Like a dog stretching out for a nap, Barrett settled the rest of his weight. "What happens when it's not me you're fighting off, but a German? An SS officer has stormed into your home in the middle of the night. Your mother and sister are wailing as they watch that Nazi take the very life from you."

The distress in Anton's eyes burned to hatred. *Good. Finally hit the right button.*

Barrett leaned farther down, his nose almost bumping Anton's. "Your sister is next."

With a cry from a medieval battlefield, Anton rammed his closed knife into the tender kidney at Barrett's back. Barrett rolled off as the shock jolted down his legs. He stared at the cracked ceiling for several long minutes as the pain subsided.

Anton's pale, worried face hovered over him. "All right, *Patron*? I'm so sorry if I've hurt you."

Barrett grinned and clapped him on the arm. "All right, lad. You did fine, exactly what you needed to do. Now, go take a break. You deserve it."

Scrambling to his feet, Anton hurried to the table covered with cups of water and plates of bread and cheese. His comrades crowded around him, thumping him on the back.

"Not dead, are you?" Auguste, his second in command for training, extended a meaty hand.

"No, but I can feel the bruise setting in. Right nasty come morning." Barrett grabbed his hand and eased to his feet. "First spark of anger that lad's given us."

Gus's pulverized face twisted with appreciation. A famed boxer in his younger days, he'd found his next calling in teaching the recruits combative skills. "Found his sticking point, didn't you."

"Aye, but it's not enough."

Skirting around the practice mats where three groups of men grappled, they sat on the bench on the opposite wall from their students. The fluorescent lights flickered overheard. Anton glowed with pride as he showed the others his knife. He fumbled with the safety before it finally sprang open.

"He's going to get himself shot. Probably the rest of us as well." Barrett sighed and leaned his sore back against the cool stone wall. His closed eyes watered in relief.

The bench creaked as Gus shifted his massive frame. "Take him out."

The boy had so little and yet worked twice as hard as the rest of the students. Trouble was, he didn't have their knack for picking up on the tasks and skills. One false or slow move in this game and it was all over. The world wasn't always fair to lads like Anton. No matter how hard they tried, they couldn't seem to make the cut. But even the Antons of the world had a place to serve.

"No. Put him on correspondence drops. As long as he can stay upright on a bicycle, he'll stay out of trouble."

"And if he can't?"

"I'll figure out something else. For now, keep training him on the side." Barrett frowned as Anton tried closing his knife. It refused to stay shut. "Start with the blade. Don't want him stabbing himself and getting blood all over the messages."

The bench groaned as Gus stretched to his feet. "Can't tip off the Gestapo so easily."

"Don't tell him. I want to ease him into the new position."

The scarred flesh over Gus's eyes scrunched together. "He's got to know he ain't cut out for this."

"A man's got his pride." Pride covered a multitude of sins and weaknesses, but in this game it was a fatal chance to take. Some were born risk-takers, like he and Gus, but others like Anton found their strength in more subtle ways. He just needed to figure out what that was before the boy got the whole group killed.

Shrugging with disagreement, Gus headed off to start the dynamite assembly session. The ache that had crowded the edges of Barrett's head all morning now throbbed in full assault. He closed his eyes, but like last night, rest evaded him. It was all Kat's fault. Her horrified reaction to torching the painted trash had cost him a good night's sleep. The artist within probably couldn't help it, even if it was Hitler.

Knock. Knock, knock, knock.

"If that's Victor, he owes me four laps for tardiness." Barrett grimaced and adjusted his back against the wall. He'd feel the kidney jab for days to come. "No more excuses about his cat getting stuck in the gutters."

He pressed the heels of his hands to his eyes as the pressure mounted. Why did she get to him like this? He'd created more disturbances than he could count over the past two years, not to mention all the scuffs accumulated over his thirty-three years, and none of them left him so restless. This is what they did as part of the Resistance. Not for the thrill of arson, but as another blow to the Germans to end the war. She couldn't understand that. Hard to get dirt on one's hands from so far up in that ivory tower.

"Do you ever do any work?"

Barrett's eyes flipped open to find Kat watching him with an amused tilt to her red lips. Dressed in cream and pearls, she fit perfectly into that ivory tower he needed to keep her in. One he could never climb as her equal. She was infiltrating his thoughts much too easily.

"Ten minutes sooner and you would've caught me in the middle of a lesson."

"I would've caught you in the middle of a nap is more like it." Soft golden curls swished over her slim shoulders as she turned her head to the class gathering in the corner for demolition lessons. "Everyone else is hard at work, and yet I find you here like a bump on a log. Such an inspiration to your men."

"Did you come down here to antagonize me, or are you stopping for a breather between shopping trips?"

"Because a bar is the most sensible place for a rest before noon."

Barrett stretched his legs out, crossing them at the ankle. "I've heard worse excuses from women who simply miss me."

"And what a grand sight you are for any pining woman: rumpled shirt, unshaven, and hair like you've been through a tornado. My heart is aflutter."

"I would expect no less of a reaction, except mayhap a dead faint at my feet."

"I'll warn you should I feel light-headed." She shifted her weight, her dainty heel clicks echoing off the barren walls. "May I sit down?"

"If you're not afraid of getting your skirt dirty."

"I'm not as fragile as you would have me to be. Is that blood?"

He squinted at the dried patch on the floor. "More than likely."

She smoothed the back of her skirt as she lowered herself to the wobbly bench. "I came because I would like to learn a bit more about . . . this." She gestured to encompass the room. "After last night and thinking of the situations going forward, I do not wish to find myself without resources."

Beauty and brains had served her well so far. Time to see how far gumption could carry her. "Ever load a revolver before?"

She shook a gloved hand. "I'd rather stay away from those things."

"What if you've lost your little stick and one of *those* things is the only thing keeping you alive?"

"Why must you assume I'm always in mortal danger?"

"Firsthand observation." He pushed to his feet and offered her his hand. Noticing the powder from sorting fuses all morning, he swiped his dirty hands against his trousers before offering it again. "Come on. We'll put Eric's face on one of the targets."

She met his grasp without hesitation. "Now, that's an idea I can get on board with."

At the back table, he picked up a dismantled revolver. All students had to learn to assemble and disassemble one blindfolded before they even put a bullet in the chamber. He glanced at the froth of netting surrounding Kat's large-brimmed hat. No way a blindfold was fitting over that. "How is the workhorse for purity doing this morning?"

"Raging on the warpath." She touched a finger to the tip of a bullet lined neatly with others on the table. The corners of her mouth pulled down. "He won't stop until he finds who did it."

"Then he'll spend a lifetime at failing. If a tiny little fire is going to distract him so much, then he better sit the remainder of the war out for what's coming."

She looked up, fear leaping in her eyes. "What do you mean?"

"Things will only escalate if Hitler continues his path of destruction. The people won't stand for it, and certainly the armies won't."

"But what about you?"

"My job is to train and not much more."

"I'd call last night a little more."

"That's your fault." He held up a hand at her look of protest. "If you and your sister hadn't shown up, I'd while away my days down here and nights slinging drinks up there. As usual, the government has taken a bad situation and turned it into a golden opportunity for themselves."

"Who would've thought? You and I, the golden couple."

Her sweet perfume swept under his nose. Like a breath of fresh flowers, it blocked out the gloom and must of his underground world. Her very being stuck out like the sun on a cloudy day. Tall, shoulders elegantly held back, fashionably dressed and coiffed, she didn't belong down here. She belonged to tea and crumpets at the Savoy, afternoon strolls in Hyde Park, and operas with men in penguin suits.

He grabbed the firing pin and jammed it down into the spring. *Pointless, boy-o. Your job is here—not the Savoy. You couldn't afford to be a dishwasher at the Savoy, much less obtain a lady from her class.* The pin slipped through the coils and bounced on the floor. He swooped down and caught it.

A smile rippled over her face as she watched him.

"What's so funny?"

"Nothing, really." Popping open her handbag, she took out a gold-tipped pen and pulled one of the target sheets from the shelf. She scratched slowly over the circles. "I was just thinking if my father could see me now, working for the cause. Might give him a reason to smile."

"Not much of a grinner, your dad?"

"Not exactly." The scratches turned into thin lips and pinned-back ears. "At least not at me."

She said it on an exhale so soft he almost missed it. He'd had his doubts about Sir Alfred's fatherly affections, but the sadness in her voice was enough to twist his gut. Fathers, rich and poor, amounted to nothing but disappointment, and yet their kids never stopped striving for their approval. The haunting shadow of self-pity crept over him. He shoved it back. He wasn't his da, and he'd prove it until the day he left this world. He'd die fighting and not shrivel into a drunken shell moaning about life's lost love.

"Where did you learn this kind of fighting?"

Her voice pulled him back from the blackened thoughts as her pen scuffed out combed hair. "Back rooms of the brewery and hard streets of Glasgow. Couldn't call yourself a man if you hadn't bloodied at least one nose."

"How awful."

"That's life. At least for the lower class of us." He slid the rear sight onto the frame, locking it in place.

"How did you escape the backyard brawls and come to serve British intelligence?"

"Didn't have much of a choice. This or jail."

Her pen stopped scratching for the faintest of seconds before continuing. "Dare I ask the circumstances?"

The memory of that night over three years ago swept over him like a stale wind. He touched a finger to the white scar above his lip. "I was tending the counter one night when three university lads came barging in, bragging loud enough to drive off the locals. When I asked the drunks to leave, they threatened to close me down after I refused to serve them. How dare I throw out Lord Charles Bounty's son?" He paused, remembering their pathetic insults. Rich chaps never knew how to curse properly. "That little peacock dared to call himself a man after he got his two lads to hold me down. He'd obviously never punched anyone before, but the beer gave him determination. That and the bottle he found."

Sadness rippled in her eyes as she looked at the scar. "Ethan Bounty."

"You know him?"

Nodding, her gaze rose to meet his. "His father and mine served together on the finance committee some years ago. Ethan deserves every insult you gave him and then some." She tapped the capped pen in her palm, each beat whacking faster and faster until the skin turned red. "Let me guess. He ran home to squeal to his father, who had the police cart you off to jail for defending yourself against his precious angel."

Barrett rocked back. "Aye, but I was lucky that the bailiff noticed the beating I gave them, and pretty soon someone from the MI6 came knocking on my cell with an offer." He spread his arms wide. "As you can see, I didn't turn it down."

She shook her head. The froth on her hat swayed gently back and forth as if it, too, disagreed with the absurdity. "My goodness. The hands of Fate are ever so strange."

"Probably seems that way to you. You must've spent your child-hood eating bonbons and petting a fluffy white cat, eh?"

"Hardly. Mother deemed both inappropriate. One to the figure and the other to her pristine furniture. There. What do you think?"

She held up her masterpiece, her anxious blue-green eyes peering over the top, waiting for his inspection. Eric's face stared back.

"If I didn't know better, I'd say the man is standing before me. You've a true skill, poppy."

"Thank you." Pink engulfed her cheeks. She smoothed the draw-ing on the table. "I'll give you ten francs if you get it between his eyes."

"I've got something better than a bullet for this work of art." He nodded to the stacked rolls of dynamite on the table. "He deserves nothing short of a proper send-off."

"I assume the brewery didn't teach you to detonate bombs."

"No, that came from the office of ungentlemanly warfare, along with a few other polishings of my hard-earned skills."

She recapped her pen and slipped it back into her handbag. "Bit of a soldier buried deep in there, I think."

Memories of his drunken da tugging on his old Tommy uniform and stumbling around their basement flat in search of *her* seared his brain. The war had cost them too much, he would cry to the bent photograph of *her*. It was the only picture Barrett had of his mother. If he ever found that little hovel she'd worked and died in, he'd tear it apart with his bare hands.

He shook his head. "An opportunist. Nothing more."

"You keep saying 'nothing more' as if you're too afraid of your own possibilities. Look around you. Do you not see the bravery it takes to accomplish what you and these other Resistance members are doing? Don't sell yourself short, Barrett."

A thrill shot through him at the sound of his name coming from her lips for the first time. *No. No, no, no.* He wasn't giving in to her charms. They'd do nothing but shackle him to eternal misery. And yet those wide eyes offered him something he hadn't seen in a long time, something he dare not trust in: hope.

He placed the revolver parts back on the table and shifted closer to her. "This evening, if you're—"

Bang! Bang, bang!

Trepidation sliced over him like freezing water. The emergency knock. "Take positions!"

Grabbing an assembled revolver, he checked to make sure it was loaded while the students flipped over tables and jumped behind them with muzzles peeking over the tops and sides. He shoved Kat into the corner and barred her with his body. At his nod, Gus cracked open the door. A few whispered words and the door shut.

"Germans ransacking upstairs."

Curses streaked through Barrett's brain. Second time in three months those SS dogs had come sniffing around. Last night—no. No possible way they could know he was the culprit. What if they'd finally come for Sam? He spun around to Kat. "Stay down here and wait until I come back and get you."

"She's gotta go." Gus crossed the room, frustration knitting his black eyebrows like spiderwebs. "They found a glass with lipstick on the rim and want to know where the woman is."

"I'm sorry. It's so hot outside, and Henri was kind enough to offer me a glass of water." Kat's lower lip pushed out on a quiver. "I'm so sorry."

He grinned to cover the turbulence flaring inside. Not her fault she'd picked the wrong time to breeze in, but it added to the strain. Especially with last night's disturbance still thick in the air. "Keeps things interesting."

"They still haven't come down to the cellar," Gus said, prying open the heavy door. "Take the back stairs. I hung a new lantern in there only yesterday."

"Get everyone out the secret exit. You stay behind. If those Nazis come sniffing down here, blow the place. We can't lead them to the other Resistance cells. Make sure you get yourself out before the fuse goes, eh?" Instructions done, Barrett motioned for Kat to follow him back into the cellar and to the far corner where three large wine barrels tall and wide enough to fit three grown men lay on their sides. He stuck his finger into a tiny hole in the last barrel's lid and popped it off. Walking to the back, he pushed open the secret door and motioned her forward. "Keep your head down and watch your feet. The stairs haven't been used much."

Securing the door firmly back in place, he brushed his hands along the wall until he found the lantern. A quick flick of the lighter had a flame burning low and steady to guide them up the creaky stairs.

"If you see a rat, try not to scream." Musty dust settled on his shoulders like an old cloak as he climbed the stairs. "We're inside the walls, and there's a good chance the Germans will hear us."

A breath shuddered from her lips as she reached for his hand. They moved steadily up until another wall blocked them. He pressed his ear to the rough boards. Nothing. They hadn't made it up this far yet. Fumbling once more, he found the latch and pushed out into his private office's water closet.

He secured the full-length mirror back in place. "Stay here."

"Barrett." Barely contained fear streaked her face. She squeezed his hand and dropped it. "Please be careful."

Hurrying through his untouched office, he took the stairs two at a time and strode into the barroom. His gaze flicked to the stage where the band sat quietly with their instruments, practice having been interrupted. Sam caught his eye and gave a minuscule shrug.

"Who's in charge of this disturbance to my establishment?"

A shorter and wider version of Himmler himself turned from his examination of the bottles on the shelf behind the bar. His black pencil mustache wiggled with disregard. "Captain Schmidt of the *Schutzstaffel* here on personal orders from Major Keiffer."

Schmidt's tiny eyes narrowed with delight as he waited for the admission to strike fear, but even knowing the man enjoyed inflicting torture and death on his victims, Barrett wasn't about to admit the name of the head of Gestapo did more than strike fear into him.

"Major Keiffer has sampled more than one bottle of my finest scotch." Understatement of the year. The major's fondness for drink went far beyond sampling, especially when he had a detachment of officers and rouged French girls with him. He could march to the Fatherland and back on the length of his unpaid tab.

Two corporals barely old enough to be out of short trousers flipped over the table closest to the bandstand. Carefully folded napkins floated to the ground like shot doves. Barrett shoved his clenched fists into his pockets. "I only hope your men haven't smashed my latest offering for him in their haste to—By the way, you never mentioned what you're doing here."

The hairy pencil twitched. "Didn't I?"

If he wasn't on the verge of breaking the man's neck, Barrett might've laughed at his pathetic attempts at intimidation. Schmidt's neck inched farther and farther out as if to prod a response. Barrett merely waited.

Schmidt's shoulders dropped back with disappointment. "We'll go to your office to discuss the situation further."

Heart dropping to his stomach, Barrett jumped to block him from the back door. His fighters needed time to escape should Schmidt and his hounds decide to take a detour through the cellars. "Afraid we can't. There's a lady up there, and I'd rather not subject her to business matters."

"Ah, the lady in question." Schmidt's eyes darted to the lipstick-smeared glass sitting on the bar in front of a seething Henri. Like a watchdog, he refused to move from his precious bottles. "This pertains to her as well."

Fangs of dread stabbed into his chest. He'd been so careful, and now to drag her down through his own arrogance. Poor lass. He'd doomed her before they'd ever met.

The sudden quietness clanged like a bell at midday. The SS men had stopped dragging chairs across the floor to watch each excruciating second tick by. The fangs sank deeper, cutting off his breath. Those guards had no qualms hauling in innocent citizens. A loud-mouthed bar owner didn't stand a chance. For the sake of the fighters in the room below and to keep the attention from Sam, it was best to play along.

"This way, Captain."

Upstairs, Kat perched on the edge of his desk with long legs crossed, reapplying lipstick with the help of a gold compact. "Darling, there you are! I was beginning to worry." The compact snapped shut. "You brought a guest."

The chills that had raced down his spine coming up the stairs turned to drenching sweat. "Captain Schmidt, may I present Miss Whitford."

Kat nodded but didn't offer her hand. She swung it out to Barrett instead. "Major."

Though her words and smile didn't falter, her hand shook like a leaf in a storm. Barrett wrapped his fingers around it as she hopped off the desk.

Ignoring the seat Barrett offered, Schmidt walked behind the desk and plopped down in the leather-backed chair. He motioned for Barrett and Kat to sit in the leftover seats. "Unannounced as the disturbance is downstairs, I assure you it's necessary before we could go any further."

The window shade fluttered as a trickle of wind pushed hot air around the room. Kat sat ramrod straight on the edge of her chair, curling her fingernails into her knees. Barrett angled his chair closer, brushing his knee against hers. Her hands slowly folded into her lap.

"Maybe I could ask your boys to stick around and help clean up. They'll never know tedious until they've refolded two hundred napkins."

"Unfortunately, they have more important things to attend to than napkin folding, Herr Anderson." Schmidt's mustache wiggled as he leaned back in the chair and folded his little hands over his soft belly. "But the thorough search is necessary if we are to proceed."

"Search all day if you like, but as with the previous visits, your boys won't find anything out of the ordinary." His man would have it blown up long before discovery.

"That is what I hope, but I must make certain. Orders are orders, you understand."

Barrett understood slow and deliberate torture. He'd seen enough arrests to know the Gestapo preferred making a grand entrance with their intent stated right away to show their power and provoke fear. If Schmidt was there to arrest him, why the cat-and-mouse game? Even more frustrating, why couldn't they send someone with a half a brain? If he was going down, he'd at least like an opponent worthy of a fight.

Knock, knock, knock.

"Come in," Schmidt called before Barrett could open his mouth.

One of the napkin-flinging boys popped his head in with a few quick words in German. Schmidt nodded and the door closed once more. The shade fluttered again, teasing escape. Sweat trickled down the back of Barrett's neck.

"Well. It seems everything is in order." Schmidt leaned forward, resting his hand on the carved wooden box of postcards and maps. Barrett clamped his fingers together to stop from snatching it away. "Congratulations, Herr Anderson. You are to host a party for the screening of Buch's latest masterpiece, *Menschen im Sturm*. The star Olga Chekhova is to attend, and if we are very lucky, Goebbels himself."

Barrett's tongue fell flat. He wasn't being arrested. He was safe. They were all safe. For now. Relief slammed over him like a barrel knocked sideways.

"Darling, how exciting!" Kat grabbed his hand. "A movie premiere with such glamorous guests."

At her fingernails digging into his skin, Barrett found his voice. "Very flattering for them to think of my humble establishment for the celebration."

"*Ja*, well, your name is not unknown in our circles." Schmidt stood and walked around to the door. "Someone will come by with further details. For your own sake, do not let us down."

Chapter 10

If not for the woman in his arms, Barrett would have cracked hours before. Light as a feather, Kat stepped in perfect rhythm to the hideous music wafting around them. Goebbels himself had selected the greatest hits of Charlie and His Orchestra, the pride of the Rhineland. But Kat felt the strain as well. With each brilliant smile she flashed at their fellow dancers, her nails dug further into his shoulder.

"Loosen up that grip or you'll break my shoulder."

"What? Oh, sorry." Her fingers relaxed. "I'm usually very good with a fox-trot."

"Do you normally dance it surrounded by half of the Third Reich's propaganda ministry?"

"No."

"Then I'll forgive the distraction."

The corners of her red mouth flipped up. "Thank you ever so."

Dressed in deep-green satin that dipped low in the back to showcase creamy skin and the soft curls of hair pulled back with diamond combs, her simple elegance outshone every woman in the place. After days of nagging, he was glad he'd given in to her demands that he learn to dance these fancy steps. Integrating into higher circles required the must-learn skill, along with eating from the correct fork and ironing his shirts. Or so she claimed. With her warming to his touch, he had to admit dancing had its advantages over ironing.

His arm circled tighter around her. "If tonight didn't demand our presence, what would you be doing?"

"Plotting new ways to put strychnine in Eric's coffee. He boils it so hot, he'll never notice."

Barrett laughed, startling the couple next to them into missing a beat. "Imaginative, though I was thinking outside of Paris. Outside of the war."

Her lips pursed in thought, tempting him. "Cocktails followed by supper, then card games while the men finish their brandy, and finally finishing the dreadful evening by dancing with whichever power-hungry bore Mother and Father have lined up for me."

"As thrilling as that all sounds, I didn't hear what *you* would want to be doing."

Surprise flitted across her face. "I'm not sure. I've never been allowed to consider it before." Her eyebrows knitted together as she drummed her fingernails on the back of his neck. After several seconds, her brow relaxed. "Travel. With no itinerary. And no protocol to adhere to. And cake for breakfast."

"Yet you've never considered it before."

"I've never had the luxury before."

His fingers brushed the bared skin at the small of her back. Silk was never so soft. "Care for a travel companion?"

"I don't share cake."

"All right with me. Never eat much of a breakfast."

Her fingers curled around the back of his neck, stroking the hairs to stand on end. The green in her eyes glowed like jade. She moved closer, her red lips parting, beckoning. "Your turn."

His turn. His turn. For what? He dragged his attention from her lips. "My perfect evening might be considered too lowbrow for your set."

"Does it involve explosives?"

His gaze zeroed in on her mouth again, forgetting all manner of distinctions from low to high class. "Fireworks of some kind."

"Kat." Ellie popped up next to them. Grinning from ear to ear and doused with perfume, she was in her element. "There's someone you simply have to meet. He's had way too much of the sherry, so hold your nose."

Once again powerless against her sister's will, Kat was yanked from Barrett's arms. She glanced back over her shoulder with an apologetic frown as the sea of gray uniforms swallowed her wake, leaving him alone without his anchor. Not knowing what else to do, he turned to the bar.

Or what was left of it after being festooned with Nazi flags. With a clipboard in one hand and half an apology, Ellie had breezed in that morning to rearrange chairs, create a larger dance floor, throw snowy white cloths over tables, and ensure the music list was set up. It was the first time he'd seen her so focused on the impeccable outcome of something other than her nails. Now, after hours of polishing every surface with beeswax, beer stains covered the floor and cigarette smoke clogged the air.

"They're really lapping it up, *Patron*." Henri leaned close as he uncorked another wine bottle. Delight flitted across his face as he read the label from one of the worst bottles down in the cellar.

Taking a break from a trumpet-less arrangement, Sam plopped on a barstool and mopped his sweaty face with a handkerchief. Henri slid him a fresh glass of water. "Highest order of German scum we've had in the place yet. Your girl to thank for that. She brings nothing but the best, eh?"

"They're hoping her riches and social status will rub off on them. Not sure how far it'll stretch since all her power is tied up in England, and at the moment they're the enemy."

"Something's rubbed off on you. You clean up nice." Sam's eyebrows waggled with delight.

"Feel like a starched puppet." Barrett tugged at the starched collar rubbing his neck. It was the most expensive suit he owned, and that wasn't saying much, but Mrs. Bonheur had scrubbed and mended the pants and jacket to good as new. "Don't fill those glasses to the top, Henri. Our guests are lit enough, I don't need the extra spills on the floor."

"No need to take your sour mood out on me. I don't like having these *crétins* stomping around in here any more than you, though I can understand when they're clamoring around your girl the entire night." Henri filled the glasses to halfway and tossed the empty bottle in the bin below the bar.

"You'd think they'd stay far away from the English, but they're the toast of Paris, aren't they?" A toothy grin split Sam's face as he drained his water glass. "She could do wonders for you, eh?"

"You two gossip worse than old women." As per orders, Kat had swept him into the restricted upper echelon of society. Whether English or German, money and the right name got you into any door. Or in his case, *her* money and name. He didn't have much to offer her but a pair of fists. A woman like her deserved the best of everything. And the best he was not.

He nodded to the men at the far end of the bar gesturing for their drinks and turned back to Henri. "Get back to work. Both of you."

Grumbling, Henri took his drinks to the other end of the bar while Sam jogged back to the stage, leaving Barrett alone again. Solitude never bothered him. Years of being shushed in a pub corner while his da finished off a last pint made it easy to keep to himself. The barkeep had even offered him his first job in wiping spills from under the tables. Doubtful his English rose had ever stooped to such an existence.

He snorted. Kat wasn't his. No more than he was hers. She was an inconvenience with a paycheck attached. A means for a fresh start. He'd never be caught in a back-alley fight with a snot-nosed politician's son ever again.

"For a bar owner, I've yet to see you raise a glass." Dressed in his finest monkey suit, Eric appeared next to him with full glass in hand.

Barrett leaned his back against the bar, crossing his arms over his chest. "I like to keep a clear head during business hours."

"Here I thought Scots couldn't stand up properly without a wee drink." Eric laughed at his attempt of humor and slapped Barrett on the back. "Have one on me. Or should I say have one from me on the Führer."

His rusty laugh chafed down Barrett's spine. The bill for tonight was footed by the mighty Führer's government, but they'd only paid for half of the expenses up front. Demanding perfection, Schmidt had assured him that the rest would be paid after the party. The rest of that money coming to the Stag was as sure a bet as Hitler giving up the war anytime soon.

"Thanks, but I prefer my own bottle of Ballantine's after we close."

"Ballantine's? I've not heard of it." Eric's pale eyebrows knitted together in deep thought. Suddenly, his face lit up. "Maybe later I can join you to celebrate what a glorious evening this has turned out to be."

How much had he had to drink already? His eyes were their usual pale blue without any glossiness, his words unslurred, and yet he appeared more relaxed and cheerful than ever before. Uneasiness pinpricked the back of Barrett's neck.

"Good mood tonight, eh?"

"*Ja, wunderbar.*" Propping an elbow on the bar, Eric leaned close and pointed a finger to the opposite side of the room. "Look at my girl. So lovely, like a pearl among chunks of coal. She put together this entire soiree for me."

Surrounded by four officers, Ellie did indeed shine like a pearl in head-to-toe white, but next to her Kat dazzled like an emerald.

"Quite a boon for you."

"*Ja.* Dr. Goebbels sent me a telegram an hour ago expressing his sorrow at being unable to attend but delighted in our magnificent success for the Fatherland tonight."

"Too bad I missed the movie, though I wouldn't have understood a word."

"Frau Chekhova's performance transcends language barriers. You can see, even now, her vivid facial expressions and articulate gestures enrapturing her audience."

Barrett ducked as Eric's arm swept in front of him to indicate the small woman who had joined Kat's group. Her back was turned, blocking her vivid expressions from view. "Oh, aye. I see what you mean."

Sam swung the band into another song with an upbeat tempo. They'd been given only a week to learn all the requested new German songs but sounded as if they'd played them for years. Sam had fallen out of his chair howling with laughter when more than one arrangement required an accordion and an alphorn.

"I didn't get a chance to thank you for recommending the Stag." The words didn't stick as bad as he'd thought. Without realizing it, Eric had shoved his compatriots into the wolf's lair.

"I was pleased to hear Schmidt's report after his inspection. One can never be too careful with the locations of such significant events."

Such as giving him, his workers, and his fighters another scare? The Germans might as well set up camp with the number of times they'd plowed through his door. "Happy to oblige his curiosity."

"To tell you the truth, it was upon Eleanor's insistence. She wouldn't hear of any other venue for the honor, and I couldn't bear disappointing her." Eric set his unfinished glass on the bar and smoothed a hand over the worn wood. "I believe she did it for Kathleen's sake. Quite a bond they have. Makes me jealous sometimes."

The catch in the man's voice took Barrett off guard. Feelings were the last thing he'd suspected Eric of having. "You really care for her, don't you?"

"Does that surprise you?" The lines on Eric's angular face softened, making him almost bearable to look at. "Perhaps you saw the uniform and interpreted only coldness."

"You haven't given me much else to go on."

"Perhaps that will change."

Tigers never changed their stripes. Uniform or not, a Nazi was a Nazi even if he fancied himself in love. More likely, Eric was trying to cozy up to keep him close. At least they had the same game plan. "We'll see."

Across the room, Kat rolled her eyes at him as the officers continued to drone in her ear. How easily she fit into this party world, nodding politely at the men around her, smiling when appropriate, and laughing without a care in the world. Yet the straight line of her shoulders and pushing back of her hair gave away her complete boredom. At least to him. He'd seen the stance every time she was around Eric.

Excusing herself, she looped her arm through Frau Chekhova's and pulled her through the crowd to him. "I couldn't listen to any more about airplanes and their individual wingspans."

Barrett shifted, brushing his shoulder against hers. An act he found himself doing more and more. "Flyboys like to talk, especially to pretty girls."

"Yes, they certainly do." A faint smile flitted over her lips. Barrett fought the urge to grab her in his arms and tilt her back on a big kiss, the wee kipper. She'd gotten more out of them than airspeeds and wind gauges.

Feeling the need to defend his countrymen's antics, Eric straightened and lowered his brow as a schoolmaster would to an unruly pupil. "Captain Gurtner and Lieutenant Sudman are two of the Luftwaffe's finest pilots. Count yourself lucky, for they do not recite their exploits to just anyone."

Unimpressed, Kat patted a curl behind her ear. "Really? Because they're over there telling anyone willing to stand within earshot."

Eric's chin notched up. "Well, they have much to be proud of."

"Or they've had one too many. Yes, that's probably it. Come morning, I'm sure their pride will revert back to revered stoicism." She turned to the woman next to her with a conspiratorial wink. "I'm glad we got away when we did. Aren't you, Olga?"

Olga waved a ringed hand dismissively. With thin eyebrows, sleepy eyes, and wide cheekbones, she hardly stood out as the darling actress of the Third Reich. "Men and their technical prowess. Why do they think it impresses us when all we'd like is a compliment, a few jewels, and a helping hand with the dishes?"

"I'll take the compliments over jewels any day."

"Tut-tut, *liebling* Kat. Jewels last longer than a compliment and are always sincere, dear. Never forget that." Olga's deep red lips dipped into a smile as she turned her attention to Barrett. "If I guess correctly that you are the owner of this establishment, will you recite Burns for me in that brogue that I find oh so charming with Scotsmen?"

Heat flushed up Barrett's neck at her brazen request. "I am the owner, but I'm verra sorry tae say I've no' much learning with Burns, ma'am."

Olga squealed with delight at his put-on accent. "Positively charming. I do love men with strong accents. Makes me feel like they truly stand for something. How lucky you are to find such a charmer, my dear."

Kat shook her head in wonderment. "Sometimes I simply don't know what to do with so much charm."

"Lock him down before some other girl comes by to snatch him up. Now, Eric, dear, don't look so put out. You're as charming as Mr. Anderson here, just in a more Teutonic way." She grabbed Eric's hand and pulled him to the dance floor. "Stop holding up the wall and twirl me around. Tell me all about my beloved Adolf. I'm thinking of traveling to Bavaria to see him soon."

Barrett watched with amusement as Olga draped one of her fringed arms over Eric's shoulder to show him the proper steps. She counted in Russian. "Quite a friend you've made there."

Kat clasped her hands and pressed them to her cheek. "I'm verra sorry, lad. I couldna hear ye over mae rolling *r*'s and charming smiles sure tae make a lass weak in the knees."

"Come on. It's not that thick."

Her hands dropped to her hips, her eyebrow spiking in challenge.

"Oh, perhaps ye put it on a wee thick for Frau Chekhova. Am I tae be jealous, then?"

"You're throwing in a wee bit of Aberdeen when you know very well I'm from Glasgow. Get your particulars straight, woman."

"So sorry."

"You'll be sorry all right when I step on your feet for this waltz."

The waltz was another propaganda take on "You're Driving Me Crazy," but thankfully Sam opted not to sing the words of hatred to Britain. Kat fell easily into Barrett's embrace as he swept them around the floor. Without prompting, she followed his lead as if each step were a continuation of his own. As if an invisible string tied them together, they each shifted to follow the slightest vibration of the other.

"Have I told you how splendid you look tonight?"

"You can ease up. No one can hear you over Sam's trumpet."

His arm tightened around her waist, pulling her closer. "I mean it, poppy."

"Thank you." She ducked her head as pink blossomed across her cheeks. "Certainly better than hearing I'm like a patch of grass after a long flight."

"That's one I've never heard."

Her head popped back up, angling closer to his. "Bet you didn't hear that the Luftwaffe are going to hit Moscow hard in the next few days, or that Hitler has ordered paperwork outlining a final solution for the Jews."

Chills sprayed down his spine. "'Final solution.' What does that mean?"

"Not sure, but they seemed awfully giddy about the prospects." She paused as Olga and Eric spun past. "There are also rumors about edging into open waters to see what the Americans will do."

"Blast them out of the water, most likely. You did a great job getting this information. Command will be thrilled." As much as he hated this spy business, at least they were getting vital information to those who needed it. All the sooner to finish off these murdering Nazis.

"Hate for them to think I'm falling down on the job." She shrugged. "Besides, drunks are only too eager to please when you show interest. I merely smiled and laughed when they wanted me to."

Dutiful to a fault. Had she ever stepped a toe out of line without obtaining permission first? "A man doesn't need drink to fall for that."

"Your flattery is on a roll tonight. Careful you don't overdo it and regret it come morning."

His eyes dropped to her full mouth. It begged for his attention, to savor the softness and linger over the gentle curves. Forbidden fruit ripe for the picking. How much more would he regret come morning? "It hasn't been so bad, has it? All this pretending. Spending time together as we climb our way up the social ladder of snakes."

"I find myself pretending less and less with you."

The music stopped, but he didn't move to release her. Nor did she.

Voices buzzed, colliding in a cacophony that grated his ears. Elbows and shoulders pushed into them as the crowd backed away from the front doors.

A single frantic voice screeched above the others. "Look at you all here. Celebrating and carrying on as if nothing is happening outside these doors! Murderers! Thieves!"

Warnings pounded in Barrett's head. Shoving Kat behind him, he motioned for Sam and the band to get down. He'd heard those words before and they never brought anything good.

The crowd surged back as a small Frenchman bounced around like a wobbly top. His mended black suit hung on his thin body, his black whiskers were too long for his thin face, and his wild eyes protruded like golf balls.

"No one asked you here, yet you storm in here as if it's yours to take. It's not! It's ours!" He sneered, balancing his bony hands on his hips and jutting his head out like a rooster. "You think you're so much better. That you deserve life and we don't."

Don't do it, friend. Shut your mouth. But the man had signed his end simply by walking in here. No way the Germans were letting him walk free. Unless there was a way to get him out before the Germans got their hands on him.

He turned to Kat. "Stay here. At the slightest incident you go straight to Sam. Understand?"

Her face blanched with panic. "What are you going to do?"

"Something stupid."

Shoving down his own clawing fear, Barrett pushed to the front of the crowd and faced the man. "What do you say you and I go and talk about this in the back room? Let these people get back to their party, eh?"

Hatred pricked the Frenchman's eyes like needles. "You're one of them."

"I'm just a simple bar owner, but I've got a dram of whisky and a willing ear if you want to tell me about what's wrong."

"You're not shutting me up in a back room. What I've got to say is for the scum in here."

"I'm more than willing to listen to your troubles, but I'm sure the ladies aren't. Come on, let's go up to my office—"

"My mother was a lady. My sister too. That didn't stop the pigs from barging into our home and forcing themselves on them. When my sister fought back, they dragged her into the street and beat her, leaving her to die as an example for those who would refuse." Reaching into his shirt, he yanked out a small gold Star of David on a chain. *"Juif!* We are nothing to you. Dirt beneath your feet, animals to slaughter. You rape and kill the innocent. Who are the true animals?"

Behind Barrett, feminine gasps mingled with German curses. Like sharks around a drowning man, the Gestapo edged closer. Helplessness swallowed Barrett. The poor man, and Barrett couldn't lift a finger to help him now. The curses grew louder as the men pushed forward. The little man's eyes darted like a caged tiger's. With a twist of his wrist, a revolver glinted in the lantern light.

The crowd fell back. A woman screamed as he waved the gun in the air with a shaking hand. "Get back, all of you!"

Barrett stepped forward, hand out and palms up. "Put the gun away, mate. You don't want to hurt anyone. You're not a killer."

The man's hand shook. "They've made me one. I don't have a choice."

"I don't believe that."

"They deserve to burn, every last one of them."

Fervent agreement burned at the back of Barrett's throat. How he wished he could tell the Jewish man that he wasn't alone, but doing so would forfeit his life and every one of those he'd sworn to protect at all costs. "Put the gun down, please. Come and talk with me."

Bang!

A dark hole blasted out the front of the little man's chest. Stunned, his mouth fell open on a gasp. Eyes rolling to the back of his head, he fell to his knees and slumped to the floor, facedown. Blood circled around him.

Barrett spun around to find Eric behind him with a shining black Luger raised.

"The time for talking is over."

Chapter 11

"Do you want a magazine?"

Not turning from the window, Ellie shook her head. A long, low whistle rent the air as the train next to them spun its wheels, chugging it forward on the dirty tracks of Gare de l'Est. Leaning forward, Kat peered out the large window. A small family struggled by with their patched suitcases. Large, yellow stars blazed on their clothing. Two German soldiers sauntered by and snatched the suitcases from their hands, dumping the personal contents onto the platform. As the husband scrambled to gather his belongings, one of the soldiers shoved the butt of his gun into the man's stomach. The woman and her children cowered, crying, as the soldiers laughed and turned to walk away, but not before catching Kat watching. The soldiers offered her a polite smile and saluted as if they'd served their duty to her. Hatred burned in the woman's eyes as she stared at Kat sitting comfortably in her first-class seat with her starless fashionable jacket.

She thinks I'm one of them. She thinks this is the world I want.

Kat swallowed back the burn of tears. This was the role she'd agreed to, to keep Ellie safe. But there was more at stake here. More to risk than her sister. If she could put aside her own immediate desires and play the part she'd been given, she could help bring a swift end to the injustice raging like wildfire.

The clock hanging over the now-vacant platform clanged. Her stomach dropped. Ten thirty-five. Barrett was late. How was she to pull off the next four days without him? Smiling and laughing during cocktail hour was one thing, but she was no spy. Foolish British command. Sitting in their high offices and holding their breath as she descended into the very heart of the viper's pit. The fear that had roiled in her stomach since the day Eric purchased their tickets quaked up into her chest. How could they expect her to pull off a minute of this ridiculous charade? She was a simple girl from Berkshire, not a trained assassin or saboteur. They needed Barrett.

She needed Barrett.

The fear in her chest hurled into shock. When had she allowed herself to become so reliant on him? To wish for him to kiss her on the center of a dance floor? She might be a simple girl, but she was university educated and the daughter of the great Sir Alfred Whitford, war hero of the Somme and tactical advisor to Churchill himself. As her father said, even the great bulldog needed an ally.

But why did her ally have to be so disarmingly handsome?

The car vibrated beneath their feet. A low whistle hissed as the wheels churned. Stacked boxes and trunks, waiting ticket holders, and patrolling armed soldiers passed by the window as they pulled away from the platform. Relief hovered as the guns faded into the distance, but knowing what lay a short ride away, she refused to let it settle.

Plucking an outdated Parisian magazine from her travel bag, Kat flipped it open to the feature article. "Oh, look. Ten new patterns for transforming your faded dress into updated pieces using tablecloths and window dressings. Look, Ellie. Isn't that darling? You can cut up a floral drape and make stripes on a white skirt. *Voila!* A new skirt."

Ellie flicked a disinterested eye to the page then back to the window. The Bastille column rose in the distance. "What kind of fashion magazine touts dresses out of tablecloths?"

"Practical ones."

"Fashion isn't about practicality."

"These days it is. Most women don't have the luxury of running down to Madame Grè's for a new frock when the fancy hits."

Ellie picked at the polka-dotted chiffon floating around her knees. "No, I suppose they don't."

Closing the magazine, Kat slipped her arm around Ellie's shoulder and pulled her close. "I wish you'd talk to me."

"What's there to talk about?"

Shoving aside the impending horrors, Kat tried to focus on the good. Though they dwindled with each passing second. "Well, we're going on a lovely holiday to Bavaria, where we've never been. Eric says the lake there is clear as glass to swim in."

"Eric." Ellie stiffened and pulled away. "Think he'll shoot anyone while we're there? Bad table service. *Bam.* Ducks quacking too loud. *Bam.*"

"That other man had a gun. There's no telling what he would have done with it."

Like a desperate man searching for scraps of food, Ellie's wide blue eyes bored into hers. "Do you honestly believe that? Really, Kat?"

Kat's heart pounded in rhythm with the clanging train wheels, faster and faster until it squeezed the air from her lungs. Of course she didn't believe it. That man had dangled from the end of his frantic rope, and Eric had wasted no time in eliminating what he deemed an unworthy existence. At last Ellie had sensed the truth of the monster lurking within her shiny soldier. But one overanxious push from Kat would send her careening back into his arms. The girl resisted any head-on approach simply on principle. She required the patience of subtle suggestion to finally reach a conclusion on her own. If she thought it her own, she was more likely to believe the truth in it.

For Kat, it was a delicate balance of concealing the truth without outright lying, for which she'd had a lifetime of learning in gossiping parlors. It was becoming quite the flourishing skill as a spy. "It's not right to take another life, no matter what they've done. Only in the direst of circumstances could I fathom such an action, like trying to save a loved one."

"Isn't that what he was trying to do? The Jew, I mean. He felt he had no other choice when he couldn't save his sister and mother." Ellie raked a hand through her platinum hair, dislodging her small, round hat. She shoved it back in place. "Eric could have talked to him. He didn't have to . . . do what he did."

What if it had been Sylvie or Pierre standing there with a gun, driven to such absolute hopelessness? How long until she was forced to throw off this cloak of deceit and make a stand against this evil tyranny? "No, Eric didn't have to do what he did. Perhaps that essence of his character has been hidden from you all this time."

Ellie sighed. "Sometimes I wonder if . . ."

"Wonder what?"

"I wonder if I've made a mistake with him." Tears shimmered in the corners of Ellie's eyes. Blinking, she dropped her head to study her hands in her lap. "There are things about him, things I haven't told you. Maybe because I've been so happy and didn't want to admit them out loud. Especially to you."

"You can tell me anything."

"I used to, didn't I? We shared everything. But this you won't understand."

Kat took Ellie's hands and held them. "Try me."

Dread swam in Ellie's eyes, threatening to drown the glimmer of hope in spilling her burden. "Promise you won't hate me."

Tears pricked the back of Kat's eyes. The bands of fear warping around her heart eased. All hope was not lost for her sister. "You drive me crazy, but I'll never hate you. Never."

The corners of Ellie's mouth twitched, but didn't quite form a smile. She took a shuddering breath. "The truth is—"

"Made it."

Suitcase at his side, red cheeked and panting, Barrett towered over them. "Thought I wouldn't make it, didn't you?"

Relief stabbed Kat's fear square in the chest. She wasn't alone. "I was beginning to give up hope."

"Almost had to." Shoving his suitcase onto the rack above them, he dropped into the plush green velvet seat opposite them and waved his hat in front of his face. "Supply man got stopped on the way to see me this morning. Gestapo decided to rifle through his papers and toss all his crates out the back of his truck. Random search, they claimed. He spent a good two hours trying to get them all sorted back inside again."

The conductor hurried down the aisle and peered at Barrett through the spectacles perched on the end of his short nose. "Are you the young man who leaped from the platform to the caboose?"

Barrett nodded sheepishly. "Aye, but only because you wouldn't slow down."

"That's the trouble with trains, isn't it?" The little man's lips pushed out. "I presume you have a ticket. Or did you leap without it?"

Digging into his trouser pocket, Barrett pulled out a crumpled ticket and held it out for the conductor to punch. His task completed, the conductor hurried back down the aisle to his hole in the back.

Shoving the ticket back into his pocket, Barrett dropped his hat onto the empty seat next to him and looked around. Only eight other passengers occupied the first-class car with velvet seats, oak-paneled walls, and brocade curtains. "Impressive ride. Your beau spared no expense for our comfort."

"That's Eric for you." Ellie surged to her feet, tucking her handbag under her arm. "I'll go see what they have in the dining car."

Frowning, Barrett watched her stumble to the back of the car and disappear into the next one. "Did I say something wrong?"

"Eric's a touchy subject of late." Kat sighed and settled back in her seat. She'd come so close to finding out the truth about him. Maybe after the drinks Ellie was sure to have in the dining car, she'd be willing to bring it up again.

"Then why are we going on this trip?"

"He's been trying to make it up to her. Over the past two weeks, he's sent over six dozen red roses to the flat to say how sorry he is."

Unbuttoning his light-gray jacket, Barrett slipped his arms out and laid it on the seat next to his hat. Perspiration glistened at the base of his throat where the top button of his shirt was undone. "Think she'll forgive him?"

"I think she wants to, but she's torn. As am I in wanting to wrench her away from that monster yet needing to remain in his graces for the sake of gathering intelligence that could save thousands. Bring this war to an end even." Kat shook her head as the thread of events and decisions tangled together until she could no longer tell one apart from the other. "That night at the Blue Stag . . . It's not something she can forget. Not something any of us can forget."

Resting his forearms on his knees, he leaned forward. His fingertips brushed the edge of her skirt. "I'm sorry you had to witness it."

"You were heroic to try and stop it."

"Didn't do much good in the end except maybe underline my name on the Gestapo's bad list."

"No one else was brave enough to step forward like you did. I'd say there's plenty good in that. In the end, you couldn't have stopped what happened."

"Couldn't I?"

She ached to grasp his hands. Of late, the urge to touch him had become more and more overwhelming each time she was near him. As if a part of her had lain dormant until he revived it. She clasped her hands together, squeezing the blood from them. Ridiculous. She was perfectly fine on her own, always had been, and would go right back to it once this whole terrible ordeal was done with.

But the ache didn't subside.

"You're too hard on yourself." Unfurling her fingers, she brushed his.

He started as if she'd burned him. "I don't think I'm hard enough on myself." Taking her hands, he held them between his own as if cradling a bird. He turned them over each in turn, tracing a finger along the sensitive skin between her index and thumb. A slow smile curled his mouth. "Then again, why create the extra work for myself?"

"Ah, yes. The lazybones conundrum you often find yourself confronted with."

He raked his fingers across her palm, fanning tingles across the surface. "Would you rather have me running around trying to please everyone but myself like you do?"

The tingles turned to ice water. She pulled her hand back.

His hands fell open. "I'm sorry. I was only teasing."

She turned her face to the window. The gray cityscape had given way to thick green trees and golden fields. A blessing to finally shrug off the city's shackles and breathe the country air again.

A jeep and motorbike with German soldiers trundled by on the dirt road next to the tracks.

Who was she kidding about breathing fresh air again? Even out here, their jailers remained vigilant. "Always a bit of truth to teasing, isn't there?"

"Or a fellow is just being stupid. Don't comment on that."

"As long as you know the truth."

"About myself, aye, and most of it not very interesting. But you . . ." He sighed and leaned back into his seat. Exasperation laced his tone. "Why are you here and not your father? Or some other emissary?"

The ever-present knot in her chest tightened. After finding Ellie's runaway note, there had been no other course but for her to go after her. Her father had turned himself purple with rage when she demanded to take his place, while her mother fainted dead on the couch after stating that a proper young lady could not travel without a proper chaperone. It had taken months, but in the end Kat's reasoning and threat to thumb her way to Paris had won.

Late at night when her thoughts belonged solely to her and the light of day couldn't penetrate their harshness, she wondered why her father hadn't put his foot down and kept it there. Was his allowance of her going to Paris merely a preservation for their good name with safety a secondary concern? Father had always been a distant figure, but could he so easily betray daughterly trust in favor of social standing? Was she so blind to it all?

"I'm the only one she'll listen to," Kat said. "If she ever glimpsed my father, she'd be on the first train to Berlin simply to spite him. Ellie's always been childish that way, but deep down she has a tender heart. She just needs someone to properly care for it."

"Like you?"

The corners of her mouth tugged up. "I was thinking a man, but yes, me too."

He shifted, catching his reflection in the window. "You don't want to hear this—bah, I don't even want to say it—but Eric cares for her in his own twisted way."

"I know. I think . . ." The knot clenched around her lungs, squeezing out a hiss of air. "I think he wants to . . . make plans with her."

"You mean marry."

Yes stuck in her throat like a thorn. She nodded.

"Intelligence would love that, with all the information they could get, but what a diplomatic mess. Can't imagine how the foreign secretary would handle it."

Her head whipped back to face him. Anger quaked down to her toes. "Is that what this is about? Gaining unprecedented access for Parliament? And when it's all over they mean to forget my sister like a worn-out shoe and trample my family's name in the mud? You right along with them, eh?"

He shot to the edge of his seat, hands braced on either side of him. "Don't you dare lump me in there with those cold ba—warmongers. I'm here to help you."

"At what price?"

He reared back as if she'd slapped him. "I've my own reasons, as do you. Let's stop there."

"Fine by me."

"Good." Grabbing his hat, he surged to his feet. "I'm going for some air. Don't get into trouble while I'm gone."

"Don't trip and fall off."

Crossing her arms, she slumped back in her seat. Her elation at seeing him had soured faster than a glass of milk in the sun. If only the Nazis could see them now. Not so golden a couple after all. That's what she got for dancing too close to the line of possibilities. No more. She'd come here to take Ellie back—willingly or not—and that's exactly what she would do. No more distractions. Not even ones with deep-blue eyes, a smile charming enough to tempt a saint, and arms that held her as if no other woman in the world existed.

She dug her fingers into her arm, vanquishing the memory of his touch. He was impossible. They had nothing in common, they had opposite views on just about everything, and her father would certainly never approve, because he hadn't handpicked Barrett himself.

Her hands dropped to her lap to flick over the water print of yellow daisies across her knee.

Trying to please everyone but myself. Like a bullet, his words pierced her. He was right, and that truth was enough to rip her carefully poised thoughts in two. Why did he have to be right? Why did he have to know what he was doing in almost every situation? Why couldn't they have assigned her someone short and fat who smelled like onions? The yellow daisies bunched in her fist. And why, oh, why, whenever a German walked by, did she wonder if Barrett was going to kiss her?

As if her thoughts had called him back, Barrett fell into the seat next to her, chest heaving and eyes intense. "Adore me."

She snorted and rolled her eyes back to the window. "I'd rather not."

"There are two Germans coming behind me whom I may or may not have hit with my suitcase when I tossed it on board."

"Oh, Barrett."

"Save the lecture. Right now I need you to act like you can't keep your hands off me and maybe they'll keep walking."

Kat glanced over the top of the seat. Dread plunked in her stomach as the soldiers stopped by each seat to glare into the faces before moving further up the aisle. She slapped a hand to Barrett's cheek, covering the side of his face from view, and drew him close. "If we come out of this alive, you owe me."

His lips brushed her ear. "Keeping score isn't a good idea in this game."

"Not afraid of losing, are you?"

"Losing to a woman isn't really losing in my book. Ow!"

"Oh, so sorry." She uncurled her nails from where they'd crimped his ear. Two seats away, the Germans barked at a young Frenchman. Dread bowled up her chest. "How hard did you hit them?"

"In the back of the knees. The tall one lost control of his cigarette, and it bounced onto the other's shoulder." With the touch of a lover, he grasped the back of her neck, brushing the sensitive skin into tingles. "Ready for the second-greatest performance of your life?"

Heart thundering in her chest, she nodded. The slight stubble on his cheek scratched her palm, shooting tingles down her arm and spreading all down her body. His lips grazed her jaw and hovered just over her mouth. Blood rushed to her head as her eyes fluttered closed despite the danger lurching closer to them.

"*Umdrehen damit wir dein gesicht sehen können.*"

Barrett's hand dropped to her shoulder as he turned to face the soldiers. "Hello, again. I am sorry about bumping you earlier. I was running late, and this lady here would have my teeth if I missed the train."

"Papers," the taller one barked. "Both of you."

As they handed their papers over, Kat folded her shaking hands in her lap and counted the silver ranks on their collars. She had no idea what they meant, but it was fewer than Eric sported. What she wouldn't give to have him here now.

"*Englisch*," the shorter one spat and pointed to the black smudge on his shoulder. His round face mottled red. "Do you see what you did? You burned the Führer's uniform."

"Actually, your friend there burned it with his cigarette."

Shut up! Shut up! The shaking trembled down Kat's legs as she pressed closer to Barrett, willing him with all her silent might to close his big mouth.

The soldier's face shaded to purple. "Get up! You're under arrest for defacing and destroying property of the Third Reich. Next stop, you're off and straight in for questioning. What are an Englishman and woman doing here?"

"Oh, yes. I thought it might come to this." Barrett sighed wearily and reached into his shirt pocket to pull out a small cream envelope sealed with red wax. "Mind you, I don't like showing this lightly."

The burned guard snatched it from his hand and tore it open. Scanning the paper, his eyes grew wider and wider until they looked ready to fall out. By the end, he was pale as a sheet and ready to faint. His friend took three seconds longer to reach the same reaction.

"Pardon, Mr. Anderson." With shaking fingers, the guard thrust the paper back into the torn envelope and handed it back to Barrett. "Please accept our deepest apologies. As you said, it was a mistake. We should have been more careful of where we stood."

"Hope this unfortunate misunderstanding doesn't badly color your report upon your arrival."

The taller one grabbed his friend's shoulder, and as one they backed away. "Good morning to you both."

Spiking adrenaline receded enough for Kat to string together a coherent thought. She waited until the soldiers disappeared back into the car they'd come from before ripping the letter from Barrett's fingers. The blood drained from her face as she tore through the contents, but for an entirely different reason than the soldiers'.

Her words slipped out on a breath. "What have you done?"

"Thought it might come in handy. Was up half the night fretting over those angled *p*'s." Plucking the letter from her motionless fingers, he tucked it safely back into his pocket. "Shame about the seal, though."

"Where did you learn to forge Eric's handwriting?"

"I've got many hidden talents. Stick around long enough and you might get to see a few more shine."

"What if someone catches us in this ridiculous lie you've cooked up? Do you know the serious consequences for making such a proclamation?"

"A few lowly soldiers aren't sticking their necks out to question if we truly are or are not dear and personal friends of the Führer." The humor dropped from his smile. "Stop worrying so much. I know what I'm doing."

That makes one of us. Dumbfounded, Kat leaned back in her seat. Adrenaline drained from her veins as her heart rate thumped back to a moderate pace. "This isn't just about you and your brawn."

"I know it isn't, poppy. Everything I've done has been mindful of keeping you safe."

Like a record player, he played from one emotion to the next. At first jovial, then sweet, a crescendo to brassy, and back to tender. It left her spinning and light-headed. And tired of dancing to someone else's music.

She popped back up in her seat. Neutral Switzerland was close by, if she could get through Austria. She could even build it up as a spa retreat for Ellie.

Her palms tingled. She shoved them between her knees. British intelligence would be furious to lose part of their golden couple, and Barrett would be left with the fury aimed directly at him.

Shame prickled her heart. She didn't want to leave him in trouble, but he had to know this was no place for her. Every day she and Ellie remained in France put him at risk, and the guilt of that was enough to stop the breath in her lungs. It was better for them all if she and Ellie left for England as soon as possible.

"Calm yourself, now." Barrett gently pried her hands out and held one between his own, his strong, steady pulse reassuring. "You'll need all the rest you can get before our grand performance."

Kat snorted. "Grand performance, indeed. Likely to be our last."

"Scoff all you like, but it's not every day the enemy gets invited to Hitler's home for the weekend."

Chapter 12

So this was what Nazi mecca looked like. Cream, salmon, and buttery buildings in the medieval style with traditional Bavarian timber roofs lined the impeccably swept streets. Flower boxes overflowing with trailing ivy and red alpine geraniums perched on windowsills. The magnificent snowcapped mountains of the Obersalzberg rose like a majestic ring around the town as a warm breeze fluttered the Nazi flags draping from each building.

"Welcome to Bavaria." A grinning Eric pushed his way through the smartly dressed Nazi citizens and soldiers on the platform. He clutched a dozen blood-red roses to his chest. "I got here an hour early to make sure I didn't miss your train."

Rushing to Ellie, he leaned down for a kiss, but she turned her face to catch it on her cheek. She didn't move to take the flowers. "Hello, Eric."

Slightly deflated, but determined, he juggled Ellie's two small vanity bags and roses under one arm while tucking her gloved hand into the crook of his other. "I have a car waiting outside to take you to the hotel. This way, porter."

Barrett gathered his and Kat's things and fell in behind the porter and his trolley of Ellie's trunks. "Think he remembers we're here too?"

"Nope." Not that she cared much at the moment. She felt sick to her stomach, and it had nothing to do with the stale baguette she'd eaten on the train.

"Berchtesgaden is famous for its salt mines. There's even a brine lake that you can paddle across." Eric chatted away as the porter loaded the trunks into a black auto. Packed and ready to go, they climbed into the back with Barrett sitting up front next to the uniformed driver. It was a short drive to their hotel, but it seemed an eternity. When the wheels finally slowed to a stop, Kat's ears felt ready to burst from Eric's persistent prattle.

The Berchtesgadener Hof was a long, four-storied building with a cream exterior and wrought-iron balconies. As with all of the other buildings in the town, a proud red-white-and-black flag flew from the roof.

"I've reserved rooms for you on the top floor because they offer spectacular views of the mountains." He handed out their keys, not quite letting go of Ellie's. "You'll have the same room the Duke and Duchess of Windsor stayed in. You did tell me you'd met them."

Ellie slowly took the key and nodded. "Once. Not long after they got married."

Poor man. Kat almost felt sorry for him. *Almost.* "Come on, Ellie. We should freshen up after that long ride."

They started for the stairs, but Eric caught Ellie's arm. "Can I speak with you?" His eyes flicked up to Kat and Barrett. "In private."

Ellie hesitated, but nodded. "I'll meet you in the lounge in ten minutes."

Kat shoved her luggage into her room before walking next door to Ellie's. It took up the entire south corner of the floor. Pale-yellow walls, gleaming oak floors covered in deep-blue rugs, colloquial paintings, and a massive canopied bed were a statement of wealth and charm. Red and pink roses in crystal vases sat on every available flat surface. Chills ran over her heart. All the beauty in the world couldn't hide the true ugliness festering in this Nazi lair.

"Mine looks like a matchbox compared to yours."

Ellie shrugged and dragged aside one of the damask drapes at the balcony. "He's trying to impress me."

Pulling the hat pin from her straw hat with its navy ribbon, Kat stepped to an oval mirror and fluffed the hair around her shoulders. Travel was never easy on curls. "Of course he is. He wants back in your good graces and seems willing to break himself in half trying to do it."

"Maybe. I don't know what to do."

"Clearly, you want to do something or you wouldn't have accepted his invitation to travel hundreds of miles for holiday. If you don't want to be here, if you've changed your mind, we can leave." She thought of Barrett down the hall. He'd be furious, but he wasn't her concern. "We can go to Switzerland, check into one of those spas for a few days of mud masks and sulfur springs. Smells like the dickens, but it's supposed to do extraordinary things for your skin."

Ellie shrugged a shoulder. "Maybe."

"Oh, for heaven's sake. You need to do something. Make some kind of decision instead of letting the wind blow you where it wills." She hadn't meant to say it, but the frustration of drawn-out nerves boiled over before she could put a lid on it. She was in no mood to coddle another one of her sister's moods, especially not in this place. Her nerves were jumbled enough.

Flipping open her cosmetic travel case, Ellie swiped fresh red lipstick across her mouth, ran a comb through her hair, and brushed off the flake of mascara under her eyes. With nose tilted in the air, she headed out the door. "I am. I'm going to see Eric."

An hour later, Barrett found Kat out on the sun terrace at one of the green-and-white umbrella tables. The spicy scent of aftershave wafted around him. "Enjoying the scenery? Bit different from England."

"I never imagined I'd travel to a place so beautiful. For a moment, I found myself relaxing at the tranquility, until I remembered whose backyard we're sitting in."

"It's up there."

She followed his pointed finger to the rising green mountains of Obersalzberg. "What is?"

"The home of the devil himself." He plopped into the wooden

chair next to her and stretched his long legs out in front of him. "The bigwigs back in London couldn't even pull off an invitational coup like this, but you did it."

She—or correction, she via Ellie—had done what no one else of military or intelligence power had yet to achieve. She'd smuggled in the spying eyes of London to the wolf's lair. No powerful connection of the Whitford name required. "I wonder if he's there now plotting his next horror to inflict."

"If so, that dynamite I brought along will come in handy. Kidding."

"Half of me wonders."

He moved closer, brushing her arm with his. Seriousness hovered in his eyes. "We could end the war. No one may get this chance again."

"It's not our assignment."

"Always playing by the rules, eh?" He leaned back in his chair, pillowing his hands behind his head. "Of course, if we took matters into our own hands, then there'd be no need for a rulebook anymore. Something to think about."

A bead of perspiration trickled down between her shoulder blades. She couldn't tell if it was the late-afternoon heat or Barrett's absurd suggestion. She shifted in the chair to stir a breeze beneath her skirt. "Has this been your plan all along?"

"Nope. Just came to me."

"I'd rather not get blown up, if it's all the same to you."

His dark eyebrows slid down into a frown. "Do you dare to insult my skills of detonation? I'll have you know that I've yet to lose a man—or woman—in an explosion of my own making. That's what timers are for."

"Probably the closest I'll ever see to you doing work."

"We're on holiday. Don't want to overdo it."

"Holiday, yes." She pinched the skirt fabric between her fingers. "While the rest of Europe groans in battle, we sit here on cushions drinking from crystal-cut champagne glasses. Does it not sicken you?"

"Every day. I learned long ago that each person has a part to play. Some in the mud, some in a pub, and some waltzing behind enemy lines. No job is easier than the next, but I have to admit it must be a relief to stare at your enemy across a muddy field rather than a dance floor. At least out there you can shoot them outright."

"The simplicity of showing one's true side."

"Aye." Closing his eyes, his face relaxed. How the man seemed so at ease in the middle of a town where one had to be a Nazi to be a citizen was beyond her. Ever since they'd stepped off the train, she'd yet to take a full breath that didn't pinch her lungs with fear. Each step he took threatened to be his last, but the grim knowledge never seemed to cripple him. Never had she witnessed someone bear such an enormous responsibility with such strength and true grit.

His chest rose and fell in a steady rhythm, as if the glowing sun overhead had lulled him to sleep. His rolled-up shirtsleeves revealed tan forearms with long, defined muscles stretching the entire length. The always-on-guard cut of his jaw smoothed into relaxation, and long black lashes rested gently on his cheeks. The pinch in her lungs eased, but the air still caught in her throat.

"Like what you see?"

Kat jumped, creaking the chair beneath her. Heat burned her face as if the sun itself had scorched her. "You had a bee buzzing around your head."

"You'll have to let me return the favor sometime." One blue eye cracked open. "And I don't mean the bee."

She smoothed a hand over her skirt. "I'm sure I don't know what you mean."

"Aye, you do."

Her heart skipped as both of his deep-blue eyes pinned her to the chair. Yes, she knew. All too well. Deep down in the scarred places of her heart, she longed to have a man near to admire her, to whisper tender things with the promise to fulfill them. But promises were broken much too easy, betraying her to pain unimaginable. She couldn't bear the same loss from him.

Heels clacked across the concrete patio behind them, quickly followed by the dull thumping of boots. Without needing to turn around, Kat's heart sank.

Ellie flung her arms around Kat's neck and squealed. "Everything's all right now. I'll tell you all about it later." Jumping back, Ellie grabbed Eric's hand and pulled him into view. "Come on, darling. Don't be shy."

For his part, Eric had the decency to look uncertain of his presence. He held tight to Ellie's hand. "I must apologize for our last meeting in Paris. It was not how I wished the evening to go, and certainly my actions were unforgiveable in the presence of ladies." He glanced down for reassurance from Ellie before turning a more intense gaze to Barrett. "Any damages your business incurred because of the incident will be seen to immediately at no cost to you."

Incident? He dared to call killing an innocent man a mere incident? Kat balled her fingernails into her palms while Ellie's eyes shimmered with forgiveness and heartache.

"Thank you," Barrett said. "Not much damage beyond a stain on the floor. Took two of my washers an entire day, but they got it scrubbed out."

Kat made a small, sickened noise in her throat. Barrett grabbed her hand and squeezed. "Thanks for inviting me. Nice to have another man to help balance out these ladies."

"I knew it would make Eleanor happy to have both of you here." Eric laced his fingers through Ellie's. "Besides, I'd never leave you alone for too long."

Though said with a smile, the words hung in the air like a low, dark cloud that crackled with lightning. A storm was brewing. Time would tell if they would make safety before it hit or get caught in the downpour.

Ellie broke the tension. "Let's go swimming tomorrow. Eric, didn't you say there was a lake around here?"

Eric nodded and pointed north. "Lake Königssee is about six kilometers that way. The clearest waters in all of Germany."

"We can have a picnic. Won't that be heavenly?"

Doubt niggled his fair eyebrows. "We have an invitation for tea tomorrow at the Berghof."

Kat swallowed a groan. If the gallows stretched before them, she wanted the memory of a perfect day as she faced the executioner. Hitler himself. "With tea in the afternoon, that gives us plenty of time to swim and lounge in the sun beforehand."

"Can't all be work and no fun." Barrett's fingers laced through hers, warm and reassuring. "You promised to show us a good time."

Certainty slid across Eric's face, smoothing his brow. "*Ja*. An unforgettable time awaits you, *meine freundes*."

Kat pressed a hand to her roiling stomach. *Don't get sick. Don't get sick on Hitler's living-room floor.*

Worry creased Barrett's brow as he reached over to rub her back. "How're you feeling, poppy?"

"Nauseated."

"Not surprising considering our whereabouts." He scrutinized a Bordone painting of Venus and Amor. Bewilderment flitted across his face. "Never understood the appeal of painting naked bairns."

"It's a favorite painting style of sixteenth-century Venice."

"Well, it's not my favorite."

"Try the Panninis. They're a little more manly with their ruins of Rome." She moved to the fireplace. The red marble gleamed like dull garnets with milky-white strands racing through it. The inside panels showed a farmer sowing seed and a lederhosen-clad man with a scythe. A simple country existence was not what she'd imagined Hitler celebrating in his home.

If living the high life with Nazis in occupied Paris wasn't enough to peg her with treason, afternoon tea with *Der Führer* was the final loop of a noose around her neck. How were they ever to come out of this alive?

Turning around, she caught Barrett lowering himself onto one of the red-and-gold floral-printed chairs.

"Don't sit!" He stopped inches from the cushion, panic freezing his face. Kat dropped her arm back to her side from where it had involuntarily flung out as if to stop him. "It's not proper to sit without first being invited to do so by the host."

Frowning, he straightened. "You really expect me to engage in social niceties, considering who our host is?"

Kat nodded. "Just because we are surrounded by bad ilk does not mean we lower ourselves to their level."

"Whatever level he's operating on, he's taking his sweet time."

"Perhaps he's too busy bombing Russia to notice the clock." The bitterness rolled too easily off her tongue, as if the evilness hanging in the air had soaked into her skin. She'd scrub herself raw as soon as they returned to the hotel. "Apologies. That was tasteless."

"You don't ever have to apologize to me, especially when I'm of the same opinion." Slipping his hands over her shoulders, he gently drew her closer. He smelled of soap and fresh air from the lake. "We'll get through this. Quiet-like or guns blazing, we'll get through this. Promise."

"Will we? I doubt the confidence you stock in this situation."

"Trust your instincts. They're more spot-on than you give them credit for."

He pressed a kiss to her forehead. Like a break in the heavens from a storm, her roiling stomach calmed. In the worst of situations, how did he always know how to keep her steady? They had been coerced into a mission that neither one of them wanted, but their time together had shifted the relationship from one of service into one she feared defining, such was the fragility of feelings burgeoning each passing day. How much more difficult it would be to leave him.

"Ugh. It's so hot outside." Ellie breezed past the door from the terrace with Eric right behind her. Slight perspiration marked the armpits of her stitched pink dress. "I'm positively dripping."

Tension lined Eric's mouth. "The Führer does not like cigarettes inside. The smell soaks into the furniture and ruins the paintings."

"Well, unless he likes cleaning up sweaty puddles he might want to reconsider that little rule." Ellie slipped her silver cigarette holder back inside her handbag and looked around the room with confusion. "Where is everyone? The invitation was for four o'clock, wasn't it?"

Kat shrugged. "No one has come back in since you stepped out on the terrace. We've been admiring the artwork."

Eric's eyes lit up. "*Ja*, the Führer has a precise eye for art and a sensational ear for music. I have had the privilege of viewing a few of his sketches. He's mentioned allowing me to exhibit one in Paris."

Kat forced her mouth into a smile. "That's wonderful. I'm sure it'll draw dozens of crowds."

Eric wagged his finger back and forth. "*Nein*. Not dozens, but thousands."

Before he could wax on about Hitler's pathetic attempts at painting, a woman in a worn dirndl came through the east door. The white blouse with puffy sleeves, navy skirt, and red-checked apron suggested she belonged at a *biergarten* and not afternoon tea. With fluffy golden-brown hair, a doughy nose too large for her face, and a small smile, she was pleasant looking but not overly pretty.

"Eric, *schön sie wiederzusehen*."

Taking her outstretched hand, Eric clicked his shiny boot heels and bent over her hand while speaking in German. He gestured to his guests. "Eleanor Whitford, Kathleen Whitford, *und* Barrett Anderson."

The woman nodded to each of them in turn. "*Guten tag und wil-kommen.* Eva Braun. Apologize tardiness. Misunderstanding kitchen. Outside tea?"

Ellie's face twitched at the broken English instructions to go back outside, but she dutifully followed Eva to the prepared table under a large blue umbrella. A lush green valley with the mountains of neighboring Austria spread before them like a painting from the genius brushstrokes of a Renaissance master.

"Spectacular view," Barrett said, accepting the tea Eva poured for him.

Eva uncovered a tray of delicate pastries and glanced expectantly behind her. "*Ja.* Herr Hitler—"

"The Führer spent many happy years in this area and purchased the house when the old owner died." Eric selected a biscuit and bit into it as he continued his interruption. A habit of his. "Nothing like watching the snow fall outside that large picture window and listening to the logs crackle in the great hall's fireplace."

Ellie's eyes shifted back and forth between them. Her arms crossed and uncrossed in her lap. "How do you two know each other?"

Surprise raised Eva's thin eyebrows. "Related through my—"

"Cousins. Distant cousins." Eva's chin dropped at Eric's glare.

Awkwardness rippled as they all feigned interest in their tea. After two long minutes of silently staring at the scenery and sipping the watery drink, Kat couldn't take it any longer. She turned to Eva. "What a beautiful dress."

"*Danke.* Had many years." She smoothed a hand over the embroidered bodice. Her eyes slowly traced the scalloped edges of Kat's green-and-white-striped Rouf skirt. "No new clothes, no elegant."

"We should change that. The next time you're in Paris, we'll go shopping down the Champs Élysées." Kat tried to offer her an encouraging smile despite the sourness still curdling in her stomach. Maybe the tanks trundling under the Arc de Triomphe would inspire the woman's fashion sense. Whoever she was, she didn't deserve to dress like a milkmaid every day.

"Not sure . . ." Eva glanced over her shoulder again. "Kindness, *danke*."

Eric jumped to his feet, rocking the table back. His arm flung out and up. "*Heil* Hitler!"

All the warmth and brilliance of the August summer day evaporated like a hiss of steam on a frozen tundra. The devil in human flesh strolled across the terrace, upright and solid as a brick, with dark-brown hair slicked to the side and a rectangular patch of hair balanced on his upper lip. Kat had often reminded herself that men were just men and women just women, be they a king, duke, shopkeeper, or bus driver, but staring into the intense dark eyes of Adolf Hitler, she realized she'd been mistaken to think he was like any other. This was a man set apart.

Eric made introductions all around. He fairly burst at the seams with pride when he gestured to the rat-faced man hovering behind Hitler as Dr. Joseph Goebbels, the propaganda minister, his direct boss.

Kat resisted the urge to wipe her hand on the grass after shaking his clammy one.

Hitler's dark eyes lingered on Ellie. His lips fumbled to tilt up into a smile. "*Sprechen sie Deutsch?*"

Still standing at full attention, Eric dropped his hand to Ellie's shoulder and shook his head. "*Nein, mein Führer.*"

No, Ellie didn't speak German, nor did she understand it. But thanks to their governess's keen interest in languages, Kat did, at least rudimentary conversations. Anything beyond "Will you please pass the butter," and she was lost.

"I hear you are doing wonderful things to promote German pride and expand our society in Paris," Hitler was saying through Eric's interpretations. Though he settled back in the chair and took a cup of tea, he didn't unbutton his box-cut pinstriped jacket. He sat rigid, as if his back detested the plush cushions.

"I don't know about spreading pride—that's Eric's forte—but I do know how to put together rather a smashing party." Ellie's hands pinched together under the table. "Eric's very resourceful when it comes to helping me plan, like acquiring Mr. Anderson's bar for Ms. Chekhova's latest movie debut. Such a shame you couldn't attend, Dr. Goebbels."

"What a triumph for our nation until that Jew ruined it," Goebbels spat out like a sullen child.

Hitler leaned forward, drawing the attention back to himself. "It must never happen again. Great precautions must be taken all around to ensure that the Fatherland is not weakened by such radicals. Our noble cause will thrive, and all opposition must understand that they no longer have a place in which to fester their ideas and lies."

Ellie's hands pinched white. "Next time will be better."

"How infallible our cause would be with supporters of like minds outside Germany." Hitler's voice remained steady, as appropriate for afternoon tea, but the tone sharpened as his intent narrowed to its purpose.

Kat slid her gaze to Barrett across the table. Hands laced across his flat stomach and head tilted slightly back, he was the perfect picture of ease. If not for the rapid rise and fall of his chest, she might have thought him immune to the conversation imploding around them.

Of course that's why Eric had lured them here. He'd very cleverly found a girl with social connections in the upper echelons of British circles and bent her to his will with gifts of a fine flat, beautiful clothes, and champagne. Unfortunately, her only real connections consisted of dressmakers, debutantes, and the rich sons of nobility. The only powerful ties could come through her father.

Kat leaned back in her chair, eager to see how Eric was going to manage landing that big Whitford fish.

"Ah, yes. I suppose I could always ring up John Purcevel. He's always up for a good time." Ellie turned to Kat, panic leaping in her eyes. "Do we know anyone else who might want to spend a week or two in Paris for some fabulous parties?"

Who in their right mind would turn down an invitation to Parisian parties? Oh, that's right. The rest of the world's population who didn't belong to the Nazi party. Kat flushed as Hitler, Goebbels, and Eric stared at her. Eva munched quietly on an apple tart. Kat's gaze slid to Barrett, who nodded slightly. Encouragingly. *Trust your instincts.*

"John does love a good party, but I'm not sure if his all-night carousing reflects positively on his hosts. Besides, you want guests who can carry their weight in intelligent conversation and thought like, say, the Duke of Buccleuch or Lord Brocket." Kat tapped her chin. She detested crawling back to use Father's connections, but at least in this instance she wielded the power for her own uses. "Of course, Lord Mount Temple or Mr. Tennant, whom I believe is a friend of the German ambassador, Herr von Ribbentrop, would be delighted to receive an invitation. They've often expressed a desire for relationships with our German brethren during meetings for the Anglo-German Fellowship."

Kat held her breath, waiting for the pin to drop and shatter the stunned silence. Eric sat proudly erect as if he had anything and everything to do with that name drop.

Hitler's stare defrosted. Slightly. "Can you get these men?"

Relieved, Ellie flashed a dazzling smile that stopped men in their tracks. Most warm-blooded men, which of course excluded Hitler. "It's impossible to turn down one of my invitations. I was thinking for Eric's next exhibit—"

The devil didn't care about Ellie's ideas. He had his own, which he embellished upon for the next twenty minutes. Eva excused herself only to return a few moments later with a camera. Kat tried to ignore the constant snapping as the woman circled around and around the table.

As the shadows grew longer and the light dimmed to burnt orange, Hitler wound to a close and Goebbels dared to speak. "*Wunderbar, mein Führer.* Precisely what I was thinking, though I could not have expressed it so vividly."

Hitler nodded slowly as if such praise was expected and turned to Barrett. "I understand you operate the establishment that hosted the film premiere. Tell me, what is an Englishman doing in France?"

Barrett smiled despite the comparison to an Englishman. "My mother's family is French, so when it came time for me to run my own refreshment business I could think of no finer place than Paris. Simple as that."

"You did not flee like all the others."

"My life and business are here. I have no ties elsewhere. As long as money fills my till—which thanks to Major von Schlegel, is overflowing—then Paris is where I stay. A small group of the *Deutsch-Englische Gesellschaft* meets once a month at the Blue Stag. You can imagine my surprise to find Miss Whitford already familiar with its sister organization in England."

Pushing his teacup aside, Hitler leaned his forearms on the table. The orbs of his eyes grew darker against his sickly skin as he didn't blink. "So money is your encouragement, but that was not the case when that Jewish madman barged in with a gun. I heard you tried to console him."

"Money was very much the point then. Lunatics like that, especially ones on the wrong side of the law, have no place in my establishment. They drive out good patrons like the major and your soldiers." Barrett tipped his head to Eric, sincerity stirring in his eyes. "My only regret is that it may have caused a slight embarrassment on such an important night for him. It might have turned out a lot worse if not for his quick thinking."

Ellie grabbed Kat's wrist. "I need some air."

Moments later, leaning against the stone terrace wall several feet from her sister, Kat gazed into the valley below. Smoke curled from the chimneys as evening meals bubbled on wood-fire stoves and families gathered around tables for a hearty meal of venison stew or schnitzel. What she wouldn't give to be down there and not here. Far in the distance, clouds darkened. The air ripened with moisture.

"Don't know why they feel the need to keep bringing that up." Ellie jammed a cigarette between her lips and inhaled deeply. "Eric promised he'd never mention it again. Guess he can't refuse the Führer. Have you ever seen such eyes?"

Kat stretched her foot out, rotating it around. One by excruciating one, her muscles relaxed from the cramped tension they'd curled into since arriving at the Berghof. "They are rather intense. Barrett's holding up well, though."

"I can imagine him standing before Death and not ruffling."

Isn't that what he's doing now? He lived and breathed danger with the Resistance, each second possibly his last, but never once did he back down from the mission. She was no expert in men, but she'd met enough to know a lesser man would have buckled by now.

As Hitler prattled on, Barrett's gaze drifted to her. One eye slid down for a wink. Warmth ignited in her pulse. "Cheeky lad."

Ellie picked a piece of tar from her tongue. "Cheeky and cuts a nice figure in the water. All that practice from the lochs in Scotland certainly paid off this afternoon. I think we'll have to go swimming again before we leave just so we can watch him do laps."

"Why must your mind always wander there?"

"Because it's the most interesting pastime I can think of."

Kat bumped her hip into Ellie's. Ash tumbled from the cigarette onto the terrace. "Only a pastime?"

"Okay, all the time." Ellie bumped her back and giggled. Eva swung around and clicked her camera in their direction before returning to the men. "What do you make of her?"

"Strange duck. Relative? Houseguest, maybe?" Eva circled around the table, careful to get every angle with all the men. After each click, her eyes flitted up to Hitler as if asking for permission to continue. He ignored her. "And yet there's something oddly familiar . . . as if she's constantly waiting for his approval, much like a—Oh, no. No, that can't be it."

"Please don't say lover. Oh, Kat, why would you say that?" Ellie's face scrunched with disgust. "That man as a lover is the last thing I want to think about."

Kat threw her hands up in defense. "You said it, not me."

"But that's what your observation jumped to, isn't it?" Ellie exhaled a puff of smoke on a groan. "He's terrifying at the best of times. No woman could possibly want an attachment with him."

With the slicked-back hair, a voice that was two notches too loud, and that patch of hair on his lip, he looked like an angry otter ready to chew off the nearest person's face at any second. Yet somehow the crazed man had been elected chancellor of Germany with flying colors. Revulsion slithered down Kat's back. "Power is appealing to some."

"Please stop."

"Look at how his speeches whip crowds into a frenzy, how men sign up in droves to fight for him, how women push their babies in front of him for a pat on the head."

Ellie flipped a hand. "Fine. I admit that power is intoxicating, but at the end of the day you want to snuggle next to a man who doesn't make your skin crawl."

"Are you saying the Führer makes your skin crawl?"

"Doesn't he yours?"

"Of course."

"Of course. Then what are we still doing here?"

Kat nodded her head in Eric's direction. "I believe your gentleman is the only one who can answer that."

Sighing, Ellie picked more tar off her tongue. "He thinks I make a good publicity image."

The revulsion flared to anger. "You mean he wants to use you to promote Nazi ideas to a wider circle? Say, England?" At her sister's glum nod, Kat wrapped her arm around Ellie's waist and turned them to the deep-green mountains of Austria. "You don't have to go along with it."

"He's difficult to say no to. You see the kind of pressure he's under. How can any person say no to men like them?"

"Ellie, Eric wears the uniform, not you. You have no obligation to be here. We can leave tonight if you like. Go to those Switzerland spas I was telling you about. Wouldn't it be nice, just you and me, away from these egotistical boys?"

"Even Barrett?"

Pain notched in Kat's chest. "Yes, even him."

"You'd miss him too much, just like I would Eric. He's pushy, I know, but I really think he could be different if I could get him away from all this."

It was the greatest lie that woman had invented since the day of Creation. That a woman could truly change a man was downright laughable at worst, naïve at best. Kat dropped her hands to the cool stone wall. "I think he's in this for the long haul, but that doesn't mean you have to hitch a ride."

"I might as well."

Trepidation plunked in Kat's stomach. "Are you . . . Has he made a declaration?"

Laughter tumbled from Ellie, startling a pair of pigeons nesting in a bush below them. "'Declaration'? What are we, stuck in the Victorian age? No, he hasn't asked me to marry him. Yet. But he speaks of our futures twining together."

"And what of the future if Germany doesn't win this war?"

"Then we'll leave. We'll go somewhere this war hasn't tainted, like America." The end of Ellie's cigarette glowed cherry as she puffed hard. "No more strings to tie us down."

Once again, her sister proved her lack of thought before leaping off a cliff. Kat gripped the stone rail until her fingers hurt. Sense needed to be shaken into Ellie, if not smacked. "This is a messy business, and no matter how pretty you smile or how many earls' names you drop, you may not get out so easily."

"What about Father's name? Think that could pull any weight?" Acid dripped from Ellie's tongue.

"I'm sure some, but I wouldn't expect his grace to extend very far with Parliament, should you decide to go down with the ship."

"If Eric's on the ship, then that's where I stay. That's what you do when you're in love. Not that you'd know."

The barb hit Kat with over twenty years of loneliness. Raw and exposed, pain seared to the top. She turned away and opened her eyes wide for the air to dry out the surging emotion.

"Oh, Kitty Kat, I'm sorry." Ellie touched her arm. "I didn't mean it the way it came out. I only meant to say that you haven't found the *one* yet. We have to kiss a lot of frogs before we get to the prince, right? Like that horrid Marcus Father set you up with."

The pain ebbed, but the sting of betrayal remained. Kat blinked and turned back. "I think I'm destined for frogs."

"I'd hardly call Barrett one. How do you know he isn't the one? Frankly, I never thought I'd see you with someone of his class, but it suits you. He suits you. You're different around him. Looser, softer."

Barrett had always seemed lacking in class consciousness, never allowing himself to be subjected to one predetermined station or another. As if he existed outside the boundaries. And so she had never considered putting him in one. He was simply Barrett. Or rather, not so simply of late, with unexpected feelings twining about her heart whenever he was near. Feelings extending beyond dependence on his help for the mission and stretching into longing for his presence. Simply for him.

"He hasn't taken his eyes off you since we've come over here." Ellie practically vibrated with glee.

A thrill spun through Kat. Ridiculous. Just because he kept an eye on her didn't mean he was admiring the view. Then again, it was Barrett. "Probably to make sure I don't jump."

Stubbing out her cigarette, Ellie plunked her hands on her hips. "Well, if you jump, then I jump, because you're not leaving me alone with those bores. He can find us later down in the brambles."

"At least that would keep him on his toes. Seems to be my problem with most men—I'm too predictable. Boring. Dutiful."

"Not lately. Barrett's brought out a spark in you, one I haven't seen since we wore our hair in braids. He's good for you."

Kat snorted, spreading her hands wide along the rail. Good for keeping up appearances on behalf of the British government, and once that was over, life would try to slip back to mundane normal. She could never go back to that ignorant existence. Not after today.

She shook off her serious thoughts. "Yes, I'm sure Mama and Father would flip for joy if I brought him round for dinner. A Scot with a talent for slinging drinks and back-alley brawls."

"Who cares what they think? At some point we have to live our own lives for our own happiness."

Her own life with her own happiness. Ellie made it look so easy. If only Kat could allow herself one inch of the freedom her sister lived for without apology. Never at someone else's beck and call, never failing to reach standards enforced upon her, no more wondering if her true self was enough. But then, she'd never had Ellie's tenacity to reach out and grasp it.

Like a homing beacon, her eyes tracked back to Barrett. Settled between Hitler, his henchman, and his minion, he looked ready to smack them all in the face with the empty pastry platter. Pushing back his chair, he mumbled something to Eric that went unacknowledged and walked toward her.

"Ladies, you have the right idea." Leaning over the rail, he took a deep breath and exhaled slowly as if to horde all the fresh air before the coming rain hit.

Kat smoothed a wrinkle from between his shoulders. Sitting for too long never did well for clothing. "Lose track with the one-way conversation?"

"I believe I was dismissed when it all switched to German."

"Maybe you bored them."

He leaned up on one elbow. "Probably. Don't know what kind of interesting information they hoped to get out of a simple pub owner, though I think they're quite impressed with you."

"Find that surprising, do you?"

Reaching out, he took a loose curl slipping over her shoulder and rubbed it between his fingers. "I'm finding that you surprise me around every corner."

Tingles danced across her scalp as she leaned into his touch. "Good to keep a little mystery in the relationship."

His lip curled up at the edge, vaulting a hundred different scandalous suggestions into the space between them. Her breath stilled, burning her lungs in anticipation of discovering what they meant.

A clap like thunder erupted behind her. Eric rushed over, rubbing his hands together and grinning like a fool on parade. "We're invited back tomorrow night for dinner. A few more guests are expected to arrive who will be most keen to hear about forging new connections while in Paris."

Anxiety danced in Ellie's eyes. She fumbled for another cigarette, but put it away at Eric's frown. "I'm afraid our social circle is somewhat small in Paris."

"Surely there are friends and potential friends of Deutschland in

France." Hitler's voice carried across the terrace and surely down into the valley below. Rising from the table, he came toward them. "If there is an Anglo-German Fellowship, then why not a French one? I'm eager to hear of anyone you think is welcome to the idea."

Kat gripped the wall behind her as Hitler's dark eyes, depthless without blinking, bored into her. Her soul quivered. "I shall make a list tonight and be more than happy to share it with you tomorrow over dinner."

"I look forward to it."

Kat nodded and smiled. He could look for it all he wanted, but he'd be waiting for a long time. She was weary of listening to dictates from those with their own agenda. It was high time she made her own judgment about the right course of action. This time tomorrow, she'd have Ellie on a train bound for Switzerland.

Chapter 13

With feet like lead, Barrett trudged up the hotel stairs, a bottle of champagne under one arm and a white envelope tucked inside his inner jacket pocket. With each step it burned his chest like a brand of betrayal. The fourth-floor hallway stretched before him like the dreaded path to the gallows. Only it wasn't his funeral. It was hers.

Pausing before her door, he took a deep breath to calm his boiling blood. *Just give her a chance to explain.* He blew out the breath. *Then throttle her.*

Knock. Knock. Knock.

Seconds ticked by.

Knock. Knock. Knock.

More seconds passed with fumbling from inside. The lock turned and the door cracked open. Apprehensive blue eyes peered out. "Barrett. What are you doing here?"

He held up the sweating bottle of champagne. "Came to celebrate."

"Oh." The door crack slimmed. "Now isn't really a good time."

"No? What a shame because I think it's the perfect time." He shoved the door open, bouncing it off the wall. Kat jumped back as he strode past her into the room. "When else will we get an opportunity to toast the success of infiltration?"

It looked like a tornado had spun through her room. Clothes and shoes trailed from the bureau to the bed, where her suitcases lay with their mouths gaping open. Colorful cosmetics and hairpins spilled out of a pink-and-white box atop the sink, and a stack of papers with a map on top littered the desk. A cool breeze ruffled the drapes hanging over the open doors to the balcony as rain pinged the cobbled street below.

He turned back to Kat, who stood next to the door, her back against the wall. "Going somewhere, poppy?"

Her eyes darted around to the telling mess scattered around the room. Panic ticked the delicate vein in her throat. "You can't be in here. It's not appropriate."

"Considering our cause for celebration, I thought it more appropriate than the hotel lobby."

"A celebration is premature. Wait until after tomorrow night's dinner and we've survived this whole ordeal."

"Tomorrow. Aye, that is something I'd like to discuss." Setting the bottle on the table in the center of the room, he went to the bathroom to retrieve two glasses. "But first, a toast for this afternoon's accomplishment."

"You must leave. Now."

"Afraid someone will get the wrong impression? Close the door."

"Barrett—"

"Shut the door, Kathleen."

Her eyes narrowed to slits. She flattened her mouth into a white line. If she could spit nails, she would have nailed him between the eyes. Fine by him. If she wanted to go down with a fight, he was more than happy to oblige her destruction.

Notching her chin, she closed the door. Finally, common sense took hold.

Grabbing the bottle, he peeled off the foil and pushed his thumb against the cork. *Pop.* Golden froth spilled down the neck and into the two waiting crystal-cut glasses. Grabbing them, he held one out to her.

"To successfully infiltrating the enemies' camp." He held his glass up in salute.

She took her glass and raised it to his. "To infiltration and getting out of here alive."

He gulped his back. The expensive liquid bubbled down his throat to fizz sourly in his belly. Kat sipped hers and placed it back on the table.

Grabbing the bottle, he poured two more fingers worth into his glass. Compared to his beloved Ballantine's, this stuff was like drinking water. Good. He needed a clear head for this event. "You did a fine job today. I doubt even a highly trained soldier could've pulled off that amount of charm in front of the devil himself."

"I've had practice with the number of politicians my father brings around."

"If you're not careful, you'll have Eric eating out of the palm of your hand."

"Not a bad advantage to have."

"No, but the closer you are, the harder it is to slip away unnoticed."

The pulse ticked harder in her neck. "That's the plan, isn't it? To integrate ourselves firmly into their confidence?"

"Aye, confidence and trust without a hint of betrayal coming straight at them." His fingers curled around the glass, fragile and cool to the touch. Just like the woman standing before him, daring to look him in the eye. Just like all the rest. What a blithering fool he'd been to think she'd needed his help. His grip tightened until the stem threatened to break. Her unfinished glass of champagne taunted him. "Not going to finish?"

Her eyes didn't leave his. "I've rather a large headache after today's excitement. Thought I'd go to bed early."

"We haven't discussed tomorrow's plan."

"Perhaps in the morning—"

"I'll have an easier time sleeping knowing what's going to happen tomorrow. I don't like surprises, especially when the stakes are high."

Her eyes dropped to the floor as the color ebbed from her cheeks. Her mouth clamped shut, refusing any words of explanation or apology. Like a bad tooth, he'd have to force it from her.

"Goebbels will be there with his wife, and the von Schiraches. The husband is governor of Nazi operations in Vienna and the wife a longtime friend of Hitler."

He walked to the open door leading onto a small balcony. Leaves tumbled down the street as the wind crashed down from the mountains and streaked between buildings. The rain turned sideways, pelting windows and spraying across the toes of his shoes. "A dinner party should be easy enough for you, but you'll have to guide me through all the social niceties of fork and spoon."

She smoothed the bottle's condensation from the tabletop, still not meeting his eye. "Not that hard. I'm sure you'll do just fine."

Rain smacked his cheek. Cold and stinging, it slithered down his neck toward the envelope searing his chest. "I'm sure I will with you beside me."

Thunder galloped across the sky as lightning split the heavens. Searing light flashed around the room as the earthen smell of burned dirt filled the air. Barrett closed the balcony door, locking it tight as the lamp on the bedside table flickered.

"Everything will be fine. Tomorrow will go splendidly." With her head down, her words barely registered above the thunder. As if she wanted to reassure herself more than him.

Tossing back his second drink, he set the glass on the table with a *clank*. Kat jumped as if a shotgun had gone off. Her eyes shone in her pale face.

Say it. Say the words. Tell me you're leaving me tomorrow. Tell me you're leaving me right at the moment I need you.

Anger spiked in his blood. He didn't need her. And she certainly didn't need him. Their forged relationship was a means to an end. All he had was himself to rely on, and more the better for him. The sooner he started to bet on someone, the sooner disappointment came knocking. Life was too short for regrets.

Windowpanes rattled as more lightning tore from the storm. The lamp flashed, then, with a soft *pop*, went out. Darkness crashed over the room.

"Where is your dresser?"

Kat fumbled around the table, jittering the champagne bottle. "What do you need with my dresser?"

"Because there are emergency candles in there." He didn't bother covering the irritation in his voice as he pulled out his lighter and struck it. A dim glow burned at his fingertips.

"It's over here." Drawers pulled open as she shuffled through the contents. "Who puts candles in a dresser? Oh, here they are."

Placing the stubby wax pillars on the table, he touched the lighter to the wicks. The light sprang against the walls, beating back the shadows that swarmed around them. Their dark weight pressed on him like a cage, blocking out everything except the pulse of survival. Primal and hard, it gnashed its teeth for release from the captor holding it back.

"Tell me why."

Her intake of breath hissed in the silence. Surprise, fear, and anger splayed across her face before she yanked a curtain of defiance around her. Reaching into his jacket pocket, he pulled out the white envelope and tossed it across the table to her.

"Tell me why you did it. And don't you dare lie to me."

Her eyes flickered down to the envelope then back up at him. Blue steel rang in their depths. "Where did you get that?"

"The porter from the train station dropped it off at the front desk. As I was crossing the lobby to bring up this bottle of champagne, the concierge asked if I might deliver it to you. Lo and behold, I found two train tickets to Switzerland for tomorrow morning." He jammed the lighter back into his pocket. "By the way, I'll need back that forged document you borrowed from me. Handy bit of paper when you need Eric's signature for travel papers, isn't it?"

A pulse ticked wildly on the side of her neck. "You had no right."

"I have every right when you put everything in jeopardy, especially our safety. Do you really think you're going to make it across the border? Do you think Eric will let Ellie set one foot outside this hotel without him knowing about it? If you did manage to get her on a train, he'd have it stopped in the next town and have her carted back here under lock and key." He gouged a hand through his hair. Of course she hadn't thought it through. Her one single focus had been on getting Ellie, and woe to anything that got in her path. Including him. "Your devotion to your beloved sister is admirable, but entirely misplaced, considering our circumstances."

"My sister and I don't belong here. This is your job. I never wanted any part of it."

"You think I want to be here? Have you spared one thought for the amount of danger you put me in with your little disappearing act? Or are your thoughts too wrapped around your helpless little sister to consider anyone else?"

"That's not fair."

"I'll tell you what's not fair. Pouring every resource I have into keeping you safe, only to have you question me at every step. You agreeing to work together and all the while plotting to slip out behind my back, leaving me to deal with the consequences. From the Germans, aye, because I guarantee Eric won't be keen on you stealing his girlfriend from under his nose, and guess who he'll turn his wrath on? That's right. Me. But also from our own side. They don't take kindly to failed missions, and guess who'll be to blame? Me again."

"That was never my intention, but you have to see that you're better trained for this type of subterfuge."

"No, *you're* trained for this. Afternoon teas, fancy dinner parties, smiling and small talk. I'm trained to kill, and whether you like it or not, we're in this. Together. Until the end."

Her hands balled at her sides as the pulse at her throat careened out of control. "Well, I don't like it. I don't like it one bit, but no one ever asked me that, did they? No. They decided what was best for them, and once more I was trussed up to do their bidding."

Her fury cleaved his reserve, spilling it out in burning rage. He rounded the table to her. "You think I volunteered for this? Spending my afternoons strolling around Naziville while breaking bread with Hitler without being able to put a bullet in his head. You think I like leaving my men to train themselves while I play sitter to two spoiled English girls who haven't the sense to stay back where they belong? You've very poor sighted to see only yourself as an object for use."

Her lips curled into a sneer. "A mistake I am more than ready to rectify. We'll no longer be in the way, and you can get back to doing what you do best. No more museum dates or late-night parties to throw you off."

"What I do best is stop this war from continuing another month longer, and right now the best way I can do that is play the adoring suitor to you. You leave, and it's all for naught. No more parties, which means no more information gathered." Heat boiled up his neck, roasting the skin behind his ears as he stepped close enough to feel her punctuated breaths blasting across his face. "But why should you care? You've got a nice home and pretty clothes to return to. Who cares if the boys out in the field freeze another winter? No, your only duty is whatever your father dictates to you."

Her palm cracked the side of his face. Fire ricocheted to the bone. Kat stumbled back as horror poured down her face.

Turning away, Barrett walked to the balcony door and pressed a hand to the window. Anger boiled down his veins, ticking his pulse hard enough to shatter the trembling glass. Outside, rain pummeled its enraged fists against the surrounding buildings before slamming into the street like a convulsing river.

He clenched his hand, desperate to gain control before the tidal wave of rage washed him down into the whirlpool below. With her one selfish decision, she'd torn up any hope of him starting over once his sentence was served. He'd go back to the same place and the same people who never expected anything to come out of him besides a good pint. And what then? Slip into the mindless rut of drinking away his problems while cursing the scraps life had thrown his way? No. That was his da, not him.

And her? Wasn't she slipping herself back into the same places with the same narrow-minded people who expected her to marry, keep her mouth shut, and do as she was told? Didn't she deserve to prove them wrong too? He flattened his hand against the cool glass. For so long he'd tried to keep her as his paid ticket to freedom, but without realizing it, she'd bared her invaluableness to him. Only together could they prove it to the rest of the world.

"We have the chance to turn this war. It saddens me that—"

"—that I'm walking out."

"—that you don't think you're clever enough to finish the task."

He turned back to her. She stood with her hands clasped tightly to her stomach. The candlelight flickered against her pale skin, drawing her eyes back into the shadows.

"I'm sorry I struck you."

"I've been slapped before."

Her head lifted. Remorse lined the edges of her mouth. "Not by me. I've never hit anyone."

Raising a hand to his cheek, he rubbed the stinging spot that was sure to sport a red handprint until next week. "Pretty good for a beginner. If my gun jams tomorrow, just slap Hitler's head off."

The uncertainty from moments before dropped. Her spine straightened until she looked ready to snap in half. "Are you really going to kill him?"

"Would you stop me?"

Her stare pierced him like a steely knife. Instinctively, his shoulders rolled forward, tensing for the assault. The wind howled behind him, counting down the eternity of minutes it took for her to finally answer. "I'm not sure."

"It's a simple yes-or-no situation."

"But it isn't, is it?" She walked slowly toward him, her bare feet silent on the plush rug. Her reflection glowed yellow in the glass. "If you kill Hitler, his second in command will simply take his place. You need Hitler, Goebbels, Goring, and Bormann to end the war, and I doubt all four will gather conveniently for you tomorrow around the supper table."

She was right. Confound the woman. "Can't blame me for trying."

"I can and will if you get yourself killed for a meaningless chance to take out Hitler."

"Good thing you'll be there to stop me."

She turned away. The silence hit him like a hammer to the gut.

"Still. After all this you plan on handing yourself straight over to the Nazis for interrogation and torture. Then, finally, when they've dragged everything out of you except your eyeteeth, they'll shoot you for spying." He grabbed her shoulder, forcing her around to face him. "That's what awaits you with those tickets. But don't listen to me. Go on and do what you bloody want."

She twisted against him, but he held tight. "Always about you, isn't it? I thought you came to help me, or is that too much of a stretch for you? To think about someone other than yourself."

"I am thinking about you. More than I care to." Like a barrel with the tap blown off, the admission spewed out with no hope of bottling back the damage. Or the truth. He'd denied it for so long, and now it stared him in the face, forcing him to recognize it for what it was. He wanted her, had wanted her all along, but now it wasn't the simple desire of a man wanting a woman. He wanted *her*.

Might as well tie the noose around his own neck. At least the pain of the gallows would be momentary, unlike the burden of needing another heart to beat in unison with his own.

Her lips parted, drawing his attention. Free of lipstick, they glowed a deep rosy pink. One taste, that's all it would take to prove to himself that she wasn't anything special. That her desires held no room for him and he could walk away a free man.

Grabbing her other shoulder, he pulled her to him and covered her mouth with his as a protest swelled in her throat. She shoved against him, but he held her tight, trapping her hands between them. He tilted his head, coaxing her flattened mouth to form to his. *You mean nothing to me. Nothing.* He took her anger, burning it into himself as he fell deeper and deeper.

As if sensing his fall, her lips softened to dissolve the last drops of boiling ire. He reared back to break the reaction before he lost complete control of himself. And immediately regretted the action. Full and red, her lips bore the mark of his commanding touch and taunted him to do it again.

"You promised you'd never do that unless there was a Nazi present." Candlelight drowned in the deep-blue currents of her eyes. If he wasn't careful, he'd fall in headlong without hope of surfacing.

"And you promised to smash a bottle over my head if I did." He grabbed the champagne bottle from the table, almost wanting her to do it. Anything to break him out of her hold. "It's not Ballantine's, but it'll do the job."

Taking the bottle, she flung it aside. It shattered against the wall, spraying champagne drops over the floor. Her arms wrapped around his neck, pulling his head down. "Not tonight."

She met him with urgency, all ties of control and restraint slipping away as she demanded his compliance. Curling his arms around her waist, he gave way with full surrender to the heat purling in his veins. Her fingers coiled in his hair, lighting his scalp with a fire that burned down his neck and winged across his chest. Dizziness swirled in his head, leaving him without a tether save her. He clung tight to keep from losing her and drifting back into his bleak darkness.

With one gentle sigh against his mouth, the reins tumbled from his fingers into hers. He pulled her closer, willing her heart's rhythm to overtake his own and never let go.

Knock, knock. The door flung open and bounced off the wall. Ellie flew in, tying a belt around the waist of her satin robe. "Kat, are you—" She skidded to a halt, eyes wide and mouth dropping open as her stare bounced back and forth between them. "The lights went out, and we heard a noise."

Eric hurtled in with hair mussed. His white shirt was haphazardly buttoned and gaping at the throat, but he'd somehow managed to get a pair of trousers tucked into his high boots. Leaving the look of shock to Ellie, he surveyed the scene with a professional eye before drawing a blank look of pretending not to see the obvious.

Like a fish gone cold, Kat's arms dropped from Barrett's neck. Red burned across her face. "I'm all right. I—we—Barrett came to help me find the emergency candles."

The shock ebbed from Ellie's face as she switched her attention to him. Coolness swept her tone. "So I see."

Like an inspector on duty, Eric's eyes swept the room, pausing briefly on the broken bottle before sweeping up to the glasses on the table. And the envelope with the two train tickets peeking out of the top. It lasted no more than a second, but it was long enough to register.

Hooking a hand under Ellie's arm, he tugged her to the door. "Come on, *schatz*. It's clear Mr. Anderson has everything in order." His pale-blue eyes lingered on Kat before sliding to Barrett. "We'll see you in the morning."

Pressing a fist into her stomach, Kat's eyes remained fixed on the door after they left. Her shoulders pumped up and down in a desperate attempt to control the situation that had spun out of control. "I think you should go."

Rain billowed against the windows, the pinging like a deluge of dull nails scraping to fill the silent void. Barrett curled his fingers in and out, flexing the muscles in anticipation. It had come, and he had only the momentary breath before the battle to prepare. And her? How was he to prepare her for what was coming?

His hand reached out to soothe the tremble from her slender shoulders but fell back to his side. Tenderness was for those who had time, and theirs was up.

"Destroy those tickets. If you had any doubt before, it's too late now." He stepped around her to the door. The cool knob stung his heated palm. "Eric knows."

Chapter 14

Kat tipped the glass of wine to her mouth, but didn't part her lips. She hated reds, especially dry ones, and they gave her a splitting headache. There was enough spinning in her head tonight without the added crowding of a migraine.

The great hall of Berghof glowed with lamplight from every corner, highlighting the tapestries and thick rugs with cheery warmth as the fireplace crackled with thick logs. Groups of twos and threes dotted around the room in easy conversation and laughter as the smell of food drifted down the hall, bringing delightful anticipation. If not for the gray uniforms spiking the evening's pleasantness, Kat might have dreamed she was back in Berkshire.

"What do you think of Bavaria now that you have been here?"

Kat pulled her attention back to the woman in front of her and smiled. "It's beautiful. I've never visited a place with its likeness, especially the crystal lakes." She was certain the landscape of Switzerland would have been even more beautiful with the freedom it offered, but such a dream had crumbled like forgotten ash. So much for her attempts to act on her own decision.

The pouf of brown hair atop Henriette von Schirach's head waved back and forth as she nodded. "We've been coming here since I was a little girl. Uncle Alf was kind enough to introduce me to Eva, and we go swimming together since he doesn't like to. I think he's afraid of going under."

The man in question sat in one of the floral chairs surrounded by a group of admirers as he waxed loud enough to be heard across the

Channel. *Don't worry about that. I'm sure the lack of a heart and soul will keep him buoyant.* "What a shame. He's missing out."

"*Ja,* but then as long as I've known him, I've never seen him give in to many frivolities, with the exception of painting and music. After dinner I'm sure he'll play a record for us, and you can witness for yourself his gifted ear." Henriette's heart-shaped face dipped. "Though sometimes I wish he would play something different simply to change things up from Strauss and Wagner. Are their works popular in England?"

"Yes, classical pieces are very popular at many of the parties I've attended with my parents, though I honestly can't tell many of the composers apart. My musical ear is sadly lacking."

"Baldur has said that you and your sister may help open many doors into these parties."

Alarm clanged in Kat's ears. Instinctively, her eyes swept the room for Barrett. He stood next to the crackling fireplace talking to a young girl and a man whom Henriette had pointed out as Hitler's private secretary and valet. The only man in civilian clothes, the cream jacket stretched tight across Barrett's wide shoulders, the erect straightness of his spine readying to rip the seams. Her heart sagged as he failed to turn at her silent call.

She wrapped her fingers around her glass, willing the coolness to draw the panic from her blood. "We hope that, ah, how can I put this delicately? Communications can be made between our two countries."

"That's good to hear." Henriette leaned close, the sterile scent of soap thick on her skin. "Many would question why two English women and a Scot are allowed such privileges as hosting parties and coming here to Berchtesgaden when you are not known members of the Party, but they must understand that for our cause to succeed we must find like-mindedness in all different countries."

Kat smiled past the sickness bubbling up her throat and softly clinked her glass to Henriette's. "I couldn't say it better myself."

Henriette sipped her wine, then looked up and frowned in disgust. "Ugh, that vulgar woman is here. Uncle Alf adores her, but must she always turn up as if a party is thrown in her honor?"

Olga Chekhova, the actress from Eric's big premiere night, swept into the hall with a rustle of black taffeta and string after string of jet beads. Accepting a glass of wine from one of the white-coated servers, she kissed Eva on both cheeks and glided over to the circle Eric and Ellie stood in. As Ellie turned her cheek for Olga's greeting, she caught Kat's eye and quickly looked away.

She hadn't spoken to Kat all day past a "Good morning" over breakfast and "After you" when they got into the car to come up to Berghof. Ellie was never one to hide her feelings, and the silence scratched Kat's nerves like nails on gravel.

"She's coming over. Please excuse me." Henriette made her escape as Olga sashayed around the guests and furniture to stand by the large picture window with Kat. Chanel No. 5 floated around her like a fragrant cape.

"Kat, how wonderful to see you again!" Olga's soft Russian accent rolled off her tongue like claret as she leaned in to kiss both of Kat's cheeks. "And how lovely you look."

Kat smoothed a hand over her wine-colored crepe dress with flutter sleeves and satin belt. "I'm afraid I'm a bit overdressed for the evening."

Sniffing, Olga waved a bejeweled hand in dismissal. "Don't mind those bores. Herr Hitler believes modesty and plain looks are most suitable for a woman, but I will never forgo my lipstick, no matter his opinion." She cocked her head, and her red lips parted in a smile that didn't quite meet her eyes. "Appearances must be kept at all times, mustn't they?"

Bands of dread squeezed around Kat's lungs as Olga's stare bored into her like a corkscrew drilling for the sweet liquid bottled below. Across the hall, a white-jacketed waiter tossed more logs into the massive fireplace. The red flames leaped like dancers, their heat twirling across the floor for her own private ensemble. She adjusted her arms as the heat scored up her sides. *Who lights a fire in August?* "Yes, they should."

Olga nodded, allowing the smile to soften her face. "Speaking of appearances, I see Eric is doing well. I haven't seen him this proud since Goebbels recommended him for the Paris posting."

Like a peacock crowing for chickens, Eric's gloating soared inches higher than those gathered around him. Talking and gesturing, he didn't allow anyone else time to reciprocate. At his side, Ellie's head lolled back and forth from boredom as Eric never thought to speak English for her benefit, as if it would slow down his storytelling. "Personal recognition from his Führer suits him well."

"Not only for himself, but his lady friend. For an English woman, she certainly seems in her element."

"Ellie never had a problem socializing." *Except lately with me.* On a third head loll, Ellie's eyes met hers and quickly looked away. The rouge on her cheeks stood out against her pale skin. "She's never lacked for good times or friends."

"And you are not that way. Very different, but very good. We all have our parts to play, yes?"

The woman's words unnerved Kat's already frayed sense of calm. She'd had a lifetime of learning the social ambiguities of what a person might say versus what they actually meant. A simple miscalculation earned one embarrassment or, at the very worst, a cut from the social group. Here it meant death.

Hesitation flickered across Olga's powdered face. "Kat, I like you very much. I like your young man there. Quite a charmer and worth hanging on to. If I found myself twenty years younger, I'd give you competition for him, though I would lose. His eyes are for you only, I see." Polishing off her glass, she set it down on the nearby table. She took Kat's hand and looped it under her arm. "Some days I feel so far from home without a friendly face to warm me, but there is something about you that makes me not so sad. I do hope that we can be friends."

"I'd like that."

"Good." She patted Kat's hand as the smile slipped from her face. "As your friend, I advise you to keep your sister close. These are dangerous times, and threats often make men do ugly things. Love is the most dangerous weapon of them all."

The last string of Kat's calm snapped. Her gaze swung to Eric and slammed into his icy glare. The corner of his mouth pulled back like a tiger with its kill in sight. Barrett was right. Somehow, he'd found out about the tickets. Her fingers dug into Olga's arm as the room tilted. If he knew about her escape plan to Switzerland, what else had he found out?

A gong sounded, shaking Kat down to her satin-covered feet. Guests started down the hall to the dining room, following the savory smell of roast and gravy and the promise of more wine.

Gently disengaging her hand from Olga's arm, she corralled all the terror quaking down her body and summoned it into what she hoped was a convincing smile. "Thank you for your concern, dear friend. I shall bear it in mind."

"I hope you do, my dear. I truly hope you do." Concern blinked quietly in the actress's hooded eyes. "If you should ever need a hand, mine is at your disposal."

Kat fell in line behind the other couples converging into the hall, Olga's words rattling in her brain like a tin of marbles. The German voices and laughter bounced off the walls and pummeled the cacophony in her head. The air grew thin in her lungs, distorting the shapes around her. She reached a shaking hand out to the wall for support, but instead of finding solid coolness, warmth enveloped her fingers.

"All right, poppy?" Barrett's voice pulled her back from the dizzying edge as his arm slipped around her waist. Though concerned, his tone was void of the usual affection she'd come to know.

Another fault of hers. She hadn't wanted to kiss him, but as his lips touched hers she hadn't been able to stop herself. He had elicited passion from her as easily as plucking a string on a violin, the slumbering chords within her stirring to life under his masterful attention. And then it was over, leaving her cold and confused. And angry. What was she doing giving in to a man who offered her nothing but headaches? Where had her common sense gone? One kiss had drained it from her, leaving nothing more than a fleeting moment of mutual desire.

And yet . . . As much as she tried to justify the moment as a collision of desperate souls seeking reassurance within the darkness, she couldn't forget his tremble of surprise and longing as her passion surged to meet his.

After avoiding him all day, she'd been forced to sit next to him in the car. Each dip in the road bumped her up against him. He'd stiffened like a board in the wind each time.

"I'm fine, thank you. Too many people in the hall." She pulled away, not meeting his searching eyes. "Or that fireplace is putting off invisible fumes."

"Who lights a fire in August?"

She smiled at her echoed words, but the string of tension still vibrated between them. Before she lost her nerve, she broke the silence. "I'm sorry about last night. For taking my frustrations out on you, and for attempting to leave you high and dry. Hardly the honorable actions of a person you're meant to trust. I broke that trust, and for that I'm truly sorry."

"I got pretty heated myself. I'm sorry." He rubbed the back of his neck. "Is that all? I mean, about last night. Uh, is that all you wanted to say?"

"Is there something else I should apologize for?"

"No, I . . . Em, a lot of things happened, and I didn't know if you regretted . . . That is to say . . ."

The kiss. Was that what he was talking about? Did he regret kissing her? She certainly didn't, and she didn't think she was too bold in claiming that he'd quite enjoyed being on the other end of it. Unless her own passion had overexaggerated his returned eagerness. Considering all that had transpired—a yelling match, lies, and a slap—his rejection would be nothing less than she deserved.

It would also be a pain worse than death to her. A torture of the most heartbreaking kind.

She knotted her hands, forcing the words past her lips. "If there's something you feel I missed—"

"No. No, I don't mean that. Unless you were having second thoughts about something." His words tripped over one another as if to reassure her he held no grudges.

Relief poured through her. Not such a terrible move, that kiss, after all. "I apologized for what I needed to."

"Ah, good, then." Barrett looked away and cleared his throat. "I see Ms. Chekhova is taking an interest in you."

"A little more than passive." She slowed to a stop beside the staircase, allowing the other guests to pass into the dining room as she rummaged in her handbag for an excuse. "She warned me about Eric."

Barrett's eyebrows slanted together. "What do you mean?"

Kat stepped closer, dropping her voice. "Somehow I think she knows more than she lets on and that Eric may do whatever is necessary to fend off threats. Including using Ellie against me."

He didn't move except the deep rise and fall of his chest that swayed the red-and-gray-striped tie over his flat stomach. Unblinking, he stared over the top of her head to the window and the inky night beyond. Finally, he blew out a breath that ruffled the wave of hair around her face. "Not a surprise."

"I find it quite surprising and alarming that some Russian actress is aware of our problem. Has a broadcast been made without our knowing?"

"There's a rumor in the intelligence circle that Ms. Chekhova's acting does not stop after the film quits rolling. She may be playing the same game we are for her own country."

"Truly?"

He grimaced and shifted his shoulders, stretching the back of his jacket. "It's only a rumor, but she has the perfect cover giving her access to Hitler's private circles. And it would explain her tip about Eric."

"Are we suddenly trading secrets with Russia, that she could know so much about us?"

"We do enough dealing to keep the upper hand against Germany. 'The enemy of my enemy' and all that."

As if the fireplace fumes had followed her around the corner, its heated fingers trickled down her sides. She resisted the urge to flap her arms to stir the air. "And Eric? What are we to do about him? How are we so sure what he knows and what he doesn't?"

"Beyond the tickets we aren't, but it's safe to assume his suspicions are on overdrive."

"We need to get out of here."

Barrett shook his head. "Too late now. We leave early, and he'll know something's up."

The heat surged to her head, sparking her temper like a wire shortage. "How do you know they aren't serving us for dinner? Roasted and flayed open to tortured perfection for their evil consumption."

Amused horror twisted his face. "That is the most grotesque thing I have ever heard, and as a bartender that's saying a lot. You need to stop reading those propaganda posters."

"He's got something for us, but he's going to pick his opportune moment to spring it. Like a wolf playing with his food before he devours it."

"We really need to work on your descriptions."

"Descriptions of what?"

They both jumped at Eric's voice sliding down the hall from where he stood in the doorway to the dining room. Eyes slanted and lips pulled back to reveal white teeth in the dim hall light, he did indeed fit her description of a wolf.

"Food," Barrett said without skipping a beat. "Kat smells beef, but I think it's pork. Braised, not roasted."

"Why don't you come in and see who is right?" Eric's lips pulled back even farther. "Unless you have more whispering to do about dessert."

The dining room was rectangular with a long, gleaming table in the center and sixteen red-cushioned chairs around it. Wood panels flanked the walls with a built-in china cabinet on one side and windows overlooking the terrace on the other. A small alcove curved out in one corner with a small round table for more intimate seating.

Settling into the corner chair a waiter held for her, Kat found herself across from Eric and Ellie, with Hitler's personal architect, Albert Speer, to her immediate right at the foot of the table. Despite their awkwardness, relief spilled through her when Barrett slipped into the seat on her left. Thankfully, Hitler didn't follow the English tradition of separating couples around the table to promote better conversation. Beyond the mounting atrocities and lack of nourishing food for the ordinary citizens, she had no clue what she'd converse with these people about. She couldn't even find momentary delight at the banquet spilling before her. A centerpiece of braised lamb on a silver platter sat in the middle surrounded by porcelain bowls of roasted bell peppers, rice, spätzle drowning in brown gravy, asparagus, tomatoes and squash, mashed golden potatoes, grilled sausage, sweet mustard, cabbage rolls, and *brochen* with creamed butter.

Though her insides screamed with protest, Kat took a small sampling of the foods closest to her plate. Pressing her fork into the top of her mashed potatoes, she carved out a hole for the gravy to pool in just as she had when she was kid. Across the table, Ellie did the same thing with her dumpling. Catching her eye, Kat smiled at their secret. The corners of Ellie's mouth twitched as if they wanted to return the grin but quickly flattened as she looked back down at her plate. Sadness pinched Kat's heart. What had she done?

The answer pulled her gaze to Eric, who fairly glowed with delight. Her pain was his privilege to witness as he shoveled food into his eager mouth. "Are you enjoying your evening, Kathleen?"

"Very much. I only wish our stay was longer." She picked up a forkful of the potatoes and forced it past her teeth.

"Are you going somewhere?"

The potatoes slid down into the sourness of her stomach. "I mean when we have to return to Paris in a few days. I will miss Bavaria."

Coolness glinted in his tone without a hint of surprise. "Is that true? Here I was thinking it didn't suit your tastes."

"On the contrary, I find the scenery breathtaking and the peacefulness refreshing after the bustle of Paris. In fact," she said, forking a sausage against the roiling of her stomach, "I was hoping Ellie and I could take a weekend in the Alps. We used to visit the lodges there with our parents, didn't we, Ellie?"

Next to her, Barrett set his wineglass down with a loud *clink*. His foot pressed down on top of hers in warning. She slipped it away and crossed her legs. If Eric wanted to play cat and mouse, then she'd beat him to it. Barrett could yell at her later.

"Remember the year we built an entire family of snow people?"

Ellie nodded, moving her fork around the dumpling. "Mother was furious we used her fur boots and cashmere shawl for decoration."

"The Alps. In Switzerland." Fair eyebrows lifted on Eric's brow. Ellie dragged a plate of cabbage rolls closer and hovered her fork over the offering as she decided which one to spear. Reaching across her, Eric pushed the plate away. "No, *schatz*. The odor clings no matter how many times you brush your teeth."

Grabbing her glass, Ellie drained the potent contents and signaled the waiter behind her for a refill, all while glaring at Eric, who munched contentedly on a crusty roll. Kat gripped the underside of her chair to keep from vaulting over the table and cramming it down his throat until he choked.

Brushing the crumbs from his mouth, Eric leaned back in his chair and sipped his wine. Reflecting the ruby liquid, his eyes dimmed to black as he stared at Kat over the rim. Kat's fingernails curled farther into her chair until she felt a tiny pop as the fabric tore.

"As this trip has been mostly business, I think a true holiday is in order." Eric rotated a finger around the stem of his glass. With each pass, Kat could almost feel his invisible finger circling around her throat. "Once we've arrived in Switzerland—"

An explosion from the opposite end of the table silenced the room. Hitler's fist lay beside his plate, his vegetables overturned from where he'd pounded the table. Pale faces turned in horror to Henriette, who sat motionless, eyes wide with fear, shrinking into her seat. Her bloodless lips moved, emitting a catlike mewling.

Eyes raging like a demon, Hitler smacked the table again and shouted like a madman.

Baldur, Henriette's husband, pulled his wife to her feet and drew her from the room. Silence crackled in the air, the slightest noise poised to ignite the stillness into a blaze. Hitler's eyes darted around the table, daring anyone to speak again. A few chairs down, Eva sank lower and lower in her seat as she shook her head slowly back and forth. Pushing back his chair, Hitler threw his napkin on top of his uneaten vegetables and stormed from the room.

A full two minutes passed before the first voice whispered, followed by another and then another like the rising drone of a beehive.

"What was that about, I wonder?" Though whispered, Kat's voice bounced off the wood panels to hit her ears like cymbals.

Mr. Speer, who had ignored everyone thus far, cleared his throat. "Frau von Schirach related an incident involving Jewish women and children she witnessed while in Amsterdam. It seems she thought their treatment too stern." Working a piece of food from his back teeth with his tongue, he laced his fingers together around his finished plate. "She dared our Führer to consider what was happening to the Jews."

Kat returned her fork to her plate and pushed it away as nausea crept up her throat. "A bold demand."

Speer scratched at his receding hairline, boredom drawing his mouth down. "Quite so. The Führer was quick to inform her that his duty is to his people alone, and the Jews are not his people. A shame about the von Schiraches. Hetty's such a lovely woman, but she's just ruined them."

Eric nodded, his sleek blond head shining from the overhead lights. "At uncertain times such as these it's important to keep only those loyal near, for you never know when a traitor will rear its ugly head."

Air squeezed out of Kat's lungs, battering her heart against the restraints of her chest. "Then we must take precautions for those we most care about."

Eric took another sip of his wine. "I couldn't agree more."

A scraping of chairs broke the ring of vibrating tension as the other guests declared the dinner ruined.

Barrett stood from his chair and offered his hand to Kat. His head bent to her ear. "I thought after all this time you'd learned to keep your mouth and emotions shut. You know we have the chance to do something here, something greater than us that can put an end to this bloody war. Prodding Eric like that won't help us in any way except to the Gestapo's secret room."

Kat stood to shaking legs. "He thinks he has the right to command people because no one stands up to him."

"You're being reckless."

"At least I'm doing something."

He dropped her hand as if she'd burned him. "Guess I was too busy stuffing my mouth to help hang ourselves right along with you."

"I guess so."

Turning on her heel, she left him and his glare, hurrying out of the room to catch Ellie. She grabbed her sister's hand and yanked her to the side of the staircase as the rest of the guests made their way back into the great hall. Eric was buried too deep in conversation with two other uniformed men to notice.

"Ellie, why won't you talk to me?" As the words crossed her lips, her floodgates trembled with release. Tears pricked the backs of her eyes.

"I . . . I've been busy today, getting ready for tonight, and Eric had lists and lists of things to talk about with me."

"That doesn't explain why you won't even look at me. Ellie, please."

Ellie raised her eyes, taking a deep breath as if to steady herself. "Last night I came to your room to check on you and found you in Barrett's arms like that with an empty champagne bottle and clothes scattered about . . . I didn't know what to think. No, that's a lie. I know exactly what I thought. You're supposed to be the good sister, Kat."

The disappointment tinging her last words pierced Kat like a double-tipped arrow. "Nothing happened beyond a simple kiss."

Ellie's face scrunched in doubt. "That kiss didn't look so simple to me."

The memory of Barrett's insistent lips and the way she'd given in to their persuasion burned through her. There was nothing simple about that kiss, or the judgment in Ellie's tone. *People-pleasing again, eh?* Barrett's voice rattled in her head. *What do* you *have to say about all this?* "He left right after you did, if you insist on knowing. Don't give me that look of innocence. I tire of turning a blind eye to your indiscretions and flighty whims."

"You were always jealous of the attention the boys showed me."

"Hounds panting at your feet is more like it, leaving me to shoo them away when you tired."

"Don't blame me because you can't say no when asked to do something. Learn to please yourself for once instead of always doing what's right."

"Kissing Barrett wasn't right enough for you?"

Ellie's focus dropped to her bright-red nails. Paired with her mint-green dress they made her look like a Christmas candy. A hypocritical Christmas candy. "I've always been the one caught in the corner with a boy while you're always the picture of purity. It's too late for me, but knowing you're all right . . . Well, it was nice to think that some things never changed."

"I can't tell if that's a compliment or not."

Ellie looked up and smiled. "It is."

The bluster that had so filled her with indignation slowly diffused. Who would've considered truth as a balm to latent hurts? Kat hooked an arm around Ellie's shoulders as she slipped her arm around Kat's waist. Together again.

They turned to the entrance of the great hall where the other guests had disappeared. "Come on, let's see what they've got for us next. I hear Herr Hitler has a masterful ear for music."

"Ugh. It's probably something with a polka band. Everyone here sits enraptured by him, too afraid to tell him that his tastes are as dry as week-old milk."

"Do you want to tell him or should I?"

Ellie shivered. "The sooner we get away from him the better. Do you really want to go to Switzerland?"

For the first time that day, excitement threatened to overtake Kat's constant fear. Hope stirred in the pile of discarded ashes. "Yes."

Ellie nodded slowly but didn't say anything more as they entered the great hall. A large group clustered in the center of the room with Eric's shiny head in the middle. Scanning the room, Kat found Barrett next to the fireplace, leaning one arm on the mantel. The flames danced indecipherable shadows across his face as he watched the group.

The crowd shifted to reveal a tall, solidly built woman with chestnut hair and a square face. A feathered hat perched atop her head, and despite the sweltering heat, she had a fox shawl draped across her angular shoulders. She nodded and smiled coolly while Eric hovered at her elbow. When she looked up her smile froze as she saw Kat and Ellie in the doorway. Her chin notched up as she slipped a gloved hand under Eric's arm.

Kat turned as Ellie's suddenly cold fingers dug into her ribs. "Who is that woman?"

"His wife."

Chapter 15

She yelled, then I yelled. She yelled, and I yelled some more. It was ugly." Kat swirled her glass of ginger ale around. The fizz had long since gone since she'd stormed into Barrett's office over two hours ago. A long walk down the Seine hadn't been enough to cool her off, and the ease of railing at someone else was too good to pass up. How he'd come by that honor he had no idea. Possibly because she was still angry at him for discovering her plot to flee to Switzerland with Ellie in tow. As if she stood a chance under Eric's unblinking eye. From the moment he'd spotted those train tickets in Kat's hotel room he hadn't let Ellie out of his sight. The fiasco also known as dinner with Hitler two nights ago had been the perfect excuse to whisk them all back to Paris the following morning. He had more control in the city.

"She couldn't understand why I was so angry. Hmm, not sure, but probably something to do with my baby sister having an affair with a married man. And not just any man, but a Nazi. Are you even listening?"

Barrett looked up from the Resistance flyer, *Défense de la France*, he had spread in front of him. It was the only true source of information being printed since the Nazis had seized the national papers for their own bloated propaganda. "Yes. Contrary to popular belief, I can do more than one thing at a time. I need to see what the other cells are up to since we've been gone."

That and if he looked at her for too long he'd be forced to remember the last time they'd been alone together. That night in her hotel room where he'd lost complete sense for the sake of needing to prove something to himself. Only thing he'd proved was that he couldn't trust himself when it came to Kat.

He watched her over the top of his paper. A picture of pure grace and beauty in her blue dress, though she would probably argue and proclaim it something fancy like Aegean blue. Either way, it turned her eyes to a mesmerizing shade of watercolor. One he found himself drowning in with no wish of a life preserver. She was the brightness to his gloom. The lightness to his burdens. The call to his heart, and how difficult it was not to answer it in full.

She traced a watery bead down the side of the glass. Lonely in its solitary journey, it stuttered and stopped in resistance to its fall until the heat of the air pressed it down to plop meaningless onto the desk. "Do you know what she kept saying? 'He's going to leave her. He's promised me. It's a loveless marriage and she's vicious.' As if that makes it any better."

He turned the page on his paper. More guerilla attacks near Chaville. "Men like him never leave their wives." Her sharp intake of breath jerked his attention back up. "Sorry. Didn't mean to rub it in."

Pain ebbed in her eyes as she shook her head. With the blond waves pinned back to her neck, the lines of fatigue washed uncovered across her pale face. "No, you're right. Ellie's floating on ignorant bliss, and I'm just worldly enough to realize it." Moving the glass aside, she dipped her small finger into the watery ring left behind and fanned it out into long lines. "She was always the carefree one, much to our parents' never-ending vexation. Dutiful Kathleen and Rebellious Eleanor. Different as could be, but still tied with sisterhood. No matter what came, those ties never broke. Until now. Her sneaking off to Paris is more than an act of disobedience. It's an irretrievable loss. One I feel may never mend between us."

"Would you want things to return to the way they were? Duty and rebellion shackled beneath the same roof, reporting to that list of rules your family has mapped out for you. You might find the fresh air more to your liking if you give it a chance."

"You mean be more like Ellie."

"No, more like you. The you locked beneath the rules. The woman who didn't hesitate to step into Naziland. The woman who faced down Hitler at teatime. The woman who loves Benny Goodman and wants to eat cake for breakfast. The strait-laced woman who relaxes in my arms when she's dancing."

A smile ghosted her lips. "That doesn't sound like the Kathleen Whitford I know."

"But it's one I've come to know." *The one I've fallen head over heart for.*

Kat quietly worked the water over the varnished planes of his desk. Art, the expression of her working mind. "She accused me of over-reacting."

"Did you?"

Kat flipped her gaze up to him, spearing him to the seat. "She's angry at her lover for having his wife show up unexpectedly, and yet she's furious at me for daring to point out that she's a mistress. Who here is overreacting?"

He conceded with silence. That sister of hers needed to have her hide tanned for all the misery she caused people. People trying to help, no less. Her own sister had risked her life coming here, and look how she repaid her. By slapping her in the face with insolence and selfishness. Ellie was running herself into the ground and taking Kat right along with her.

The water under her finger curved into a bow with two high stacks on top. Slowly, her nails looped circles and billowing smoke. A ship that gleamed with varnished oak from the desk beneath. For a woman so tightly held together she possessed the most surprising imagination. Dipping her finger into the glass, she rippled waves of ginger ale over the sides of the ship. The waves rushed forward to the edge of the desk and dripped to the floor. Where did she imagine it going? As far away as he wished to go?

Turning in his chair, he filed the paper in the folder for burning later that night. Get rid of all evidence, leaving nothing to come back and hang himself with. Unlike paperwork, he couldn't rid himself of her so easily. Bottle after bottle of Ballantine's couldn't purge her from his thoughts, his very system of existence.

A crumpled message caught his eye at the bottom of the stack, and once more anger burned in his veins like wildfire. Command had denied his request to end the mission and get the sisters out of Paris. They couldn't afford one extra man for escort service, especially not when the women in question were vital to retrieving information from Hitler's private circles. He slapped the folder closed. Their safety was in his hands. Her life was his to protect.

Who would protect his heart?

"Is this your mother?"

He spun back around. The air froze in his lungs as he stared at the faded tintype of a beautiful young woman with unbound dark hair swinging down to her waist. Innocent sweetness curved her face as two large eyes pierced the lens. Eyes he saw every time he looked in the mirror.

"Pieces of a forgotten past. I'll thank you to return it."

Pink burst across Kat's cheeks as she gently placed the photo on top of his other meager savings from a life he'd tried to piece together. Postcards of New York City and Washington, DC, and Coney Island, newspaper articles about the building boom in major American cities and new immigrants at Ellis Island, and even a few American coins his cousin had sent him from Pittsburgh. Seeds of hope.

Closing the lid, she slid the box he'd carelessly left out back across the desk to him. "I'm sorry. I didn't mean to pry. It's just that we've been together for some time—" The pink deepened to red. "I mean, we've worked together, and I hardly know anything about you."

He brushed his thumb over the intricate carving on the lid of a thistle and fleur-de-lis intertwined. Scotland and France. "Thought you wanted to keep all the personal particulars private. Keep things uncomplicated." Taking the box, he eased it down into a lower desk drawer and locked it tight. Out of sight and mind. No use dwelling until the mission was complete. "Besides, there's not enough about me to keep you interested."

She, on the other hand, had enough to keep him reeling for more years than he could count. Distance had been his ally, but she'd broken through every barrier to leave his defenses in tatters. If he'd thought to keep anything from her grasp, that kiss had wrenched it free.

Her head cocked to the side as she studied him for second. Her mouth parted as if to speak, but a quick shake of her head stopped the words from escaping. She jumped to her feet. "Care for a walk?"

"Thought after the past week my presence was intolerable to your sensibilities."

"In light of my less than stellar morning, I'll give you a reprieve."

No. Stay away, lad. You know what happens when you get too close to this one.

Hopefulness and loneliness clashed across her face. "You can help me think of new complaints about Ellie and Eric."

"Can't turn down that offer." So much for staying safe.

The waters of the Seine lapped against the stone embankment below as they walked along the Right Bank. To the left stretched the fancy Pont Alexandre III, and beyond it towered the Les Invalides, where the remains of Napoleon lay in silent slumber under a dome large enough to hold the man's godlike persona.

"I'll never understand man's ingenuity to build things over water." Afternoon clouds rolled across the sky, darkening the waters of the Seine to a muddy green. He should've thought to bring a hat. "All those statues and gold. Don't know how it keeps from collapsing."

Hatless herself, Kat pointed to the four gilt-bronze statues at the corners. "I believe Résal and d'Alby designed the *Fames* as stabilizing counterweights for the arch."

"Sneak into a few engineering lectures while at university?" Another marker in the distance between them.

"Not exactly." Her hand dropped to the rail, fingers curved over it. "My fiancé—ex-fiancé, that is—was an engineer."

His mouth slacked open. "You were engaged?"

"Years ago. It didn't end well. He . . . wasn't who I thought he was."

Tendrils escaped from the pins at her neck to dance unchecked behind her ear. A far cry from the prim and proper image he'd come to expect. Just one more expectation about her he had all wrong. The strand weaved down her neck to brush her shoulder like a yellow ribbon of silk. All other times she had a perfect comb to hold everything in place, yet here before him she let it fly free.

He curled his fingers against his leg to keep from reaching out and touching the temptation. "So no engineering. What else don't you like?"

She ran a hand over the weathered stone base, a wry smile twisting her mouth. "Poetry. The subtle intricacies baffle me. I prefer not to have to guess what the artist is trying to say."

"Maybe that's why you're having so much trouble with Ellie. The situation she's created for herself isn't exactly straightforward."

"She forgives his horribleness time and time again, dancing to his tune and making excuses for his behavior, while I get the silent treatment for daring to question his motives. Does that make any sense to you?"

"People in love do stupid things."

"Well, if that's love, I hope it never happens to me, because I can't bear the thought of losing all common sense for no good reason."

His mother's photograph crept to the edges of his mind. He wished he'd been old enough to have a memory of her. His father had been too busy hoarding his to bother sharing. "You're preaching to the converted."

Love. The sickness of all mankind. He'd managed to avoid the disease his whole life. Sure, he'd dipped into the pretense when a pair of pretty eyes fluttered his way, but by the next morning he was resolved once more to remain alone. Only in the deep darkness of night would he admit to the loneliness and the need to share it with someone. To share anything with someone.

Next to him, Kat stared silently over the water as they walked down the bridge. Despite the Nazi patrols marring the city around them, she exuded quiet assurance. Not just someone to share with but someone he didn't have to hide from. She saw him for all the things he was without fear. If their time together had proved nothing else, Kathleen Whitford was fearless.

The hairs tingled on his arms. Her eyes on him always did that. "You're doing it again."

She jumped as if a gun had blasted. "Doing what?"

"Last time you claimed it was a bee buzzing around my head, but since there aren't any flowers around here I'm reluctant to believe that excuse again." He stopped and turned to face her, leaning an elbow against the stone rail. "Care to tell me the truth this time?"

"When will the pretending end?" The current of blue dipped and rolled in her eyes. The same look he had seen during the storm in Bavaria shuddered in their depths, but unlike that night she didn't move toward him. "Aren't you tired of it all?"

Aye, more than you can possibly know. Tired of fighting, of pretending, of answering to someone else's beck and call, of running from the shackles that sought to hold him prisoner to the past. Alfred Whitford's deal was the chance to change his life. Get the man's daughters out, and his debt would be cleared with enough money in his pocket to start over anywhere he chose. The last thing he'd expected was the daughter throwing a wrench into his well-laid plans. In fact, she'd managed to overturn his entire being.

He glanced to her mouth. Those full lips now pressed into a line had demanded everything from him, only softening as his eager response surged to meet her insistence. Was he tired? Aye. Tired of needing to resist her at all costs and failing miserably.

Keep to the task at hand. The sooner it's done, the sooner you can forget about her. "But here we are, and here we'll stay until the agency relents and gets us out of this boggy hole."

The surging current in her eyes stilled. "A few days ago we managed to walk free from the very heart of evilness, a feat I didn't believe possible after staring into Hitler's hideous black eyes." She shuddered and turned to face the water, folding her hands on the rail in front of her. "Now, we're right back where we started, and if I have to smile one more time over some Goebbels movie premiere destined to glorify the Nazi magnificence, I'll scream. I don't know how you do it day after day."

"A dram of whisky and a little bit of fight training at the end of the day help release all that pent-up rage."

She snorted. "I envy you. Grappling around on the ground is at least a useful skill. Planning the next party and practicing dance steps fall woefully short of such value and, if anything, merely increase the frustration after seeing firsthand the danger you and your men put yourselves in every day."

"Not everyone is meant for cloak and dagger or shouldering a rifle. You're doing what no one else can do, and if making small talk with Russian movie stars and hobnobbing with the enemy elite is going to help win this thing, then I can think of no one finer for the job."

"Gee, how thrilling it is to know all my fine education and etiquette lessons are finally reaching their pinnacle of power." Her shoulders drooped as if the stint in Bavaria had added to their invisible burden. "All my life, my name has been offered as a golden key to unlock the gilded echelons of money and popularity, but it's only served to lock me away. Until you gave me a new set of tools to pick the lock and find freedom. All I wanted was to get my sister out of here—make no mistake, that is still my intent—but I can't return to that cage. I've witnessed too much to simply sit at home while this Nazi poison spreads. Not when there's more we can do."

His heart thumped. After all this time, all these struggles together, did she finally wish to work alongside him? Give them a new reason to fight? Blood hummed in his ears at the memory of their kiss in Bavaria and the ghost of it pressing against his lips every night as he tried to sleep. "You really think you can do this?"

She drew herself up and narrowed her eyes, the coolness of her gaze freezing the ghost kiss in its tracks. "I most certainly do." Brushing past him, she strode away, her heels pocking against the pavement in angry clips.

He cursed, but luckily it was lost on the wind kicking up from the river. "Wait a minute. I didn't mean—"

"Oh, I know what you're thinking. Poor little rich girl thinks she can do whatever she wants because she lives in her own plush world of fantasy. Like slipping into Paris when no one else can because of dear Daddy's connections, or that brilliant move to kidnap her sister to Switzerland."

"True, not your finest hour."

They reached the other side of the river, but she didn't slow down. "Believe it or not, I can and will do this."

"Never thought you couldn't. I just don't want you to have to do it alone." The weight of his words hit him in the gut. Not until that moment did he realize their trueness.

Her feet faltered. She swung back around, delicate brows furrowed. "You leave me dizzy at times. Oscillating between concern and wanting to leave me in a gutter."

"Don't think you don't deserve the gutter sometimes."

"How touching."

A low roar split the engine noise of the autos chugging by on the Quai d'Orsay. Two steel-gray motorcycles zoomed by, clearing the way for five char-blackened tanks. The ground shook as the massive beasts rolled by with guns pointed straight ahead, daring any to block their passage. People stopped along the sidewalk to stare at the invaders with repulsion and sadness shivering in their eyes.

"Think they can take whatever they want simply because it pleases them." Though murmured, the viciousness in Kat's voice rang loud as a Howitzer.

Not bothering to turn her rage from the tanks, she stepped off the curb without looking. A horn blared. Barrett jumped forward, grabbed her arm, and yanked her back onto the footpath as a wayward Nazi rider motored by on his cycle.

Kat swooped down and grabbed her handbag that had tumbled into the street. "*Deutsch schweinhund!*"

Shock rang in Barrett's ears at her less than prim and proper outburst. "Never studied German, but I'd guess that wasn't very ladylike."

"You'd guess correct. Please don't mention it. Ever." Shaking, she pulled her arm from his grip. "Thank you for saving my life, I believe for the second time, but it's best we part ways here. Good morning, er, afternoon."

Her cool dismissal snapped the last strand of his patience. He gouged a hand through his hair to keep from reaching out and shaking sense into her. "Can't learn your lesson, can you? When is it going to get through that thick head of yours that you can't navigate this without me? Getting on a train or crossing the street, you need me."

"Strange how you keep saying that. It's beginning to sound like you need the reassurance."

"Hardly. Every second with you proves it." He dropped his hand and slid it into his trouser pocket. Like a match, his irritation sparked and slowly burned out to smoke. "I will get you out of here. You and your sister. And the more you cooperate the sooner I can do it, which means the sooner I can get out of here. Think you can keep yourself out of trouble long enough to accomplish that?"

Indecision warred in her eyes. "Think you can stop patronizing me long enough to make a plan?"

"Deal." He stuck out his hand.

"Deal." She clasped it and shook. "We certainly make a lot of deals. Think we'll keep this one?"

She'd forgotten her gloves. Most likely too frazzled from the row with her sister, she'd walked out into public improperly attired. Or so she would say. He, on the other hand, liked this unbound side of her. The warmth of her bare fingers wrapping around his swam down his palm. "With our track record . . ." He shrugged and let go of her hand before his thoughts crashed in on one another. "Time will tell."

Skirting away from the Les Invalides, they turned onto Rue de l'Université. He counted down to the sixth building on the left and up to the top flat, where the braw fight between the sisters had taken place. Hopefully, Ellie had cooled down by now to no longer endanger the crystal vases.

The familiar yet not quite right smell of bread from the corner bakery drifted down the street. Barrett wrinkled his nose. Rice? If nothing else, wartime rationing gave bakers the chance to stretch their limits for product creativity. War brought out the oddity in every situation. Like the woman next to him. Rigid and stubborn, yet daring without thought to herself.

She stopped before they reached Ellie's building. "Thank you for walking with me, but I'll find the remaining few yards by myself. I'd hate for you to get clocked by a hurtling flowerpot that's meant for me."

"Still that angry, eh?"

"I'd rather not take any chances."

"Appreciate the concern."

A smile flitted across her face. Her body started to move, but her feet stayed rooted to the spot. His pulse quickened at the hesitation.

"Thank you for not giving up on us. I know it's your assignment, and a less than desirable one at that, but it's been nice to have an ally for once. I truly wish to do everything I can to help you."

"I'm not so bad to have around after all, eh?"

"Of late, there are more places you prove a danger to." She briefly touched a hand to her chest, just over her heart, then straightened her lapel and walked away.

It was the closest she'd come to admitting the connection binding them together more than the mission. And it was close to driving him mad. Her gratitude would die a quick death as soon as she found out she was only a paycheck to him. Or so he kept telling himself.

Kat hurried down the street before her mouth ran away with more than she wished to admit. She should never have gone to the Stag in the first place, but not going there meant she had to deal with her frustration alone. And she was tired of being alone. Alone without Barrett.

She'd all but declared the place he'd claimed in her heart, what with that indication of her hand that had moved of its own accord. Of late, too many brave little audacities had sneaked out before she could stop them. Speaking to strangers without proper introductions, walking down the footpath without an escort—an inebriated Ellie not counting—flinging herself at a man not her betrothed. All improprieties forbidden in a lady of good breeding, yet Barrett had swerved his way around the rules, taking her right along with him. Dare she admit to the rush of liberation or the bravado it gave her? Had it been inside her all along waiting for the right person to unlock it?

As she crossed the last block before Ellie's flat, a car door slammed across the street. A sleek black auto with chrome finishes lurked between the closed florist shop and a newspaper stand. A uniformed German stood erect next to the driver's side door while a dark-haired woman draped in green crepe and brown fur trim reapplied her lipstick in the back seat. The woman turned, catching Kat's eye. Her red lips twisted, slicing a knife straight into Kat's gut. Eric's wife. Snapping closed the lid of her compact, the woman fluffed the fur on her shoulders and settled back into the seat with a cold dismissal.

Controlling her thundering heart until she got inside the building, Kat raced up the stairs and panted to a halt on the final floor, where two more guards stood at attention outside Ellie's door. Her lungs burned from the sprint, but she shoved down the flames and glided past them into the flat. Oddly, Pierre wasn't at the door to greet her.

"You will think on this, Eleanor, and in the end you will see I'm right." Eric's voice carried down the hall like a spear. "Tell me you understand."

"I didn't leave England and my father's insufferable rules only to fall into the arms of another man's controlling schemes." From the sound of it, Ellie wasn't playing target to his aim.

"He did not pamper you the way I do. He did not attempt to lay the world at your feet the way I am trying to do."

"What good is the world if you won't allow me to think for myself? When we first met, you hung on my every word, you made me feel special in a way no one else has. But now your voice is the only one that matters. The only opinion of value."

"I am a man of the world. I see how things have been changing while you have been sheltered under a family stifling your potential. Don't you trust me enough to think for both of us now? Eleanor, don't you love me enough?"

Ellie hesitated. "I do, but—"

"Then think of the glory your contribution will bring, what it will mean to me."

"To you and her."

Glee surged in Kat's heart at Ellie's venomous tone. Finally, she was standing up to that horror parading himself as a man. Kat inched farther into the room as Eric struggled with his placation.

"Outwardly to her, *ja*, but it will be you she gives thanks to. You will want for nothing, not ever again."

"Except the freedom to make my own choice."

"Now, *schatz*—"

"Don't call me that. Not when you call her the same thing."

"Eleanor—"

The front door slammed behind Kat. She jumped, knocking her shoulder into the wall. A loud moan of pain flew out uninvited.

"Kat, is that you?"

So much for going unnoticed. Rubbing her aching shoulder, Kat walked into the dining room to find Ellie and Eric squared off on either side of the table. Three cups of coffee sat on the gleaming wood surface, the one next to Eric's smudged with bright-red lipstick.

"I didn't realize we had an audience." A fierce frown carved a line between Eric's eyebrows. "If you don't mind, this conversation is private."

Not about to leave her sister alone with the wolf, Kat moved farther into the room. "I'm sorry. I didn't realize we had visitors."

Ice glinted in his eyes. "I'm hardly a visitor. That would imply my stay is short, and nothing is further from the truth. Your stay, however, I define as a visit."

Ellie circled the table and grabbed Kat's arm, looping her hand through it. "My sister is welcome to stay as long as she wants, and she certainly doesn't have to apologize for coming and going as she pleases even if it doesn't please you. I may have no control over you dismissing the butler, but you will never dismiss her."

A new dread seized Kat. "Where is Pierre?"

"With his family." Eric's unblinking stare gave away nothing. "He had obligations to attend to, and I could no longer keep him from it. He won't be returning."

Ellie hissed. "The next time you take to firing servants, consider my opinion on the matter first. As far as I'm concerned, this is still my home, and I have a right to say what happens here. One of the perks of the deal, wouldn't you say?"

"The deal, *ja*. Perhaps a better one in the 8th arrondissement with a car, should your fulfillment be carried out." Eric's long fingers reached across the table and pushed a small wooden box across to her. "A week of relaxation and reflection should be plenty of time to think over your options. See you then, *liebling*."

Ellie's nails dug into Kat's arm as Eric took his leave, ordering his guards to shut the door behind him as they had so thoughtfully done for her. The clock on the sideboard ticked the hour for teatime, but Kat had no taste for the comforting brew. She needed something much stronger to wipe the confrontation with Eric from her thoughts.

Barrett.

Taking a deep breath that shuddered down to her toes, Ellie unhooked her hand, pulled out her long cigarette holder, and struck a fresh light despite a cigarette still smoldering in the ashtray on the table. She walked to the window and stared down as gray smoke curled from her nose. "Didn't think to see you again so soon."

The sourness that had knotted in Kat's stomach all day slowly loosened at the despondency in her sister's voice. "I don't like quarreling with you."

"Were you with Barrett?"

Kat reached for the box, its top smooth and cool to the touch. "We went for a walk."

"He's good for you." Ellie nodded absently and dragged on her cigarette. The smoke bounced off the window, but she didn't wave it away from her face. "Too bad that can't be said of all men."

Unable to resist, Kat popped open the lid. Nestled on a bed of black velvet lay a slender blue-and-white iron cross with a starburst at the back and black swastika in the middle. *Der Deutschen Mutter* circled the spidery symbol.

"What is this?"

Ellie didn't bother turning from the window. "It's the highest honor awarded to a German woman."

"Why would he give this to you?"

"Because it proves how much he needs me."

Kat moved her thumb over the swastika and the poisonous inscription to block it from view, but the words had burned themselves too deep. *Der Deutschen Mutter.* The German Mother. Dread flooded her veins. "Needs you for what?"

Smoke curled from Ellie's mouth like ashes from a smoldering ruin after a night of unending bombing. Broken, with little hope of lasting until the relief of morning. She didn't answer.

Chapter 16

Kat stuffed her carefully worded letter into the silver-embossed envelope and sealed it shut. Maybe Barrett would reply to this one. She tapped the corner against the side of the desk. But what about the other four that had gone unanswered?

Replacing the fountain pen and paper in its storage box, she pushed out of her chair. Late-morning sun filtered through the gauzy curtains to shine across the water-lily pattern of her room's wallpaper, but she had no eye for the beauty. Not today. Not when it had become her prison as it had five days ago. Crossing the thick white carpet, she stared out the window as hazy clouds drifted across the blue sky. *Tap, tap, tap.* The letter pinged off the windowpane to fill the silence beating down around her.

"Please, please, Barrett. Please reply. Let me know you're all right." Unable to explain to him why she couldn't see him until next week, she hoped he would read between the delicate lines and not do anything rash to further provoke Eric's wrath.

She pressed a hand to the glass, her warmth seeping through its coolness until she dropped it back to her side, leaving a fleeting handprint. Alone, surrounded on all sides by panels. Just like her. Just as she always was. Until Barrett came. The only one to stand next to her without fear, without fleeing at the first hint of distress. Simply to stand next to her. When the time came to leave Paris, would he still . . .

Whirling, she rang the little silver bell on her nightstand. A few seconds later, Sylvie popped in. "*Oui*, mademoiselle?"

Kat held out the letter. "Another one. Are you sure they're getting to him?"

Sylvie's eyes dropped to the ground as she nodded. "*Oui.* My contact assures me that they are given to the right man."

"But there's never a reply for me?"

Sylvie shook her head, still eyeing the floor. She held out her hand.

Kat's fingers crimped the edge of the envelope. What if he didn't think it necessary to reply? Or perhaps he thought it might cause more problems if he did and Eric found out?

"Mademoiselle?" Sylvie's eyes flickered up, concern in their brown depths.

"What? Oh." Kat smoothed the edge of the crumpled envelope against her skirt and dropped it into the maid's waiting hand. "Thank you, Sylvie. I don't know what we would do without your help, especially since you're the only one allowed to come and go." She dropped her voice. "Have you heard from Pierre?"

"*Non.* No one speaks of it. There are too many gone to keep count of."

"And your family?"

"Well enough, mademoiselle. They do not go out anymore. It is safer to stay inside."

"Are they getting enough food? What about clothing? I have several blouses in my wardrobe—"

"*Non, merci.* The wages Major von Schlegel pays are more than enough for me to keep them provided for. For now."

Kat took the girl's hand. It was ice cold. "Please, if there is ever anything you need . . . Anything at all, let me know. I want to help however I can. I know people who may be able to help. Do you understand?"

"*Oui.*"

"Please be careful out there."

The girl's cheeks paled. Yanking her hand back, she bobbed a short curtsy and hurried out of the room like a frightened rabbit.

In the living room, Ellie stretched out on the couch with a dozen fashion magazines scattered around the cushions and an ashtray with two smoking cigarettes on the floor next to her. "I'm so bored."

Kat swooped up the ashtray and stubbed out the burning sticks. "Setting the flat on fire isn't the answer."

"Smoking is my only release. And it annoys Eric. Anything that annoys him right now is fine by me."

"Then maybe we *should* burn down the flat. Can't think of anything to peeve him more." She gathered the magazines and stacked them on the glass coffee table.

"Stop tidying. If I see you trying to organize one more thing, I'll go crazy." Ellie swung her bare feet off the couch and ran a hand through her hair. Usually coiffed to platinum perfection, each passing day had brought on a new round of laziness. Today it looked like it hadn't seen a comb. "Five days we've been here. Trapped in my own home like a prisoner with the building surrounded by his guards. What does he think we're going to do? Shimmy down the drainpipe?"

She leaped to her feet and fumbled in her satin robe pocket for a fresh cigarette. Lighting it, she paced around the coffee table. "Who does Eric think he is? My lord and master? My warden?"

"Yes and yes." Kat pushed the edge of a magazine in line with the others as Ellie turned her back.

"I'm going to tell him I don't like it one bit. He can't treat me like this, not if he ever hopes to earn my affection again." Gray smoke billowed around Ellie's wiry hair. "If I even allow him to."

Kat frowned. "After this week you'd still consider it?"

"No. I don't know. I'm just so angry at him." Puffing her cigarette, Ellie marched to the locked front door and banged on it. "Do you hear that? I'm angry, so the next time he comes to this door you can tell him to turn right around because there's no welcome for him on this side."

"I doubt the guards on the other side of that door understood you."

Ellie added a kick for good measure. "Maybe not the words, but I'm more than sure they understood the tone."

"It's not the guards you need to yell at, it's Eric. Tell him you're done."

"Easier said than done. Once he takes hold of something, it's not easy for him to let go."

"Ellie, you're not some *thing*. You're a grown woman, so stop acting like a child about this and end it." Kat threw up her hands in exasperation. "What man professes that he cares for you and shows it by locking you in your room to think on the ways you've disappointed him?"

"This is what happens to people who defy him. Who dare to tell him no."

"He locked us up because of that business with his wife. Whatever she propositioned, as your fellow prisoner I have a right to know. How else are we to 'ruminate on our future for our own good' when I don't know what we're intended to ruminate on?"

Ellie sank onto the cream upholstered wingback chair, dropping her face into her hand while her cigarette dangled from the other. "Stop yelling at me. Please."

But Kat wasn't done. Not by a long shot, and Ellie's self-pitying did little to assuage the frustration too long bottled. "Why do you put up with this?"

"Because he takes care of me. He lets me be free. You know what it was like growing up back home. Every move and decision was dictated to us. If it didn't have Father's approval, it ended before it ever began."

"Eric has proven no different. From one controlling man to another. For once in your spoiled life, stop and think about what you're doing before it's too late."

"Eric loves me. Like no one ever has."

"This isn't love, Ellie."

Ellie's head snapped up, eyes bright with defense. "And how would you know?"

"Because I know what the absence of it feels like. The twisted ways it contorts itself into making you believe a lie that you wished so desperately were true."

Marching to the window, Kat yanked back the gossamer curtains and threw up the sash. Cool air rushed in to dispel the cramped stuffiness. She placed her palms on the sill and took a deep breath. The air was filled with the stench of damp concrete and car exhaust, but at least it wasn't stale cigarette smoke. Five days was too long to be cooped up with any one person. Especially an obstinately blind sister.

Ferreting secrets from the enemy over the past few months had left her with a reliable scale to value what mattered and what didn't. Tiptoeing around feelings and people-pleasing fell into the *didn't* category. And good riddance. It was exhausting.

Who would've thought Kathleen Whitford could break the rules of conventional politeness and enjoy it?

Several long minutes dragged by before Ellie's voice reached out to her. "I'm sorry. I've dragged you into this mess and now you're miserable too. At least before you had Barrett to cheer you up, but now Eric's taken him away as well. It's what Eric does. He takes things away until you have no reason left but to look to him. I used to have friends, you know. Beautiful, wonderful French friends. But Eric didn't like them. Said they were too unruly. One day they stopped coming to see me. He had forbidden their company, then set about choosing who I should be spending time with."

Possessively persuasive. Eric's charms seemed never to cease.

Kat's fingers curled onto the stone ledge outside the window as the weight in her heart shifted to the place Barrett so often occupied. "I'll see Barrett in a few days, and I can explain why I haven't been around. That is, if our jailor deems our confinement sufficient."

A swift breeze swept by, blowing the hair from her shoulders. Though carrying the scent of freedom beyond her four walls, it did little to dislodge the uncertainty hanging in the air. She needed something much stronger than a south wind. Her fingers curled tighter, her nails biting into the stone ledge. She wanted Barrett. Longed for his solid reassurance that calmed her shaking fears and set the world to right again, to feel his secure arms around her once more, his steady heartbeat beneath her cheek. To hear him say her name in that soft burr that melted her soul down to its core.

A key turned in the front door lock. Heart dropping, Kat turned. It was much too quick for Sylvie to have met her contact and returned by now.

Eric slid in the open door, a tight smile on his waxy face. A yellow-and-white-striped bag dangled from his hand. "*Guten morgen.* Anyone home?"

"Where else would we be?" From the couch, Ellie stared at him through slitted eyes.

Eric's smile didn't falter as he closed the door behind him. But not before Kat saw the muzzle tips of the armed guards outside. "I come bearing gifts."

"We have all the excitement we can bear in here, thanks." Cigarette smoke curled from Ellie's nose.

Walking into the room, Eric swung the bag back and forth as if to entice her. "It's from your favorite shop on Rue Leroux. With the birdbath out front. Remember? You always broke off pieces of your cake to toss to the birds."

"I remember. I always met you there after you had a meeting at Gestapo headquarters right around the corner."

"*Ja*, I suppose it is right around the corner."

"They're not looking to expand, are they? I'd hate to think of the Gestapo taking over a patisserie. No telling what kind of ingredients they'd use. Black market, or maybe whatever they find leftover in the house they raided the night before."

Eric's smile flattened. The pastry bag dropped to the coffee table. "That's enough."

"Is it?"

"Eleanor, I don't wish to warn you again, but one more word—"

Ellie leaned forward, tapping her ashes into the pastry bag. "One more word and what? You'll lock me away? Too late for that."

His face mottling red, Eric clenched his hands at his sides until they shook. Ellie leaned farther back into the couch cushions without the sense to look frightened.

Kat stepped forward, bringing his wrath around to her. "Eric, please consider that we've been in here for five days and tempers are less than ideal."

The buttons down the front of his tunic swelled on a deep breath. Slowly, his hands stopped shaking as the red drained from his face. "Ever the voice of reason, Kathleen."

"Reason or not, an entire week of punishment is unacceptable for two grown women. Please reconsider and allow us to go out again." Kat swung her gaze to Ellie. "Ellie will be so much happier."

The lines drawing Eric's mouth flat softened. "All I want is for her to be happy, but she must realize that. Truly understand that without distractions telling her otherwise. I gave my word for one week of contemplation on the proposition, and I cannot go back on it."

Ellie snorted. "That is the most ridiculous, selfish thing I've heard from you. And that's saying a lot."

His pale eyebrows spiked. "'Selfish'? For wanting you to see the happiness I offer to you on a gilded platter? I'm trying to give you the world, but you slump in here as if life's misery perches on your shoulder. Really, Eleanor. The least you could do is try for my sake. Wash your hair perhaps, cast off that robe you've no doubt worn since yesterday."

"The day before, actually."

Around the coffee table in a blink, he grabbed her arm and hauled her to her feet. "That changes immediately. The green dress with the wide belt and matching shoes I bought you for Valentine's. It'll wipe away the sallowness from your cheeks." He turned to Kat as he pushed

Ellie toward the bedroom. "I had hoped you could take better care of her than this. Seems the job is best left with me."

Kat pressed her palms against her sides to keep from scratching her nails down his face. If she angered him now, there was no telling what he would do. His power gave him infinite solutions. "Eric, please let her be. This has not been an easy day."

Eric's hand rose from Ellie's arm and brushed a stray hair from her cheek. With exquisite tenderness, he tucked it safely behind her ear. Ellie jerked away, but Eric grasped her chin and held tight. "You need not concern yourself any longer. If you truly desire what's best for all. And I do mean all, Kathleen."

Brick crumbled beneath Barrett's crushing grip as he peered around the side of the building. Several doors down, Kat leaned out of a window, arms braced on the ledge and pale face drawn tight. Five days and he hadn't heard from or seen her. Five days of losing his mind. He should never have left her to enter that flat alone.

Jean, the watchman he'd placed on the block to keep an eye on the girls, had reported unusual activity around the building. More guards, only the servants coming and going, the window closed up, and Eric stopping by only twice when he was accustomed to visiting every day, often with overnight stays.

At first Barrett contributed Kat's silence to their rather heated conversation on the bridge. But it had ended pleasantly enough, hadn't it? She had said she was glad he was there. She had wanted to say more, something that was tinging her cheeks a rosy red with the mere thought, but she'd held back. Deep down in a place he forbade himself to venture, he had hoped she was glad to have him there as more than an ally.

"*Papier, m'sieur?*"

Barrett turned to the newspaper vendor behind him. The boy brandished a smudged copy of that morning's paper. Barrett started to shake his head until he noted the hole in the kid's shoe where his big toe stuck out. Rooting in his pocket, he fished out five francs.

The boy's large eyes rounded. "*Non*, too much."

Shrugging, Barrett pressed the bit into his grimy hand. "All I got, kid."

No doubt fearing his benefactor would change his mind, the boy skipped on, and Barrett handed the newspaper to a man passing by. He'd read that morning's headline and had no desire to go over the lying details that bragged of a German victory in Belgium.

Kat gazed over the tops of the buildings in the direction of the Stag. Was she imagining seeing it? His pulse kicked. Did she imagine seeing him? Her head whipped around to something behind her before swiveling back to the window. Her hands clenched. Whatever was going on behind her, it was taking an effort not to involve herself. Most likely Eric. Less than ten minutes inside and he was already causing problems. No surprise there. If there was a problem—and her face told him there were too many to count—why didn't she tell him? Why didn't she phone or send a letter? Surely one of those servants could have ferreted one out. Their families served in the Resistance faction of the 2nd arrondissement.

Curling her hands over the ledge, Kat turned in his direction. He inched away from the building, far enough out that she might see him but not enough to draw the suspicion of the guards posted by the front door. If she could see him, maybe then she would know he hadn't abandoned her. That he was close enough should she need him.

He had taken another step, raising his hand, when the front door opened and out walked the little brown-haired maid. What was her name? Sophie? Sylvia? Kat turned back inside as the maid looked left and right and hurried to the next block with head down and arms crossed over her chest. She was his best bet of finding out what was going on inside that flat. Tilting his hat to block the side of his face from the guards, he shoved his hands in his pockets and followed the girl from across the street.

Three blocks down she stopped on the corner, glancing left and right as Eric's car pulled up next to her. Leaning through the passenger window, she handed the driver a sealed envelope and raced back to the flat.

Chapter 17

"I hate this music." Ellie swigged back another glass of champagne. "I hate this food, I hate that art, and I hate . . . this dress." Lolling her head to the side, she plucked at the pale-pink pleats across her chest. "Makes me look like Aunt Mildred."

Kat grabbed the crystal glass from Ellie's hand before it spilled onto the marble floor. "We don't have an Aunt Mildred."

"Well, if we did, this is what she'd wear. Dusty old spinster. Can you believe he made me wear this?"

Maneuvering around to the back of a seven-foot-tall plaster replica of the Strasbourg Castle, Kat handed the glass to a white-jacketed waiter and waved him off as he offered yet another libation. "Yes. He's controlling. Haven't you figured that out by now, or do we need another week of solitary confinement?"

Ellie shook her head. "I can't stand another second in there. Those walls are closing in on me."

"Me too, so let's try to behave and not spill our glasses all over the ambassador's coattails."

It was their first night out since their weeklong imprisonment. The previous evening a box had arrived with Ellie's curtain-like dress with a note from Eric asking her to please wear it as she joined him in welcoming the party chancellery, Martin Bormann, and Goebbels to the National Museum of Architecture and Monuments. A postscript at the bottom stated that Kat was also invited as Ellie's escort.

Scanning over the slicked-back heads of the Nazi officials crowding the floor, she spotted Eric standing next to a plaster collection of saints from Notre-Dame de Reims. Dressed in his most starched uniform, with medals gleaming, he preened like a peacock as he attempted to explain the importance of the masterful works surrounding them. Shining like a statue, his wife had poured herself into a gold-lamé halter-neck dress with the side seams nearly bursting from her added curves. Her dark eyebrows arched in challenge at Kat before sliding back to her prize, Eric.

Disgusted, Kat looked away. She was no escort. She was a referee to keep the mistress and wife from having a go right in front of Eric's superiors and ruining his night. And what a night it was. All the top brass had assembled to oversee the unveiling of new plans for the museum. A place that had once held plaster recreations of French Medieval and Renaissance monument art, it was now destined to house German architectures. *Wonder if they plan to tear down the frescos and erect an iron eagle?*

She should make an effort to remember everyone's names in case the information proved valuable to their London contacts.

"Oh, look. There's Franz who does something that I can't bother to remember." Ellie pointed to a rounded fellow stuffing his face with cocktail shrimp. The buttons down the front of his tunic strained with the added morsels. "And look. He brought his mistress with no sign of a wife. She's probably doing her duty back in Dusseldorf by raising their ten Aryan brats. See, these are the kinds of people Eric wishes me to make friends with. Old buzzards."

Kat shot her a quelling look. "Keep your voice down. People are looking."

"I don't care."

Kat yanked Ellie around to face the window before her outbursts brought over the black boots to march them before the Gestapo. Outside, patrol boats paddled down the Seine, flashing their lights along the banks in hopes of catching curfew breakers. "You need to. Fuming over your self-inflicted misery as a mistress is one thing, but sneering at their Aryan philosophy is another."

"You don't think it's right. One race superior to another and all that." Ellie's pale reflection drooped in the window. "Eric tried convincing me, but I simply couldn't buy it. I mean, the hatmaker back in Berkshire was an undesirable, but I never noticed her growing fangs. She picked out the loveliest ribbons for me."

A patrol light skimmed up the sides of the Eiffel Tower, its form tall and ghostly in the misty night air. Goosebumps prickled over Kat's skin. "No, I don't think it's right, but we're in the minority here, so the less they know of our true feelings the better. And no human is an undesirable." *Unless it's Eric.*

"That's my Kitty Kat. Always trying to do the right thing."

"It's exhausting."

"So stop."

"I can't. It's ingrained in me. Like teatime and the British flag."

Ellie giggled. "I believe that's the most English thing I have ever heard." The smile slipped from her face. "Sometimes I think about home. All my friends, how I could understand what everyone was saying and could recognize all the food on my plate."

Kat pushed down the bubbles of hope popping up. "Do you think about going back?"

"Sometimes. And then Mother's and Father's reprimands come flying at me like a hailstorm, and I remember why I left. I never wanted to fit the mold they had made for me, but now look at me." She spread the pleats of her skirt. "Just like you said, I let myself become a ball of clay to someone else all over again. Under the misguidings of love. A glutton for repeated mistakes."

"Going back doesn't mean you need to live under their roof or fit any kind of mold but the one you create."

"Where else am I going to stay? The only way I can afford my lifestyle here is because Eric foots the bill, and now that's all about to change."

The reminder smashed Kat's bubbles of hope. She moved closer, but it still wasn't close enough to block out the dark world pressing in all around them. "I wish you would tell me what it is. I hate seeing you mope around in misery day after day. Whatever he's promised you can't be good if it brings you so much agony."

Ellie shook her head as a silvery tear slipped down her rouged cheek. "Doesn't matter anymore. I don't have many options here, and no good man will take me back in Berkshire."

Kat brushed away the next tear trickling down Ellie's chin. "We never have to go back to Berkshire again. We can rent a place in the city. We'll be the two sisters who collect doilies and cats."

"I hate cats."

"So do I."

"No, I've feathered my bed, and now it's time to lie in it. Who knows. Maybe I'll get a bigger flat out of the deal." Ellie patted away another tear and smiled, but there was no light in her eyes. "Excuse me for a moment. Need to powder my nose before all these sauerkraut vapors give me a shine."

"Ellie—" Kat's hand reached out to grab her, but her sister disappeared around the corner before she could stop her.

So close. No matter how hard she tried, she couldn't seem to yank them free of the millstone Eric had thrown around them. What she wouldn't give to tie a weight around him and knock him into the Seine. Atrocious man. Why must he always make things so difficult?

"Are you enjoying the gallery?"

Kat jumped, banging her elbow into the window. Pain screamed down her arm, but curbed to alarm as Eric grinned before her like a wolf cornering a lamb. She notched her chin up in the most unimpressed way her mother had taught her. "Architecture was never a passion of mine, though I appreciate the beauty and skill."

"Did you see the new design plans?"

"I did." His head inched forward, willing her to go on. "I admire each new artist putting his stamp on the world, but I believe the collection is complete as is. Anything new or added would take away from the original intent."

"That's what I like about you, Kathleen. Straightforward yet diplomatic. You should consider a career in politics."

"If their on-goings didn't prove so disgusting, I might consider it."

He smiled, a valiant effort for one with no soul. "I hate to see you standing here alone. Might I introduce you to a friend of mine? He's in town for a few days and is in desperate need of a proper guide for all the must-sees Paris has to offer."

Revulsion slithered up her throat. She'd seen the roving looks she and Ellie got while at the parties and knew of the desperate women who sold themselves to keep their families from starving. She'd die before draping herself over the arm of a Nazi, no matter the information she might glean from such an encounter. "While I appreciate the consideration, I'm afraid I'm too much of a bore to properly entertain company. That is Ellie's department."

"Eleanor is already spoken for."

The challenge hung in the air like a shard of ice. Its coldness slithered out to chill the blood pumping around Kat's heart. "So am I."

The ice surged into Eric's eyes. "Ah, I nearly forgot. Mr. Anderson. I know it's been a long week without seeing him, but hopefully the quiet days have been enough to inspire an understanding of what's truly important and what should be left behind."

Kat curled her fingers into the folds of her navy crepe skirt. The beaded floral motif dug under her nails. "You think I needed that lesson along with Ellie?"

"Not precisely, but Eleanor couldn't stay there by herself. She's not a solitary creature."

"No, she isn't, and at times like these she needs all the support she can muster."

The overhead lighting slid off Eric's thickly pomaded hair as he tilted his head. "Very admirable. A trait I hope to uphold upon your departure. Incidentally, you've yet to tell us when that is."

"As long as my sister needs me, I remain here. Excuse me, please."

"Of course. And don't forget to smile, Kathleen. This is a party."

Kat walked away, determined to keep her pace even and unhurried despite her hammering heart. The minute he noticed her losing control was the second she'd lose this cat-and-mouse game he was resolved to play out. Every nerve in her body shivered with warning as the creature closed in to strike.

Where was Ellie?

Leaving the red walls of the Galerie Davioud behind, she picked up her pace in search of the nearest ladies' room. "Ellie, are you in here?" Her voice bounced off the empty stalls.

Perhaps she'd sought out a quieter hall without the strains of Wagner blaring in her ear. Oh, how the Germans loved their Wagner. But two more galleries and still no sign of her sister. Kat's pumps clicked against the marble floor like anxious ticks on a clock. Where had that girl gone?

A dim light glowed on the cold white floor where a large wooden door stood ajar. A nameplate on the door read *ADMINISTRATION*.

Kat pushed open the door. "*Excusez moi, je cherche*—There you are. I've been looking everywhere for you, and so is that nightmare you call a boyfriend. Why are you hiding in here?"

The single lit lamp on the clunky desk outlined Ellie's form in the center of the room, turning her bleached hair to silver. Floor-to-ceiling bookshelves stuffed with ancient volumes lined the entire room except for the west wall with two long windows facing the outside garden. A low couch stretched in front of the windows with a dark figure lounging in the corner.

"Oh, dear. I know he has his trouble spots, but a nightmare?" The figure leaned slightly, catching the edge of her golden straps in the lamplight. "Maybe a little too far, *ja*?"

Ice sliced down Kat's back. Eric's wife. Moving into the room, Kat stood next to a shaking Ellie. Kat resisted the impulse to grab her hand for comfort and instead slipped the ice from her back to her tone. "No, I don't believe it is too far a conclusion."

The darkness of the room couldn't hide the smirk of the woman's blood-red lips. "My cousin Eva Braun told me of your directness when she met you at Berghof."

Kat startled at the revelation of kin, but quickly recovered. Now was not the time to pull out the family tree. "Odd, I've only recently discovered your existence."

The woman's crossed leg jiggled as her hooded eyes raked Kat up and down. Flicking ashes from the tip of her cigarette onto the floor, she held it to her stained lips and puffed. "Then I believe a round of introductions is in order." Puffing again, she raised her pencil-thin eyebrows at Ellie. "Would you care to do the honors?"

The tremor from Ellie's body leaped to her throat. "No, I wouldn't care to at all."

The thin eyebrows lifted higher into the dark hairline. "I see directness runs in the family. Not sure if I'll appreciate that trait, but it can be curbed under the right hand." Flicking more ashes to the floor, she turned her gaze back to Kat. "I'm Hildegarde von Schlegel."

"Kathleen Whitford." Kat almost laughed at the absurdity. If not for the woman's heavily accented voice, they might have been back in a London drawing room. Of course, social introductions never occurred in dark back rooms with one's sister's boyfriend's wife.

"I would say it's a pleasure to meet you, but I think we're all honest enough to know that's not true. You understand that, don't you, Kathleen? As with me, your pragmatic sense forces you to see things as they are to decide the best outcome, unlike others who prefer to dream. My husband, for example."

Kat crossed her arms over her chest, protecting her vulnerable spots in case the woman jumped to attack. "I never took Eric for a dreamer. The starch in his uniform prevents any kind of ridiculousness."

"That's true in a sense, but Eric believes in a world where he can have his cake and eat it too. No world like that exists. Something I've been chatting with your sister about."

Ellie's hands clenched to fists. "Spin your stories all you like, but I won't change my mind. Eric doesn't love you."

"Oh, I'm quite sure he does, at least in his own way. If he didn't, he would never have agreed to this deal for me." Hildegarde crossed one leg atop the other, swishing the golden material around her ankles. "You see, love isn't about flowers or sweet whispers in the dark. It's about facing the cold truth together. About rising against the injustices of life together and sacrificing everything so the other may succeed. You can't possibly understand this because, like Eric, you live in a dream world where every problem is worked out for you. It takes realists like me, and your sister, to keep the cogs turning."

"You mean keep the arms twisted."

Hildegarde shrugged a bared shoulder. "Whatever it takes, but a medal and lavish accommodations are hardly arm twists. They are rewards for a generous service to be provided."

Kat stepped forward, forcing Ellie behind her shoulder. "And what service is this?"

"One of the highest honors for the Fatherland."

"Ellie isn't German."

"*Nein*, but the blond hair and blue eyes certainly are."

"A bottle of peroxide works wonders."

Hildegarde's dark eyes narrowed as smoke spiraled from her mouth. "Eric said you come swooping in every time the girl needs saving. A bit of a cumbersome trip coming all the way from England this time."

"I hardly consider spending time with my sister in Paris cumbersome."

The blood-red lip curled up. "Spending time—is that what you're calling this?"

The hairs sprang up on the back of Kat's neck. She smoothed the peplum skirt of her cream jacket to steady her trembling hands.

"I would think scrambling after your philandering husband just as cumbersome."

Hildegarde snapped to her feet. A few inches taller and several stone heavier, she towered over Kat like a shimmering monolith. Her rich brown hair was piled high atop her head, her heart-shaped face was perfectly powdered and rouged like porcelain, and thick black lashes crowded her brown eyes. Without the sneer she was quite beautiful.

"You know nothing. This conversation is private. Get out."

"Rudeness to my sister won't win you any favors, Frau von Schlegel. Not from me." Ellie stepped away from Kat's protecting shoulder. The ruffles on her bodice fluttered from her frantic heartbeat. "I'd watch my tongue from now on."

Hildegarde's red nails bunched the golden fabric at her sides. The seams groaned in protest. "Ungrateful child. Do you know the number of strings I had to pull to get that medal without proof?"

Ellie's laughter screeched like nails on glass. "'Ungrateful'? You should be the one throwing yourself at my feet. I don't want that ugly medal."

Fingers turning white, Hildegarde twisted forward like a gnarled branch. "You think I'm grateful for having to grovel in this situation? To throw my last shred of hope into your filthy English basket?"

"It's not my fault your husband came looking for me because you're barren."

Cold sickness grabbed Kat by the stomach and twisted. She grabbed Ellie's arm, forcing her to look at her. "Ellie, what deal has Eric made you?"

Ellie tried to wrench her arm free, but Kat held fast. Ellie shook her head, not meeting her eye.

Hildegarde's contorting rage simmered as she stood straight and tall, her molten dress glistening in the lamplight. Sparks of triumph flared in her dark eyes. "She's going to bear my and Eric's children. The perfect Aryan family."

Chapter 18

S he's *where?*"

"At a party. Jean saw them leave an hour ago with instructions to the driver for the Museum of Architecture. Said they didn't look happy, though you'd think they would after a week locked up." Sam flicked a speck of dust from his bony shoulder as the warm-up notes of the band drifted up through the floor planks. "What do you suppose the party is for?"

Barrett yanked the tie from his neck and threw it on the stack of papers cluttering his desk. "Nazis. Does it really matter the reason?"

With pointed eyebrows, Sam picked up the discarded tie. "You really should leave this on."

"And you really should mind your own business."

Undisturbed, Sam dangled the tie like a fish on a line. "Our customers expect to see you during the band's second set."

"They can expect all they want. I've no mind to trot down there and parade around for their amusement."

Grabbing his bottle of Ballantine's, he ripped the cap off and pressed the cool bottle to his lips. No time for a glass tonight. He needed the relief now. Between Kat and the Germans downstairs, he couldn't decide who the winning contributor to his urgency was. Not that he would consider anything about this night as amusing. Far from it. Over the past three days, the women had trickled out, leaving only soldiers to finish their pints at smoke-clouded tables. Sam and the band played as lively as ever, but the room once filled with clapping and after-hours laughing had grown thick with quiet. The customers now sat straight in their chairs, one hand around their glasses and the other dropped to their knees. With feet braced apart, their eyes moved to and fro with calculated interest.

Barrett took another swig that burned down his throat. No, he was anything but amused tonight. "Don't you have music to play?"

"I could ask the same of you."

"What do you think I'm doing now?"

"Trying to stifle your anger that your girl is at a party hosted by a Nazi whose thumb she happens to be under."

Barrett stared at him for a long second, wishing he could deny it. "If you weren't so right most of the time, I'd fire you."

"And if you were any other kind of patron, I'd have resigned."

"Glad we're on the same page."

"As am I." Grinning, Sam folded the tie back onto the desk and left.

Lifting the bottle to his mouth, Barrett caught his reflection in the glass window. Same brown hair, same shoulders, same grip on the bottle's neck.

He was his father.

Disgusted, he screwed the lid back on and dropped the bottle into the wastebasket. No. He wasn't his father. He wouldn't crawl into the deep end of the bottle in search of relief from his problems. He'd meet them head-on.

But first he'd apologize to Sam for his bitterness moments ago. Solidarity had been a comfort throughout Barrett's life. He got along well enough with others, but he never allowed himself to be a part of them. It was simpler, cleaner, without the entanglements. Sam was the first person he'd been able to sit down and share a drink and a laugh with and not get annoyed. Best not to annoy his only mate now.

Then he needed to see Kat. See with his own eyes that she was all right after her weeklong sentence, and pray to God Eric wasn't there. He'd kill the man, if that was what he was, with his bare hands if he saw him too soon.

The beating rhythm of a drum stuttered to a halt. Odd. Hugo never lost count or dropped a stick. Feet thundered up the stairs until they crashed through his door. A white-faced Corbin followed by six of the kitchen staff tumbled in.

Corbin threw the door closed and shoved the boys into the washroom. "Nazis are raiding the bar! They've come for the fighters. Anyone harboring them will be pronounced guilty on the spot. They're here for your blood, *Patron*."

Barrett yanked open the secret door behind the washroom mirror and shoved the washers and Corbin into the passage. "Get the lantern on the wall. Keep quiet, and make your way all the way down. Don't do anything until I get there."

He started to close the door, but Corbin shoved it open. His eyes filled with panic. "Where are you going?"

"To get more people."

"Too late. The Germans are overrunning the place. We barely made it up here without them seeing us." Heavy boots sounded on the stairs outside the office door. Corbin grabbed Barrett's arm and yanked him into the secret passage, sealing the door behind them. "We tried. It's too late, *Patron*."

Barrett's curse echoed in the darkness. Terrorized breaths pounded off the close walls around them. Fumbling for the lantern on the wall, he drew the lighter from his pocket and struck it. The orange light bounced around to the frightened faces.

Holding the lantern up high, he made a quick examination of each. "All right, lads? Keep quiet and follow me. Careful now."

It seemed an age ago when he'd traversed this stair with Kat clinging to his hand. Thank God she wasn't here now as the sound of breaking glass and tumbling tables bumped through the walls as they picked their way farther down. He tried to focus on the steep steps in front of him as his mind raced with what was happening to his men on the other side of the walls. Worrying did no good now, not when he needed to get the handful behind him to safety.

The door to the cellar loomed before him. Pressing his ear to the cold wood, he listened for movement. Corbin's quick breaths shot across the back of his neck. Nothing on the outside, but that didn't mean the Germans weren't close by. The Resistance training room was the most fortified place in the area, but he couldn't risk creeping out just as soldiers came down the stairs to catch them. That room stored too many lists of identities and he wasn't about to put them at risk.

He turned to the men behind him. Boys, really. Though some of his trainees, this was their first real encounter with the enemy. "We have to leave by the sewer. There's a grate in the corner to the right." He moved the lantern to highlight Luc, his youngest but also the swiftest. "Move the grate as quietly as you can and slip down. The rest of you will follow on my signal. Be quick and watch your feet. They'll be down here in a matter of minutes."

Listening once more to ensure the cellar was empty, Barrett pushed open the secret door. Darkness. Motioning Luc behind him, they crept to the edge of the oversized wine barrel. Barrett pointed to the corner where the sewer grate was. Soundless as a rabbit, Luc slipped out and opened their escape route. One by one the boys disappeared down into the hole. As Corbin hurried across the stone floor, he slipped, thumping into the stack of barrels next to the grate.

Light flooded the stairwell to the upstairs. "*Was wer das?*"

Barrett motioned Corbin into the sewer. Extinguishing the lantern, he pulled the *sgian dubh* from his sock and crouched in the barrel. His heart hammered in his ears, drowning out all thought beyond survival.

Two pairs of feet moved slowly down the stairs as a flashlight bounced before them. The yellow beam skipped across the stone floor and swung over the tops of the barrels and bottles lining the walls. The two corporals, one heavyset and fair and the other tall and bony, moved along the rows to read the labels and peer between the cracks.

The fat one shrugged and pointed back up the stairs. "*Es gibt nichts hier unten. Komm schon.*"

His companion moved closer to the corner where the grate still gaped open. The small Scottish blade twitched in Barrett's hand as the boy leaned down to examine the bottom row of red wines. Tapping the bottle's neck in appreciation, he leaned farther over . . . until the edge of his flashlight beam danced off the edge of the grate. Straightening, he jerked the light to the gaping hole in the floor. From the short distance, Barrett saw the calculations of a soldier behind his dark eyes. Gripping his knife tight, he leaned forward to spring.

Slinging his rifle behind his shoulder, the soldier squatted down and peered into the hole. It proved to be a fatal mistake. A flash of metal surged out and sliced across his exposed neck. Luc's blond head popped out as he stabbed the end of his blade into the soldier's chest. The corporal fell back, clutching at the red spilling from his neck.

With a guttural cry, his companion raced across the cellar with his rifle aimed straight for Luc. Barrett sprang from his hiding place and rammed the boy into the floor. A bone crunched on the soldier's shoulder as they hit the hard stone with Barrett landing on top of him.

Howling in pain, the boy raised his knee up to jab Barrett in the stomach. Barrett rolled off and kicked the rifle aside just as the German grabbed his ankle and yanked him back down. They grappled, but the busted arm sealed the corporal's fate. Lifting his *sgian dubh* high, Barrett stabbed straight down into the German heart. Guilt hit him like an arrow as he watched the life disappear from the boy's round face. Another shred of his humanity gone in this bloody war effort.

Yanking the blade from its hold, he wiped it on the uniformed sleeve and threw himself into the sewer before he had time to think on it.

Chapter 19

"And where do you propose we go? Switzerland or back to England? I doubt they have ships bobbing in the harbor ready to head into enemy lands."

Having fled the nightmare party on the plea of a headache right after encountering Eric's wife, Kat hadn't wasted a second thought as they scurried back to the apartment. No more missions. No more polishing of their good name. No more jumping to someone else's command. They were leaving. That night.

Kat tossed a blouse into the open suitcase, uncaring of the jumbled mess within. She could repack it later after they escaped this horrible place. "Ships sail on waters, not lands."

"Waters, then. Is that it? We're sailing?" Ellie paced in the doorway of Kat's room. Her pale hands wrung together as if squeezing the life from them.

Kat didn't answer. If she knew Eric half as well as she thought she did, he most likely had the apartment bugged. That and she didn't want to frighten Ellie with the threadbare plan she'd thrown together on the ride back to the apartment. The situation would remain calm as long as she appeared in control.

She grabbed a pair of lacy underthings and hurled them into the suitcase to steady her shaking hands. Slamming the lid shut, she locked it tight and tucked the key into her pocket.

"Are you packed?"

Ellie stopped pacing and stared. "Was I supposed to?"

"Unless you want to leave Paris with nothing but that hideous frilly gown on your back, then I suggest you throw a few things into a suitcase."

Panic flared in Ellie's eyes, wide in her pale face. "But I don't know what to—"

Kat brushed past her into the hall and down two doors before turning into Ellie's room. Cream, gold, and satin, it shimmered like a frozen palace in the moonlight that streamed in from the floor-length windows. "Get your suitcase and put it on the bed. Grab two sturdy outfits, one pair of sensible shoes, and a few underthings. I'll get the toiletries."

Hurrying into the adjoining bathroom, Kat ignored the man's razor and comb perfectly lined next to the sink and plucked out a few essentials from the cabinet. A light popped on, reflecting in the mirror. "Turn that off! Do you want everyone to see what we're packing?"

Thumping came from the other side of the wall. "Sorry, but it's so hard to see in this closet without a little light."

"Make do." Tossing the toiletries into the suitcase, she noted the outfits Ellie had selected. White and yellow with chiffon sleeves and pleated hems. She yanked them out and tossed them on the floor. "Find something else that doesn't stand out and that you won't notice if it gets dirty."

Ellie's head poked out of the closet. "Gets dirty? Why are we getting dirty?"

"Just do it and hurry!" Kat disappeared back in her room to grab the extra cash and passports she had hidden under the bed as Ellie continued to thump around. Tucking the precious commodities into her girdle, she patted them into as comfortable a place as she could manage and ran back to Ellie's room. "Done?"

"Almost." Ellie stooped over her vanity. Dainty metal scraped over metal. "Just need a few earrings—."

"We don't have time for such ridiculous—"

"—to sell if we need extra money." Ellie dangled a large teardrop orb between her fingers. "An emerald should fetch a pretty price or a hot meal."

A laugh choked on Kat's lips. "Yes, it should. Tuck those close to you."

Gathering their suitcases, they headed for the door. Ellie stopped, bumping her suitcase into the back of Kat's legs. "What about the guards out there?"

"We'll simply tell them we're meeting Eric at the train station because he's surprised us with a trip to Switzerland. All last minute so he had no way of informing them of our plans. By the time they get it all sorted we'll be long gone."

"Oh." Ellie nodded before turning and running back in the direction of the kitchen. "Just a minute. I have to leave a note for Sylvie so she's not worried."

"Unnecessary, *schatz*. That little Jewess is more concerned with other things from now on."

A sledgehammer of fear whacked Kat square in the middle of her back as a lamp sprang to life from the couch-side table. The light filtered around the room, marking the furniture in ghoulish shadow. Eric sat in the corner of the couch, one booted foot propped atop the opposite knee while his arm stretched along the back of the low couch. The faint smell of red wine hovered in the air.

Eric's gaze drifted down to the suitcases then back up. "Going somewhere?"

"On holiday. The city has gotten a bit crowded of late. Too many wives." Ellie's chin notched up. "Where is Sylvie?"

"The same place as that butler, where they can no longer contaminate society. I've been on to them for some time as possible links to one of the underground Resistance movements. Placing them here under my constant eye was a stroke of genius, and eventually my patience paid off." His eyes drifted to Kat. Cold and motionless, they froze straight through her. "I suppose I have you to thank for that."

Kat gripped her suitcase handle tighter to keep the blood from pounding out of control in her head. "How did I help?"

"*Tsk, tsk.* I told you this past week was for rest and contemplation, but you couldn't help writing to your boyfriend, using that little maid as your go-between. Or at least she would have been a go-between if the letters had ever reached him." He sighed and held out a slim hand to examine a fingernail. "Baffles me the information people are willing to offer with the right amount of persuasion. She was much easier to induce than that butler."

"You mean threaten." The words of the brief notes Kat had scribbled out for Barrett raced through her mind. She'd kept them clean of any kind of incriminating messages and only sought to reassure him that he would see her again after a few days. She didn't dare ask how those innocent letters connected Sylvie to the Resistance lest it circle back to Barrett. Sorrow crushed her heart for Sylvie and Pierre. "You monster."

He shrugged, barely creasing the shoulders of his uniform. "Don't take it too hard. We'd have found out sooner or later. We always do."

The suitcase handle creaked in her twisting hand, ready to splinter. "Where are they?"

"Waiting for a train to take them to their final destination at a camp in Poland. Oh, don't worry. They're traveling with their families. We left no one behind. Now, back to this business of your holiday."

Ellie stood ramrod straight with white fingers curled around the handle of her own suitcase. "We're off to Switzerland just like Kat planned before. I need a break, Eric."

One slender blond eyebrow spiked. "A break from me?"

"And your wife."

If she wasn't standing perfectly still for restraint, Kat would have rushed across the room and thrown her arms around Ellie out of pride. Why hadn't that backbone come in sooner?

"I see." The eyebrow dropped back into place over his emotionless eyes. Steepling his fingers, he rested his chin atop them. "It's out of the question. Things are much too dangerous for me to allow you to wander around without my protection."

"I'm not asking for your allowance."

Darkness flickered in his eyes. "The contract states that you do not leave the city without my permission."

"I never signed any contract." Ellie's chin trembled. "And I don't intend to. Ever."

"That's unacceptable to me."

"Learn to live with the disappointment, as I will. Come on, Kat."

Kat saw the red spots creeping up Ellie's neck as she brushed past her to the front door. She was on the verge of losing control if they didn't get out of there fast.

Eric rose from the couch. Unhurried, he tugged at the bottom of his tunic to straighten the wrinkles. The scent of wine grew stronger. "Where do you plan to go? Do you think any train station in Paris will let you on without my go-ahead? If you do manage to make it out, stop to consider that your name is at this very moment being wired to every guard station in the country. You'd never make it past the border. You'd be escorted right back here where you belong with nothing to show for it except embarrassment. Don't embarrass yourself or me, Eleanor."

Ellie's shoulders sagged as her head dropped forward. She fought to throw him off, but his shackles refused to break. Fury whirled inside Kat's chest like a thunderstorm. "Can't you hear a word she's saying? She doesn't want to be here, and she certainly doesn't want anything to do with the sickening deal you and your wife have schemed up. Find another desperate vessel to spawn your seed."

Eric's dark expression crackled to hatred as his gaze rolled to Kat. "You've put this pathetic idea into her head from the start."

"Nonsense. You're the one driving her away. I'm only too happy to escort her."

"To Switzerland? Do you think for one minute I believe that trope? Or that you came here for merely a sisterly visit?"

"Of course she did, Eric. There's no way—"

"Silence, Eleanor!" Eric's eyes didn't leave Kat. "She has plenty of ways. Don't you, as the daughter of Sir Alfred Whitford? There's no end to the number of strings you could pull to get into occupied Paris unnoticed and then slip back out with your acquired treasure."

Like a wobbly top, Ellie hovered at Kat's elbow. "What's he talking about? What treasure?"

"You, *schatz*. You are the grand prize we are both fighting for. Unfortunately for your sister, I'm going to win."

Kat stepped in front of Ellie, blocking her from view. Her fingers stretched back, grasping the handle of the club she had hidden up her sleeve. "Arguing isn't polite for a lady, but in this instance I'll make a concession."

Surprise sharpened the ice in his eyes to icicles. "You think to shield her from me, as if I would harm her?"

"I'll do what's necessary."

His lip curled. "You? By yourself. I have guards standing just on the other side of that door plus more on the sidewalk to come at the snap of my fingers. Oh, no, lest I forget, you, too, have assistance. Mr. Anderson and his swinging musicians. Do they propose to bludgeon me with their trumpets? As if they could from where they're bound."

Fear shook through Kat. Barrett. "What have you done?"

"Precisely what I said I would do to all the rats scampering about underfoot. I have uncovered their filthy lair and flushed them out. Or rather my men will within the hour if they have not already. Their rat leader, in particular, will answer for his crimes. Such a shame, as I was growing accustomed to Mr. Anderson's rough ways."

"You are the vilest form of evil."

"I've done what I had to. Those people are a threat to everything we are. Every pure thing we are trying to create." Flattening his lips, he peered around her to Ellie. The icicles warmed. "Is this what you want, *liebling*? To have the two people who love you most fight over you until one is declared the loser? All I wanted was to give you everything. Furs, jewels, beautiful apartments and cars, Paris itself on a silver platter. One day soon, London, and eventually the world. Don't you want to share these things with me?"

Behind her, Ellie shook her head. She grasped Kat's arm and the hidden club beneath her sleeve. "I wanted love, Eric."

"That's what I'm offering you."

"No, you're offering a life of servitude in giving you beautiful Aryan babies because your wife can't."

"But we'll be together. Unlike your sister, who only wishes to drag you back to England in chains to the misery you escaped from."

Ellie's fingers squeezed Kat's arm, bruising the skin. She turned and looked at Kat, her forehead creasing. "You mean to take me back?"

"I mean to take you away from him."

"And back to England. The only place on earth I have no wish to ever return to." Her face shifting from uncertainty to anger, Ellie's hand fell away as she dropped the suitcase to the ground. Slowly, she edged away from Kat and turned to Eric. "Do you promise we'll always be together?"

Eric nodded, hope springing to his eyes. "Always."

Ellie smoothed her hands up the front of his tunic to circle around his neck. "And I'll have the finest furs and diamonds? Even the world?"

Like petrol poured onto a wilting flame, desire crackled in his voice as he drew Ellie closer. "With the might of the German army behind me and the powerful Whitford name behind you, no one will dare to stop us."

Kat's mouth dropped open as shock rippled down her body. After all that had happened, her sister had betrayed her for a fur coat. The shock turned to crippling anger as Ellie kissed his cheek and laid her head on his shoulder. And yet . . . the burning love Kat had expected to see blossoming across Ellie's face was consumed by contempt. Hidden from Eric's view, her sister's gaze darted from Kat's face to her arm and back up.

Kat shook her head, not understanding. Ellie's eyes widened as she tried to force her silent message across, again looking from Kat's arm to her face and then up to Eric.

Her arm . . . The weight of the club pressed against Kat's wrist. *Oh.*

But that club wasn't enough to do the damage she needed. She needed something heavier. Like herself.

Ever so slowly, like a cat walking on glass, Kat moved around behind Eric, who was nuzzling Ellie's neck. Then, in one swift motion, she launched herself onto his back, knocking Ellie away and wrapping her legs around his waist with her arms squeezing around his neck. He thrashed about, but she locked her ankles and wrists and held on, choking off his air with all her might. His movements became weaker until, wheezing, he finally tottered to his knees, then fell unconscious onto his face. Kat rolled off of him.

Ellie stared in horror. "You killed him."

"I didn't. Merely incapacitated him for a few minutes."

"Where did you learn to do that?"

"Barrett. Get the cords from the drapes."

Doing as Kat asked, Ellie ran back with a jumble of strings in her hands. "We can't strangle him!"

Kat grabbed the cords and dropped to her knees next to the motionless Eric. "As much as that would make my day, we're letting him live."

She made quick work of securing his hands and legs together in a series of knots that would make a sailor proud. As she tied everything off, a part of her mind assessed the situation. She'd certainly never thought she'd have the tenacity to do something like this—and certainly not to succeed. Perhaps one day when their lives weren't at risk, she might find the time to gloat about it.

Grabbing Eric's bound hands, she motioned for Ellie to take his legs, and together they half carried, half dragged him to the servant's closet down the hall. Stuffing him inside, Kat balled a semiclean rag into his mouth in case he woke up early and decided to alert the soldiers of their escape.

Ellie slammed the door shut. "Did Barrett teach you to tie knots like that?"

Kat shook her head. "I used to watch Mother's lady's maid tie her corsets tight enough to eliminate breathing. The girl's father was in the admiralty." She brushed back a loosened hair from her forehead. "For a minute there, I thought you wanted to stay with him."

"And lose this cracking figure to ten brats? No, thank you." Ellie ran a hand over her hip. The smile faltered on her lips as she glanced at the closet door. "I almost feel sorry for him."

"Don't. He deserves it plus a whack for good measure." Grabbing Ellie's arm before her bleeding heart got the best of her, they hurried into the kitchen, where Kat threw open the large window that Pierre always opened when he burned the toast.

Ellie backed away, bumping against the counter with arms outstretched. "You can't be serious."

Kat hiked her evening skirt up and hopped up on the counter. She had to warn Barrett and his men before it was too late. "Unless you'd rather meet the soldiers about to bust down your front door, I suggest you stop talking and get yourself through this window."

"To do what?"

"Shimmy down the drainpipe."

Ellie balked. "What about the suitcases?"

"Leave them."

"You've picked up the most criminal behaviors since I last saw you in England."

"Seems I'm to use all of them to get you out of here. Come on."

Hefting Ellie up behind her, Kat swung her legs out the window and wiggled her body onto the ledge just below. Her heart thundered in her ears until it drowned out every screaming fear. Except the one of plummeting four stories down into the courtyard garbage heap. *Don't look down. Don't look down.* Grabbing the drain, she took a deep breath and swung out to wrap her body around it. Inch by inch, she wormed her way down with Ellie huffing right above her. Two stories from the ground her heel caught the edge of her hem, jerking her body down. Her fingers clawed into the pipe, breaking nails as she struggled to regain her footing. Sweat trickled down her back, soaking her silk blouse.

He made this look so easy.

With air weighing like lead in her lungs, each inch an eternity to descend, it seemed forever until finally her foot touched solid ground. The inner courtyard was silent, the brick pavers slick with late-night dew as the last days of August turned cool.

Click click click. Ellie's heels bounced off the stone walls like gunfire.

"Take your shoes off." Kat snatched off her pumps and rolled down her stockings, tossing the silky pair into the communal rubbish bin. Another lovely pair gone. Barefoot, she and Ellie hurried across the courtyard and peered around the corner. Not a soul to be seen, but that didn't mean one didn't see them.

"Uh-oh. I think they're about to find Eric." Ellie pointed back up to her apartment where lights flickered on.

Time was up. Creeping out into the darkened street, Kat held her breath as she waited for the bullets to rip through her body. When she remained in one piece, they dashed across the street and didn't stop until the Seine lurked before them.

Kat peered around an abandoned newsstand, eyes darting left and right for movement. The mustiness of the towering buildings unfurled along the street like choking gas. "We need to get across the river."

"Then let's go."

Kat grabbed Ellie's arm and pulled her back down. "The river is the most patrolled area of the city. We can't just stroll across."

"So we'll crawl."

"Because that's not suspicious." Kat rubbed a hand over her forehead. Sweat pearled between her fingers. She had one plan: get to Barrett. If that failed, they had nothing. Why hadn't she thought through this sooner? Father wouldn't—No. Father wasn't here. She was. "After this next patrol boat, we'll run across. Stay close to the rail in case we need to drop down. Keep your head down and don't look back."

Ellie's hands wrung together as her nervous breaths came out in tiny gasps. Kat patted her fingers, stilling them. "We're all right. Trust me?"

Ellie nodded.

Hauling her sister to her feet, they crept out of hiding as the silence of the city enveloped them like a scratchy cloak. With each step, their ragged breaths threatened to tear it open. Fear of Allied attacks plunged the city into darkness each dusk, but what she wouldn't give for a sliver of light to guide the path. Anything to reassure her she wasn't about to step into a crack and plunge into the infested waters below. And Ellie didn't know how to swim.

Lights probed the black riverbanks. Another patrol boat. Adrenaline pumped down Kat's legs, numbing the pain of the coarseness raking her tender feet.

"Kat!"

Kat whirled back at Ellie's frantic hiss. She was stooped over tugging at her dress, which had caught a loosened nail in one of the boards. "Rip it!"

"I'm trying, but it won't give way."

The lights drew closer. The long yellow rays bounced off the water below and up the cracks at their feet. Kat hurtled herself at Ellie, flattening them both to the ground as the lights swung up to pass overhead. The bridge shook as the boat motored underneath, petrol fumes wafting up to choke her nose. Peering through the crack, she counted six uniformed men with guns strapped to their shoulders.

As the search lights turned down the bend, Kat peeled herself and Ellie off the ground and yanked the skirt free. "All right?"

"Let's not do that again."

"Agreed."

Off the bridge, they turned right, darting between alleys and behind shrubs. The farther they crept along the more unease spiraled into Kat's bloodstream, paralyzing her thoughts beyond putting one foot in front of the other. Surely Eric had raised the alarm by now. The streets should be swarming with Gestapo agents and their ferocious dogs to close in for the kill. She would never forgive herself if they got to Barrett before she did.

"I think we're about six blocks away from the Stag. If we take the next alley over, we can cut out at least five minutes." Ellie shifted behind her, but didn't answer. "Caught your breath yet?"

When she still didn't answer, Kat turned to find a short, bulky man with his paw clamped over Ellie's mouth.

"If you want to live, *cherie*, I'd keep your mouth shut."

Chapter 20

The rock hit the far wall with a satisfying *thunk*. Barrett looked around for another one to pummel his rage into. After all these months they'd finally come for him.

"It smells like rotting fish down here." Corbin whipped a spotless handkerchief from his black jacket pocket and sniffed with disapproval.

A rock rolled under Barrett's toe. "Is that your only complaint for tonight, or are you adding another to your tab?"

"Fish makes me gag."

"Then hold your breath."

Corbin's mouth opened, but he quickly clamped it shut and stormed off. Good riddance. Barrett was in no mood for coddling or patience. He kicked the rock. It hit the sewer stream and plopped straight down. Aye, it smelled like fish to high heaven, and worse, but they were alive. The same might not be said of the poor lads caught back at the Stag. Sam. Would he ever see his dear friend again? He kicked at the crumbling wall, desperate for more stone to bear the brunt of his frustration.

"Someone's coming!"

A hush fell over the sewer antechamber as the lid for the ladder leading down slid away and two long legs climbed down the metal rail. The air sucked out of his chest and hit him square in the stomach. He'd recognize that figure anywhere. But what was she doing here?

Shoving his way through the people, he waited until she was within reach before grabbing her off the ladder and pulling her against him.

"Unhand me!"

"Calm down, you cat!" Kat's arms flailed as her foot sought a solid spot on his leg to kick. Pinning her arms down, he spun her around to face him. "What in blazes are you doing here?"

Terror, surprise, and finally exhausted relief passed over her dirty face. "Barrett." His name came out on a sob as she sagged against him.

"It's all right, poppy." He stroked her silky hair, wild and unpinned with a slight curl from the late-night mist. "I've got you now."

Her fingers dug into his chest like grappling hooks, clinging to him as if the threat from outside had chased her down the ladder to rip her away once more. He circled his arms around her. He'd never let that happen. The days without her had been pure torture. Time after time he'd set off to bang down that flat door and carry her away, but each time Sam had yanked him back. Eric would have had him arrested, and what good would that do her then? Sam was right, but it didn't stop Barrett from wanting to punch him for it.

Her fingers slowly unbent themselves from his chest as her breathing calmed. She turned her face to rest her cheek against him. In one night, the world had been turned inside out, but now, together, they could right it. He could right anything holding her like this.

Movement up the ladder drew their attention. As quickly as she had fallen into his arms, Kat left to help her sister down the last few rungs. Coldness pricked Barrett's heart. Once more she'd left him for the sister who couldn't even help herself.

White, shaking, and tear streaked, Ellie collapsed against her sister as Kat wrapped her arm securely around her shoulders.

Jean, the man he'd sent to watch after the sisters, pulled the sewer grate over his head and shimmied down the ladder to land easily as a cat on his feet. "Found them crossing the bridge. They must've come out the back way and not the front where I was hidden. Only thought to follow when I heard those shoes clicking on the pavement. Made them easier to track."

Kat frowned over the top of Ellie's head. "You were watching us?"

"I had a man posted to keep an eye on things. Didn't want to leave you alone should anything happen," Barrett said.

Jean swiped at the sweat streaking his face. "I was going to bring them to the Stag, but the street was crawling with Germans. Figured something happened and brought them to the rendezvous point instead."

Barrett clapped him on the shoulder. His men knew how to pull through. "You were right to do so. Thank you."

"Is there somewhere we might sit down? Kat asked.

"This way." Barrett led them to an empty makeshift table and three chairs along the back brick wall. The stench wasn't as bad back there. He pulled out two of the chairs. "Here, have a seat."

Easing Ellie into the one behind the table, she sat opposite from Barrett. Her hand never left Ellie's. Slowly, her eyes rose up to his. "Where are we?"

"A Resistance stronghold several feet below the maze of catacombs. Renauld, their section leader, was kind enough to offer it as a meeting point should the bar ever be raided."

"Eric knows who you are. I was running to warn you."

"We got out just in time." He should've closed the doors as soon as the women customers stopped making appearances, but if Kat had come looking he didn't want her finding shuttered windows and him nowhere in sight.

"However did you escape?"

"I had a split-second's warning to get out before the Gestapo stormed up to my office and found me. Managed to get a few others out, but not nearly enough."

"Sam?"

His friend's name stabbed like a hot poker. He picked out a splinter on the plywood tabletop. "Don't know."

"Oh, Barrett. I'm so sorry." Her hand reached out, covering his.

"You take a lot of credit for things you've had no part in."

"Only one person to take credit for this." Her face hardened. "Eric."

The splinter snapped between his fingers. He shoved it to the floor. "Should've known he was behind this evening's unexpected meeting. Didn't think he'd hit us on the same night."

She looked to Ellie then back at him. "I'm afraid our part was a little more spur of the moment. He forced my hand, so to speak."

Ellie threw her arms on the table and buried her head in them with a low moan. Barrett stood and motioned for Kat to follow. Whatever she had to say probably didn't sit well with Ellie.

She stooped down and smoothed Ellie's platinum head. "Right back. Promise."

In a corner stacked with munition boxes and radio equipment, he pulled them away from the Resistance members clustered together discussing the events and the best way to hit back. He wasn't hitting back. He was done. He had the girls, and by the looks of Kat, any safe cover they had was blown. Scraped bare legs, a fancy evening getup that had probably been much prettier hours ago, and hair like yellow brambles clouding her blanched face. Shaken, but unhurt, she was on the verge of dropping. Best to get the information out before then. "What happened?"

She started, haltingly at first from the minutes after she'd left him on the street outside the flat over a week ago, then rising in intensity through the confrontation with Eric and his wife. She reached out and took his hand in both of hers, kneading his fingers as she told of their harrowing climb down the building and the boat patrol under the bridge. Her fingers laced between his as she shuddered to a halt after explaining how Jean had found them on the street just a short hour ago.

Anger quivered in Barrett's veins. If he ever laid eyes on that despicable bag of scum, he'd thrash him within an inch of his worthless life for torturing her like that. "Aye, I'd say he forced your hand. Shame you didn't choke him longer for good measure."

"Blame my last string of human compassion."

"As if the blighter deserves it. I've had Jean watching the place since you came to Paris. Thought an extra pair of eyes would come in handy. Turns out I was right."

He'd been worried sick when he didn't hear from her, but Jean had assured him that she was safe enough sequestered inside. The assurance hadn't been enough to keep him from waking in the middle of the night drenched in nightmarish sweat. What if something happened and he couldn't get to her? He'd never forgive himself.

She squeezed his hand. "I wrote to you several times, saying I was quite all right and for you not to worry, that I would see you soon. I'd hoped you would read between the lines, but I know now you never got them."

"When I didn't hear from you for days, I went to see the truth of Jean's reports of your imprisonment." He swallowed hard as the helplessness from that day swarmed him. "You leaned out the window, and I thought about climbing up to you if not for the armed guards by the door. That and the little maid sneaking down the block."

"Sylvie is Jewish. Eric was blackmailing her." Her eyes squeezed shut on a groan. "When he no longer needed her, he sent her and her family away. To a camp of some kind."

Barrett cursed. "Deportation camp."

"What are those?"

"Work camps that the Nazis have tried to keep hidden from the public. They've been rounding up anyone they think undesirable—Jews, Gypsies, political dissidents—and deporting them to ghettos and other places no better than pigpens for containment. A cleansing for the new Aryan utopia they want to create. More often than not, those poor souls are tortured or worked to death."

"Sylvie." Tears streamed down Kat's face. "How does no one know about this?"

"The Nazis are clever. They control just about every output of news, and they only report things they want the public to know or to believe are true. This way, their evil deeds can be accomplished with none the wiser."

"How utterly stupid of me to think I could slip anything past him, and now my foolishness has ruined her entire life and family. Can we find them? Can you rescue them?"

"A rescue attempt is out of our hands."

"We could try."

"We would fail." Her agonizing plea burned coal-hot in his chest. Too many lives had been shattered. He wouldn't risk hers again. "It was likely Eric's plan all along. She was probably spying on Ellie long before you came." Unlatching her fingers from his, he turned her hands over. Red scratched down her wrists, and several bluish-black bruises spotted her knees from falling on the bridge. "He didn't hurt you, did he?"

She shook her head and curled her fingers around his. "He wouldn't dare in front of Ellie. I'm sorry for involving you in this. I couldn't think of anywhere else to turn."

Reaching out, he brushed off a bit of gravel sticking to her collar. She'd nearly killed herself trying to get here. To get to him. "I would have you turn nowhere else."

"I'm leaving this place. I don't care what it means, but I'm taking my sister and going h-home." Tears crowded her bottom lashes. She turned, dashing them away. "Excuse me, please."

Before she could retreat and curl into herself, he pulled her close, wrapping his arms around her, and allowed her to use him as a barrier to the world. "There now, my braw lass."

Then, the woman who'd been forced to stand tall and brave the punishment on her own curled into him like a child as the kept emotions found release. He cradled her, murmuring words against her hair as warm tears soaked the front of his shirt. Her slender shoulders shuddered as she burrowed further into his chest, curving herself to mold against his embrace. Too long she'd held it in, but tonight had broken her. For once in his life, he was glad to be the one to pick up the pieces.

Tomorrow, he'd figure out a way to put them back together. And it started with getting them out of Paris.

Chapter 21

Three days passed before Barrett decided it was safe enough to leave their rendezvous point in the sewer and make for the countryside. A frenzy had swept the Parisian streets with news of the disappeared English socialites. According to Jean, an enraged Eric was desperate to keep it quiet, but the scandal had proven too big for even him to cover up. Especially when his wife was seen at the opera sporting a rather large ruby that had once belonged to Ellie.

Women. What they wouldn't do to get one claw up over another.

Barrett splashed tepid water from his canteen over his face in an effort to cool the sticky heat from the whiskers covering his chin and jaw. Disgusting and itchy, but they served the purpose of helping him blend into the population fleeing the city. Him and his "cousins."

A few feet away, the bushes rustled as Kat—or his first cousin, as the forged papers claimed—came out from where the two women had gone to freshen up. As if that potato sack of a dress could be freshened up. But it was durable and the shoes sturdy. The time for evening dresses and perfect manners had ended.

For wearing commoner's clothes for the first time, Kat still eased herself down on the grass and spread the woolly gray skirt over her bared knees like a queen. "Care to let me in on the plan now that we're safely outside the city?"

Outside the city, aye. Safe? Not a chance. He looked all around the sloping embankment and back up to the dusty road behind them. Birds chirped in the scattered treetops, oblivious to the danger encroaching on their lands.

Kat sighed with impatience. "For heaven's sake. There is no one here but us."

"First rule in this business: never assume you're safe." Another quick take around the perimeter before looking back to her. The sun had pinked her nose and cheeks, but not even the fresh outdoors could push away the wanness haunting her face. "Have you eaten?"

She shook her head. "Not hungry."

"Then where's the apple I gave you?"

She glanced to where Ellie sat by a small stream washing her face. "I gave it to Ellie. She needed it more than me."

Of course she had. The woman would starve herself before letting her sister do without. The sister who hadn't said a word since their journey began beyond a gasp when she'd found out his Resistance connections. Not to mention that look of anger and disbelief she'd thrown at Kat for keeping it from her.

He took a deep breath in an attempt to tamp down his irritation. "This is going to be a hard trip, and food supplies are limited. The last thing I need is you fainting in a ditch, so you'll eat your portion from now on."

"Are you quite finished lecturing?"

"Only if you're finished giving away your sustenance."

"Fine. Now, may we return to the escape plan?"

Screwing the lid back on the canteen, he tucked it into the canvas haversack next to him. "We're making our way to Salbris, a small town near Bourges where the local faction of fighters will be waiting for us. As long as the messenger didn't get shot on the way."

She blanched and looked away. "How will we know where to find them?"

"By the clues they've left out."

"Which are . . . ?"

He shook his head. "The less you know the better in case we're captured. And Kat, you do have to believe that that is a very real possibility."

She plucked a blade of dried grass and slid it between her fingers. "I do realize that, but you have to accept that we're in this together, and refusing to tell me everything is just as harmful as not. If you get taken, Ellie and I are left alone without the slightest clue of finding a safe place."

"Your father never gave you a backup plan after that Red Cross boat?" His tone was sharper than he'd intended, but a man who threw his child into such danger without so much as a map was worthy of contempt.

Intense eyes with pinpricked pupils bore into him like nails. "My father never had a say in the details of this trip. It was all left to the SIS, and their only instruction was to meet with a man named Crowder a week after I had arrived. I waited nearly four hours at the meeting spot, but he never showed. I was told to assume if that happened he was already dead." Dropping the blade of grass, she stuck her hand out to him. "Do we have a deal?"

"We seem to make a lot of those."

"So you've pointed out before." Her fingers wiggled in the space between them. "Honesty or no?"

Honesty. The very word sliced between his ribs and straight into his heart. Honesty required he tell her that she was nothing more than a paycheck, a means to his detested circumstances. At least she'd once been. Now, she'd beguiled her way into something more that he was loath to admit out loud. He wasn't ready for that amount of honesty, not with himself and not now.

"I'll do my very best." He shook her hand and dropped it immediately lest the longing to hold it coaxed forth the words that he was desperate to keep in.

A dry midafternoon breeze ruffled the lazy stream at the bottom of the embankment. The smell of sweet grass and dirt churned in the early September air. Back home, autumn was rolling in to pluck the purple from the swaying heather and spin it into red and gold for the treetops. The lochs would be too chilly for a quick morning dip, and the cold, crisp nights would sparkle with frost. How he would miss it. A tightness squeezed in his chest. How he would miss one other thing in particular.

"I've lived my whole life trying to do what was right, what was expected, but I see now it was out of fear of disappointing that I agreed in the first place. I should have said no to a great many people along the way."

"You should've told them to take a flying leap."

Her lips quirked. "In hindsight many of them probably deserved that. But in all those people you were never one I tried to please out of wanting to curry favor. I can be myself without fear of reprisal. A situation I have rarely been in, and yet here I find it with you."

"We'd have gone on the run long ago if I'd known these sentiments were waiting for me."

Blushing, Kat curled her legs and tucked her feet under her skirt. "Will we ever get out of here, I wonder? Home seems so far from here, so distant. Will it feel the same after seeing all of this?"

"It won't, but it's not a bad thing to start over."

"Like in America?" He twitched, but it wasn't fast enough for her not to notice. "The postcards from your office, and you said you had nothing to return to in Glasgow."

"It's as a good a place as any." *No demons to haunt me there.*

"No past to shackle you to its demands. How nice that sounds."

"Come with me. Pretty sure they don't care if you're a blue blood or a bartender over there." He clamped down on his back teeth to hold back a groan. What was he talking about? A woman like her up and leave for a strange place with a penniless nobody like him? The sun was wreaking more havoc on his senses than he realized. "Unless you're tired of me by now. I know I would be if I were you."

"I'm very grateful to have you. Not that I have you—I just mean that you're always here. Always with me. I mean, no one's always with me." Red rushed across her face. "I'm bobbling this, aren't I?"

"A wee bit." A blond strand unfurled across her burning cheek. Without thinking, he reached for it, weaving it between his fingers like a satin ribbon. Last week, such an impropriety would have had her reaching for her nearest hairpin to tame the errant hair back in place. Or stab him with, depending on her mood and who was around. "Dinna worry, lass. Yer secret is safe with me, for I willna tell ye dinna have it all together all the time."

She turned to him, slipping her hair from his fingers. "Your slip into brogue hints at mockery and I'll tell you, I dinna appreciate it."

He grinned. "I'm remembering a certain English lady with her nose in the air curbing me to stay out of her private affairs. About time you started appreciating my usefulness."

"I was quite detestable in the beginning, wasn't I?"

"Only in the beginning?"

She brushed a dried blade of grass from her skirt with an agitated flick of her wrist. "As if you've been perfectly affable this whole time."

He leaned back on his elbows, stretching out his legs and crossing them at the ankles. "I've been told I'm extremely affable. You're just not used to those slicks you usually encounter in your perfumed drawing rooms telling you how it is."

"No. They're much too polite, but in the end the truth always came out."

"Such as they didn't have the cleverness to keep you entertained? Just another injustice to the Englishmen when compared to a strapping Scot." His poor attempt at a joke fell flat, earning a modest twitch of her mouth.

"Other way around, I'm afraid."

"About the injustices to a Scot. Oh, aye, I've got a complaint list a mile long."

Her eyes dropped to her lap. She picked slowly at the pills rolling at the seam as she tried her best to hide it, but her poker face was terrible. He knew the pain that burrowed in her heart as if she'd shouted it. He'd gathered enough from her dropped comments to piece together the picture, and it made him want to thrash the man who'd used her for his own gain. "His loss, poppy."

"The all-important Whitford name and ties. Yes, quite a loss."

"He wasn't man enough for you." Her head cocked back and forth as if weighing his words until a small snort dismissed it. "You don't believe me."

"Times are hard now. Men want a girl they can go out and have fun with and forget about their troubles." She plucked one of the gray pills from her skirt and flicked it into the dirt. "I'm the boring girl you take home to Mother."

"You show me a boring girl who scales walls and beats down Nazi soldiers in back alleys, and I'll show you a three-legged talking coo."

"I don't know what a coo is."

"It's a Highland cow, with the big horns and shaggy fur. My point is a mere boy does things like that. A real man sees the treasure before him, and will fight tooth and nail to be worthy of the claim. No matter how long it takes him."

Worthy was something he'd never be accused of. The opposite, in fact, for every corner of his life. Bastard born, with the town drunk for a father, wasn't much to instill confidence in a kid, but street fights with the bullies was. He'd had to earn every ounce of respect one scrap at a time, but never could he earn enough to stand in the same circles as Kat Whitford. A lifetime of trying could never prove him worthy of her.

She stared off to the trickling water below, the blue sky and thick white clouds reflected in its shallow depths. Calmness curved her features, but the deception couldn't stop the running of thoughts behind her singular gaze. Finally, she turned back to him. "Do you really have a talking cow?"

He snorted. "Do you always get uncomfortable with compliments? For a woman who prefers the truth, you sure don't take them well."

"Truth is one thing, false flattery another."

"You really don't see it, do you?" Angry frustration crackled to the surface. He surged to his feet. "You really don't see what an incredible woman you are just because a few barmy dunderheads were too intimidated by the challenge. A man comes along to tell you differently and you don't believe him. You don't believe me."

"I've been led astray by men proclaiming they speak the truth, but in the end the words all twisted into the scenario they wanted. Never what I wanted. Never what I needed. But like a fool I went along with it because I wanted to believe that he had my interest at heart."

The breaking of her voice on *he* pierced his anger like an arrow. "Your father set it all up, didn't he? The chump, the engagement. All because he needed something from the boy. What was it? A title, land, investments?"

"The Richmond family lost most of their fortune after the Great War, but their name is one of the most respected and affluent in the county. Marriage to a powerful family, like mine, could make them great again. I thought Marcus liked me well enough on his own until I found the signed contract between him and my father a week before the ceremony." Her face twisted with the betrayal. "Father couldn't trust me to make my own match. Had to do it himself."

"I'm not this Richmond bloke, and I'm sure not your da." Guilt knocked out the anger as soon as the words left his mouth. Of course he was like her old man. He was on this very mission because Sir Alfred didn't have faith in his own daughter to bring Ellie back without his help. Her trust betrayed again, and he was to pay the price once she discovered his part in it.

"Those two never saw what I see." Bending down, he grabbed her hands and hauled her to her feet. Desire shot through him, but he resisted the urge to pull her close and prove his words until she had no breath left to refuse. "For once, save me the headache and agree with me."

Her slender eyebrow rose. "If I start agreeing with you now, it'll set a bad precedent. And we have a long road ahead of us."

"Indulge me."

Her eyebrow dropped to furrow into doubt. "I'm surprised my headaches haven't driven you off."

"Haven't so far." Only as the words left his mouth did he realize how much he meant them. For the first time in his life, he wanted to be there for someone. For her. And the admission terrified him to his soul. "And before you say I had no choice in the matter, let me just say that any other mission chap would've left at any one of the troubles you've found yourself in the middle of. The movie premiere, the train station, Hitler's dinner party—take your pick."

She eyed him for a long minute. "All right. I concede. Your life has gotten exponentially more problematic since we've met. But if I'm to get into trouble with anyone . . . I'm glad it's you."

Her hopeful smile was all the encouragement he needed. Placing his hands on either side of her face, he stroked his thumbs over her soft pink cheeks that warmed with each passing second. In return, his pulse throbbed with the need of her. Lifting her face, she grazed her lips over his to press a kiss to his cheek. Her soft breath washed over his skin, tingling the hairs to stand on end. With excruciating slowness, her lips traced the short path back to his mouth to hover inches away from them. Her eyelashes swept up, liberating the bold blue and green to reach into his soul and break the boundary between them.

Every instinct of self-preservation told him to turn and run, but something deeper begged him to stay and let her in.

She closed the distance, her lips firm and absolute in their need as she curved his mouth to submission. Her hands kneaded the front of his cotton shirt, digging between the buttons to brush the skin beneath. He groaned as he shoved his hands into her hair and pulled her to him until there wasn't a space of relief between their bodies. He'd dreamed of her so many nights—the smell of her perfume, the heat of her hair when the sun hit it, the way her laugh warmed everything around her. His imagination was a far cry from the realness of her in his arms.

He slipped an arm around her waist, every muscle tightening to keep her close. A gasp of surprise tumbled over her lips as the possessive hold forced the air from her lungs. He captured it, drawing it deep down until it crushed his barrier of preservation to dust—

A gunshot blasted in the air. Kat jerked back. "Please tell me that wasn't what I'm sure it was."

Another shot cracked the sky. Rifles. And not just any rifle, but a bolt-action Mauser issued to the Germany army. "Afraid so. Hunters looking for an easy target. Run!"

Tall grass slapped around his waist as they grabbed Ellie and raced away from the encroaching voices.

"*Der hase! Diesen weg!*"

Rabbit. They hunted rabbit, but it didn't mean they wouldn't take a potshot at a civilian's back. The open field stretched before them, offering nothing but high dead grass and a copse of trees two hundred yards away to hide in. The perfect spot for vermin to cower and a stray bullet to hit one of them in the confusion. Pushing Kat and Ellie from behind, he veered them to the stream bank. "Jump into those reeds there!"

They dove behind the thick green reeds just as three German soldiers crested the mound he and Kat had sat on moments before. Dirty and ripped uniforms hung off their lanky frames, their hair shaggy beyond regulations, and two weeks' growth of whiskers covering their jaws. The fear racing through Barrett plummeted to his stomach. Deserters. The worst kind of man. Dishonorable enough to leave their duties and ruthless enough to do whatever it took to survive.

Kat's trembling hand brushed over his. "We can't stay here."

He scanned the area. There was nowhere to hide except the reeds crawling along the stream. Canteens hung off the men's belts. They'd need to refill them, and when they did, they were sure to spot the platinum of Ellie's head lurking in the greenery.

"*Was ist das?*" The shortest of the bunch, with copper hair, held up a slender white object.

On the other side of Kat, Ellie gasped. "My comb."

Barrett held his breath. Maybe they would pocket it and continue their hunt elsewhere.

The copper-haired boy tossed the comb high in the air and caught it with a wicked gleam to his eye. Barrett's breath hissed out. He knew that look, and it didn't bode well. The boy ribbed his comrades, making crude illustrations with his hands and pointing out to the field around them. The others nodded, malicious smirks curling their lips. Rabbit was no longer on the menu.

Fanning out, the deserters scanned the ground and grass with the tips of their rifles. Obsession lit their eager faces like the taste of water in a wasteland. Kat's fingernails dug into the back of his hand as they drew closer. A few more yards and the copper boy would have them in sight. Barrett flipped his hand over to squeeze Kat's. She couldn't stay here. He needed her gone, now. If he could get that Mauser, he might stand a chance.

Reaching into his pocket, Barrett pulled out his switchblade and pressed it into Kat's hand. "Creep backward and edge along the bank of the water. On your belly if you have to. Keep Ellie in front of you. Don't stop, don't look back. No matter what. Keep going."

"You'll be behind me?"

He smiled ruefully. "I'll be somewhere back behind. Now, go."

Making only the slightest of efforts toward following them, he watched them steal away, his heart wallowing in his throat as the distance between him and Kat widened. Mud caked up her sides, but she didn't stop or look back as she urged Ellie ahead of her. With one final glance of her burning into him, he stopped and turned back to wait for his prey.

Chapter 22

Rocks scraped under Kat's stomach as she crawled along the bank. She spat out the mud that Ellie's feet in front of her kicked back. How far had they gone? They must've been moving for at least an hour . . . a day. Twisting her head, she sighted the fading sun that had barely moved in the orange sky. Ten minutes was closer to the mark. She tugged on Ellie's leg, pulling her to a stop. Silence all around. No gunshots, no voices, not even a whisper of wind.

And no movement behind her.

Uneasiness prickled along her skin.

He'd told her not to stop, not to turn around, but the stillness behind her rang like a death peal. She looked back. A wall of reeds surrounded them. She twisted left and right, frantically pawing at the stems for a glimpse of him. Barrett was nowhere to be seen. Icy fear spilled into her blood, freezing the air in her lungs.

He'd promised to be behind her the whole way. The fear lunged into her brain. No, he'd said *somewhere* behind her.

"Oh, Barrett. You didn't."

Ellie twisted around. "What's going on? Where's Barrett?"

The anguish in her heart threatened to stop the words before they spilled out. "He stayed behind."

"What? Why?"

It didn't matter. All that mattered was pulling him back from the danger that he'd placed himself in so that they could get away. Kat sat up and looked over the tops of the reeds. The setting sun slanted across the deep-orange sky, turning the field around them to a blaze of gold. But nothing else stirred.

He wouldn't leave her with such a stupid decision, and she sure wasn't about to leave him. Stupid decision or not.

She turned back to Ellie. "Stay here."

Ellie shook her head. "I'm coming with you."

"I'll be back within an hour." Reaching into her pocket, she pulled out the knife Barrett had given her and pressed it into Ellie's hand. "Take this."

Ellie's eyes widened with terror. She grabbed Kat's hand. "And if you're not?"

Icy fear warped the words on Kat's tongue. She pushed it back. "I will be. Promise."

Sidling away before Ellie could latch on to her, she scanned the area across the field, down the small valley the stream sank into, and back across to where a clump of trees stood a hundred yards to the east. Wisps of white curled above the fading green boughs. Fire.

She hunched over and ran toward the trees. Dried stalks slapped her face, stinging her ears and crunching beneath her feet. *Please, please, Barrett. Don't do anything stupid.*

She stopped just inside the cluster of trees. Heart racing, blood rushed to her ears. She took a long, deep breath to calm the intensity, forcing herself to focus all around her. Just as Father had instructed her during shooting parties. The slightest detail might give away your quarry, he'd said. But it would also give you away to them.

As the blood abated from her ears, voices carried from far in front of her. She picked her way through the brambles until the faint orange glow of a fire came into view. On the edge of the tree line, one of the soldiers hunkered down over the flames, coaxing them to brightness. The other two bent over a log with a rope tied around one end. The other end of the rope had been thrown over a tree branch. Kat crept closer as her heart thundered in her chest. Where was Barrett?

The two men finished tying off the rope and stood. Kat's heart raged into her throat. Not a log. Barrett.

His shirt was ripped at the collar with bright-red splotches of blood down the front from where they dripped from his nose. Bruises curved around his neck, and raw, pink rope burns slashed around his wrists. Curled into a ball on the ground, his body heaved with ragged breaths.

A soldier with greasy black hair falling below his ears squatted in front of him waving Ellie's comb. "*Wo ist die frau?*"

Barrett shook his head.

The soldier smacked him on the cheek with the comb. "*Wo ist die frau?*"

Once again, Barrett shook his head, refusing to tell him where the woman who owned that comb was. The black-haired man motioned to his comrade, who yanked on the other end of the rope, jerking Barrett up. He scrambled to his feet before the rope pulled his wrists out of socket, but it didn't stop the men from yanking harder to lift him up in the air with his toes brushing the ground.

The man with the comb circled Barrett like a jungle cat. Coming around to the front, he slammed his fist into Barrett's stomach. A moan of pain shot through Barrett's clenched teeth. Kat's fingers dug into the dry earth to keep from rushing out and clawing the hateful soldiers to death.

Drawing a knife from his belt, the black-haired man ran his thumb across the tip to prick a drop of blood. With a rotting grin, he held the knife to Barrett's throat. Barrett's strong pulse throbbed against the blade as his breath hissed out between his busted lips.

Though he spoke in German, his meaning was clear enough as he ran the tip of his knife down Barrett's front, ripping off the buttons with a flick of his wrist. He parted back the halves of Barrett's shirt to reveal a muscled chest and flat stomach that sucked in and out with labored breaths. The soldier traced a line from Barrett's exposed collarbone diagonally across the hard chest and planes of his stomach. A thin red line seeped up.

Kat's heart drowned in agony. She clamped a hand to her mouth to keep the pitiful sounds from lurching out. He'd sent her on to keep them safe, and now, with his life's blood trickling down his battered body, he refused to give them up. Everything he had done was to keep them safe, and now he'd strung himself up a tree to get her to safety. She bit down on the inside of her palm as a sob clawed up her throat. Oh, Barrett. She'd been so terribly, terribly wrong about him so many times. Why had it taken seeing him stripped bare and beaten for her to finally admit the truth to herself? The truth that her heart was being killed before her very eyes and she had to get him down before she lost it forever.

The copper-haired man hunkered by the fire slowly turned a long piece of metal over the greedy orange flames. A bayonet. Next to him on the ground lay a rifle.

Sickness hurtled up Kat's throat. She clamped her lips closed. Not now. Later, much later, when she could recount the foolishness she was about to throw herself into. Grabbing a sharp rock that wedged itself between the tree roots, she hefted it in her hand. It would do.

Crouching along the perimeter, she stopped just behind the copper-haired man to block the other two and Barrett from sight. As quietly as she could, she slipped through the bushes and ducked directly behind her target. Air pinching tight in her lungs, she raised her hand and brought the rock down into the back of his head with a solid smack. He crumpled over oozing dark blood from the back of his skull.

The bayonet clanged into the burning wood, shooting sparks up. The other two soldiers whipped around as Barrett's head lolled to the side. More blood spilled from his nose to splatter across his bare chest.

The dark-haired man's lip curled up like a wolf's as he saw Kat. Lust, hot and vicious, sizzled in his dark eyes. He brushed the comb over his palm. "*Die wir hier haven?*"

His question slithered around Kat's neck, threatening to choke off her breath. "*Français.* I speak French."

The soldier's eyes roved over her body like a starving man seeing steak for the first time. "I speak French enough you obeying when tell you what want."

The snaking words spoken in horrible French squeezed tighter. Dots danced before her eyes. "Last chance."

He stepped toward her, rubbing the comb against his thigh. "Give you one chance push skirt down."

"I'll kill you if you touch her!" The rope jerked against Barrett's hands, strangling the words from him. The vein in his neck pulsed wildly as red burned up his chest and face.

Kat locked eyes with him. The expression she found there stole the sickness and pulverized it into fury. She dropped to her knee and grabbed the rifle. Praying to God it held bullets, she squeezed the trigger.

Bam!

The greasy-haired man fell back clutching a gaping hole blown into his shoulder, howling obscenities.

His comrade dropped the rope, sending Barrett crashing to his feet. In a flash, he whipped a knife to Barrett's exposed throat and shouted in German.

The gun shook in Kat's hands. Her eyes skittered to Barrett's. White-hot rage burned in his eyes. *Shoot him.*

"*Nein, nein, meine lieben.*" The knife nicked into the side of Barrett's neck, splatting red onto his torn collar.

The gun fell from Kat's cold fingers. Lips twisting with hideous glee, the man slammed the handle of the knife into Barrett's stomach. Barrett doubled over on the ground wheezing for air.

"*Treten die waffe weg.*" Evil intent shook the deserter's body with each step he took toward her.

Barrett groaned and rolled to his side. Blood drummed in Kat's ears. Her eyes fell to the ground, searching for anything. The tip of the bayonet gleamed next to the sparking fire. Neck, bicep, stomach, groin, kidneys. Target spots. She'd told Barrett she couldn't do it, but the man stalking toward her forced the exception. He reached his filthy hand toward her.

Dear God. Give me strength. His hand inches from her neck, Kat squatted and grabbed the bayonet, stabbing it upward into his belly with as much force as she could draw. The blade pierced skin, tissue, and organ like a knife through butter. Warmth spurted through her fingers.

He veered back, his ugly mouth parted in surprise as he fumbled for the blade sticking out of his kidney. She clutched her trembling hands to her chest. Hot tears spilled down her cheeks as the man gurgled to his death.

Swiping at her eyes, she pushed to her feet and swayed as dizzying dots crowded the corners of her brain. Movement by the tree sent the dots scurrying. Barrett grabbed the dark-haired man's knife and rolled to his feet in one swift motion to slice the blade across the soldier's neck. The deed done, Barrett's knees buckled, driving him to the ground.

Kat sprang toward him. Taking the knife, she sawed through the rope binding his hands and caught them between her own. Red and raw, but skin unbroken. Shaking beyond control, her hands clambered up his arms, across his bare chest, up the sides of his neck, and across the broad planes of his face. Tears scorched her throat and eyes. "Are you all right? Barrett, are you hurt?"

"Besides all the blood and a possible broken nose?"

She grabbed his face and pressed her mouth to his, hard and possessive. "Yes, besides those. Stupid man, what were you thinking?"

He raised a hand to her cheek, rubbing a thumb roughly across her cheekbone. "About you, daft woman."

The fire popped and hissed behind them as the copper-haired man tried pushing to his feet. Blood streamed down the back of his neck, staining his filthy jacket to black. Barrett swooped down and pulled a pistol from the belt of the dead man at his feet. With his free hand, he pressed Kat's face into his shoulder.

Bam.

Barrett tossed the gun. "Let's get out of here before someone decides to come investigate the gunshots."

"We should keep that pistol."

"If we get caught with a German officer's Luger in our pocket, it's a death sentence for sure. Likely these filth stole it themselves."

Not bothering to turn her head to see the deadly damage behind her, Kat wound her arm around his waist. He tried pulling away. "Don't. My blood."

"Too late for worrying about ruined clothing now." She tucked him closer, caring not at all if he bled all over her blouse. She had him alive, and that was all that mattered.

"Where's your sister?"

Kat pointed as they picked their way back through the trees she'd come from. A night sky of dusty blue and smoky stars barely lit the fields stretching before them. "A few hundred yards that way. I didn't want her to . . . This would be too much for her." More tears scorched her eyes, clogging the back of her throat as the past few minutes rushed over her senses like a tidal wave. "I killed those men."

Barrett hugged her close. "We'll deal with that later. There's a small crossroads about an hour's walk from here. Should be a few towns near enough to find food, maybe shelter for the night."

She reached up to attempt pulling the cut ribbons of shirt back into place. He winced and pressed a hand to his side as red seeped through the cloth. She tried prying away his fingers. "What's happened here?"

He shook his head as his pale lips twisted into an unconvincing smile. "Naught but scratches, poppy."

Tall grass brushed her waist as they picked their way over the uneven ground beneath their feet to where Ellie waited. "No, Barrett. What happened back there was more than scratches." Her arm tightened around him as she looked up, her gaze locking into his. "Much, much more."

Chapter 23

Kat leaned up on tiptoe and peered at the faded sign. Why couldn't they have a full moon tonight? "Troyes twenty kilometers and Chablis six. Which way are we to go?"

Barrett braced a hand against the post holding the sign, his head down. "What was Chablis?" Ellie stood beside him, arms wrapped around herself, silent.

"Six."

"Chablis, Chablis. That sounds familiar. Like a friend's name I knew once, or something."

Kat dropped her gaze to him. "Maybe you read it on a map once? Perhaps it coordinates with a rendezvous point for us?"

His head rocked back and forth. "Maybe. Maybe not."

Kat frowned. He wasn't usually so uncertain. "If it sounds familiar, then it's possibly the way we're supposed to go."

"Or not." Rolling his head up, he blinked several times at her as if to focus. Sweat beaded his forehead. "Maybe it's on the unwanted list. I mean . . . places we're not wanted . . . no, places we don't want to go."

"You're acting strange." She held a hand to his damp forehead. "And you're burning up."

Straightening, he stepped away from the post. His feet tripped together and sent him tumbling to the ground before Ellie could reach him. Bright red soaked the entire left side of his shirt. Kat dropped next to him and peeled back the shirt to reveal an oozing gash the size of her palm.

"Why didn't you tell me how badly you were cut?"

"Because it's nothing. A scratch."

"A mere scratch doesn't give you fever, clot-headed man." Wriggling out of her slip, she pressed it to the gaping wound. "Ellie, I need yours, too, to wrap around his torso and hold this one in place."

Without a word, Ellie shimmied out of her silk slip and ripped it down the seam, carefully wrapping it around Barrett's torso and tying off the ends in a knot. The last of their finery staunched the blood flow. At least for the moment.

Unscrewing the lid to the canteen, Kat pressed it to his lips. "You need to drink."

Barrett flapped a hand to push it away. "No, you take it."

"No. We need to bring down the fever and keep you on your feet. We can't drag you the whole way to town, and we need to find something to disinfect and properly bandage this wound before infection sets in." She pressed the canteen to his trembling lips. "Drink."

He glugged back the tepid water and pushed it away as shivers ran down his body. Screwing the lid back on, Kat slung the strap over her shoulder and hooked an arm around Barrett before motioning Ellie to take his other side.

"I'm not a child."

Kat slipped his arm over her shoulder, careful she didn't bump his wound. "Sometimes I wonder, but we can move more quickly and safely over the terrain if we keep you upright from the start rather than tripping behind us."

He blinked heavily. The sooner they got moving the better. He was ready to fall like a tree, and once he was down she was sure they'd be unable to move him again. Fear twisted around her heart. They would make it. There was no other choice but to make it even if she had to drag him the entire way.

Bang! Bang! Bang!

Kat's fist ached from bombarding the oak door repeatedly.

Ellie shivered on the other side of Barrett as the early air of morning swept around the corner of the wooden building. "No one's home."

"It's a brothel. Someone is always home." *Bang! Bang! Bang!*

Heavy footsteps pounded against the floor inside. Several locks and chains slid behind the door before it cracked open. Yellow light flickered out. *"Qu'est ce que tu veux?"*

"Je suis désolé de vous déranger." Kat gestured to Barrett's mostly limp body slumping against her. "He's hurt, and I need to dress the wound properly."

The door widened to reveal a large-boned woman with thick skin drooping around her face and neck. The remains of garish red lipstick stuck to the corners of her downturned mouth while thick kohl rimmed her eyes. A black shawl with too many holes to count wrapped around her wide shoulders to cover her stained nightdress beneath. "It's after four in the morning. I just put my girls to bed."

"S'il vous plait, no one else will help us."

The madam's eyes narrowed at the now-crusted-over bandage wrapped around Barrett's abdomen, then slowly grazed up to his lolling head. Her suspicious eyes snapped open. *"Mon Dieu!* Bring him in."

She stepped aside as Kat and Ellie urged Barrett inside. A lantern flickered on a small Queen Anne side table, casting eerie shadows on the worn velvet settees and faded paintings of girls dancing and bathing. To the left stood a closed door and to the right a rickety-looking staircase that wound up to a second-floor balcony. The scents of cheap perfume, sweet powder, unwashed linens, and stale beer permeated the air.

Grabbing the lantern from the table, the madam motioned them upward. "This way."

Kat brushed the damp hair covering Barrett's eyes. "Can you make it up the stairs?"

He nodded with a shiver. She needed to bring his fever down and fast. "Just don't let me tip backward."

The madam waited impatiently at the top of the stairs as Kat and Ellie aimed Barrett upward. By the time they got to the top, all three of them huffed and puffed from the exertion. They followed the large woman to the end of the landing, and she unlocked the last room and stepped in. A kerosene lantern sprang to life from a small vanity table next to the door. A bed on a metal frame took up most of the room while a lace curtain and blackout sheet covered the window next to the bed. A large trunk in the corner made up the entirety of the room's contents.

"Girl in this room died last week, so you can have it for the night. Maybe tomorrow if I can't find a new girl by then. Sheets are in that trunk. Make the bed yourself. A little worse for wear, but I boiled 'em in lye soap, so they're clean." The woman cast an eye around the room as if daring them to find fault in her offered accommodations.

Ellie touched the foot of the bed. "What did she die of?"

"The clap, same as every other girl here who's gone on before. A returning sentiment from the last war." The madam's eyes cut over to Barrett.

Barrett sagged against Kat. His weight buckled her knees. "Ellie, help me get him on the bed before he collapses."

The madam made no move to help as Kat and Ellie struggled to get Barrett onto the mattress. With his head all the way at the top, his feet still hung over the end.

"Bring that lantern over here so I can see." Kat peeled back the shirt to reveal bright-red blood seeping through the bandages. Not good. She clamped her teeth together to keep her heart from leaping out as she unwound the bandage to see the gaping wound. She turned back to the woman standing silently in the doorway, eyes never blinking from Barrett's face. "May we have some strips of linen and fresh water to cleanse the wound?"

"You'll need to close that wound before you wrap it up again." Turning, the woman disappeared.

Kat bit her lip as she looked to Ellie. Was the woman coming back? Barrett groaned as his arms and legs twitched. Kat brushed back the hair from his forehead. "It's all right. We're going to get you cleaned up. Bring this fever down."

He grabbed her hand and pressed it to his lips, then let it fall limp at his side.

As one minute turned into two, Kat turned to the door. If the woman had no intention of returning, then she was going to knock on every door until she found the supplies needed.

Footsteps in the hall stopped her. The woman came back in, her arms loaded with supplies.

"Get that area cleaned off so you can see what the real damage is. Here's sulfa powder to sprinkle over it." The woman tossed her a small package, then held out a handful of linen to Ellie. "Tear these into long strips." Pulling out a round cord and needle, she held them to the light next to Kat. "Know how to sew?"

Kat swiped a damp cloth across the dried blood at Barrett's side. "Needlework and embroidery on hankies. It wasn't very good."

The woman grunted. "I'll do it."

The dirty cloth dangled from Kat's fingers as she eyed the unrolling catgut and long needle. "Shouldn't we call a doctor?"

The woman's eyes drove into her like nails. "There is no doctor. My girls get beaten up often enough. You don't think I know how to take care of them?"

"Of course, I'm sorry. It's just that . . ." Kat bit her lip to keep it from trembling. "Tell me what you need me to do."

The first rays of morning peeked around the corners of the blackout curtain by the time they had Barrett cleaned, sewed up, bandaged, and sleeping. Kat stood at the foot of the bed, arms crossed over her stomach, as Barrett stretched out before her. Stripping him from the waist up, she'd examined almost every inch of him for any other unseen wounds needing tending. His chest rose and fell on deep breaths, the dark hair glistening with sweat as the muscles concaved down to his flat stomach. His head twitched back and forth as if assaulted by dreams. There would be more to come if the fever didn't break soon and if they couldn't keep infection from setting in.

Her throat ached from tamping down the swelling emotions. It had taken him throwing himself on the brink of death to realize her heart belonged with him, and now he was slipping from her fingers like sand. Taking her heart right along with him.

"Staring at him won't help the recovery any sooner." Kat turned as the madam wiped her flat hands on the edges of her black shawl. The kohl around her eyes had sunk into her crow's feet. "Best take a rest like your sister." She gestured to Ellie passed out in the corner, strips of linen covering her legs.

Kat shook her head, dislodging more hair from the pins barely holding it back. "A few more minutes until I know the valerian has eased his sleep."

The woman shrugged a thick shoulder. "Suit yourself. Girls usually sleep till noon. Don't have much to eat beyond plain porridge, but you're welcome to it. Looks like you've all been through the wringer a few times."

"You've been so kind. Thank you, Madame. You know, I don't even know your name."

"Madam will do." Her gaze shifted to Barrett. For the first time all night, the hardness softened from their depths. "Don't normally let girls in here, especially nice ones, as they often have a way of never leaving. This ain't a good place for nice girls like you and your sister. I did it for him. And the memory he brings."

"What do you mean?"

The softness fell from her eyes. "Get there right at noon or there'll be none of the porridge left for you."

Chapter 24

Fire burned down his throat, snaking down to smoke out his lungs. Trapped in a wooden box, he opened his mouth to scream and choked on the ashes smoldering his tongue. The heat shot out of his mouth to set the box ablaze.

In the far corner, the vapors receded to reveal a woman curled on her side. Kat.

He dragged her head to his heart, willing his breath to fuse to hers. But he was too late. He'd exposed her to this peril, and he'd failed to protect her as she perished among the flames, taking his soul with her. Tears spilled down his cheeks, dropping to her hands like ashes where they burned up her arms, across her chest, up her neck and face. His breath blew out, scattering the last bits of her into dust.

He clawed at the ashes, desperate to piece her back together. A wail, deep and primal, exploded out of his mouth to shake the fiery beams overhead. With one final burst of heat, they collapsed on top of him.

"Shh, shh, now." A voice, soft and low, tugged him from the pyre. Cool fingers brushed his temples, tamping out the flames engulfing him. "You're safe, Barrett. I'm here with you now."

He grabbed at the hand to keep it from leaving him to perish. The muscles around his eyes twitched as he worked them to open. Just once, a glimpse of her to make sure she was real. They cracked open, and her face blurred before him. His free hand reached up to touch her cheek. So cool, so alive. The ashes shifted on his tongue. "Y-you're all r-right. A-alive."

She brought his hands to her warm lips, pressing a kiss to the fingers. "Yes, darling. We're all right now."

The kiss burned down his arm, igniting his head to flames once more. His eyes slipped closed. At least if he was to die, she was the last thing he would see.

Floating in darkness. The heated pain ebbed away with the cooling currents sweeping over him. Grayness circled above him. Pushing against the blackness drifting below, he surged to the surface. But instead of the anticipated face, he was greeted with dark-rimmed eyes set into a flabby face. A lantern flickered on the bedside table. No other light permeated the room due to the blackout sheets drawn tight against the window.

"Who are you?" His voice sounded rough as unsanded wood.

The woman didn't blink. "No one of consequence. But you, on the other hand, are something else entirely."

He struggled to sit up, but she shook her head. "Don't move or you'll tear my handiwork. That poor girl's been through enough. She don't need to come in here and find you bleeding out again."

A cracked vase filled with lilacs sat on the bedside table filling the air with sweetness and the lingering presence of Kat. "Where is she?"

"Resting. Finally." She fluffed the lace barely covering her ample décolletage. "As you should be doing, Monsieur Anderson."

The headache hammered behind his eyes as the darkness unfurled once more along the edges of his mind. "Did she tell you who we are?"

The orange-and-red feather sticking out of the woman's hair wobbled back and forth as she shook her head. "*Non*, but she didn't have to."

He blinked rapidly to stop the encroaching darkness. "But you know me."

A slow smile curved her garish red lips. "*Oui*, and you know me, *mon coco*. But you don't remember."

The words drowned in his throat as the darkness swarmed over his head, pulling him down to the depths once more.

"Where are you?" Barrett staggered against the handrail, peering down to the parlor below. Strangely quiet. Wasn't a brothel supposed to ring with laughter and bedsprings? His stomach growled, urging him on.

His head spun by the time he made it down the creaking stairs. "Poppy!"

Opening the door on the left, he stepped into a gaming room filled with tables, chairs covered in faded green velvet, plush curtains, and crude paintings of women dancing together. Voices drifted under the crack of a door to the far right of the corner. Sweat trickled down his brow. What if the Nazis had found them?

Kat! Sliding between the tables, he wrenched open the door and hurtled into the room. Ten pairs of painted eyes fluttered up to him, spoons dripping with colorless porridge hung in midair to their painted mouths.

Kat shot up from her seat at the far end of the kitchen table. "What on earth are you doing out of bed? Upstairs, immediately."

"I . . . em . . ." His gesturing hand fell flat. "Didn't realize we had company."

"We don't, as we are their guests." She hurried around to him. A thin cotton dress that was at least two sizes too small clung to her figure, and her hair had been recently washed as damp strands swung over her shoulders. "Madam has graciously allowed us to stay for a night or two until you're well enough to travel once more."

His gaze shifted to the thick woman presiding at the head of the table. She met his stare without blinking her dark-rimmed eyes, just as she had last night. Was that only a few hours ago?

Her bold eyes inspected the white linens wrapping around his naked torso. "*Bonjour*, monsieur. You're looking better than when they dragged you in here."

Why hadn't he thought to grab a shirt or blanket to wrap up in before charging down here? "Aye, feeling better for sure. Thank you for letting us stay here."

"Any enemy of the Germans is a friend of mine. No questions asked."

Good. Kat hadn't told her anything, and the woman hadn't asked. Yet she still knew his name. Uneasiness wriggled in his mind. He squinted at her in a feeble attempt to recall her face, her voice, her unnerving presence. Nothing.

"Wish you'd woke me up to help tend those wounds." A skinny girl from the corner seat giggled. "I'm good with my hands."

The girl next to her tittered as the strap of her slip fell off her shoulder. "And I'm good with everything else."

Madam's palm smacked the table. "*Silencieux*! There are ladies here, and I won't have your rough talk in front of them."

Kat touched his elbow. "Back upstairs with you. I'll bring you a bowl of porridge."

"No, I can't be in that room a minute longer. I need air."

"There's a bench out back. Wait out there, and I'll join you in a minute." Stretching up, she pressed a kiss to his cheek, to the howling delight of the room.

He had no mind to sit outside eating, not when that madam followed his every move as if she knew the secrets he carried. But he wasn't getting any answers with ten pairs of roving eyes fixed to his naked chest.

Outside, weak sunlight filtered through hazy clouds. Crispness stippled the air as the long, hot days of summer sloped into the cooling of autumn. He sat on the bench and leaned his sore back against the building, ignoring the rough wood that chaffed his skin. Half-smoked cigarettes and cigars littered the dirt courtyard stretching around the area. The shambles of a leaning barn sat fifty yards to the right, its occupants and usefulness long since departed. A towering oak tree threw shade over the golden grass farther out, with what looked to be a flower garden sprouting at its roots. Even farther, low hills rolled and dotted with snaking vineyards, their fruit picked weeks ago for the harvest.

He leaned his head back and took a deep breath. Too long since he'd relaxed in the open air, unclogged with city dirt and Nazis.

The slight cut angling from his shoulder to his hip had scabbed over, and his ribs ached from the pummeling they'd received. He turned his wrists over. Rope burns snaked around them. But he was alive. Thanks to her, he was alive. He closed his eyes.

Footsteps sounded on the dirt. "I know my shirt was a wee bit torn, but I hope you've at least found a bedsheet for me to wrap up in. Don't need those women getting any ideas before the regular customers come in. Besides, I've got my own nurse that I'm quite pleased with."

"She's worn herself out making sure you pulled through."

Barrett's eyes popped open to see Ellie standing in front of him. Wrong sister. He leaned forward to cover his chest with his arms. When the swath of bandages proved too difficult a barrier, he gave up. Not like she hadn't seen a half-dressed man before. "Just a few scratches. Nothing to worry about."

"But worry she does. Lifelong habit." Her toe scratched in the dirt.

Silence stretched between them. Barrett cleared his throat. "Out for a walk?"

She nodded. "Wanted some quiet. A change for me when I usually prefer the hustle and bustle."

More silence and toe scratching. Barrett looked to the closed door leading inside. Where was Kat?

Ellie shifted her weight and tugged the patched shawl closer over her shoulders. She, too, wore a dress several seasons past its prime. "She, uh . . . She didn't tell me exactly what happened when she went back to get you." She glanced up from her feet, biting at her lip. Without all the war paint covering her face, she looked like an innocent young girl. "By the looks of you, well, I managed to piece together the gist of it."

He shrugged a shoulder. "Nothing I couldn't handle." He could've handled the torture all on his own for however long it took, knowing it was to keep Kat safe, but in the end it was she who had saved him. He owed her everything, but didn't have two bits in his pocket to offer her. Nothing except himself. What a pitiful offering.

"I know you went back to save us, for Kat."

He shifted uncomfortably on the bench. "It's the least—"

"But it wasn't, was it? So many times over the past month you've swooped in to take care of things, keeping Kat out of trouble when her mouth got the better of her temper, and then getting us out of Paris when Eric's true colors came to light."

Had they not been flying high before? The girl was more delusional than he'd given her credit for. "Look, it's all been a part of my job."

"Maybe at first, but if you hadn't come along, I'd probably be carrying Eric's child while he locked my sister away in one of those work camps. We wouldn't be standing here today if not for you." Her pale hands wrung the corner of the shawl. Tears swam in her eyes. "Thank you."

If he hadn't been sitting down, he would've fallen down from shock. "Em, you're welcome."

"And if I were you, I'd stop lying by saying it's only a job. A job doesn't require what you do for her, and duty has little to do with what she's done for you." She blinked back the tears and offered a wobbly smile. "I used to think I knew all about love. What a joke. But with you two . . . I see it for what it truly is now."

Barrett's jaw slacked open. Love? Who was using that four-letter word? He shifted again as heat flushed up his chest, blood pounding to his head. Kat had never incited a four-letter word from him. Well, except the times she refused to listen, which was almost all the time.

Irritating, maddening, utterly charming woman that his heart cried out for. He dropped his overheated head to his hands. What was he supposed to do now?

The door flew open and Kat walked out holding a steaming bowl of porridge. "Not as tasty as bacon and crumpets, but it's filling and warm, which is more than we've had of—What's wrong?"

Setting the bowl on the bench, Kat dropped to her knees in front of him. Her hands ran down his arms, up his neck, across his face. "Are you in pain? Dizzy? I told you to stay in bed. Ellie, help me get him back upstairs."

"No, no. Just, em, chilled." His head snapped up to see a blanket draped over her arm. "Good, you brought something." He grabbed the blanket and threw it around his shoulders to cover the exposure keenly bearing down on him.

Somewhat appeased, she tucked the edges of the blanket around him and sat next to him. "Ellie, did you not want lunch? Or do they consider this breakfast? Though it's going on four o'clock, they did say this was the last meal before they open for business."

Ellie laughed. "Never thought I'd see you say that with a straight face, and no, I'm not hungry. Had a big lunch, or was it breakfast? Their meal schedule is off."

Barrett swallowed his laugh on a spoonful of bland porridge. Two English ladies debating the mealtimes of a whorehouse was not a conversation he wanted to get into the middle of.

Shifting her gaze between her sister and him, Ellie tapped a small pebble into the dirt with the toe of her shoe. "Guess I'll go see if our clothes are ready to take off the line. Don't know how much longer I can stand being stuffed into this dress."

Kat tugged at her own plunging neckline and nodded. "The sooner the better."

Silence settled around them as Barrett dug into his porridge as if it were a steak and potatoes while Kat gazed quietly at the courtyard and empty vineyards far beyond. Accustomed to all the flurry usually accosting them, the constant danger stalking them, and the ever-present falsehoods to keep in place, how peaceful it was to simply sit together without words.

Polishing off the porridge, he chugged back the tankard of water she'd brought out. He'd ask for more, but by the looks of the women back inside, they needed more nourishment than he did. Even if it tasted like old wood chips. "Did you get plenty to eat?"

"Yes, though I hated taking portions away from those girls. Two of them are barely sixteen."

Tightness pinched his chest. Same age as his mother when he was born, and probably in a place too similar to this one. He pulled the blanket over his shoulder as it slipped down. "We need to leave by nightfall. Dangerous to cover ground at night, but more dangerous to keep to the roads in the day. We can reach Salbris in two, maybe three, days."

"More like three to four. We're not leaving tonight." She shifted on the bench to face him. Dark circles haunted her eyes. "I am not dragging your body for however many kilometers it is to Salbris because you simply needed one more night to rest. Madam has already given consent, so that's all there is to it."

His rebuttal collapsed on a huffed breath. "So you're calling the shots from now on, are you?"

"Yes, and I think I quite like the change." She grinned. The lipstick long gone, her lips flushed rose. Delicate, perfectly shaped, inviting.

Desire swept through him. He brushed his thumb over her satiny cheek. Her skin was white as milk, and it took only a moment for the blood to sweep to the surface and tint it an exquisite shade of pink. Her black eyelashes swept down to graze her cheeks as gracefully as butterfly wings, concealing the green glinting from the inner depths of her blue eyes. She tilted her head to greet his mouth, the corners of her lips curling up as he brushed against her. He angled his head to fully cover her mouth with his own . . . and bumped his nose into her cheek.

He jerked back and covered his pulsating nose with his hand. "Ow!"

"Let me see." Kat pushed his hand out of the way and gently touched the bridge and tip. He tried to squirm away as the angry sensation pulsed to his brain. "Just hold still. You move worse than when we have to give the eardrops."

"You're not the one with a broken nose."

"It's not broken, merely bruised." She dropped her hand and fixed him with a raised eyebrow as one might a raving child. "Would've thought a man with as many brawls under his belt as you would know the difference."

"Still bloody hurts."

She inched closer, brushing her shoulder to his with one hand on the bench between them. He dropped his next to hers so the sides of their hands touched. Long, pale, with perfectly rounded nails, her hand looked out of place resting on the rough-hewn bench next to his calloused and blunt one. He lifted his little finger and stroked it over hers. So soft that if he wasn't looking straight at it, he would've imagined he was touching air. His other fingers lifted up to brush over the top of her knuckles and down the length of each finger. He held his breath as he wondered if she would draw back from the impropriety. Ridiculous considering she'd seen him half naked, but there was something so intimate about touching another's hand, brushing over the skin, tracing down the lines of the palm. He'd never given much thought to hands beyond their usefulness as a tool to eat, lift things, and fight. But now . . . Out of the times he'd kissed her, he'd never been so nervous as now when all he wanted to do was lace his fingers between hers and share the flow of his heart pulsing through his palm to hers.

She flipped her hand over and captured his fingers between her own. With a deep sigh, she settled against his shoulder. He closed his eyes, grateful for the small reprieve they had together, and just for a few moments tried to imagine their world without Nazis. Ironic that that was what had brought them together in the first place.

"Why did you do it?"

He cracked one eye open. "Do what?"

"Go back."

His other eye slid open. "I had to."

"Without me? I thought we were in this together. No lies. You promised you would never lie to me. You said you would be right behind me." She turned to him, pain drawing her face taut as anger spiked her words. "You weren't there."

"I said I would be somewhere behind you, and I was. Those men would've caught us."

"So you turned back to use yourself as bait."

The crack in her voice drove through him like a hatchet. He crushed her fingers between his. "I did it because I had no other way to keep you safe."

Her lips pinched white as if trying to hold back a heated rush of rage. Ever so slowly, she pulled her hand from his grip and pressed it to the side of his face. Fingernails dug into his skin. "Do not *ever* leave me alone again. Hear me, Barrett Anderson? *Ever.*" Her other hand rose up, capturing his face in a viselike squeeze. "If you do, I swear you won't live long enough to regret it."

She kissed him, hard and quick, to drive her fatal threat home.

The door banged open. "*Excusez moi.*" One of the girls from inside with too much eyeliner leaned a bony hip against the doorframe and took a long drag from a cigarette. "About to open for business. Unless you feel like entertaining with us, Madam suggests you get upstairs."

Chapter 25

Morning brought news of the RAF bombing half of Berlin, and Madam promptly closed down the house for the night to celebrate. With any luck, it was the beginning of the end for this bloody war.

Picking up a table stained with whisky and other unsavory spots, Barrett carried it across the room as his dark thoughts crashed in on one another like thunderclouds.

"Don't lie to me."

I'm going to betray your trust.

"Don't lie to me."

I'm working with your father because he expected you to fail on your own.

"Do not lie to me."

He's paying me enough to start my life over far from here, and I only get payment if I hand deliver you in person.

"Do not ever lie to me."

I ache for you more than my own soul.

Barrett set the table down harder than he expected. Two girls hanging colorful shawls like banners rushed over, their hands a flurry of concern over his arms and face.

"M'sieur, est-ce que tu vas bien?"

"Fine, fine." He waved them off before Kat could turn around and catch them at it again. Any time he made the slightest noise the girls took it upon themselves to offer their nursing services, promising that every one of their "patients" always left feeling better than when he came in.

Standing in the corner with the violin player going over song selections, Kat stood out against the dark-wood walls, stained floors, and soiled doves like a beacon on a night of pitch black. Not even the poorly patched dress and golden hair tied back with a simple pink ribbon could diminish her radiance. She glanced over her shoulder at him, a smile blossoming across her face that sent a heated thrill racing through him. But the thrill turned cold. One day soon, when she found out about his deal with her father, she wouldn't smile at him like that. Not when his betrayal pierced her just like the time before when a man had used her to gain what he wanted.

Outside, the sky glowered in steely gray. Trekking across the courtyard, he wandered up the slope to the towering tree and the small garden beneath. A thin wrought-iron rail ran around the rectangular plot with the gate hanging off one hinge. The entire space was run over with climbing weeds and dead leaves, and a single crooked wooden cross sat in the center. Long forgotten, the wood was faded and worn from the weather, with dead weeds tangling over its arms. *Petite Colombe* was carved in the center.

"I tried to keep up the flowers, but my thumb is black as tar." Like a hulking shadow, Madam appeared next to him, black shawl knotted around her thick shoulders. "Roses, daffodils, and lilies once grew here. Beautiful, just like her."

The last thing he wanted was small talk with the woman. But considering they were under her roof, politeness was required. "Who was she?"

"Just another girl who fell here many years ago, like so many of them did during the war. Family was dead, and she was starving. She didn't belong, but I knew if I turned her out, then the Germans would get her."

Desperation came in so many different forms. He crossed his arms and studied the little cross. One single cross. "Why is only she buried here?"

"Because she was special. My Little Dove. Dark of hair, eyes of deepest blue, soft of voice, and kind as a saint."

"What happened to her?"

"What happens to many girls here. A victim of the occupation and too many soldiers far from home in need of a woman's touch. The doctor declared it consumption, but I believed it was a broken heart." Her gaze shifted to him, eyes dark and penetrating. "Had herself an *amoureux*, a man far from his country during the war. He left with a promise to return for her."

"He never came back."

Madam shook her head. "*Non*, but he left a piece of himself for her to always remember."

Barrett turned back to the cross and the sad story it marked. Images of his father crying himself to sleep over the loss of his true love haunted him. "Perhaps he did want to come back, but never could."

"Perhaps. I believe they loved one another, but he never darkened our door again. Not even after the countless letters she sent him."

Barrett often came home to find his father sitting on the cold floor surrounded by letters from his love. He'd look up at Barrett with despair spilling from his eyes. *"She wrote me, but I never knew. They were delivered too late."* Then he'd cry like a baby curled up on the rug.

His jaw worked back and forth. "Guilt often keeps a man from doing the right thing."

"*Oui*, she deserved a happy home, a baby to love."

Barrett could feel the directness of her stare boring into the side of his face. Did she like unsettling everyone like this, or was it his lucky chance?

Reaching into the bosom of her black-fringed dress, she pulled out something. She carefully smoothed out the slight curls to the edges and held it out. "Would you care to see her?"

An odd pitch colored her words. Alarmed, he turned to see a photograph in her shaking fingers. Of course she was emotional. The girl obviously meant a great deal to her. Barrett took the photograph and scanned the faces of sixteen girls, all scantily clad and perched on the same rickety staircase that stood inside now.

"Third row from the bottom, next to the wall."

He stopped on the indicated face. Long dark hair, bright round eyes, small nose turned up at the end. His heart stopped. He knew this face. Had stared at it for nearly thirty years, desperate to call back the woman who had left before he had a memory of her to call his own. His mother.

"Where did you get this?"

"I had it taken to celebrate the end of the war." Madam's fat finger edged over the top of the picture, pointing at *her*. His mother. "She was barely three months pregnant with you here."

His heart sped up, pounding in his head as vile anger pierced his veins. "And you still had her as a whore? A pregnant woman?"

"The day she found out she was carrying you was the day she quit. She cooked, cleaned, mended the girls' clothes, anything she could do to earn a few coin. She put it all away for you." Her face hardened as the memory spewed out. "It was her dying wish to see you safely to your closest kin, so I used the money and bought your passage to Scotland with a sister from the House of Mercy as your caretaker for the voyage. You didn't belong here, but you sure didn't deserve belonging to the likes of him." She spat on the dry ground.

The need to defend his father clashed with the burning memory of the hunched-over weeping man after a long night of drinking. Barrett swallowed back his anger. "My da was many things, a father not being one of them, but he wasn't low enough to spit on."

Red flared on Madam's fleshy cheeks. "He left her here. Knowing how she loved him, he left her here. You're probably not the only bastard he left behind."

"My father was a shell of a man after the war. He turned to drink and never recovered. At night I could hear him crying for *her*." His tongue faltered on the name he'd tried so hard to repress. "For Marie. The letters she wrote never got to him until it was too late, and soon after I showed up on his doorstep. Unannounced. He was too buried in grief for my mother to give a second thought to me."

Though flung with as much venom as he could, the words seemed to assuage the woman's own. She looked back to the forlorn cross. Her face softened. "You look just like him. That's how I knew who you were when you showed up at my door. Like a ghost from a distant time. Everything except the eyes. You got that color from Marie."

For the first time in oh so many long years, sadness crept in. He'd shoved it away, barring it from his existence, but the picture in his trembling hand broke the barrier of his resistance. Longing slashed his soul. Longing to know the woman who smiled so sweetly up at him, who had scrubbed the stains from a whorehouse floor to keep him fed, to once remember a mother's touch and gentle kiss good night, to find joy in her smile when she looked at him. The ache swelled to unimaginable pain. He held the picture out to Madam before it consumed him.

"*Non*. You keep it. I don't need the picture to remember anymore."

Not trusting his voice, he nodded his thanks and carefully tucked the photo into the breast pocket of his shirt, just over his heart. He'd never again see the one he'd kept of her in his carved box back in Paris, but this . . . This he would never let go of.

"This is yours too." Fishing again in her ample bosom, she pulled out a pale-yellow handkerchief wrapped around something round. "Your grand-mère's. It was the only thing left after the fire that consumed your mama's family. She was all alone after that."

"Did she ever speak of them? Where they lived?"

"I know what you are thinking, but it is useless to cling to that. She only spoke of them once before locking away her memories forever. I know nothing more about them that may bring you peace. I am sorry."

The brief hope of finding living relatives flared like a firework and burned out just as quickly with only the smell of momentary brilliance smoking in the air.

Barrett took the handkerchief and peeled back the corners. Nestled inside was a brooch with a single large blue stone surrounded by tiny dark-green ones. He quickly covered it back up to prevent seeing his reflection, filled with angst, in the stone's shiny surface. "Thank you."

He turned around, putting his back to his mother's grave and the incredible sorrow it weighed on his soul. The brothel stood before him. Worn, with the wooden panels warping off, and discolored patches in the roof. He'd sworn to tear it down with his bare hands if he ever found it. But now, with his mother pressed to his heart and his grandmother heavy in his hand, he lacked the strength for it.

The packed dirt beneath his feet was hard, unrelenting. The tangle of weeds crawling over the simple mound within the plot a cruel ending to the woman buried beneath as the world marched on unknowing of her. Here she had been for the entirety of his life and here she would remain. To have come so far to find her, to stand so close only to be separated by a sleeping eternity of dirt. Would he ever be so near her again? Would he ever see all of those snatched away from him again? His mother. Sam. Or was Barrett doomed to walk on with only their fleeting memories to haunt his guilt? Their lives might have turned out different without him shouldering in death.

He would not allow their sacrifices to go without atonement. If he couldn't save them, he could save Kat. He would take her far and away before she, too, fell victim to the curse of those linked with him. This filthy place and the blackness that carved his path were the only things he had left to offer her. She'd never want him now.

"And thank you for not turning us away, especially when I've brought back less than pleasant memories." He started down the slope, eager to flee the grief behind him and dreading the heartache before him.

"She would've been proud of you. Saving these women at great cost to yourself."

Barrett stiffened but kept walking as the bleakness gnashed at his heels.

"You were the light of her life."

The teeth of anguish bit, wrenching a cursed single tear from him.

Chapter 26

I'm sure he just went for a walk."

"All afternoon and evening?" Kat scanned the room for the two hundredth time. Night had fallen well over an hour ago, and still no sign of Barrett. "He knows how dangerous it is to be outside at night with Nazis patrolling the area."

Ellie shouted over the din of the music and dancers' feet stomping over the floor in what was supposed to be a quadrille. "And I'm more than sure he can take care of himself should he be questioned."

Kat swung back to her sister. "By now, Eric has our faces plastered on every piece of paper available in France and probably Germany. No amount of clever talk and finely crafted false identifications can stop us from being rounded up and slammed into a hole the Gestapo have specially carved out for us. With any luck, they'd shoot us on the spot instead."

Ellie blanched, hands halted midclap. "You've been talking to Barrett too much."

Perhaps she had, or perhaps it was the first time her eyes had opened to what truly lurked around them. They weren't safe. Not even their next breath was guaranteed as long as they remained in occupied territory. But scaring Ellie wasn't helping their situation any either.

She patted her sister's pale hands. "Forget I said anything."

"How can I? Eric is all I think about." Ellie's eyes dropped to her newly mended skirt, washed and patched up from crawling over the ground. They were finally back in their old clothes. A little worse for wear, but at least they fit properly. "He'll never stop looking for me."

"As soon as we're back in England, he'll have no option but to give up. He can't touch you there."

"Maybe not, but he's always here." She pointed to her head. Without the constant use of peroxide, the dark roots were creeping out. "It's his face looming over me every time I close my eyes. Sweet and gentle at first, and then the murdering coldness like he had that night he shot that man."

She hunched over with a shudder. Kat wrapped her arm around her. "We'll be all right. I'll never let anything happen to you. Believe me?"

Ellie looked up at her and nodded. "Of course. You never fail, Kat." Her eyes slid over Kat's shoulder. "And he never fails you."

Kat turned as Barrett hovered in the doorway to the card room now turned dance hall. If he'd hoped to go unnoticed, he was unsuccessful. Standing well above every other person crammed into the room, and one of only four men amongst the women, he was like a flashing red beacon on a pitch-black night. He scanned the crowd, searching, searching, until finally his gaze landed on her. She smiled with relief, but he didn't smile back.

As the musicians eased into a slower tune, the girls launched themselves at Barrett. The town's baker, cobbler, and farmhand were left grumbling in the middle of the floor as their painted partners vied for the attention of the fresh bait. Brightly dyed feathers bobbed in their curled hair as they clucked around him, but Barrett merely flashed them a melting smile and shook his head.

A squatty girl with a yellow feather, henna-red hair, and a purple dress shoved through the throng, grabbed Barrett's hands, and hauled him to the center of the dance floor. Her flabby arm curled possessively around his waist, as she was too short to reach his shoulders, and she stepped off in time to the music, leaving Barrett no choice but to follow.

Their prize partner taken, the other girls grabbed one another and fell back to dancing. None had obvious training, but they were happy enough to celebrate for one evening without having to spend it on their backs.

The baker—a tall, skinny man for such an occupation—shifted through the crowd and stooped in front of Kat. "*Puis-je avoir cette danse, mademoiselle?*"

Rice powder stained his trouser cuffs and a spot behind his ear, but Kat inclined her head and took his hand as if he were a nobleman of the highest rank. Certainly the men back home, with all their glittering finery and noses stuck too far up in the air, never looked at her with such reverenced awe. "*Mon plaisir.*"

He had two left feet, but he kept up a lively conversation of rations, baking without flour, and the flowers he hoped to plant once the Nazis were gone.

Barrett whirled by, spitting at the hideous yellow feather fluttering against his mouth. "Having fun?"

He was close enough to touch, but years of dance lessons kept her hand resting on her own partner's bony shoulder. "Of course."

"You're mine next."

"Who else's would I be?"

His flabby partner spun him around before Kat had time to read the churning current in his eyes. Not soon enough, the violin lurched into a lively country dance.

Barrett barreled through the throng of grabbing hands and swept her into his arms and around the floor before she had a chance to catch her breath. "Got you."

"You didn't give me time to put a feather in my hair."

"No feather, please. I'll be spitting out pieces for days." His eyes traveled up to her hair, which she'd left loose with a slight curl at the bottom. "Besides, I like your hair like this. Not bound up like an English socialite."

"But I am an English socialite."

"Not like any I've seen." His arm tightened, pulling her closer. "You're not like any woman I know."

Desire flashed in the deep blue of his eyes as his heart pounded against her chest. Steady and strong, it whirled her pulse to drown out everything around them. Her fingers traced up his neck to brush the stubble covering his jaw. Ever so gently, she cupped his cheek and raised her lips in invitation. The desire surged in his eyes as he leaned down . . . and stopped. Blinking, he visibly reined himself in and drew back enough to put a space between their bodies.

"Where did you learn the Scottish dance?"

Stunned by the subtle rejection, Kat shook her head and tried to focus on his words. "I . . . that is, we had to learn all of the dances for our coming-out ball and presentation at court. Many of them are antiquated beyond words, but the reigning powers that be feel the tradition is best kept alive." With all eyes skittering to them, envious toward Kat and longing toward Barrett, she had to concede this might not be the best place to kiss. "I love the country dances best of all, but your footwork is a little off from what I learned."

"That's because you had English teachers, and I had the true Scottish lessons passed down for generations to guide me."

"You told me you couldn't dance. It's why we practiced so much before the movie premiere."

"Fancy ballroom nonsense. A Scottish reel is another thing altogether."

Did he realize how pronounced his brogue became when he spoke of his home? Or how his hair gleamed like polished mahogany in the lantern light? How secure she felt in his strong embrace with his scent of clean cotton and outdoor breeze tantalizing her senses? How she could think of nothing beyond wanting to press against him and kiss him?

A dark figure over his shoulder drew her attention. Madam watched the proceedings like a hawk, with her gaze lighting on them every few seconds. Kat tightened her grip on Barrett's shoulder. "Where were you all afternoon?"

He studied the top of her head. "Walking."

"It's dangerous."

"I was careful."

"That's not the point. You're always telling us we can't go out alone. This isn't the time for double standards."

His gaze dropped to her face. Her mouth. The banked desire stirred once more in his eyes. "Worried about me?"

"Always."

Tingles fanned across her skin as his hand brushed up her back and curled around her neck. Warm fingertips caressed the sensitive skin behind her ears, and her breath caught in her throat, threatening to explode from the pressure building within. She raised her hand and grazed a finger across his broad mouth, warm to her trembling touch.

"Kat," he said, voice hoarse. "There's something I need—"

A girl with a red feather yanked him from her arms. Kat was left standing in the center of the room with her hand still in the air, the impression of his warm lips turning cold on her finger. Heat flamed her face, threatening to set her ablaze right then and there. Turning, she ran for the exit.

None too gently, Barrett unlatched the painted woman's arms from around his neck and headed for the door Kat had gone through. He'd come too close to letting her convince him that everything would be all right, that they belonged together. The desire burning in her eyes ignited the yearning within him. She'd pressed against him. Surely she'd felt the barely controlled erratic beats of his heart. And when she brushed her thumb over his lip, he could have claimed her right then and there.

But they didn't belong together. Could never be together. Every obstacle blocked their happiness, not least of all this squalid place he'd been born to. She might be able to overlook that, but he never would, and he would never set such a decision to her. She deserved better than having to choose. But her father . . . She needed to know. And it was the ultimate betrayal from that that would seal their fate. That would set her to hating him and him to a lifetime of misery without her.

She wasn't in the parlor, nor was she upstairs or in the kitchen. That left outside. He hurried through the kitchen, shoving the crooked bench aside, and threw open the door. Cool, night air hushed the courtyard. He'd told her and Ellie a million times to not go outside at night. German patrols often scouted the area, and just because Madam had closed her doors for the night didn't mean one of them wouldn't come sniffing around in hopes of a lark.

Pulling the blade from his pocket, he circled the corner and stopped. With her back pressed to the side of the building, Kat tilted her face up to the pale moon. Her skin glowed like smooth alabaster.

She turned her head to him, lips parted. Every thought and determination he'd had vanished.

Shoving the knife back in his pocket, he closed the distance between them in three unbearably long strides. Crushing her to him, he found her mouth without hesitation in a hard, fiercely possessive kiss. Her arms came around his neck and pressed him closer until there wasn't a breath left between them. Her cool lips turned to velvet heat beneath his touch, branding him. He felt her intense desperation seeping into him, wrapping around his soul and pleading with it to join hers. His fingers tangled in her hair as complete surrender engulfed him like fiery darts hitting the ground and setting a blaze all around them.

It wasn't enough. No matter how tight he held her, how hard her heart beat against his, it wasn't close enough. His soul ached to cling to hers.

Her fingers dug into his hair, raking through it to send fire all over his scalp. She branded him. Hers for always. And he . . . he wanted her more than anything he had ever wanted in the whole world. More than his freedom, more than his next breath, more than his own life.

Slipping his arms around her waist, he tore his mouth from hers and kissed the satiny skin of her cheek, her ear, trailing the delicate sweep of her jaw and her offered throat. She smelled of lilac water, sweet and fresh. He kissed down her neck, lingering over the shallow indent at the base before traversing up the opposite side. Her pulse ticked wildly, and he could hear his own thundering to eclipse hers. Did she know what she meant to him?

Her hands kneaded his shoulders. "Barrett . . ."

The ragged cry of his name edged him back up to claim her mouth once more. This time not as hard, but still with enough longing and passion to blind him beyond all else except for her. She sighed against him as one hand slipped down to cup his cheek. Long, soft fingers grazed the stubble on his jaw. He felt her lips curl up in a smile. Taking her hand, he laced his fingers between hers and pressed his face into her palm, kissing it.

She dropped her head to his chest and sighed again. "Never let me go."

Never tripped on the edge of his tongue.

You won't say that in the morning.

He hated himself for what he was about to do. His arms tightened around her, savoring the feel and smell of her one last time. In the coming days and years, when the hatred burning in her eyes no longer stung as badly, he'd remember this moment and the perfection that existed between them.

"Kat." Blast his ragged voice. "There's something I need to tell you. Something I've held back for a long time now."

She nodded, tickling the underside of his chin with her hair. She tilted her head up but didn't step back from him. "I've been holding back something too. I think I knew a long time ago but didn't want to admit it to myself." A shy smile curved her beautifully swollen lips. "Barrett, I l—"

"We have to get out of here *now*!" Ellie's voice rent the air like a rifle blast. Racing toward them, she grabbed their elbows and yanked. They didn't budge. "Didn't you hear me?"

Barrett shook the fog from his head. Only then did he notice the terror slashing Ellie's face. "What's happened?"

"German soldiers came to the door demanding to join in the party." Ellie panted and glanced over her shoulder. "Madam stalled long enough for me to grab the bundle you made, but we have to go *now*! They're inside as we speak."

Barrett tamped down the fear rising in his throat. "How many?"

"Three, but they said more were on the way. The others had to stop at the houses along the way. To search them."

Kat gripped his arm, squeezing the blood from it. "Search for what?"

"Us."

Chapter 27

Kat ducked her head under the low-hanging branch. The fourth one in the past hour that had tried to take her head off. Blast those clouds hanging over the moon. Tonight of all nights they needed its light.

Ellie huffed and puffed in front of her as they hurried to keep up with the grueling pace Barrett set. Only if they had wings could they go any faster. That or a torch. Or a match or anything close to resemble light to see the ground by.

Ellie stumbled, her small cry of surprise shattering the stillness of the night. Kat reached out to help, but Ellie brushed her off. "The rocks are out for me tonight."

Barrett's head whipped back with a silencing glare before continuing on. Kat swallowed back her own curses for the rocks rolling beneath her feet. Damp night air seeped through her jacket and pitifully thin wool skirt, chilling her to the marrow of her bones. Exhaustion batted at her mind. She fought against it, desperate to keep her wits in order to survive the night.

They'd slogged through grassy fields, over rolling hills, and around treacherous fallen trees with nothing but their ragged breaths to punctuate the stillness of the night. No one dared to whisper aloud their fears lest they give away their position to the beasts tracking them. But now the crunching sound of their footsteps on dead grass and packed dirt was softened with gurgles. Kat's ears pricked to the gentle noise. A stream. Pushing through knee-high grass, they found the dark waters rippling around a rocky bend. Barrett knelt down on the marshy bank and scooped a handful of the wetness into his mouth. Declaring it clean enough, he quickly refilled their canteen and stuffed it back into the haversack slung over his shoulder.

"We need to cross." He pointed to a few rocks and a rather wet piece of log dotting the shallow stream's surface. Seven feet across at best. "It's not deep, but the last thing we need is wet feet."

Nimble as a deer, he hopped across the rocks and waved Ellie forward. Arms outstretched like a cat over her bathwater, Ellie wobbled on her toes as she timed each footstep to the next rock like a dance step. Her foot touched the log. With a *snap*, the log gave way. Ellie lurched forward with arms flailing, and Barrett caught her and swung her to shore before she landed facedown in the muck.

He set her straight and turned back to Kat. "You'll have to jump the last step."

Her right foot slid forward on the first step. Ridiculous hobnailed shoes. Why hadn't she taken them off beforehand? The next sharp-tipped rock found her foot teetering for a grip. Oh, that was why. One, two, three. She stopped to judge the jumping distance to shore and Barrett's outstretched arms.

She misjudged.

Her toes sank into the water lapping the shore mud. Barrett's arm snaked around her waist and yanked her out before her heels had a chance to land.

His face loomed over her, mere inches away. "What did I say about wet feet?"

She curled her fingers into the front of his shirt, soaking in his warmth as the night air threatened to chill her from the outside in. "Good thing you caught me, then."

The corner of his mouth curved, then quickly flattened. Straightening, he set her on her feet and stepped back. The warmth evaporated, leaving the chill more pronounced than before.

"Keep moving."

Barrett twisted his head left and right as they crested the slope up from the bank. Gone was the tender lover from a few hours ago who had held her so passionately in his arms, kissing her with the urgency of a dying man. Before her now was a man on a mission. But something had changed that wasn't due to the Nazis on their trail. He'd held her for the briefest of moments after she almost slipped into the water, his strong arms tightening around her and his mouth eased into that smile that made her heart turn somersaults. And then it was gone. As if he'd dropped an iron curtain to divide them.

A wind whipped up and tugged at her jacket. She held the flimsy material closer to her chest, wishing she'd had time to grab an extra pair of . . . pair of what? The brothel girls didn't own anything beyond flimsy to offer them. She shivered. Barrett had been so warm. Surely the chill or adrenaline from the escape had twisted her perception. He would never push her away, not now, not when they had dared to bare their innermost needs to one another. Not when *I love you* reverberated in her heart.

A deserted vineyard stretched in the valley below. Dead vines tangled together in row after row of what had surely once been a prized harvest of grapes. A reminder of ordinary days not so long ago, it had crumbled beneath the never-ending march of jackboots.

Like gnarled snakes coiling together, the vines provided somewhat of a break from the wind squeezing between the threads of her jacket and skirt. Kat plucked a dead leaf still clinging to one of the branches. She didn't know much about wine except which was proper to drink with each food course, but the leaf was a sole reminder of the bounty once produced here. Perhaps the grapes had even made it into one of the bottles gracing her father's table. The dead bleakness stretching down the rows on either side of her assured her they'd never know.

Nazis. They killed everything, from people to ideals and right down to the simplest pleasures in life.

Nearing the end of the row, Barrett held his hand up for them to stop. "There's a road up here. I'll step out and see if there's a sign to tell us where we are."

Ellie latched on to Kat's arm. Her body shivered from head to toe. "Hopefully far and away from where we were."

Kat chafed her hand over her sister's to stir blood back into the icy extremities. "We've been walking three hours, so that's roughly fourteen kilometers."

"That's it? I'm surprised the Nazis aren't breathing down our necks by now. Do you suppose that madam gave us up? Or one of those girls?"

Kat stamped her feet to keep them from freezing to the insides of her shoes. What she wouldn't give to turn this vineyard into a burning inferno right about then. "She assured me that everyone in that place was loyal to *la liberté française*."

"Nazis have ways of making people reconsider their loyalties."

"She would never give us up. Never." Barrett's vehement words sliced through the air like a sword, brooking no further argument. "Stay here."

Ellie pulled Kat down to the ground next to her and huddled close. Cold soaked through her wool skirt, but her legs sighed with relief from the break of constant movement.

"What's your boyfriend's problem?"

"We're being hunted like rabbits. What else do you think?" Kat pressed closer, desperate for the body warmth. Across the dirt road, Barrett headed toward the faint outline of a road sign. "And he's not my boyfriend."

"Beau, suitor, kissing partner. Take your pick." A foggy breath puffed out from Ellie's lips. She'd had more than one glass of Madam's offered wine, and the sweetness mingled with the mustiness of un-turned earth. "How did they find me so soon? This is a huge country."

"I'm sure Eric's put every one of his dogs on this search, but it's not just you he's after. Barrett alone is worth a king's ransom for all his connections."

Ellie dropped her chin to Kat's shoulder. Short little breaths shot to the back of Kat's ear. A few seconds passed before the telltale grinding of back teeth came.

"Spit it out before you grind your molars to dust."

Shifting her pointy chin, Ellie took a deep breath and blew icy air onto the back of Kat's neck. "I just . . . I don't have a good feeling about this."

"We're freezing to death in the middle of nowhere with armed Germans on our tails. Of course you don't feel good. I feel positively sick."

"No. It's something more than that." She sat up straight, digging her fingers into Kat's shoulder. "I don't think this is going to end well. Eric will find us no matter where we go."

Kat grabbed her hand before her collarbone snapped in two. "He no longer has a say in the matter."

Ellie slowly shook her head. The fear that had burned so strongly in her eyes moments before succumbed to something infinitely more dangerous. Resignation. "You don't know him. He won't let me go."

In some ways Kat agreed with Ellie. She knew him well enough to know he wouldn't go away without a fight, and the thought of engaging him in such a showdown was enough to sour the sickness coiling in her belly. She tilted her face to the hazy night sky and drew in a ragged breath. The coolness slid down her throat and stymied the acidity eating at her. She had to believe they'd get away. Just a few more days, and this would be a nightmare left far behind them.

"Why did you come here, Ellie? Truly, because hiding in a vineyard with the enemy hunting us is no longer a time for flippant lies."

Ellie sagged next to her. "I was suffocating. Each day in that house was a slow death. Sure, I loved the money and clothes, but I never wanted all those responsibilities that came with it like you did. I wanted to be able to make my own choices. If I wanted ice cream for lunch, then by golly that's what I wanted to eat. Not the soup and salad Mother had arranged. I wanted a chance to see new things and meet new people and know they were my friends because they liked *me*, not my family."

"I want those things as well." It was softly spoken, but Kat's whole heart shouted with the admission.

"Then why didn't you reach out and take them?"

"I've never had your gumption. We were given our roles to play at birth, and I've upheld mine all these years to be the perfect daughter, to conform to our family image. Then you left, overturning every-thing I felt was supposed to be dear to us. I felt betrayed because you didn't seem to care."

"That's not true, Kat. I never meant to hurt you. Never. I'm sorry I've been such a terrible sister."

"*I've* been a terrible sister, trying to force you back into a mold you were never meant to occupy. But now I think, perhaps, it's time to change our molds. I've done everything I can to keep you safe, and despite the hardships, every effort has been worth it. I just don't think we can ever return to what was."

Ellie clasped Kat's hand between her own. "That's not such a bad thing. I kinda like this new and daring version of the Whitford sisters."

Kat squeezed her sister's fingers as a lightness settled over her that blinded the shards of rooted bitterness. "You know something? I think I do too."

Dim yellow lights bounced down the valley. The sourness surged up her throat. Headlights. And the only people allowed out past cur-few were Germans.

Kat crawled to the edge of the road and hissed. "Barrett! *Barrett!*"

The headlights stuttered along the rows of vines. Barrett was no-where to be seen.

"Barrett!"

Praying he'd seen them coming, Kat dove back to the coverage of the vines and pressed herself flat into the dirt next to Ellie. The mustiness of dead leaves ruffled under her nose from her shuddering breaths. Like the prongs on a spinning raffle wheel, the lights blurred down the road, catching between the twisted branches. *Tick. Tick.* Ticks of headlights slowing, slowing . . . until rumbling by in a plume of exhaust. Kat lifted her head enough to count two jeeps with four soldiers each. As their lights flickered off the road sign, the snouts of gleaming deadly metal scanned over the sides of the vehicles. Looking for their rabbits to shoot.

The lights jogged ahead and their hunters motored on, leaving nothing but a cloud of dust to settle over the prey. Kat's heart slowly receded back down her throat to lodge like a bolder in her chest. Minutes ticked by before she allowed her head to raise up.

A dark object hurtled at her. Kat rolled to the side as it careened past and dropped between her and Ellie.

"Are you all right?"

Kat pressed a hand to her chest as her heart threatened to jump straight out. "Don't scare me like that. I tried warning you."

"I jumped behind a bush when they came around the corner." Barrett held out his hand and yanked Ellie to her feet, then offered it to Kat. "They're heading in the direction of Clamecy, but that doesn't mean more aren't fanned out in the area."

Gaining her feet, Kat tried to knit her fingers between his. He pulled away and rubbed a hand over his side. A frown flattened his mouth.

"Is it your wound? You didn't pull the stitches did you?" Kat moved to examine the bandage, but he knocked her hands away.

"Twisted the wrong way. I'm fine," He turned away from her and pointed east. "We need to find shelter before dawn breaks. Rest up and get ready to move again at dusk."

Brushing the dirt from her sleeves, Kat tried to hide her disappointment in his sudden distance. "How soon will we reach Salbris?"

"If we keep this pace, we can be there before daybreak tomorrow." His gaze skimmed over her and back to the road. "No point in wasting any more time here."

Chapter 28

It wasn't the Savoy, but such splendor could never compare to the relief this decrepit old barn offered. White paint peeled off the walls, cobwebs clung to the rafters, and the gray light of dawn dripped through the holes in the slatted roof. Wet wood, mildewed hay, and animal hair mixed in an old recipe that assured them the structure hadn't been used since well before the war.

"Never have I thought a patch of moldy straw looked so inviting." Ellie peered into one of the deserted stalls and wrinkled her nose.

"Try to resist." Kat dug into the haversack to scrounge together a semblance of a meal. A slice of rice bread and an apple. Her stomach gurgled in challenge to the feeble offering.

The side door creaked open and Barrett walked in, sheathing his knife in his belt. "Perimeter's secure."

Kat palmed the bread and apple. "We hardly have any food."

He plowed a hand through his hair, standing it on end. Dark circles smudged under his dull eyes. "I'll ask the contact for supplies when I meet him."

"How does he know we're here?"

"I tied a white strip of cloth to the cemetery gate like I was instructed. Hopefully he sees it sooner rather than later. I'd rather not spend all day hiding behind gravestones on the off chance he missed the signal."

Kat noted the torn fabric at the bottom of his shirt. At least he had sense enough to not use his bandages. "Why not meet us here?"

"In case the Germans are watching, I'd rather not lead them here." He didn't bother stifling a yawn. "Don't know when I'll be back, but if I don't return by sundown then you'll know I've been caught. Stay hidden until dark, then head straight to the church. It's on the other side of town, so you'll have to circle around in the fields. Ask for Father Lucian. Understand?"

Fear bobbed in her chest. She nodded.

"Still have that club of yours?"

She patted her jacket pocket. It did little to persuade her of bravery. "Of course, but I won't need it, because you'll be back soon."

A muscle worked in his jaw as he studied her with hooded eyes. His fingers twitched over the handle of his knife. "Remember. Father Lucian."

The bobbing fear pricked and spilled out like oil, sucking the air from her lungs. "Please stop saying that like you're not coming back. We've come so far, Barrett. We're leaving together."

His muscle ticked harder, pulsing a vein in his neck. As she said his name, he looked at her. For the first time since they'd fled Chablis really looked at her. Weariness hung on his face, and his shoulders rolled forward. The teasing light that so often danced in his eyes was smothered beneath deep, penetrating waves of misery.

His despair harpooned her.

She reached out, desperate to soothe the sorrow from him, but he reared back as if she came at him with fire. The iron curtain crashed back in place, separating them. Turning on his heel, he marched to the door.

"Wait! Take these with you."

He eyed the apple and bread she thrust toward him and shook his head. "Not hungry."

"Liar."

Warring with himself for a second, he finally grunted and grabbed the bread, shoveling it in his mouth. "Keep the apple. Never cared for them much." Swallowing, he leveled her with a stare that could freeze water. "Stay out of sight."

The door slammed in her face. Its resolute finality echoed off the empty stall and crumbling walls and hit her from behind with a force to shake back her senses. Tossing the apple into the haversack, she raced out the door after him.

"What is your problem?"

He spun around, the angles of his face hard in the steely predawn light. "I told you to stay inside."

"For the past two days you've barely spoken to me, never once looked at me, and recoil from my touch as if I'm a leper. What's happened, Barrett? Please tell me, because I can't take the silence anymore."

"What's happened? Have you not noticed the Nazis on our trail? I've been doing everything I can to keep us safe and get out of here, so excuse me if I've been a little too preoccupied for long conversation by the fire."

"It's more than the Nazis, more than just getting out of here. I know you well enough by now to know when something deeper troubles you. Whatever this is started when you came back from that long walk in Chablis." She stepped toward him, pleading. "Won't you tell me what you're hiding deep down in there?"

"You have a bad habit of prying where you're not needed. Stop thinking your guiding hand is needed at every turn, because it isn't. Your sister will tell you that."

She tried to ignore the barb as his callous words hit their mark. "I pry because I care."

"You shouldn't."

"Well, I do. I care very much for you. More than I've ever allowed myself to care for anyone."

A warning ticked the vein on the side of his neck. "Go back inside, Kathleen."

"Not until you tell me what's going on."

"Nothing is going on except your flat-out refusal to listen to me for your own good. Now, do as I say and get inside."

His words cracked at her like a whip. A whip she'd felt time and time again her entire life, though wielded by a different hand. A fatherly hand that insisted it knew what was best. She'd had enough of that nonsense.

"The only thing I refuse to listen to is your continued lies. I know something happened that day. Something that twisted you inside, and now you're shoving me away because of it. Do you think it'll frighten me like some skittish shadow? I tell you true, Barrett Anderson, I'm not going anywhere."

"You should. You should flee as far away from me as possible."

"No."

Anger flashed in his eyes, hands curling at his sides. "Don't you get it? I'm dangerous for you. Every second near me taints you, and I won't witness you so far covered in my muck that there's no hope of escaping." His jaw ground back and forth, tempering the searing anger. "Leave me be to crawl back into the hole I came from."

"Barrett, I know your past holds many ghosts, and the roads you've taken have been less than desirable, but they do not make the man I see before me. A good, strong, intelligent, and honorable man."

He jerked forward, face hard as granite. "I am nothing but what my past has made me. A bastard. The son of a soldier and a whore. I was born in that festering brothel in Chablis. The same one that tended my wounds is the one I swore to tear down with my bare hands if I ever found it."

Kat's hand flew to her mouth to smother the soul-wrenching cry. Selfish to her own struggles, she'd never seen the anguish drowning him. She reached a hand out to him. "Oh, Barrett."

Jerking away, he turned to stare across the overgrown fields around them. Beyond a split-rail fence, the hazy fingers of a dull sun poked over the horizon. When he spoke again, his tone was heavy with dis-illusion. "My father died a drunk because he couldn't be with the woman he loved, the same woman who's buried out in a pile of weeds behind a brothel. So much for your honorable man."

"Honor doesn't restrict us to our past, only what we do now." Kat's heart broke for him. He carried the unbearable weight of unworthiness, thrust on him by circumstances beyond his control. But the greatest sin of all was that he believed it. "My family, its history, and its stand-ing have been an exclusive identity for me since birth, much to my own detriment, while you have lived with no family or history to center yourself upon. We deserve to break free of those bindings."

"I think many in your social ring would balk at that."

"Those stuffed shirts wouldn't know a real man of worth if he kicked them in the money bags." She reached out and lay her hand on his cheek. Compassion, longing, and hope trembled through her fingertips. "They could never hope to amount to you."

Sneering, he twisted his head away. "You live in a fantasy world, one you need to return to and forget all of this."

The bobbing fear swelled to unsurpassed pain in her chest as his words pushed her further and further away. "I'll never return to that world, not anywhere without you."

"I have nothing to offer you but dirty hands and empty pockets."

"Don't care about those things. This is what concerns me." She tapped her heart. "This is what I'm after."

"I'm afraid you're to live a life of disappointment, then. Go back inside, Kat."

In the dim morning air, she could make out no flicker of light in his eyes, as if he stared out at her from a bottomless black pit. Shoul-ders slumping, he turned away. Each step hit like a hammer of defeat to her heart.

"Don't you want me anymore?"

She couldn't stop the last word from cracking any more than she could stop the world from spinning out beneath her feet. Helpless, she held her arms out and waited to see where she fell.

His feet faltered. Staring across the field in front of him, his shoulders dropped even more on a heavy sigh. "Yes." He turned to face her. Desperation creased his face. "God help me, yes."

Closing the distance between them, she wrapped her arms around him until the air gasped from his lungs. His erratic heartbeat thumped against her ear as he stood stiffly in her embrace. She rubbed her hands along his back, across his shoulders, up his neck, and pressed her mouth to his, pouring every ounce of love she had into him.

Tentatively, his arms circled her as if afraid to trust himself. He didn't kiss her back, but he didn't pull away either. His hand cupped the back of her neck and gently pressed her head to his shoulder.

"You shouldn't do that." His hoarse voice rasped in her ear.

"But you wanted me to."

He nodded, knotting his fingers in her hair. "Yes."

Leaning back, she looked into his face. "Then that's all that matters. Your family, mine, they have no rightful say in our happiness."

He snorted, ruffling the hair from her face. "Spoken like an upper-class blue blood."

"Blue blood or base-born, it makes no difference. This war has changed everything. Boundaries like that don't exist, not anymore, not when people are fighting for the right to simply live in peace."

His hands dropped from her waist to ball into fists on his hips. A deep *V* creased between his dark eyebrows. "We go back to England, and that's all that will matter. War or not, some lines will never be broken."

"So we'll leave. We'll go to America, where there are no lines to compare ourselves to. Start fresh with no ghosts haunting our every step. A new life all our own. Isn't that what you've wanted all along?" As soon as the notion bolted from her mouth, it was suddenly and clearly the only thing she wanted to do. The promise of a new beginning, together.

"America." The word whispered like a dream on the fog. Something stirred beneath the hopelessness in his eyes. "You want to go to America with me?"

"Yes, I do. Despite what people may believe, I can actually think for myself. But if you keep making ridiculous statements like that, then I'm bound to change my mind." She grasped his face, bringing it inches from hers. No more hiding. "Whoever we were before and from wherever we came no longer matters. It's just you and me, Kat and Barrett."

His hand closed overtop hers, warm fingers sliding between hers and drawing out the early morning chill from their tips. Deep within his blue eyes, something dared to stir, dared to slip out from its restraints and bare itself to her. She recognized it in an instant as the same hope that swelled in her breast. Brought together and tested by the searing fire of war, their fates were sealed. No longer two broken pieces but one solid entity made stronger together.

"Do you truly mean that? You and me, no more family names, no more lineages, no more past? We can start anew?"

"How many times do I have to say it? Yes, I mean it."

He gripped her hands tight. "There's something I need to tell you. I should have long before now, but I can't keep it from you any longer. No more secrets." Raising her hands to his lips, he pressed a firm kiss to her knuckles and raised his beseeching gaze to her. "I have to meet our contact first, but when I come back we'll talk."

A tiny worry snagged her feeling of complete elation, but she waved it off. Nothing he could say to her would top the nightmare of lies and horrors they had experienced. Whatever his confession, they would overcome it together. As they always had.

She smiled at Barrett with all the love brimming in her heart. "Yes, we'll talk. Hurry back."

Only a few more hours and he'd finally put this accursed place behind him. His contact, a burly man with the burnt, metallic smell of a smithy clinging to his faded coveralls, had outlined the plan in just under an hour. They would wait until nightfall, then meet him in the apple orchard two miles north of town where a Lysander plane would touch down shortly before midnight to ferry them back to England under the cloak of darkness.

"Simple as that, eh?" Barrett had said.

The smithy had shrugged. "Long as the *Boche* don't see us and you make that plane on time. It waits for no man—or in your case woman."

Adjusting the sack of food the smithy had given him over his shoulder, Barrett grabbed the top rail of the broken split-rail fence and hopped over. Across the field leaned the decrepit barn. And Kat.

Her pleas had hammered at the walls he'd bricked up to keep her safe. It had taken every last shred of defense not to give in to the passion of her kiss, but it was the hope sparking in her eyes that proved to be his undoing. She didn't care where he came from, nor that he had nothing to offer her. She was under no illusions as to what kind of man he was and yet wanted him still.

An itch stretched up his side as the knife wound did its best to heal. He pulled his jacket tighter across his stomach to keep from scratching away Kat's hard work to keep him alive. She deserved better than he could hope to ever offer her. But no man could care for her the way he did. No man could—he swallowed against the tightness building in his chest—love her the way he did. Aye, she had his heart now and forever.

He started across the field, his footsteps lighter than the past few days when he'd trudged along with no hope. America was his dream, but she had changed it. Without her in it, it was a spit of land, bleakness that stretched on and on until his dying day. Only she offered him the light and rest he so desperately craved, and he could spend the rest of his life giving her the love and loyalty she was more than worthy of.

Except there was still that business with her father.

His feet faltered. Before anything, he had to tell her the whole truth. If the betrayal cost him her love, then . . . He shoved down the heaviness piling on his chest. He'd deal with the fallout later when he had a bottle of whisky at hand.

Pushing open the barn door on its one hinge, Barrett blinked several times to adjust his vision to the dimness inside. Though with the steely clouds covering the sky, the light inside was hardly much different from outside. Eerie quiet greeted him. Pulse leaping in his veins, he reached for the knife on his belt. Dried straw and cold dirt crunched beneath his boots as he stepped farther across the floor.

"It's you." Kat and Ellie popped up from behind a trough tucked in the far back corner. "Back so soon."

Sheathing his knife, he took a deep breath to calm his heartbeat. "The contact was waiting for me when I got there."

She brushed dry bits of hay from her skirt with a precise flick of her hand. "Are we leaving soon?"

"We're to meet him after nightfall when a plane will be waiting to take us back to England by midnight."

Ellie sidled up next to her sister, eyes large in her pale face. "Does this mean we're going home?" At Barrett's nod, Ellie squealed and threw her arms around Kat. "We're finally leaving!"

Kat's arms circled her sister, but her eyes shone for Barrett alone. A welcome of happiness between them. "Yes, it's wonderful." Unlatching Ellie, Kat moved toward him. He could almost feel her kiss brushing over him as she closed the distance. "Thank you."

The door behind him eased open on its rusty hinge. "Don't thank him just yet."

Barrett's blood froze. Eric had found them.

Chapter 29

Eric's iron-gray uniform blended in to the gray swath of sky behind him, its severity punctuated by the silver buttons gleaming down his chest. A Luger sat strapped to his side.

Stepping into the barn, he glanced around at the sagging beams and broken farm tools with a frown. "Come down in the world since you left me in Paris, *ja, schatz*?"

Color drained from Ellie's face. "Eric. What are you . . . How did you . . ."

Eric smiled at the tremble in her voice. "I think what I'm doing here is fairly obvious. I've come to claim what belongs to me. And as to how I got here, let's just say that you should be more careful where you leave things, *schatz*."

Reaching into his pocket, he pulled out a woman's comb. Dirty, with a few of the teeth broken off, and last seen in the hands of a man Barrett had sliced open.

"*Tsk, tsk*. I gave this to you, Eleanor." Eric slowly waved the comb back and forth. His teeth gleamed like razor blades in the shafts of lights streaking through the roof as his cold eyes moved to Barrett. "With all the blood you left trailing behind, I didn't think to find you still alive. Must have had a good nurse to tend you. It was only a matter of searching the nearby towns until by a stroke of pure luck I saw you crossing the field here. By the way, I am surprised at how quickly you traveled with such injuries. And with two women."

Barrett moved to block the women from Eric's view. "What's your plan now, Schlegel?"

"Take back what belongs to me, or weren't you listening? Perhaps your head is too full of Resistance news to comprehend anything else."

Smirking, Barrett crossed his arms over his chest to get his breathing even. What he wouldn't give for a gun to shoot the man dead on the spot. "'Bout time you realized I wasn't some pub owner slinging drinks for a living."

"I knew for quite some time. You didn't actually think I'd allow your kind to our parties, much less the Führer's home, without reason, did you?"

"More reason than to make Ellie happy?"

Eric's sinister sneer slipped into a second of vulnerability. "Her happiness is foremost in my thoughts and actions."

"Something you showed to a *T* when you locked me in that flat for a week." Ellie shouldered past Barrett to square off in front of Eric. Red splotched across her pale cheeks. "Or do you define my happiness by how many blond-haired, blue-eyed heirs I'll push out for your horrid wife? Think that ugly medal is enough to make me feel better when I'm no longer fit for a decent man to want me?"

Eric swallowed hard. "*I* want you."

Ellie's hands fisted on her hips. "Well, I don't want you. Not anymore. Not now that I know what you truly are."

"I'm sorry to hear you say that, but in time you'll feel differently."

Shouldering past Barrett from the other side, Kat stood next to Ellie. "Get it through that dense skullcap of yours: my sister wants nothing more to do with you. Nothing in this whole forsaken world is going to change that."

"Least of all you, her dear sister." Hatred burned like blue fire in Eric's eyes. "If you'd never shown up, everything would have been perfect. You've tainted her mind with your poisonous words."

"You did that all on your own, *Sturmbannführer*."

The hatred flared in his eyes, burning Kat to the spot. "I honestly do not understand what you see in her, Anderson. Sir Alfred must be paying you a shiny coin to keep you around her for so long."

Kat's back went rigid. "What about my father?"

"You didn't actually believe this man would pant after you if not for your father bankrolling him, did you?" He sneered. "Oh, dear. You actually did believe that."

"That's enough, Eric."

Ellie's reprimand crackled with animosity as Eric tore his stare from Kat back to her. "I'll forgive your sister's mouth for your sake, but stop this nonsense at once, Eleanor. Come back with me."

Ellie shook her head hard enough to loosen her hair from the ribbon tying it back. "Are you crazy? Do you realize what I've done to get away from you?"

Eric smoothed down the front of his tunic with a trembling hand. "Something I'm willing to forgive if you return with me now."

"Your compassion is your undoing, husband."

A shadow moved away from the doorway to stand next to Eric. His wife.

Leveling a silver pistol at Ellie's head, Hildegarde's blood-red lips parted in a smile. "The time for negotiations is over."

Barrett groaned. This party kept getting better and better. The hard edge of his knife pressed against his hip. Little good it did him in the moment. One move to that, and he'd have two beads trained on him with no way left to protect the women.

Eric's spine straightened, his tunic creaking stiffly. "I told you to wait in the car, Hildegarde."

"How long does it take to grab one simpleton girl?" Scoffing, Hildegarde fluffed her fur collar with one gloved hand while the other remained trained on her target. "I should have known you couldn't come by yourself to complete the task. Sure enough, I come to find you pleading like a dog with your *Englisch hure.*"

Hardness twisted Eric's face as he shifted to stand between her and Ellie. "She is not a whore."

"Mistress, lover, paramour. Different names for the same performance in your bed." Hildegarde shouldered past him and held the gun at arm's length from Ellie's temple. Bitterness burned in her dark eyes. "I didn't drive to this godforsaken place to stand around in a barn and have my expensive clothes mauled with the stench of pigs. Get in the car. Or better yet, the trunk. You reek of filth."

With a violent shake of her head, Ellie scooted back, bumping into Kat's shoulder. "You are out of your kraut mind, lady, if you think I'm going anywhere with you."

"Hildegarde, I told you to let me handle this quietly with no fuss. Now, put the gun down. What good is she to you and our legacy if she's dead?"

Hildegarde laughed, a cold, high-pitched noise like metal grating over gravel. "Her or some other girl, it makes no difference. It's not too difficult to find a vessel. But you have to have this one. How many times have I told you your sentimentality will be your undoing?"

"I'm warning you, Hilde." Eric's hand dropped to the Luger at his side, the sleek black metal sharpening the whiteness of his fingers.

"Fine. Have it your way." The woman's dark orbs rolled in disgust. She swung her aim to Kat. "This one shouldn't matter as much to you, and it will give me great pleasure to shoot that mouth off for good."

"If there's anyone whose shooting will be for the good, it's you." Ellie leaped forward and grabbed for the gun, but Hildegarde twisted and smashed the butt into Ellie's mouth.

Ellie fell back with blood dripping from her lip.

Dark victory surged in Hildegarde's eyes as she took aim once more at Ellie. "No matter what Eric thinks, you deserve to die. And how much sweeter it will be at my hand." She laughed as Ellie struggled to scoot back. "Look at you. Miss High and Mighty, crawling over the ground like a pig at my mercy. I'll remember this pathetic sight always."

"Get away from her, Hildegarde." Eric's drawn pistol didn't waver from his wife's back.

Hildegarde's head snapped around to him. "Or you'll what? Shoot me? You don't have the guts. You've never had the guts. If it weren't for me, you'd still be filing paperwork back in Berlin. You could never do anything on your own. You don't know how."

Eric's hand shook as red shot up his neck. "Last warning."

Without turning back, Hildegarde pulled the trigger.

Bam!

Ellie fell back, limp as a ragdoll. Kat screamed.

Hildegarde's white teeth gnashed like a wild cat's at Eric's gun still pointed at her. "You don't have the guts—"

Bam.

A bright red spot spread from a hole in Hildegarde's chest. Her mouth slacked open, dark eyes widening as the gun tumbled from her fingers. She dropped to her silk-stockinged knees and crumpled to the ground on top of her gun as crimson stained across her cream blouse. Two final gasps escaped her lips, and she lay still, staring up at the ceiling.

With a cry, Kat dropped to Ellie's side and pulled her head onto her lap. Blood oozed across the girl's shirt, making it impossible to tell where she'd been hit. Kat rubbed her sister's face. "Ellie. Ellie, can you hear me? Wake up!" Tears spilled down her cheeks as she looked to Barrett. "She's not moving."

Horror drenched Eric's face. His eyes ricocheted from Ellie to his wife. "What have I done?"

Eric stumbled to his wife and fell to his knees at her side. The Luger slid from his hand. He pressed shaking hands over the gaping hole, knitting his fingers together as if to form a patch, but the blood trickled through them and dribbled down his wrists to stain his uniform cuffs. "The blood . . . There's so much of it." He pressed down into the wound. "It won't stop. Too much."

Barrett held his arms out and shifted in front of the women. His pulse careened. "She's gone, Schlegel. Let her go."

"I can't stop . . . There's so much." Eric raised his crimson-coated hands before his face. The color drained from his cheeks as the pulse at his neck surged. His pale lips trembled together until the clacking of his teeth filled the silence. "What have I done?"

Gut roiling, Barrett grabbed at words, any words, to bide him time. He needed to get Kat and Ellie away from the madman. "Keep calm, now, Schlegel. I'm sure you didn't mean it."

"But I did. I meant to scare her, to cut off those slandering words." Eric raked his gory hands through his hair, staining the blond strands. His eyes, whites shining like billiard balls, slashed down to his wife's body. "She's made me a monster."

"You made yourself the monster!" Kat shrieked, tears flowing down her cheeks in angry torrents. "Curse your blackened soul!"

Barrett shot her a silencing glare. They needed to keep Eric calm before he waved that gun around and blasted off another victim's head. He took a deep breath past the rush of blood in his ears and turned his attention back to Eric. "You only meant to protect Ellie."

"Little good that did." His voice broke on a sob. "My Eleanor. What have I done to you, Ellie, *liebling*?"

Pushing to his feet, Eric staggered over to Ellie and dropped beside her. He took her hand and gently stroked the back of it, leaving red streaks on the pale skin. Eric's gun lay several feet away, but Barrett dared not leave Kat for one second. Any move, any twitch, and he'd slam a fist into that Nazi's face and crack it right off his neck.

"On your feet, Schlegel."

"What have I done?" Tears streamed down Eric's face as he stared at Ellie without blinking. Slowly, he shook his head. His eyes jerked to Kat. "No, no. Not what I've done. What *you've* done."

"I'm not the one with blood on my hands. Don't you touch her!" Kat snatched Ellie's hand from his. Her lips curled up like a wolf's at full moon. "No one is to blame but you. I came here to save my sister from your clutches, and now she bleeds out before my very eyes because of you. *You've* done this. You and you alone."

Eric sloshed his head back and forth. His teeth gritted together, breath heaving out in short rasps. "We were happy. Then you showed up and ruined everything. This is your fault!"

He lunged, grabbing Kat's throat and flinging them backward. He had only a moment before Barrett launched himself at Eric's back and ripped him off of Kat. Head down, shoulders forward, Barrett charged and hit the man straight in the stomach. They toppled back in a flurry of kicking legs and swinging fists. Fury raged through Barrett's veins and out his fists as he pummeled Eric's nose, mouth, and every smug muscle of his body. But the desperation in Eric fought back like a wildcat, swiping at his ears and biting at his wrists. Doubling up his fists, Eric rammed them into Barrett's stomach.

Barrett rolled over as his abdominal muscles spasmed in pain. Scrambling to his feet, Eric raced back to his wife's body and grabbed the pistol from where he'd dropped it. He pointed it at Barrett. "Don't move or I'll take your head off and then swing right over to your lover." He pulled the hammer back. "Or better still. I'll keep her alive to watch the life drain from your eyes with the knowledge that she brought all this on. There is nothing more painful in existence than to watch your loved one die."

Not about to die like a dog begging on the ground, Barrett staggered to his feet and sought a second's distraction to unarm the crazed man. "You kill me and you'll truly become that monster you never wanted to be. For Ellie's sake, don't. She'd never want to see you like this."

Eric stumbled around in circles, tears streaming down his face. He groaned and pressed a fist to his forehead as if the gnashing thoughts inside were too much to control. "How could I have done this? I only wanted to love her, to take care of her. And now she's gone. And taken everything I wanted, everything I hoped for, with her."

"Put the gun down, Schlegel. Before you hurt someone else."

"Hurt?" The whites of Eric's eyes shone bright as he gazed down at the Luger. He stroked a blood-stained finger down the muzzle. "I've only pulled a trigger four times in my life. Each time with precision, the intent to kill. But not her. Never her."

Eric gestured to Ellie's still body with the pistol. Kat gasped, covering her sister's head with her arms. Barrett lunged to block the gun's aim. "Give me the gun, Eric."

"She could never love me like this. This monster." He gazed past Barrett to Ellie. More tears rushed down his cheeks. "*Ich liebe dich.*"

The pistol flashed to his head.

Bam.

Chapter 30

"S he's still breathing." Kat lifted her cheek from Ellie's mouth. "But there's a lot of blood."

Barrett squatted next to her and gingerly pried away the reddened cloth at Ellie's shoulder. "The bullet's passed through, but we've got to stop the bleeding."

Kat yanked off her jacket and wound it around her sister's shoulder. Ellie's head lolled to the side, and Kat swiped the hair from her cheeks. "Ellie? Can you hear me? I need you to wake up."

Ellie moaned as her eyelashes fluttered. "No."

"You have to wake up. Please, come on. Talk to me." Kat looked to Barrett, panic whirling in her eyes. "We have to find a doctor."

Barrett glanced over at the still bodies and pooling blood behind him. "We need to get out of here. Someone will have heard those shots, and I'd rather not wait around to see who comes to call." Slipping his hands under Ellie, he lifted her in his arms. "Grab our sack of supplies. Leave no evidence of us for them to find."

"Where will we go? We can't carry her through town."

"We'll go to our rendezvous point at the apple orchard. The grass should be tall enough to hide us, then I can go and find help. Now, hurry!"

Barrett's heart thundered at each whistle of wind, each twitch of a tree limb, and each rock crunching beneath his foot as they hurried through the woods. Blessedly, the sun remained hidden behind a thick wool of clouds. Escaping the gore behind them in the barn and facing the dangers to come, brilliant sunshine would not do.

Finally, they reached the orchard. Barrett gently set Ellie down against an apple tree trunk, then stood to scan the area. The last fruits of the season had been picked clean from the trees. The once-sweet fragrances filling the air now gave way to the mustiness of drying leaves. Birds clattered in the boughs while squirrels rummaged in the grass for any leftover seeds. As the quietness of the place settled over him, he took a deep breath to calm his pulse. Safe enough for now, but they weren't out of the woods yet. Too many hours to count until that plane came.

He knelt by Kat at Ellie's side and took the girl's pulse. Slow and unsteady. She needed a doctor. "I'll signal our contact again. He's bound to have supplies or know someone we can trust to tend her. I'll be back as soon as I can. Make sure you—"

"I know what to do. Go."

The brittleness in her voice did little to ease his mind. He touched the red finger marks circling her neck, inciting fresh rage in his veins. "Kat. What happened back there—"

She jerked away from him, eyes never leaving her sister. "What happened back there is done. I've no wish to speak of it. Stop coddling me while my sister dies in front of me."

She was in shock. He prayed they'd be long out of France before the emotions caught up with her head. Pressing a kiss to her head, he stood. "I'll be back as soon as I can, poppy."

She didn't acknowledge his leaving.

The Lysander glided through the darkness. Not a pinprick of light to guide its descent, and only the subtle hum of an engine to mark its nearness. Kat's ragged breathing filled her ears with anticipation of their freedom. But inside her heart was breaking. Another illusion of happiness struck down by her father's interfering hand. The love she had to offer dashed upon the rocks by a man who found it unworthy of his attention. At least attention beyond money. Just like Marcus.

She bit the inside of her lip to keep back the tears. It mattered not. In a few hours they would be back in England and she'd never have to lay eyes on Barrett Anderson ever again.

Touching her fingers to Ellie's pulse, she found it weak but steady. Their contact, Madon, had brought a field kit and set to work immediately, cleaning and bandaging the nasty wound. As long as they didn't have to bail out of the airplane she would make it.

"A little while longer, Ellie, and I'll have you stuffed into clean sheets with a feathery pillow to match."

Ellie lightly squeezed her fingers in response.

Barrett squatted next to her and checked the pulse at Ellie's throat, nodding approval. "Madon says it should take about three hours before we touch down again. Compared to the last few months, it'll go by in a snap." Barrett touched Kat's elbow. "Your sister is going to be fine."

Usually so calming, his voice scraped down her nerves like fiery darts. She jerked away from his warmth seeping through her jacket. "Yes, she will."

"I didn't think any of us would make it out of that barn alive." He stroked her cheek, scorching her skin. "I thought I was going to lose you today."

Turning her cheek away, she dug her nails into her palms and struggled past the well of tears in her throat. "Yes, I can see what a terrible loss of an investment that would be for you."

He stiffened. "What are you talking about?"

"Don't play dumb with me. Eric lived long enough to spill your secret deal with my father. Paying you to pretend interest in me." A laugh, dry like a winter's wind, scratched up her throat. "I'm such a fool. How did I not see it before? A man of your clandestine occupation should have given us a wide berth, but you edged closer and closer. He must've paid you handsomely. He always does my suitors."

"I never pretended interest in you."

"Don't tell me you fell head over heels of your own volition."

"And what if I did?"

"Then I'd say you were lying."

He moved close enough for her to see the warning flashing in his eyes. "I told you from the start that I am many things, but a liar isn't one of them."

She leaned forward to give him full view of her own threats brewing. "Then what do you call this mission you've been on since the unfortunate day we met?"

"Precisely that. A mission to keep you and your sister safe at all costs because you couldn't be trusted to keep out of trouble on your own. I was going to tell you everything, but Eric got there before I could."

"Yes, he did all the dirty work of your confession for you. If you had any kind of honesty, you would have told me from the start instead of leading me on."

"I was sworn not to tell you no matter how much I wanted to."

"Lies again."

As their voices rose higher than the humming airplane closing in, their contact, Madon, looked up from where he kept watch next to Ellie. Barrett grabbed her arm and hauled her a few feet away. Air hissed from between his teeth. "I've been working for the SIS just as I've told you. Days before you arrived in Paris I received a proposition from your father. A side job to fetch you and Ellie back to England."

She tried prying away his fingers, but they held tight. "A paycheck too irresistible to turn down."

"Not irresistible enough to put up with you half of the time." A half smile curved his lip. His grip eased. "Are you really so upset that your da wanted you safe?"

She looked away as the pang of inadequacy hit her hard. "He didn't trust me, my abilities to do the job myself, before swooping in like always."

"Mayhap he did, but it came from a father's love."

She clamped her lips together as her throat ached with rising tears.

She shoved the weakness down. "I suppose he threw in a few extra coins to kiss me. What else did he promise you? A seat in Parliament? Land? The pick of his finest horseflesh?"

"None of those things matter to me."

"Then what does?"

"A ticket to start over in America. And you. Above all, you." Grasping her face, he pressed his mouth to hers. Hard and demanding, it sought to possess her.

Oh, how she wanted it to. Her traitorous body sighed at his touch, longing for more. But the betrayal was too much for her heart to bear. She shoved him away. "The plans we made this morning belong to another lifetime. Before Eric, before the blood, before the deaths. From the beginning, you've made it clear that we have no place together. We should never have allowed that to change."

"You're right. There is nothing in this world that should keep us together. I've done everything I can to believe that, but I'm done lying to myself. And to you. Nothing solidifies the mind faster than a gun to the head."

"Gun or not doesn't change the facts. Too much separates us. All Eric did was put it in greater perspective."

"I'm not about to acknowledge some murderous Nazi did us a favor, but coming within an instant of losing you made me realize how foolish I am to think I can extricate you from my very being."

He reached out for her, but she stepped back as anger boiled to the surface. "It makes no difference now."

"Why? Afraid to have a real man desire you, care for you, help shoulder the burdens you've too long carried by yourself?"

His heated words scorched her core, but they were no match for the burning fury shaking through her. "If I ever desire such a man, it'll be one who comes to me of his own merit and not because he's buried deep in my father's pockets."

Hardness carved his face. "I'm in no man's pocket, not even the mighty Sir Alfred's. It was a job offered and accepted to get you safely back to England."

"If it was merely a job contract, then why not tell me about it before?"

The hardness dropped as if dashed in the face with cold water. Turning his shoulder to her, he plowed a hand through his hair and wrung the back of his neck. "I was afraid to."

She crossed her arms over her chest, buckling back the fury that came too close to barreling out. "Of what?"

"This. This is exactly what I was afraid of." He turned back to her. Desperation warred in his eyes. "You lumping me in with all those other deadbeats who have let you down before. For the first time in my life I wanted to be there for someone. For you."

"And you were. Just as you agreed to do with my father."

"I'm sorry I've kept things from you. Truly I am. But if you're determined to retreat behind that cold wall of wounded pride every time someone shows signs of being human, then you're going to live a lifetime alone. No one to love and no one close enough to love you back."

Her heart screamed for her to swallow her ridiculous pride and forgive him and fall into the strong arms longing to hold her. But the wounds of the past inflicted by Marcus, even her own father, flayed open, raw and stinging. She'd trusted them once, had sought shelter in their arms, but had found no comfort in the end.

A rush of wind whipped her skirt as the airplane glided in low and touched down. It looked barely big enough to hold them, much less the pilot. No matter. She'd climb inside a matchbox if it got her back to England. And far from the turmoil of emotions she didn't want to sort out.

"Come, Mr. Anderson." Throwing her shoulders back, she summoned the coldest chill she could muster into her voice. "It's time you collected your payment."

Chapter 31

Barrett kneaded his hat in his hands, careful not to touch anything. The gleaming walnut floors, portraits of fancy dressed people and colorful landscapes lining the paneled walls, the velvet drapes surrounding the dozens of windows overlooking the rolling green lawn, and the smell of beeswaxed furniture were all profound reminders of the world Kat came from. A world he had no part in.

Three days ago they'd left the horrors of France behind as they flew across the English Channel to land in what appeared to be an abandoned airfield somewhere in Dorset. Two autos with armed soldiers had been waiting. One bundled away the women while the other tossed him in the rear seat and raced off into the night. He'd spent hours at a military headquarters being debriefed. He'd begged for news of Kat and Ellie, but none was given. Not until an invitation with a single name was presented to him at the end of his interrogation.

"Sir Alfred will see you now." Above the upturned nose, the butler refused to meet his eye. He flattened himself against the door in hopes Barrett's commoner germs wouldn't leap upon his starched penguin suit as he stepped by.

A long, spacious room with dark wood greeted him. Three walls were lined with floor-to-ceiling bookshelves, filled to capacity with musty tomes. The fourth wall of windows looked out to a formal garden of green hedges and sparrows pecking the ground. At the far end of the room, situated behind a massive desk with stacks of papers, sat Sir Alfred Whitford, the man himself.

Marching across the thick rug, Barrett didn't slow his pace until the tips of his shoes hit the front of the oppressive desk.

Sir Alfred's thinning gray eyebrows flicked upward. He didn't bother rising to greet him. "Mr. Anderson, we meet at long last."

Barrett gripped his hat to keep from slugging the man across his aristocratic face. "Aye."

Blunt fingers tapped the top of his immaculate desk, while deep lines creased into the man's face as he studied Barrett with unblinking eyes. Barrett had to imagine many a man cringing under such a glare. Though every angle of the hardened face was unfamiliar, that stare was utterly and completely Kat. He shoved down the sudden pang in his heart.

The fingers stopped drumming. "The deal was to bring my daughters back safely."

"As I've done."

"As you've done?" Sir Alfred's fingers clamped into a fist. "My eldest daughter comes home with bruises around her neck and the other with a bullet hole in her."

Bitterness, swift and red hot, barreled down Barrett's veins like a bullet readying to erupt from a muzzle. "They got those defending one another from a madman."

"A madman you let them cavort with all over Paris and half of Germany. Only for him to shoot his wife and himself in a barn."

"Has Ellie recovered?"

"*Eleanor* will mend now that she is home where she belongs. Unlike the places you dragged her around." Sir Alfred twisted his head to the side as red crept up his neck. His voice rose with each word. "Dancing with the *Schutzstaffel,* drinking with movie stars. Dinner parties with Hitler. What kind of man are you?"

"The kind you and your government cronies paid to rub elbows with those snakes. It made me sick to watch Kat slog on her belly alongside those monsters."

Sir Alfred's fist banged the desk. "Don't you dare drag her name into this. I wanted my daughters returned immediately, but my 'cronies,' as you call them, went behind my back and kept them there. Two weeks ago I found out my daughters were crawling through the French countryside with you blazing the trail."

The rage Barrett had barely tried to contain spewed up and out. If justice was swift, the louse before him would drown in the venom. "Yet here you sit, their own father, behind the protection of his mighty desk. Sending out drudges to do the dirty work for you."

"You know nothing about me."

Leaning forward, Barrett drove his knuckles into the desk. Words hissed out between clenched teeth. "I know enough that you didn't have the guts to go to Paris yourself. You sent your own daughter straight into the enemies' hands without the slightest hope of rescuing herself. Not that she needed much help. That woman faced down Hitler without a quiver. She has more backbone, more integrity, than you could ever hope to achieve with all your military medals."

Ever the political strategist, Sir Alfred gave no indication of abashed humility. "You didn't think she stood much of a chance when you took my deal."

Framed pictures stood on the bookcase behind the desk. Sir Alfred shaking hands with Winston Churchill, atop cavalry horses, on the decimated ridges of Verdun, and unsmiling with family. The largest picture of all was of Kat sitting primly on a stone bench in the middle of a flower garden. The perfect English lady. But not the woman he'd come to love.

The pang in his heart splintered open to crippling pain. To love, but never to claim for his own. "It took me less than a full minute to realize her worth, which you have failed in a lifetime to discover. She is the most fearless and unselfish woman that I have ever known and is too good for the likes of you. The likes of me too."

"They told me you were one of the best, but they failed to mention your tendencies as a hothead." Sir Alfred's eyes narrowed. "Shouldn't come as such a shock, you being a Scot and all."

Smirking, Barrett straightened. "And I heard you were a war hero, a real man's man. Funny how we both seem to have been misled."

"So it seems." The blunt fingers tapped once more on the gleaming desk. A sigh ruffled through the old man's nose. "If you're done insulting me, let's get on to the business."

Opening a lower drawer on his desk, Sir Alfred pulled out a chequebook and flipped it open to the first page. He dipped his nib in the old-fashioned inkwell and scrawled an amount and his signature to it. Tearing it out, he waved it back and forth until the ink dried, then pushed it across the desk to Barrett.

It was more money than he'd ever hoped to see in his lifetime. A ticket to America, a down payment on a brand-new life, and more to set him up for a very comfortable existence. All in his name, free and clear. But the astonishment quickly gave way to disgust. "I don't want your money."

Sir Alfred's eyebrows spiked into his graying hairline. "No? After all of this, the darting on the line of death, the knife attacks, the slogging through mud? My money is no longer good enough for you?"

Barrett's gaze flicked back to Kat's picture. "It's too good."

"Surely you can use it for something. You'll need to start over."

"Aye, I'll start over. But I'll do it as my own man." Stepping back, he gave a curt nod. "Good day to you, sir."

Back straight lest his heart collapse further inside, he marched from the room. Far from Sir Alfred, his twisted blood money, Kat's picture, and the future that was never to be theirs. The butler waited for him with the front door wide open. It slammed shut almost before he reached the outside.

A slight movement to his right caught his attention. Kat. Dressed in soft pink and pearls, hair elegantly swept back, and swirling in perfume, she was once again the perfect picture of a lady. His heart clenched.

He settled his hat on his head and allowed himself one last glimpse into those beautiful blue-green eyes. Then, reaching into his pocket, he pulled out his grandmother's wrapped brooch. Unable to look at the glittering stone, he pressed it into the only woman's hand worthy of such a jewel. His own jewel. "I'll miss you all my life."

He strode down the steps to the final cracking of his heart.

Was it possible to still hear the ragged breaking of a heart after watching it walk away without a backward glance?

Kat pressed her cheek to the bench's seat as hot tears poured onto the cold stone, the rattling in the empty cavity of her chest a cursed reminder of her loneliness. She'd waited for him on the steps, each second an eternity of torture until the door had opened and out he'd walked. As she looked into his eyes, her legs shook so bad she thought she'd collapse, but instead of the usual passion she found only sorrow that stabbed her to the core. *"I'll miss you all my life."*

She beat her fist against the stone, but it remained unyielding and impervious to her grief. Life. What life without him? Her entire life had been spent drifting from one social gathering to the next at the behest of her parents, talking to the same mindless people here, funding an approved charity there. Not until Paris had she found meaning in her well-laid path. And then Barrett had crashed in and veered her onto a completely different one. She owed him everything for that.

Her nails curled into the stone. But he didn't want what she offered. He'd taken her on as a job. Nothing more.

Yet there was no mistaking the longing in his eyes that beat in time with her own. There was no denying the love.

The scraping of wheels rolling across brick reached her ears. Kat pushed up from the ground to sit on the bench. She swiped her pale-yellow handkerchief across her eyes and folded her hands in her lap. Over the brooch.

"It's no good, daughter."

Kat straightened her shoulders and gazed across the low hedge maze. "I don't know what you mean."

"I've lived amongst women my whole life. I know when one of you has been crying."

Kat shifted on the bench as her father's pushchair rolled to a stop next to her. Polio had wasted his lower half, but his arms and shoulders were still solid from his years as a soldier. His direct stare bore into her, leaving little room to argue. "I don't know what's come over me. Never been much of a crier."

"There's a first for all of us." Leaning down, he pulled his thinning legs from the footrests. "Get me out of this contraption."

Standing, Kat moved around to place his arm around her shoulders and helped lift him onto the bench. She carefully arranged his feet on the ground before taking her seat next to him. Overhead, the hazy clouds burned away to reveal the glorious sun in its soft blue setting. The late-morning air chirped with birds flitting from one tree to the next. A far cry from her mood.

Father shifted, rubbing a hand over his slim thigh. Kat noted the goose bumps at his wrist. "Shall I fetch you a blanket?"

He scowled. "Stop fussing. Too much like your mother. That woman will fuss all of us into an early grave."

"Not Ellie. She loves all the attention bustling around her."

Father snorted. "And your mama is doing enough of that. Won't let her out of her sight."

"Can you blame her?"

"I might have her chained to the bed. See she stays home and out of trouble for a while."

"I think you can rest easier these days. Ellie is different. Paris . . . matured her. All the things she went through, she's come out better for it."

"Time will tell." Father harrumphed. "For now, you're both home."

Kat threaded her sodden hankie through her fingers, the dampness cold on her skin. "Yes."

"No small credit to you."

Her head snapped up to meet his eyes. "Correct me if I'm wrong, but was it not you who hired someone behind my back because you thought I was incompetent to complete the task on my own?"

"I would have paid an entire battalion to retrieve you both if that's what it took." He slapped a hand against his leg. "Blast these for crippling me so I couldn't go myself."

Kat stared across the top of the maze at the evergreen leaves bright despite the chill sweeping the air. She'd played in there too many times to count as a child. Father chasing her and Ellie about as they shrieked with laughter. The carefree days of youth. No expectations, no calls of duty, no class restrictions or political gains. Back when she was so trusting of the world and everyone in it.

"You should not have set up deals without my knowledge, Father. Not again."

"I will not apologize for sending someone to see my own flesh and blood safely back to where they belong. Incompetent? No, Kathleen. Never that. You are *my* daughter after all."

"Then you should know to trust me more. In all aspects."

"You're so young. You haven't seen much of the world. One day, when you have children of your own, you'll reconcile the decisions you make for their own good." His hands gnarled together over his thin legs. A body once so strong now reduced to a shell of former vitality, yet the submission to atrophy had only sharpened the steel of mind. A steel Kat sharpened her own resolve against.

"Their good or the good of the family?"

"To me, they are the same."

"But not to me." The brooch weighed heavy in her hand, a solid reminder of all that had happened. Of the woman it had forged of her own wit and volition. She had changed, and there was no going back. "When I was in France, I saw families torn apart because of their family names. People put aside their differences and came together in the spirit of what truly matters. I was forced to become what I never imagined, yet in doing so I found what truly matters to me. And it's not money or position."

"That money and position has provided you with protection your whole life."

"From some things, but in other ways it's a prison. A life sentence of what we do not want."

Her father, commander of troops and starer-down of cannon fire during the Great War, flinched. "I only did what I thought right. For you and Eleanor. To see you provided for and safe. Though as any good commander I must assume blame for my tactics." His dark-blue eyes, squeezed into a perpetual squint from years of staring through binoculars toward the enemy line, studied her without blinking. Finally, a long sigh settled down his round nose. "Perhaps you're right. Eleanor would not be here, and I very seriously doubt still alive, if not for your bravery." His bristled mustache twitched. "You've done me proud, daughter."

Tears pricked her eyes once more as his words assuaged the pain that had rippled around her heart for years. She swallowed hard to keep the waterworks from overflowing, as if he couldn't already see she'd been sobbing. No matter Father's sentiment, she couldn't deny the real source of their survival. But to speak his name and remember everything they had done and gone through together . . . She might as well slit open her veins and let the sorrow flow free.

She turned away before he saw the weakness cracking the surface. "I assure you it was not all me, Father."

"Not from what I've heard."

"You know better than I not to believe everything you hear."

He nodded, fixing his gaze on the hedges sprawling before them. "Yes, a lifetime of politics has taught me that. But every once in a while you meet a person who will undeniably tell you the truth flat to your face. Such as the man I met only this morning."

Barrett. Heart lurching, she dug her fingers into the tops of her knees. "No doubt he failed to keep his mouth shut when he came to collect his check."

"I shall say this: if I were still a military man, I would have had him court-martialed from his first two words. Never in my life have I been spoken to in such a manner."

"I suppose with his pockets now loaded with your money, he feels he has the right to speak to you any way he wishes."

"Must be a fine way to live. Speaking your mind without fear of reprisal. Would hardly work for our set. The aristocracy pride themselves too much on what is not spoken." His arm brushed hers. "Perhaps I'm getting on in years, but I'm finding that what's left unsaid is most often what we regret."

Kat frowned. "You're trying to make a point."

Father's lips flattened in the exasperated way they did with his dim-witted junior lieutenants. "That is a fine young man who told me off this morning, and you're a fool to not go after him."

Kat's mouth dropped open. Words tripped over her tongue, but not one made sense. "But how . . . What?"

"You're a Whitford. And no Whitford sits around weeping their eyes red like a silly debutante. We attack and never let up until the thing we want most is in our palm." He shifted position with a grunt, drooping his ramrod shoulders. "I've tried very hard to do what's best by you, your mother, and your sister. At times I did not always think of what you may have wanted, but I assure you it came only from wanting to give you the best of what you deserved. Truthfully, I never thought a man could be your equal. I was proved wrong today."

It was the closest he'd ever come and would ever come to an apology. And Barrett had caused it. Shaking her head, she twisted the brooch in her lap. The emeralds twinkled in the sunlight while deep-blue flames leaped from the center stone. Blue as his eyes. "He lied."

"Because I made him swear to it, which makes him a man of his word."

There wasn't one promise Barrett had made and not fulfilled. She'd trusted him with her life and would do so again without hesitation. And her heart? What of that tangled mess? Had he not stirred it to beating? He'd held it so close to his own that they had fused together. As he'd left her on the steps, she'd heard the sound of them ripping apart. But her heart had left with him, and she was certain it was his heart that beat inside her now.

Father touched her arm. "Kathleen, he didn't take the money."

He didn't take his payment.

He'd done it all without claiming a cent for his own. She pressed a shaking hand to her cheek as the beginning of a smile tugged at her lips.

"What are you still doing sitting here, girl? Go get him."

Chapter 32

I'm from Glennmoore Distillery. Got the cases here you ordered." Barrett hefted the crate onto his shoulder. Last drop-off of the day, and his muscles were aching from the strain. Not that they'd stopped over the past two weeks of carting orders around, but this was a first for the docks.

The ship's purser, a short man with round spectacles, ran a pencil down his clipboard. "Name?"

"Glennmoore Distillery. You've ordered six crates from us."

The pencil hovered with impatience. "*Your* name."

"Anderson."

"B. Anderson?"

The corner of the crate dug into his shoulder. "Aye."

Scratching on his clipboard, the man nodded. "Follow me."

"I've left the other orders on the dock—"

"The porters will take care of them. Follow me."

Barrett glanced up at the towering side of the *Ulysses* and the hundreds of small round portholes spotting it. He'd never cared much for ships. Metal boxes floating on water were nothing more than a temptation to fate. If he was going to die, he'd rather not be trapped in one of these with miles of freezing ocean around him.

Pushing down his trepidation, he stepped aboard. The deck rolled gently beneath his feet as he followed the purser down the twisting passageways and up several flights of narrow stairs. Men and lads in white uniforms bustled to and fro, flattening themselves against the walls as they passed by with practiced ease. Barrett managed to keep from knocking any of them in the head with his bulky load.

Twisting the handle on a heavy riveted door, the purser led Barrett out into what he could only assume was the main passenger area. Spacious, with dark woods, colorful carpets, planted palms, and leather-backed chairs. Every bit of fine furniture was nailed to the deck.

"This way." The purser motioned with his clipboard up a flight of mahogany stairs with a grand clock at the landing. "Hurry up, now. The passengers have almost completed loading."

"I thought every ship nowadays was commissioned for troop transport."

"Most of our current roster is for wounded, soldiers, and medical staff, but the occasional civilians come aboard if there's room available. Being war, we do have our priorities." The purser stopped at the top of the stairs and glanced to the crate balancing on Barrett's shoulder. "We try to keep their spirits up as best we can."

"Glennmoore is honored to be of use."

"Hmm, we'll see."

The passageways were wider and less twisted near the staterooms. Carpets covered the floors, and the wood paneling gleamed from polish. Grand ladies in their jewels and men in white ties must have once glided down these halls while his kind rode down in steerage.

Ladies like Kat.

The corner of the crate rammed into a wall. The purser whipped his head around and glared. More scratching on his clipboard.

"Sorry." Barrett adjusted his load. Not the first time Kat had distracted him. At work, in his one-room flat, in his sleep, her face never left him.

Before he could damage anything more, the purser finally stopped in front of a door midway down the ship and slotted a brass key into the lock. Inside, cherrywood walls, deep green-and-gold wallpaper, an intricate rug, and spindly furniture of a fancy design all bespoke a life that rich people would appreciate.

He stared across the room and out the large windows to a private balcony and the ocean view beyond. No, not just rich people. He could learn to appreciate such things.

"Ahem."

The purser's throat clearing brought him back to reality. The one he needed to stick to with his workman's clothes, scuffed shoes, and crate of whisky hefted on his shoulder. "Where do you want it?"

The man pointed his pencil to the marble fireplace. "Next to it. Mind the flowers."

Aye, the flowers. Only rich people would waste money on a vase stuffed with lilacs and lilies arranged in a faux fireplace. Setting the crate down, he pushed it back to the wall lest it trip a pair of fancy shoes. The smell of lilacs wafted under his nose.

Kat always smelled of lilacs.

He jerked back to find the entire cabin dripping with the horrid reminders, all in shades of cream and purple. "Bit much for a sea voyage."

"They're for a wedding."

His gut lurched. Of course they were. Lured into a trap of memories, why would he not find more heart-wrenching evidence of the things never to be his? He moved to the open door leading to the balcony. Tangy salt air washed over him, drowning out the flowers.

"Wait a moment in here while the other supplies are brought in, as you'll need to double-check their contents and sign off for delivery. I shall return shortly," said the purser.

The deep blue-green waves crested white in the distance. If Barrett squinted hard enough, could he see the Statue of Liberty and all that she promised? Or was she one more lady he would fail to obtain?

Kat had waited for him on the steps that day. Everything in her eyes told him, begged him, to take her in his arms and kiss her until there was nothing left standing between them except their bared souls. Mayhap in her perfect world there could have been that, but it was far from the truth. Too much stood between them. He'd known it as soon as her father signed his name to that check. She was his heart. No amount of money could buy that.

Pounding the doorframe with his fist, he turned from the ocean that too closely matched her eyes. The lilacs stared back at him.

"What is it with today?"

Slashing his hand through his hair, he circled around the room in search of a safe spot. The door to the adjoining berth stood open. A dark-gray jacket hung on the back of an ornate chair. He frowned. Did he not have one just like that?

Glancing over his shoulder to make sure the coast was clear, he marched into the room and snagged the jacket off the chair. Same buttons, same patch around the cuffs. Digging into the inner breast pocket, he fished out the ticket from last week's boxing match he'd gone to with a coworker.

The door slammed shut behind him. A key turned in the lock.

He shoved the ticket back in the pocket. "You better have a good explanation for what my jacket is doing here."

"I thought you might need it."

Of all the people in the world, he never thought he'd hear that voice again. *Her* voice. Every inch of him went cold, then burned hot as blood rushed to his head. He gripped the back of the chair to keep steady. "What are you doing here?"

"I should think that was obvious. I came for you," Kat said behind him.

"You lured me here under the false pretense of malt whisky."

"It worked, didn't it?"

"Aye. It did." He swallowed hard against the sickness roiling in his gut. A wedding, the purser had said. "Now what? Shall I pour the glasses for you? Turn back the bedcovers?"

"Not yet." His throat tightened at the smile in her voice. "It would help if you turned and looked at me."

It was the last thing he wanted to do, but he couldn't continue to stand there staring at the wall. Bracing himself, he turned slowly.

A thousand years would never have prepared him for seeing her again. Dressed in sky blue with her golden hair curling around her face and his grandmother's brooch pinned to her lapel, she shone like an angel from his dreams. He struggled to keep the air from collapsing in his lungs.

"Mind telling me what you're planning to do with this?" He held up his jacket in accusation.

"I thought you might like to take it with us."

Us. It rang in his ears like a bell. "I'm in no mood for games. I've got work to do. Stand aside."

Kat braced herself against the locked door. "Not until I'm done putting sense into you."

"What sense might that be? It's a coldhearted thing you've done, bringing me here to serve at your wedding. No doubt to some army captain with shining medals for being shot on the field of glory."

"He has been shot at. Stabbed a little too. But he's not a captain. Nor in the army." Cocking her head to the side, a light sprang to her eyes. Much bluer than the waters outside. "Look around, Barrett. Haven't you figured it out by now?"

He glanced around the cabin. His small suitcase stood at the foot of the bed next to a more expensive case, while his comb and hair paste were laid out on the vanity next to a set of silver-handled brushes and a mirror. A cut-glass bottle of *Doux parfum de Lilac* glinted beside a vase filled with the purple flowers. Pivoting around, he noted his pajamas set out on the foot of the bed while an airy lace-capped nightgown floated from the wardrobe door.

His lungs constricted. "You're out of your mind."

"Probably, but then if I were sane I'd have stayed away from you long ago. Trouble is . . . I can't. And I don't want to." Pushing away from the door, she stepped closer. "And neither do you."

"What is it with you Whitfords and the constant need to bend everyone to your scheming whims? Thought you might have had enough of that from your father, but it looks like the acorn didn't fall too far from the mighty oak."

"Your ridiculous stubbornness has given me no other choice."

"Except to kidnap me. Do you not find the slightest bit of irony in that?"

"If that's how you wish to view it. But kidnapping usually involves an uncooperative party. I'm fairly certain that by this evening you'll be more than willing."

"Doubt your family will approve such relations with an ill-bred guttersnipe like me. Aren't the Whitford girls subjected to walking bank notes with shiny buttons and a pedigree?"

"Ellie is too busy heading up a fallen women's shelter in London to find a button of her own, and I've found shiny trimmings overrated."

He shook his head, but the cobwebs tangled too thick. "It'll never work. Too many obstacles."

"Only the ones we've put there ourselves. Stupidly." She spread her hands wide as earnestness shone from her eyes. "I let my pride ruin the best thing that could ever happen to me, and now I'm here. Asking you to take the rest of me back because you've already got my heart."

"You called me a liar."

"Another on my long list of errors. Hardly the last, I dare say."

"You also accused me of lacking honor."

"Look, if you're going to keep tabs, then we've got a long life of payment ahead." She took another step toward him. "I know you didn't take the money."

Every muscle stiffened in his body as her delicate lilac fragrance drifted to him. "I'm not the man for you. I work for a living with barely two shillings to rub together in my pocket. My clothes are worn, and my name lacks any kind of clout."

She moved to him, circling her arms around his neck as a smile curved her full mouth. "You're exactly the man for me."

Her lips brushed his, spiraling wildfire in his blood. He jerked back. "No. Find someone else."

He moved to the door, ready to break it down if necessary. He couldn't stand to be in the same room with her, much less the same space of air.

Something hard hit the back of his head.

"Ow!" He spun around to find the silver-handled comb at his feet.

The brush in her hand was poised for striking. "Don't make me clobber you with this one too. It was a birthday gift, and I'd rather not dent it on your hard head."

"*My* hard head? I'm not the ridiculous one thinking that anything between us could work out. Look around you. I can't afford any of this. We'd be in the galley peeling potatoes to afford wherever this boat is sailing to."

Tossing the brush back on the vanity, she sighed and crossed her arms. "First of all, this is a ship. Second, this cabin is a wedding gift as we sail to America and our new life."

Wedding gift. America. New life. He'd struggled so long to keep her out, but with every second she found a new crack to slip through. "I'll be starting over on my own terms. When I do, it'll be without a bride, and certainly without one I can't support."

"You will be able to support *us* just fine as we already have an investor."

His eyes narrowed. "Your father."

"No. He wanted to see us off, but his pushchair is difficult to maneuver up gangways. That and he doesn't like the stares."

Barrett's mouth dropped open. "You father is in a pushchair?"

She nodded. "Polio. Hasn't been able to walk in over six years."

After all these months of loathing the man's guts, he'd gone and vilified a crippled man. Barrett swallowed back a groan of self-disgust.

No wonder Sir Alfred never rose from behind his desk to knock him out for the storm of insults that day in his office.

Anger boiled up, more at himself than at her. "You should have told me."

"He doesn't like people to know, to feel their pity," she said softly.

"I'm not most people."

"No, you're not." A slight smile curved her lips as she tapped polished fingernails against the sleeve of her dress. "Now that we have that cleared up, the Bank of England has granted us a loan with two percent interest over ten years. A fair deal in today's market."

He whirled to the door. "I can make my own way."

"Stubborn fool."

Grabbing him from behind, her foot hooked around his and yanked. He tipped backward and hit the floor.

Kneeling, she leaned over his chest and pinned him to the ground. "Now, I have a special license signed by the archbishop himself, and I'm getting married today. To you. It would be much easier if you went willing, but I'm prepared to go at this the hard way as well."

Knock. Knock. A key rattled in the lock and the door pushed open, shoving Barrett on the shoulder. The purser popped his head in. "Oh, pardon me. I didn't realize the chaplain had already been here."

Kat shook her head. "He hasn't."

Suspicion creased the man's forehead as he stared down his short nose at them. "Then might I suggest we compose ourselves until he does. This ship was christened by the king himself, and I'll not have any shenanigans spoiling its sterling reputation."

He whirled out without closing the door.

Kat's gaze dropped back down to Barrett. The green tint in her eyes darkened as her lips hovered inches over his.

He cupped her cheek, grazing the delicate skin with his fingertips. Like warm silk. His heart pounded like a trip-hammer. "Why do you want me so?"

"Because I love you."

A word so foreign to him he might have thought he was dreaming if not for her soft weight pressing down on him. He'd waited a lifetime to hear it spoken to him, and to have it claimed by this beautiful, courageous woman was more than his soul could withstand.

Grasping her face, he rose up to meet her. "I love you."

Her smiling lips met his in a surge of passion. They molded to his, seeking and possessing everything he had to offer. He dug his fingers into the richness of her hair, twining the curls behind her ears. She sighed, sending his pulse pounding in reckless abandon as he deepened the kiss.

How could he have thought to ever let her go?

Her hand moved up his arm, brushing tingles down the limb until she found the opening at his collar. She brushed her fingers over the exposed skin, inflaming it to her touch like a brand. He belonged to her alone. Always.

"Oh, dear. Did I get this room already? Sometimes I have a hard time keeping track with all the departing soldiers."

Barrett's head cleared long enough to notice the black-and-white markings under the naval uniform as those of a chaplain. "No, Padre. You haven't been to this cabin yet."

"Oh." Relief curled the gangly man's lips. Pushing the wire-rimmed glasses back up his nose, his expression soured into a frown. "Then I'll ask that you release the young lady until I've performed the necessary rites."

Grinning, Barrett rolled to his feet and offered his hand to Kat. Pink tinged her cheeks as she brushed the wrinkles from her skirt. "Might you give us a moment, Padre? He's yet to ask me."

"Ask you? Ask you what?" Padre swung his gaze between them until his eyes popped open wide behind his glasses. "For heaven's sake. You're not even engaged and carrying on like . . . like I don't know what. Make it fast, lad. I should hate to think what will happen if I don't return in the next ten minutes. Or sooner."

Alone again, Barrett pulled her into his arms. "You're so certain I want to marry you."

She circled her arms around his neck, ruffling the hair on the back of his head. "Yes, very certain."

"Do I get a say in this?"

"No."

"Not even to ask you proper? To be my wife through all the years I'm granted to live at your side. Because I want you, not in a way to survive, but in a way to make life worth living." He locked his hands behind her waist, drawing her closer. "I don't know where I'll be in ten or fifty years, but I do know where my heart will be. With you."

She grazed a kiss along his jaw. "Not with some woman to simper over you and let you do whatever you want?"

"Someone who doesn't argue as much would be a nice change."

"If that's how you feel about it—"

She whirled from his grasp, but he caught her wrist and drew her back. Wrapping his arms around her waist, he held her tight to his chest and inhaled her sweet lilac scent. Touching his forehead to hers, he fell headfirst into the blueness of her eyes and let himself drown in their depths. "No. This is how I feel about it."

He moved his mouth to hers, claiming her for his own. Always.

Feet shuffled in the door. "Oh, for Saint Peter's sake. Dearly beloved, we are gathered here today . . ."

Acknowledgments

First and foremost I wish to thank Pinterest, you wonderful quirky rabbit-hole of inspiration you. Without scrolling through the numerous pins of historical oddities and fashion while I was supposed to be doing something more productive, I never would have come across a photo of the Mitford sisters. Six glamorous English socialites with wildly different takes on life and paths to happiness and sorrow. Kat and Ellie would not exist without you (or the *Vikings* TV show, but that's another story).

This book's journey would not have been half as incredible as it's been without the team at Thomas Nelson. Y'all have blown my mind with the amount of dedication and enthusiasm you put into every page and everything that goes beyond the page. A special and heartfelt thank you to Jocelyn Bailey, my editor, who believed in me and this story, talked me off a writing cliff or two, and pushed these characters and their plight to great heights. I cannot express how grateful I am to be included in this publishing family.

To my wonderful, stalwart, brave, daring, and tenacious (in the best of ways) agent, Linda. Lady, all these years you never gave up on me. There were times when I doubted I'd ever get this far, but you never did. And look at us now! This success belongs to you as much as it does to me. Kim. My writing would be no where without you, or more likely run off into a verbal ditch of despair somewhere. You're the other half of my brain and I wouldn't have it any other way. As for my heart, it belongs to my little unicorn and Viking in training. You keep me grounded when I need to be and build me wings when I long to soar. Love y'all.

Discussion Questions

1. How would you describe Kat and Ellie's relationship? How have they responded uniquely to their English upbringing? Do you relate to either of the sisters?

2. Throughout the book, many different forces work to serve the war effort. Some prefer to work behind the scenes, such as Sir Whitford, while others stride to the forefront of action like Barrett. Given the choice, which would you prefer?

3. Kat is a well-brought-up woman with all the comforts her station affords, yet she does not hesitate to abandon these conveniences to save her sister. Have you ever felt convicted enough to leave behind all you knew and venture into uncertainty? Would you do the same for someone you love?

4. Eric's title is the Minister of Culture and Social Movement in France. Why do you think the Nazis bothered with such roles amid wartime and took great pains to steal and hoard Europe's fine art?

5. Founded in the 1920s in order to unite a greater Germany after the crippling loss of WWI, Nazism grew to the height of its power under the leadership of Adolf Hitler and became the standard by which we judge evil. Why do you think so many people went along with Hitler's ideology? Did it have the power to corrupt good people, or were those who followed him seeking an outlet for their innate wickedness?

6. What motivates Barrett Anderson? Describe his code of

ethics and consider how his backstory has molded his character.

7. Kat is disgusted by Nazism but must play nice with the enemy in order to infiltrate their inner circle. How would you have handled such circumstances? What about Kat makes her the perfect spy?

8. Major Eric von Schlegel is a complicated man with a decisive view of the world and those within it. Is any part of his character redeemable? As twisted as his actions and beliefs are, do you believe Eric truly loved Ellie?

9. What did you learn about Nazi-occupied Paris that you did not already know? Though Ellie and Eric lived decadently, what do you imagine the day-to-day experience was like for the rest of occupied France?

10. How did you feel about Sir Whitford throughout the story? Did that perception ever change?

About the Author

With a passion for heart-stopping adventure and sweeping love stories, J'nell Ciesielski weaves fresh takes into romances of times gone by. When not creating dashing heroes and daring heroines, she can be found dreaming of Scotland, indulging in chocolate of any kind, or watching old black and white movies. Winner of the Romance Through the Ages Award and the Maggie Award, she is a Florida native who now lives in Virginia with her husband, daughter, and lazy beagle.

Learn more at www.jnellciesielski.com.